The Edge of America

Also by Jon Sealy

The Whiskey Baron

THE EDGE OF AMERICA

a novel

JON SEALY

Haywire Books
Richmond, Virginia

HAYWIRE BOOKS

ISBN: 978-1-950182-00-8
Library of Congress Control Number: 2019933252

Cover Design: Baxton Baylor
Copy Editor: Nicole van Esselstyn
Proofreader: Benjamin Kolp
Author Photo: Casey Templeton

First Printing

For Emily, again

I don't think that I've been satirizing the revolutionary world. All these people are not revolutionaries—they are shams…By Jove! If I had the necessary talent I would like to go for the true anarchist—which is the millionaire. Then you would see the venom flow.

— Joseph Conrad

In those days there was no king in Israel; every man did what was right in his own eyes.

— Judges 21:25

BEFORE THE $3 MILLION went missing, before the bombing, before the manhunt shut Miami down in late April 1984, Bobby West and the woman who was not his wife stood naked together in the shower. A sparrow-plump man of early middle age, with watery gray-blue eyes and woefully Germanic skin, West idled under the beating hot water and thought of nothing.

The woman, Diana Burns, massaged shampoo through her hair at the back of the tub. "Ansel Adams died on Sunday," she said.

"I saw that."

"I hate to admit I didn't realize he was still alive."

"That's what happens to icons," he said. "You forget about them in old age. How old was he?" West always wanted to know how old someone was when he died.

"Early eighties?"

"Must have been ancient," he said. "What'd he died of?"

"I don't know. Old age, I guess."

He picked up a can of Barbasol and began to lather his face. She closed her eyes to rinse her hair, edged him out of the water. Her skin was natural and loose in the water, a stark contrast to his wife's—his ex-wife's—chemical treatments. He was entirely unsuited for the flash and youthful strivings of Miami, and believed his divorce was somehow linked to the way he relished the privacy of a morning shower.

"How old do you have to be before you can die of old age anymore?" he asked.

"In this day and age? I don't know." She finished rinsing her hair, spat water, opened her eyes. "I'd say eighties."

He slid the razor along his face in front of the mirror he'd tacked up in the back of her shower. "I'm sure he qualified."

"Because if you think of how active people are in their eighties and nineties."

"My grandfather lived to be ninety-three," he said.

"Or how active people are in their seventies and eighties."

"I come from good stock."

"I'd say once you're in your eighties, old age contributes to how you died."

"There's always a cause," he said. "Pneumonia, or your heart stops. Something."

"Right, but how much of that is old age?"

"The goal is to go quietly in your sleep."

"I don't bounce back like I used to," she said. "You start declining around twenty-eight."

"I'm done if you are," he said.

"I'm done," she said.

He shut off the water. The sound of the shower gave way to the sound of a helicopter drumming low across the sky. He wiped some crud from the corner of her eye and stepped out of the shower to dry himself off.

Although pressed for time, he pulled her onto the bed and held her close. He wished he had the energy to make love to her again, but these days he felt the widening gulf between mind and body. West was not old, just a year over forty, but the weight of responsibilities had begun to sap his energy. He lived in a state of dislocation, estranged from his wife and daughter, in a house he didn't own, in a city that was not his own, and the only time he felt levelheaded and clear was with the woman who was not his wife. At thirty-one, Diana was old enough to know how to handle herself but young enough to get away with homicide. Unmarried, fertile, striking: a woman who turned heads. West was a bottom-line man, spreadsheet dull, and he lived for these moments with her. It wasn't about the sex but the moments after, when the clouds of the everyday cleared from his mind. All he wanted was stay here with her, but she had other ideas. She slid out from under his arm and snapped on her panties.

"Where you off to, speedy?" he asked.

"We landed a new account, so I've got a strategy meeting in half an hour."

"You're leaving me, just like that?"

"The account's going to pay my entire team's salary this year."

"I got to start charging you when I spend the night."

"You know how volatile the industry is these days. We can't lose this opportunity."

He reached for her wrist. "The ninety-nine-dollar Bobby West special."

She laughed. "Stop. I'll be selling cars if I'm not careful. Anyway, don't you have your own meeting?"

"I could cancel it."

"No need to do that."

"Watch how easy it is." He rolled over and reached for the phone with all the grace of a water buffalo. "See here? I'll just call Vicky and I'm off the hook. You have me all morning."

"You've made your point," she said.

As the buttons on the phone beeped, she fled to the bathroom.

"I run the show," he called. "That's the advantage of being the boss."

"Well, you're welcome to stay here as long as you like, but I've got to go."

She shut the door and turned on the faucet. The phone continued ringing until Vicky picked up and said hello in her perky receptionist voice.

"Vicky," West said.

"Yessir, Mr. West."

"Nothing. I'm sorry to bother you."

"Your ex-wife's been calling all morning," she said. "She left a few messages yesterday asking you to call her."

He hung up and lay back on the pillow.

The air conditioning chilled his bare skin as a certain dreaminess came over him, that bleak idle moment when you know you still have the rest of the day to face but nothing to face it with.

Diana returned to grab her earrings off her dresser. He closed his eyes, no longer interested in persuading her to stay. The easiest way to make it through the day would be to get to work and bury himself in some analyst's report. Diana was chattering: would he zip up her dress? He tuned her out while she finished dressing and then glided to the bathroom, where she mussed her hair and stared at herself in the mirror for several moments. When she came out, she leaned over and kissed him on the forehead. "I hate to run off," she said. "I do love our mornings together."

"Yeah, yeah."

"Don't pout. See you this weekend?"

"It's my weekend with Holly." He sat on his elbow and, on impulse, broached the idea they'd both danced around so far in their relationship. "You could come over, if you wanted to meet her."

Diana stuck out her lips like blowing through a straw. "Maybe some other time."

"I'd even cook for you." He smiled, at first a win-her-over gesture but then genuinely as he saw the image of Diana and Holly at his table, enjoying a normal, domestic evening together. It had been some time since he'd experienced such an ordinary night, like a family man again. He could use relief from the anxious life of a bachelor. Marriage had somehow made him dumb, and now the simple actions of stocking the fridge were a challenge.

She returned his smile and said, "Lock up when you leave."

When she was gone he dressed in a hurry. His office was on the seventh floor of a glass tower on Biscayne, so he wouldn't have time to go home and still make his nine o'clock meeting, a bull session in which the Artium Group's executive team would rehash the first quarter and find a few clichéd rah-rah talking points to get them through the rest of the second. Nothing about Cuba, communism, international strategy or the Cold War—all the things he once believed would define his career. Instead, he examined balance sheets and negotiated office politics. He doubted anyone would notice he was in the same shirt and tie from yesterday, but he knew the moment he arrived Vicky would have a sheaf of messages from his ex-wife, whatever she wanted. At times he felt she was more open with him now than when they were married, as though a clot had come dislodged with the signing of divorce papers.

He went downstairs and poured a finger of bourbon over ice, just enough to take the edge off while he dealt with whatever problem Isabel had for him to consider. He called her from Diana's bedroom, held the phone to his face as he buttoned his shirt.

"Bobby? Where the hell have you been?" she asked by way of greeting.

"I don't know if that's your concern anymore."

"Are you at work?"

He still hadn't heard through the tension in her voice, to the fear, when he muttered, "Vicky told me you called."

"Holly's gone," she said, the bell toll of fear unmistakable.

PART ONE

CENTRAL INTELLIGENCE AGENCY
WASHINGTON, D.C.

OFFICE OF THE DEPUTY DIRECTOR (INTELLIGENCE)

25 April 1984

MEMORANDUM FOR: Mark Brown
                    Special Operations, Latin America
                    Counterterrorism

SUBJECT: Events in Miami, Florida re: Robert West

The Artium Group is over-leveraged and appears to be hemorrhaging cash. The most recent balance sheet, year over year, is below. The "miscellaneous liabilities" suggests an off-the-books accounting. Recommend an immediate audit and suspension of Robert West.

	Mar. 1983	Mar. 1984
ASSETS		
Current Assets		
Cash	3,332,000	2,168,000
Short-term investments	-	-
Net receivables	10,450,000	10,231,000
Inventory	623,000	705,000
Other Assets	6,068,000	2,955,000
Total Current Assets	**20,473,000**	**16,059,000**
Long-term investments	-	-
Property	10,121,000	9,594,000
Intangible assets	22,019,000	21,461,000
Other assets	3,477,000	4,093,000
Total Assets	**56,090,000**	**51,207,000**
LIABILITIES		
Current Liabilities		
Accounts payable	9,857,000	10,942,000
Misc. liabilities	0	3,000,000
Total Current Liabilities	**9,857,000**	**13,942,000**
Long-term debt	51,191,000	48,331,000
Other liabilities	8,303,000	6,717,000
Deferred long-term charges	723,000	3,498,000
Total Liabilities	**70,074,000**	**72,488,000**

1

The operation had been simple. No wonder it failed. One day in the early weeks of 1984, Alexander French dropped by Bobby West's office unannounced, with a few questions about the Artium Group and sheltering assets.

When his secretary came in to tell him Mr. French was here, West was sitting at his desk in a trench coat and wraparound sunglasses. Never mind if it appeared slightly demented for the thickset, pale-skinned financial officer to work like that. This was January and the air conditioning was on full throttle in the office. Miami never really got cold, but there was no need to turn the office into an icebox. The arctic gusts swirling out of the vent made him shiver like a wet dog. To warm up he'd opened the shades as wide as they would go so that blinding winter light barreled into the office, and maybe it did warm the room a degree or two, but the sunlight also bit into his retinas. Hence, for two days now he'd worked in his coat and sunglasses, neither of which he took off for visitors. The secretaries and couriers and interns never batted an eye. The higher up a man rose in an organization, the more eccentric he was allowed to be so long as he delivered on his targets.

His secretary was a comely young unmarried girl named Vicky who wore black-framed glasses and had a penchant for leggings that hugged her slender frame and made her appear ten years younger, a teenager no different from his daughter. She was young enough to be a daughter if he'd made bad choices in high school, old enough to be a girlfriend if he made bad choices in early middle age. He often wanted to say something about professionalism, but this was the 1980s. A generation of lawyers would retire early thanks to the fees from harassment suits. Today she wore a blouse with one side inappropriately exposing her shoulder, lines of a tattoo he'd never seen before, which he consciously ignored. She smacked gum and grinned at his getup. "There's an Alexander French here to see you."

West took a breath. "He say what he wanted?"

"Only that he was here to see you."

"How's my afternoon looking?"

"You've got a two-thirty with the leadership team to prep for next week's board meeting, and before you leave you need to call the guy from Navarro Security back."

He waved that off.

"The man wants to give us a pile of money," she said.

"Everyone wants to give us a pile of money. It's what they want in return."

"That's above my pay grade. You want to see Mr. French?"

Vicky was well trained in fending off sales calls, but she must have had an instinct that Mr. French was not a man to stonewall. Everyone in the city had heard of Alexander French, though no one knew what he was famous for. Nefarious business dealings, real estate development, and a general reputation for being a man above the law.

"I guess you better send him in," West said.

"You want a minute?"

"No, I'm fine. I don't want him to get too comfortable."

"Right-oh."

As she bounded out of the room, his eyes never left her bare shoulder. An office was a treacherous place, filled with people from different backgrounds and competing motivations and degrees of naiveté or experience. You spent half your waking hours with these people, you laughed with them, you built an inside language. Then you relied on the human resources department, an unspoken moral code, and general self-restraint to compartmentalize your passions. He felt awkward around his direct reports, many of them younger women brimming with confidence but wildly lacking in perspective. As he'd grown older and his daughter entered adolescence, he'd felt less and less the sense of camaraderie with his colleagues, the veiled desire to fuck them in the elevator, and had taken on the cold demeanor of work. Tasks to complete. Responsibility. Father knows best. In many ways he'd turned into his father, a condition he tried not to dwell on. Days at the office, grouchy at home, business always on his mind.

West kept quite busy indeed these days. Such was life as an executive for the Artium Group, a holding company that owned stakes in a spread of Miami businesses: boat shops, gun shops, travel agencies, real estate agencies, private detective firms. The group also financed Florida Air Transport, a small airline that shuttled up and down the east coast with the occasional lob over to Europe. His formal title was Chief Financial Officer, but that was a convenience of paperwork, the brainchild of a lawyer or an accountant. The company's president was an old German immigrant who spent his workdays collecting art or attending high-end soirées around town. All of the Artium Group's legitimate businesses were merely fronts for the CIA, which had a history of keeping tabs on life in South Florida. The agency excelled at surveillance, but as near as West could tell, the information he filed simply went into a vault for posterity. Meanwhile, his job on paper was to ensure the businesses all paid their bills on time so the Artium Group maintained enough profit margin so as to remain invisible to other businesses and government agencies. He enjoyed the variety, the challenge, the puzzle of it all, but he was tired of making money for other people while watching colleagues in Washington ascend to power. The rules had changed in the past few years, and he saw what kind of money could be made in this country if you were willing to take the risk. Rather than continue facing a dull future of pumping information north and running numbers in Miami, he was ready for such a risk.

Mr. French came in a moment later carrying a briefcase.

West stood and offered him a seat. He then felt compelled to take off his sunglasses and say, "We're having air conditioner problems."

"I see." Mr. French set his briefcase on the edge of the desk.

"Maintenance tells me they're working on it," West went on. "Something about they'd been expecting a heat wave, we need upgraded insulation, the time-transfer of the HVAC system. All of which is to say my office is frigid."

"Whatever works," Mr. French said, and West stopped himself from rambling further and took his seat.

Mr. French was a bald, effeminate man on the cusp between middle and old age. He wore a brown sport coat over a dark-leaved Hawaiian shirt, and he had a gold hoop earring in his left ear. He could be an oddball beachcomber by all appearances, but West knew him to be a ruthless gangster who controlled the drug trade throughout South Florida, among other things. The CIA had only a marginal interest in him, in that he had close contacts in Cuba, Colombia, and elsewhere, but West would have read the man's file if he'd known he was coming. Probably why he'd arrived unannounced.

"I understand you're the one who takes care of finances around here," Mr. French said.

"I'm one of them, that's true."

"Can you tell me anything special about your operations?"

"Such as?"

"I'd like to get a better sense of how things work here." Mr. French spoke with a calm authority and an undertone that suggested he wasn't a man to play games with. "From the accountant's side," he went on, "how does the Artium Group make money, and how is that money reported?"

"It's a little complicated," West said. "Basically, we're a holding and investment company. We buy things and sit on them while they increase in value, and then we sell them."

"Help me out. You mean like stocks?"

"Stocks, yes. Bonds, real estate, businesses."

"Businesses."

"We like to think of ourselves as offering a service. We provide a little capital, and the engines of commerce continue to run. If you buy a majority stake in a business, you can direct the course of its operations, though we never do. We're not activists or speculators. We no longer make short-term bets for or against anything."

Mr. French gave a sly grin. "I hear Iran scared you boys straight."

West said nothing, a play he still had to force himself to make even after all these years in business. There were only so many types of people in the world, and he'd experienced his share of boardroom meetings gone awry. Men skittered to the edge of safe ice and danced. Shouting matches caused secretaries to cower down hallways. He'd seen it all, and could see already that Mr. French was like a boxer, the type ready to corner you against the ropes. He'd stay low and throw a few soft jabs, and then the thunder would arrive. Your feet couldn't move fast enough, like you were underwater. This was Alexander French: he wouldn't back down until you were toast. Anything West said would pin him to the side of the ring.

Mr. French spoke first. "What about futures?"

"We leave that to the farmers," West said. "We don't do fancy accounting, and we don't hide anything in our books. No unnecessary risk. Everything we do is for the sake of efficiency and accountability."

"I see, I see." Mr. French scratched his chin as though considering how much bullshit Bobby West was feeding him. Then he said, "Tell me about the CIA."

"You mean the spy organization?"

"Yes, yes." Mr. French waved off anything coy. "Rumor is the Artium Group is nothing but a front."

"I can assure you we conduct legitimate business here."

"Oh, I believe that, but I also know these little so-called businesses, your shops and even your airline, aren't the only things propping you up in this beautiful office."

The man was right, of course. The Artium Group's portfolio was nothing but CIA cover. A boat business gave them a reason to keep boats in the harbor. A gun shop gave them a steady supply of ammunition. A real estate agency gave them a series of safe houses.

But even in today's heady market, the spread of properties couldn't sustain the group's balance sheet. What sustained West's balance sheet was a constant line of tips about world events. They made a king's ransom betting against Allende in Chile in 1973, but took a hit when the Iranian Shah was overthrown. As time passed, West found it difficult not to get lost in these financial ups and downs, to keep his moral center and remain focused on what he truly cared about: Cuba and the Soviets. He'd joined the organization shortly after the Bay of Pigs, when the spirit of a thousand dead rebels hovered over the CIA. His charge from day one was to topple Fidel Castro, and thus far he'd failed. He'd made wheelbarrows full of money, but his primary mission with the agency, issued when he was twenty-two years old, was still an outstanding item in his daily to-do list.

Ostensibly, he ran the CIA's South Florida intelligence operations, filed reports about the Cuban exile population and waited for someone in Washington to make a move on Castro. Because Cuba was contained and the exiles—*la lucha*—had become naturalized citizens, Washington generally viewed South Florida as the FBI's purview, or the DEA's, so West's primary job these days was running a straight business, a role he felt entirely unsuited for. He specialized in information, one prong of the organization's Latin America operations (the others being counterterror and government relations). Cuban dissidents, front organizations, rebel training: this was Bobby West's area of expertise and, at one time, the largest division of the CIA. But these were lean years, triumphant years, diplomatic years. Officially, there was no more CIA in Miami. While the current administration had cautious interest in the Sandinistas, Cuba was contained. The Soviet Empire was out of viable proxy states. We were coming for them, the Soviets, and everyone else was in a holding pattern with no resources coming out of Washington. Nevertheless, the central rule of government was: if you didn't like the policy, wait until the next election. Every administration wanted to make its own mark, which meant you had a different flavor every four or eight years. All he had to do was float the business until something changed in D.C. That, however, was a tall order.

He said nothing as he waited for Mr. French to make his play.

The man finally got to the point. "You recently made contact with one of my employees. Felix Machado? Said you were sniffing around a source among the Cubans here. Said you seemed to have grand plans of shaking things up. Well. I don't know how much you know about me, but I'm also in the portfolio business. I have a new venture in mind, and I'd like to partner up with you. It could be lucrative for the both of us."

West sat back. "I'm listening."

"My organization has, call it, something of a union at the Miami Airport. A group mainly employed by Florida Air Transport."

"I'm familiar."

"Well, this union has an opportunity to splinter into the import-export business, but to do that we'll need some accounting help."

"It's illegal, what they're doing?"

"They're merely importing and exporting. Free trade, my friend, it's good for the economy."

"It's certainly been very good for Miami." West nodded toward the window, the skyline. "Is this import coming from Colombia, by any chance?"

"Asia, actually. Afghanistan."

"I wasn't aware they produced much of anything."

"No thanks to your people, but they've got a thriving black market now that the Soviets have packed up their toys and gone home."

West considered his options and contingencies here. Mr. French didn't have to tell him: *We're in the drug business.* Mr. French didn't have to tell him: *I'd like CIA help.* Mr. French didn't have to tell him: *This is going to make you filthy rich.* The question was: What could Mr. French's organization offer West and the CIA in exchange for financial backing?

"Let's forget any business proposition for the moment," Mr. French said. "What would you recommend in theory? From an accounting perspective?"

"Well," West said of the airport employees, sliding into his consultant's role with ease. The way to a businessman's heart—

or any man, for that matter—was to ask him his opinion. "It's good your guys already have an occupation. The first thing to do would be to set up a dummy corporation. You can't just use a union, or Florida Air Transport employees. I'd come up with something bland, maybe Florida Import-Export. FIE Enterprises."

Mr. French smiled.

"You've already done that?" West asked.

Mr. French cocked his head but continued to say nothing.

"You'll want to set FIE up as an investment firm that handles benefits for Florida Air employees. Medical, pensions, that sort of thing. Contributions from union employees would be invested in whatever portfolio you desire. Just put the money in some kind of fund, which maybe—and I'm not saying yes—maybe this is where the Artium Group could help. It would be in our purview to buy a stake in something like FIE to manage the investments. We'd bundle the money with our other interests to keep FIE activities at arm's length. We can set up an account for it and transfer the money wherever you like, minus our commission."

Mr. French was still grinning. "I presume that account could be offshore?"

"From our end, it's just an account. Could be Switzerland, the Caymans, Panama. We'd just be investing to hold a stake in the business, so we wouldn't need to know the specifics of FIE operations, other than the benefits you manage. We have some reporting obligations, but like I said, your employees have a legitimate occupation."

"One last question for you." Mr. French unlatched the briefcase and turned it dramatically. "I know wheels turn a little slowly in government, but this needs to happen fast. If dealing in cash speeds up the process, I'm ready to make the first investment." He spun the briefcase toward West.

"Jesus. How much is it?"

"Should be $980,000. You can count it if you've got the time."

"You couldn't find the extra twenty grand to make it an even million?"

"Courier's fees."

"Do I want to know where this came from?"

"Are you really asking that?"

West shook his head and began to flip through the money. Sure enough, the bills were rubber-banded, twenty $100 bills at a clip, 490 bundles. There was no way he could actually verify all the bills were real and accounted for. Easy place for fraud, but he somehow knew every single bill was genuine. Mr. French wanted him to know he had means, and wouldn't risk his reputation on counterfeit cash, not the first time.

"What am I supposed to do with a million in cash?" West asked when he finished. "I can't just take it down to the local bank. I'd have the FBI on me quicker than you could say money laundering."

"You don't have to take it to the bank." Mr. French handed over a business card with two phone numbers on it, one local and one international. "Felix will take care of it. Once a month, he'll contact you, take the cash and deposit it in a bank in Panama."

"A million in cash."

"A week."

"What?"

"We'll need to deposit about a million a week, so you'll be holding up to five million before we can move it."

Christ, West thought.

"Now," Mr. French said. "I don't know if you know me, but I've done my homework on you, Mr. West. I know the CIA can wear a man down, especially if he's in charge of Cuban relations in Miami. What does Reagan want with Cuba these days? You might as well be stationed in Akron, Ohio, for all the action you see here, right? And I know the Artium Group is over-leveraged from a few bad investments you made in the Carter years, so you have to be thinking a few things. First, how long will Uncle Sam keep floating you without seeing any financial or intelligence returns? Second, what's the point of all this?" Mr. French waved his hand out the window. "You've got—what?—fifteen working years left? That's enough time for one big move. One big chance to make an impact. Six percent of this operation is yours, for the holding and accounting. That's enough to right-size your business and maybe even get a little action going with the Cubans."

West's life was worse than Mr. French described. His body lately had been deteriorating as quickly as his ambitions. Never an operations man, always the analyst, he still wondered what his life could have been had he not married and settled into the conservative life of a businessman. Twenty years ago he'd gone through basic training at the Farm, and he continued to punish his body with running and weights as if to prove to himself what he could have done in another life. And now here he was. There were two roads to bad decisions. The first was inexperience, which got you when you were young, and the second was inattention, which got you on the back nine. Now what else did he have to do besides make money like everyone else in America?

"Our standard fee would be more like twelve percent," he said. "We mirror the Fed's interest rates."

"Twelve percent is more than half a million a month."

"I can't invest the cash and make anything off it while I'm holding it. This might be beyond my organization's purview."

"Ah, you do run a business here," Mr. French said. "Tell you what. I can go to eight percent. Cash money, no reporting. Keep it in a safe under your house if Artium doesn't want my money. I'm offering a guaranteed fixed return you can't find anywhere else in America. Give it to your Cuban exiles. Felix can connect you with the right people, and you can arm a revolution with this kind of money."

Mr. French had him against the ropes with that one. West suspected the man knew his weak spots better than he himself did. He bit his lip as the last piece of hesitation bled away from him.

"Smile, man. We're going to make you—and the American government, if you want to share—extremely rich."

"This isn't a done deal yet," West said, "but if I can arrange everything, what do you need from me?"

"I've got one catch on my end. I've got a lead on a supplier, a sort of freelancer. She and I have danced around each other for a while now, and I believe she's done some work for your organization as well. Arms purchases, nuclear cleanup, from what I understand."

"What are you buying from her?"

"Nothing right now. After the Soviet invasion, she took a lead in running goods in and out of Afghanistan. We want to play in that market, so we need her on board."

"So what's the catch?"

"I need you to come to Europe with me to meet her. She'll want to know who my business partner is in this."

"Meaning she'll want to see the CIA is on board to keep you from getting shut down," West said. "So you're here not only to ask me to launder your money, you're asking me to endorse the drug trade on behalf of the CIA, when our commander in chief has declared a total war on drugs."

"Diplomacy's a messy business. That's something even Reagan would tell you, at least in private. Look out your window. You said so yourself, this city wouldn't exist without this business."

West gazed at the Miami skyline. If his hunch was correct about FIE, a great deal of money indeed would be funneling in. Fees would be good for his personal balance sheet, and Mr. French was right. These were lean years for the CIA's Latin American sector. West's job was a game of roulette. The spin Mr. French handed him wasn't a gamble so much as an open hand to catch the manna from the sky.

Mr. French rose, left the briefcase on the desk.

West extended his hand and said, "Thank you for coming in today."

"No, thank you," Mr. French replied.

When he was gone, West continued to stare out the window for a long time. Then he picked up the phone and placed a call to Washington.

2

Amsterdam. The steely sky hung low like a tarp and the air was chilled. Ice skittered across the land and into West's bones in a way he hadn't felt since his childhood winters in Illinois. Stark contrast with South Florida, a seventy-degree forecast every day. A sheen of gloom hovered over Holland, the fields brown with a tint of gray, perhaps an optical trick played by the cracked white pavement of the runway. In the distance, two plumes of smoke funneled out of a factory. Flat country and farms, the land and the sky melding in a haze in the distance, smog or fog or just the way the country looked. Wind phalanxed across the plain and ripped at his clothing on the tarmac.

He took a train to Central Station, where the main square was crowded with pedestrians, with bicyclists weaving in and out of the throng. A bagpipe player stood nearby. A tram ambled through silently along the main drag, Damrak. The sky had darkened so that the red bricks of the city that surrounded them were gray and ashen, lit only by the red lights above bars, the tavern signs advertising Heineken and Guinness and Budweiser. Unholy lights, festive cheer for the heathen set. Narrow alleyways crosshatched the canals. Around him, the glottal chatter of Dutch harmonized into a multi-layered white noise.

Mr. French stood by a statue in the square. The two men shook hands and began strolling down the street.

"How was your flight?" Mr. French asked.

"Uneventful. She here yet?"

"She works on her own time."

"Isn't that bad for us?"

"Relax. This gal comes recommended by people who don't recommend lightly. It's not like we're outsourcing a manufacturing plant or buying paperclips."

"I'd rather be working with someone we've established a few ground rules with."

"She'll be here," Mr. French said again. "We'll talk to her, see what we can arrange, and if we get a bad vibe we'll find somebody else."

They turned into a narrow alley lit by red bulbs. Prostitutes stood in windows like merchandise. Several were clearly bored, putting on makeup, blowing hair out of their faces, while others danced in their displays. They were attractive, mostly clad in white bikinis, mostly white and blonde, though there were blacks and Latinas and Asians as well. Young, old. No redheads, or West might have been tempted. Ahead, a man stumbled out of an office, grinning like Christmas morning. His friends were in a bar across the alley, banging on windows and yelling at him. A hooker stepped out of her office and tried to hook West with a cane. "Hey, come play with me," she said. He shrugged her off and continued on. They passed a sex shop, which could have sold postcards and T-shirts but instead sold dildos, lubes, anal beads, leather, and porn. Mr. French seemed bored with the whole scene. He led West to a hotel, where they picked up West's key and dropped off his bag. Then they went to the Big House Coffee Shop that sold Amsterdam's finest.

In the dim room, a cat brushed against West's legs. It had scraggly fur and nasty eyeballs and what appeared to be a tumor growing out of its back. West shuddered and hurried to catch up with Mr. French, who waved him into a booth. He sat while Mr. French went to the bar and returned with two joints and offered one over. West held up a hand. Mr. French took it back and lit one, put the other in his shirt pocket. He puffed deeply before he said, "So what do you think?"

"About smoking pot?"

"About Amsterdam."

"Charming."

"We're in a place where you can get anything you want. Drugs, sex, an assassin, anything."

"That's..."

"Liberating, is what it is. Look around you. Where else in the world can you get away with wasting perfectly good pot?" French leaned over and wiped pot seedlings into West's lap. "No one here gives a shit. They leave you alone. A libertarian's paradise. You've got your American college students over here for a time, you've got your expatriates, you've got your immigrants and your locals and your Germans and your Jews. This is the true melting pot. The U.S. is a tossed salad. Everyone clinging to their identities and squabbling over turf. Except in Vegas. You ever been to Vegas? It's unreal. You think you're going in for something real, a gambling good time, but there's nothing underneath the glamour. You think there is. You think, surely every place has a reality to it? But no. Not Las Vegas. Amsterdam, maybe. Vegas, no."

"Tell me about our girl."

"Adriana Chekhov. She's Israeli by birth, though I don't know where she lives now. She moves around a lot, apparently. She's done occasional freelance work for your organization, when the Soviets were in Afghanistan."

"Running drugs?"

"Guns. She does whatever pays, for whoever's paying. I think CIA keeps her on retainer for your bomb-buying operation. She goes around Eastern Europe inquiring after used atomic weaponry and such that perhaps the Soviets have misplaced."

"A woman does this?"

"Women are born spies. They can get away with so much more than men because they're discreet. No pissing contests, no rash actions."

"You ever met her?"

"Never laid eyes on her."

"How will we know her?"

"She gets paid to kill people and buy atomic weapons. She'll find us."

Sure enough, a woman with long red hair and gray eyes came in and sat at their table. She had a rifle-straight spine and delicate features, and wore a dull green sweater and a brown vest that masked her curves. Without speaking, the woman rolled an expert joint, taking care with each piece of the marijuana. She licked the papers and lit the end and began puffing. She blew smoke in their faces, and after several puffs she said in a low, husky voice, "It's okay that I join you?"

"We're Americans," said Mr. French. "We welcome everyone."

The woman smirked. "Surely not everyone. I've visited your country. New York. D.C. Miami. I've seen the problems you have."

"But we solve those problems. That's what makes us great."

The woman puffed her joint and went on as though Mr. French had not just spoken. "You're a conservative country. You fear change. Take your Cuban exiles. You want them out. They want to get out. But no one has the stones to disrupt the status quo, to enact real change."

"We're working to take care of our Cubans," West said.

She cut her eyes to him. "Perhaps God will intervene."

"With luck, God will prevail."

"You believe in Providence?"

"I don't see why not," West said, "though this really isn't my area of expertise."

The woman finished her joint and chuckled. "Expertise. So, Alexander and Bobby, you've come a long way to discuss things other than God."

"So have you, Ms. Chekhov," Mr. French said.

"Adriana is fine. I'm happy to discuss God wherever there's an occasion. It's comforting, don't you think, the three of us, with our secret lives and our secret motives, should come together to discuss a higher power, a light to guide us. But. For me, Israel is only a few hours to Amsterdam. Tell me about your Miami."

"I'll turn this over to Bobby," Mr. French said.

"Right," West said. "Well, I've made all the arrangements. We have an airline to take care of customs, and I've set up a slush fund with a holding company to take care of our finances."

The woman sat back and crossed her arms and listened as West explained the finer points. The U.S. drug culture had undergone severe changes over the past decade. During the Vietnam War, Chekhov had helped a man establish a heroin supply chain out of East Asia, and business had boomed for everyone—the New York gangsters, the Asian producers, and those in the middle like Chekhov. A side business for her, really, while she scouted Malaysia and the Philippines for threats to Israel.

"You know this how?" she interrupted.

West smiled. "I keep my ear to the ground."

When the Vietnam War had come to an end, the DEA made several high-profile busts, and the Colombians cornered the market with cocaine in the ghettos. Right now, heroin was still popular in New York, and high-priced cocaine was all the rage among Miami businessmen and the Hollywood set. It was only a matter of time before the Colombians had a monopoly on the entire U.S. drug market. West and Mr. French's brilliant plan would bring back the high-dollar days of Vietnam.

Chekhov saw where they were going and said, "You want me to help you drive out the Colombians."

"We want you to help facilitate transport between Afghanistan and Miami," West said.

"Our thinking," Mr. French said, "is that Afghani farmers have enough supply to completely saturate the U.S. market. We don't have to drive the Colombians anywhere. If we can get this operation up and running, the cocaine cowboys will be out of business by 1990."

Chekhov smoked another joint while West finished explaining the logistics. She was an attractive woman, with thick and sensual lips, yet she was also somehow beyond sexual. No flirtation in her glance, no lack of control or self-understanding. The smoke clouded West's thoughts and he admired her for suggesting a meet-up here, where the woman obviously was in control. And if something went wrong? If they tried to set her up? Chekhov doubtless had an underground hiding place nearby where she could disappear, and she would resurface in six months to kill them in their sleep. The woman was a ghost who lived in the darker provinces beyond the political, the social, perhaps even beyond time itself. She was the snake who showed you the fruit. She was the devil who gambled with God, the archangel who came to collect what was due. She struck a match and watched it burn as West talked. When they'd made their arrangements, Chekhov understood not only her role and the potential payout, she also understood the subtle wedge between these two men, the gangster and the spy. There was no way for her to know how West and Mr. French were playing off each other, but she knew enough to ensure she was paid in cash up front.

She said, "You should really stay an extra day or two, if this is your first time." She dropped a card on the table. "I recommend you give her a call. Don't bother with the women in the windows. They are for the tourists. She will show you the real Amsterdam."

On the card was a phone number and the name Anna Anna. The double name struck West as funny, but Mr. French and Chekhov failed to see the humor.

"Interesting chick," Mr. French said when she'd left.

"That's one word for her," West said. "You trust her?"

"I think we can make use of her."

West nodded. Adriana had told them six to eight weeks for the next shipment, but that what they wanted would be no trouble. By the end of April the atmosphere would be totally changed and she would be just another vendor with a financial incentive to maintain an even keel.

"Well," Mr. French said as he stood up. "I'm going to find a club. You can come with me, or you might want to give her a call."

Instead of calling the girl, West followed Mr. French down to the blue light district and into a club. The club was down in a basement and had a second floor in the back. It was dark and smoky and lit in neon violet. House music thrummed and men in tight shirts or no shirts walked by and the air was hot and still and smelled of stale sweat. The doorman made West check his coat, a racket to make a few guilders. Though the music bounced, no one danced.

They went up the stairs at the back, into a narrow corridor to the bar, and the corridor had private rooms off to the left with grainy porn on TVs. They circled the club and went back downstairs and Mr. French ordered a Beck's and moved into the dance area and shook his shoulders and hunkered his head, and soon other men joined him. At the bar West ordered a Beck's for himself and watched Mr. French cut loose. A man jumped onto a pillar and began to strip and other men nodded at him.

West drank his beer and Mr. French came over to order another. "Relax," he said. "They don't teach you about this at the Farm?"

"If you let on you have queer tendencies, they don't let you in," Bobby said, "and if you try to hide your queer tendencies, they'll beat it out of you in basic training."

"No good, my friend. Look at you. No wonder the CIA has so many intelligence problems. You can't blend in. You've got to experience everything."

Mr. French pulled a hexagonal pill from a white bottle in his pocket, swallowed it with a gulp of beer, shook one out for West.

"What is it?"

"It's an opioid, Bobby. Makes you feel good."

Mr. French set the pill on the bar and went back to the dance floor. West ordered another beer and said to the bartender, "Is that true? Do I stand out?"

The bartender, a rippled hunk of muscle, shrugged.

West swallowed the pill.

"You got a phone booth in here?" West asked.

The bartender raised an eyebrow.

"Phone?" West held up his finger and thumb in a receiver shape.

The bartender nodded his head toward back and West turned and saw stairs leading down deeper below the ground. At the base of the stairs, he passed a couple groping each other, both oblivious as he headed to the phone in the back. West dialed the woman's number, listened as the ringing phone merged with the thumping bass upstairs.

3

The money came like a flood, always in cash, briefcases of it. A million here, five hundred thousand there, another million. West installed a safe in the floor of his home office, covered it with an area rug, and tried to ignore what festered under the floor. Mr. French's man dropped the money at West's house every Friday afternoon, and hung around long enough for West to count it.

Occasionally West asked, "How's business?" or, "Plans this weekend?" or, "You a baseball fan?"

("Fine. No. No.")

The drugs came in from a C130 out of Afghanistan, loaded by local Taliban freedom fighters, the same men who fought the Soviets and who had been abandoned by U.S. interests, given an empty job to do by CIA: sow the seeds of American destruction, poison us from the inside out like a cancer. The plane landed at the airport where, under Felix Machado's guidance, the drugs were transported to a warehouse along the Miami River. They were then distributed among an army of men lower and lower on the totem pole, down to boys with Mac 10s fighting for turf. The money trickled back up the layers of the org chart, salesmen to managers to directors, each middleman pulling his take. West invested overflow profits to help launch Radio Martí and listened to stories from Felix about the

Cuban cause and how it was only a matter of time before the second generation of exiles in America rose up. "Keep the money coming in," Felix said. "You'll see." Until then, West squirreled away cash in his safe, cooked books, phony transactions on behalf of the Artium Group, then phony withdrawals, and then he gave the money back to Felix or whatever thug came for it at the end of the month. That money never touched the AG's accounts, but it was there nonetheless, ghost money, real transactions, real debts.

Every Friday West would leave around four, and he would drive slow and cautious to his home in Mangrove Estates, the cash in his briefcase in the front seat. Since the divorce he'd lived in a modest house in Coral Gables near the U, an old neighborhood with mature trees and enough respectability that he could stay here as long as he needed, until he paid off the note on his old house—Isabel's house—and could invest in something nicer for himself. As he traveled down the Dixie Highway, he kept an eye on the other cars around him to ensure he wasn't being followed. He always made a few extra turns—would that Datsun exit here? Was that van driving a little too close?—and when he pulled into his driveway, he glanced around to see if any of his neighbors were out, watering their lawns or pruning shrubs or otherwise waiting for him to get home. The cash in his briefcase burned like radioactive waste, its half-life decay so gradual that everyone alive would be long dead before its poison bled dry one ion, one dollar at a time.

He tried not to think about what would happen when this house of cards tumbled down. It would, it would. He couldn't decide which was worse: having an angry smuggler fly in from Central Asia to rip out his fingernails or having a higher-up in the CIA, or the SEC, or some unnamed agency, drag him off to a life in prison for running a scam against the U.S. government. America was built on corruption and scams, from financing the American Revolution to the 20th century entitlement state. Everyone had a hustle going: the direct marketer selling junk bonds, the fitness guru selling blenders on late-night television, the president selling himself and his vision of economic recovery. *Morning again in America,* he would call it in the fall campaign. A resurgence of prosperity. This was how capitalism worked, markets in free exchange, the rise and fall of financiers, businesses, nations. In such a landscape, West merely played the game, socking away money to pay off his debts, his alimony to Isabel, his individual retirement account and perhaps an overdose of insurance.

This was the story he told himself.

There was nothing wrong with that.

A few months into his new arrangement and six figures in the bank for his troubles, West arrived home to find his daughter in his living room. At seventeen, Holly was a complete mystery to him, no longer his little girl but rather a stranger who stayed with him two weekends a month. Lanky, joints out of socket, bones jutting out in skeletal isolation from her overlong arms and legs, she nonetheless carried herself with fluidity and grace, much like his ex-wife. It terrified him.

The TV was on and a talk show host chattered and smiled. An audience roared. The host did a jig on screen, and the audience roared some more. Holly watched it with a dazed expression, neither cracking a smile at the antics nor seeming at all conscious of her surroundings.

He set his briefcase by the door and took off his jacket. "Hey," he said.

"Hey, Daddy." Her voice flat, muted, her eyes on the screen.

He kicked off his shoes. "Everything all right?"

"It's your weekend," she said, eyes still fixed on the TV.

Although he'd forgotten, he said, "I know. I just wasn't expecting you right when I got home."

"Here I am."

"I'm glad to see you."

He carried the briefcase to the couch, leaned over and kissed her on the forehead.

"I have a few loose ends to tie up from work." Already going to his office. Just let him get the money in the safe. "Would you like to go out for dinner?"

"OK," she said.

Just let him get the money in the safe and pour a drink, and he will be good to go, ready to visit with his daughter. Business in one compartment, family another.

As he was bending over the safe and unloading the contents of his briefcase, just over half a million dollars, Holly surprised him by asking, from the doorway, "How long have you had that safe?"

"For a while now." He paused with a bundle of cash in his hand. His back was between her and the contents, so he shoveled the rest of the money into the safe, haphazardly, sloppily. Don't jerk around. Don't act like this is a secret. He closed the safe and centered the rug over it. He groaned as he put weight on his arms and rose from his knees. "I'm getting too old to be crawling around on the floor," he said.

"You never used to have a safe."

"My job has changed. I've got a few more responsibilities now."

"That's a lot of money." She crossed her arms, blew hair out of her face.

"It would be a lot if it were mine to keep," he said. "In the business world, it's not so much."

"I thought you said you capitalists didn't sit around hoarding money."

"I'm not hoarding it." He clucked and took a breath and said again, more quietly, "I'm not hoarding it. It's part of my job."

"Loan sharking."

"Good god, I'm not a loan shark. It's business. Money sloshes around the world like musical chairs and has to land somewhere."

"What are you doing with it?"

"I'm just holding it for now. It's going into the stock market, eventually," he lied, "but I won't meet my broker until Wednesday." His knee popped as he limped toward her. He put his arm around her and led her out of the office.

She pulled away from him and walked swiftly back to the couch. She picked up the remote and, before channel surfing, she said, "That rug looks suspicious, you know."

He clicked off the office light and shut the door. "I don't think anyone's going to rob me," he said. "Unless you've got designs on it."

"Whatever." She raised the volume so that the commercials—click, click, click—yelled at him, muted him.

He clawed a few lumps of ice from the freezer and sloshed whiskey into the glass. His drink was Maker's Mark, something he'd once seen a businessman drink when he was in college. *It tastes expensive…and is.* An asinine slogan, but he was hooked on the brand. Funny how those early impressions followed you for decades. He sipped the whiskey and gnawed on the ice, leaning over the kitchen counter.

Holly sank into the couch cushions and continued her rapid flip through the channels—click, click, click. The five o'clock news was on the local stations, plastic anchors delivering the day's rundown. Commercials seemed to be on all the cable channels. Bleach, plastic baggies, cereal. All the things you need for domestic bliss. We live in an age of permanent prosperity. Let us celebrate by squeezing our toilet paper.

"Have you signed up for your fall classes?" he yelled over the screaming ads.

"Not yet."

"Senior year. That's a big one."

She muted the TV. "You know, whiskey's bad for your liver."

"I really enjoyed high school," he went on.

"Alcoholism's a disease. We had a police officer come in and explain."

"My favorite subject was calculus. Learning the logic of equations can teach you a lot about accounting." He took another swig.

"Right now, you're poisoning yourself with each sip."

He spat out a sliver of ice. "I just had my first sip. Nothing's in my blood yet. Besides, it's only bad if you're an alcoholic. Which I'm not. I don't drink enough for cirrhosis."

"Your liver is working overtime."

"Everything is bad for you in large enough doses. Soda pop is bad for you."

"Poison," she said again.

"All that sugar."

She found a channel without commercials, turned the volume back on. A chef was demonstrating a food processor, the half-hour segment one long commercial disguised as a show. "I'm not good at math," she said. "You know this. Numbers don't agree with me."

"You used to like it. I remember helping you practice your multiplication tables."

She rolled her eyes. "In third grade. Everything was fun back then. It's weird that you have so much money in the house."

He would think about that line later, when the money and the girl went missing. *Unless you've got designs on it,* he'd said. So trusting, so cavalier.

"Best not tell your mother," he said. He drained the whiskey. All that was left in the glass were two tiny bullets of ice, quickly melting into an amber-tinted liquid. Whiskey-water. He would drink that as well.

4

What led Holly Hernandez, in the spring of 1984 and three months shy of her eighteenth birthday, to steal $3 million and ride north with a boy she hardly knew, so that she would find herself shivering in some no-name gas station's unisex shower stall, awash in halogen light and coming to the realization that she'd made a terrible mistake, that she lacked the drive or connections to get anywhere real, New York or L.A., or even the good sense to go home to Miami?

Perhaps it started with a moment in March, when after a few drinks she felt the weight of her life bearing down on her, a subtle glimpse of wisdom beyond her years. If only she could break free of herself and latch onto something tangible in the world.

At the club one Wednesday night she made out with a man in his early twenties. He was tall and skinny and had white pants and a Jewish Afro. They did lines of coke in the bathroom. He bought her drinks and she felt the rum-buzz and the sugar-high. Sweat made her skin sticky and warm, and she felt herself flush beneath the flashing red and green lights, the drumbeat of the club mix driving her onward into the great unknown, and she pressed herself on the man. He scraped at her back with too-long nails and clamped his mouth to hers, and when they came up for air he could barely restrain himself.

He said, "Come with me, come on," and pulled her into the cooling March night.

South Beach Miami: where cool means enough of the humidity has burned away so a person can breathe.

They stumbled into the man's Trans-Am and drove. He leaned over and tried to kiss her while barreling down the highway, but she pushed him away and asked for a cigarette. As they turned onto the freeway and headed out of the city, away from the skyscrapers, she smoked and gave no indication that she cared where they were going. They were young and wild and desperate and free, and the night was theirs for the taking.

"Where you live, baby?" he asked, and it could have been a line from a movie.

"Oh, baby, I live way back there," she parroted.

"That right?" He drove on.

North of the city, he pulled onto State Route 84, into a stark, run-down neighborhood that reminded her of her grandfather's home in Hialeah, or the industrial strip by the river. They turned into a trailer park next to a swamp, crept down a dirt path and stopped in front of a brown double-wide.

"You live here?" she asked.

"My weekend house is in Coconut Grove, but I got to work at the marina tomorrow."

She followed him into a messy, cramped room that smelled of mothballs and cigarettes. He left her in the living room and she stood for a moment, the rum-buzz fading and a sense of exhaustion coming over her. The weight of the evening, the mistake she was unable to stop herself from making. *Drive,* she thought. *Take me out of this state. New York, L.A., somewhere not Miami. Just drive.*

By now her friends would all have left the club and gone home, and her mother, if she were a proper mother, would know something was amiss. But no, her mother was probably under a Valium spell, and likely wouldn't notice Holly's absence at all.

The man had a bottle of Jim Beam on the counter and she unscrewed the lid and took a sip, coughed it back up and sprayed whiskey across his countertop. She took another sip.

"Whoa, there," he said. "You don't have to drink that poison."

They did two lines of coke off a mirror on his coffee table and the buzz kicked back in.

He then wrestled her to bed where she lay back and forgot about the past and the future. This was not the first time she had been with a man, and if a voice inside her had for a moment said, *Maybe we should quit, maybe you're pushing past a wall where you can't get back,* another, louder voice would have said, *Hey, honey, you just do what you want to do,* and she did.

In the morning she woke and felt as though she were looking through a cracked windshield, splinters and fragments of glass between her and the rest of the world. The man was gone, and on the table were two twenty-dollar bills and a note that said, *Got to run, here's money for a cab.*

She moved to the bathroom and, after throwing up and wiping her mouth with a square of cheap toilet paper, she lay down on the cold linoleum and stayed there until mid-afternoon when she heard children's voices as they walked between this trailer and the next. One of the kids drummed on the wall as they slouched by. She got up and straightened her skirt and ran water over her face, and in the mirror she got a glimpse of what she might look like in a few years, after the world had a chance to batter her around some more.

With the forty dollars in her purse she sat in a diner down the street from the trailer park and ordered coffee and French toast and tried to figure out what to do with her life. She was a half-hour out of Miami, and over coffee she thought about her mother, the witchy woman who never understood her, or her father, who, while loving, was an asshole for abandoning the family for his work. She thought of school, and thought she might miss one or two of her friends, but, fuck it, why not just keep moving and see where she landed? Perhaps she could outrun this feeling that life had no more to offer than a pointless everyday sense of being.

But after she paid for her breakfast, she moved to the street and hitched her thumb in the air for passing cars. A man in a station wagon picked her up. He got her to downtown Miami, and from there she was able to catch a bus home.

5

Keith Sorrells was sick of selling cigarettes. Only job he could get out of high school that would get him out of the house, out of town, out of the state. No college for this kid: four more years of classroom drudgery as a Tiger or a Gamecock? No, thanks. The only child of a Baptist preacher and a part-time real estate agent, he'd had his fill of meet-and-greets and social affairs, and wanted nothing more than to be left alone. Oh, he'd gotten out of South Carolina all right. He was a retail sales rep stationed out of Savannah: that meant he motored around South Georgia ten hours a day, haggling convenience store clerks about boosting their display of his main brand. C-stores, they called them. Market share. SKUs. Whole slew of jargon he never understood. What he did understand is that he had consistently low sales numbers (*underperforming,* in the corporate parlance), and for this he managed to get himself fired (*terminated*) one Friday afternoon in the spring of 1984.

On the day of his termination, he got sloshed at J.E.B. Stuart's, a riverfront redneck dive amid a throng of piano bars in Savannah's commercial district. There a friend named Big Duck gave him a lead on a line of work in South Florida.

"My girlfriend's got a cousin in Miami, says there's plenty of work."

"What kind of work?" Keith asked.

Big Duck shook his head. "You name it. Selling houses, selling coke. Everything's up for sale down there."

"I'm tired of sales. How do you stay with it?"

Keith didn't know what Big Duck's real name was—Benjamin David, perhaps, or perhaps nothing at all related, Jeff or Sam or some bullshit—but the dude carried himself like a burley Irish drunk with a high forehead and a low tolerance for equivocation. B.D. was a few years older than Keith, maybe twenty-five, and had been in territory sales all his adult life. Must have driven a hundred thousand miles around the southeast, burned up I-95, pot-holed the lazy back roads, zigzagged along Carolina byways. B.D. told him, "It gets easier after six months. Most guys burn out in the first year."

"Yeah, they get fired too?"

"Some do. Some just quit."

"I ain't a quitter."

"No shame in finding something suits you better."

"And what might that be?"

"Hell, I don't know. You want another drink?"

Keith handed over a twenty, knowing he wouldn't get change. He had the look of a man smart enough to know he was being taken advantage of, yet dumb enough to let it happen.

B.D. went up for another pitcher. He came back and refilled Keith's mug, said, "You want, I'll give you her cousin's number. I think he works for a couple of movers. Maybe he needs an extra hand."

"Better than working in sales. Customers are the worst. Always got to be convinced something's a good deal."

B.D. blew a cloud of smoke across the table. "That's just human nature. We're skeptical, but we love a good deal if we can find one."

The next day Keith cashed his last paycheck, packed a duffel bag, and got in his pickup with enough money to last a month if he could land a cheap place to stay. He didn't own anything worth keeping, so he left his stuff in the ground-floor apartment he rented and headed south just at dawn. No job, no girl, nothing keeping in him Savannah and he damn sure wasn't about to head back home to live with his parents. Miami sounded like a fine spot for his next incarnation. In his two years out of high school, he'd managed to get a tattoo of the Japanese word for *crane* on his bicep (he was moved by the character's design, but thought nothing of the bird), sleep with two women (he'd underperformed with the first, and had not been invited to try again; he'd hoped the second might turn into something, but the woman had just been looking to score), read Genesis and the four Gospels (enough to know he still hated to read but also enough to reinforce the fear and guilt and wonder accompanying the belief you had an immortal soul and were a child of God), borrowed several thousand dollars from his parents (and hadn't made a move to pay it back), and lived with the inkling that his real life had yet to begin, that some unknown future still lay before him.

He drove a white Chevy pickup with a V8 and gas mileage that didn't matter now that the late-seventies energy crisis was a dim blur in the rear-view. With a phone number for B.D.'s girlfriend's cousin in his pocket, he headed south. Out of the low-country, with its tall grasses and coastal winds and palmettos, heat boiled on the roadway not long after sunup. The southern Georgia landscape was all dust, billows of it. Dust so thick you couldn't even see the sky or the sun in it, just a wall of hot light that set the red land afire. Across the state line, Florida looked the same at first—red clay and rednecks—but as you moved south and the day fired up, the land greened and the trees fell away. A casserole of gray clouds in the eastern sky created a startling contrast of sun here and shade there. The dust dissipated, replaced by wetland shrubs, cypress swamps and flatlands. Keith had always thought Savannah hot compared to the Carolina mountains, where the hills shaded you from the worst of the southern heat, the swelter tempered by a perpetual breeze nonexistent down in the low-country. What he couldn't know, of course, was how much worse Florida would be, more like a Latin American country than good ole U.S. of A. Crops here may as well be cocaine or bananas or hot peppers. This was not the United States. This was alien country. Florida: a state on the edge, an appendage isolated from the rest of America. Old people and ex-cons. Cuban exiles and Haitian immigrants and Colombian drug runners.

After eight hours meandering down I-95 and the turnpike, Keith made it to Miami around three. Tall buildings jagged out of the swamps, a hot strip of glistening banks built from drug money. From the freeway he saw signs for Miami Beach, crossed the MacArthur Causeway and landed in the Art Deco district, a strange brew of the gaudy old, their faces tanned to leather, and sunglassed thugs in white suits. Men in muscle shirts no doubt heading to or from a bodybuilding session. Women with bronze cleavage and tight asses and shopping bags. Roller skates and bikinis. Pastel colors and neon lights. Porsches, Benzes, a Maserati. A line of palm trees between the road and the beach like sentries, grown on farms and transplanted for local flavor. And here was Keith: a rube in a redneck truck.

He drove on until he found a gas station—a c-store—and pulled in. There was a payphone in front of the shop, but he felt anxious about calling B.D.'s girlfriend's cousin straight away. If the man wouldn't see him—or if B.D. had exaggerated the opportunities in South Florida—Keith was up a creek. Nothing to do but sleep on the beach and head back home. Won over by a tropical display at the front of the store, he bought an exotic soda and drank half of it in the parking lot.

He sweated in the muggy heat. Sunlight beat the pavement around him, and fumes danced across the ground. In a passing car, rap music drummed. Bass rattled loose plastic. *BOOM, rrrr, BOOM, rrrr.* The tinted windows hid the driver, but Keith felt eyes on him as the car crept by. When it had passed, Keith placed his call.

The cousin—ID'd as Felix on a scrap of paper—answered after five rings, when Keith was about to hang up. He introduced himself.

"Oh yeah, Jim said you might be calling."

"Jim?"

"Yeah. What do you call him?"

"Everyone there calls him Big Duck."

The man laughed. "He never told me that. What can I do for you, Mr. Keith?"

In the c-store parking lot, there was a break from the traffic so Keith could hear the distant hum of the sea, punctuated by the caw of seagulls overhead. He said, "I was hoping you could help me find a line on a job. B.D.—Jim—said there was plenty to do in Miami."

"You got a specialty?"

"I was selling cigarettes, up in Savannah." He added, "To gas stations, mostly."

"Got it. Salesman then."

"If you want to call me that," Keith said.

"Hey, this is America. This whole country's about sales."

"I hate it."

"What, you want to repair air conditioners or something?"

"You know an easier way to get rich?"

Felix laughed and said, "Maybe. Tell you what, why don't we meet this evening. Where are you now?"

"Near the beach."

"Hey, beaches are everywhere here. What beach?"

"I don't know. The beach. The sign said South Beach."

"I'm a ways from there, but what the hell. We could hit up a few clubs. You up for it?"

"I could do that."

"There's a spot called Willow 57, right on Ocean Drive, near Sixth Street. You want to meet me there, what, nine o'clock?"

"How will I find you?"

"Just sit at the end of the bar, near the register. I'll find you. We'll have ourselves a good time and see if we can't find some reason for you to stay in Miami. You like seafood?"

"Sure?"

"You're searching for something to do, there's a great little shrimp shack called Smoky's. The woman who owns it, Carol something, she'll hook you up with a bottomless basket of fried shrimp. It's right down at the bottom of the key—you probably passed it on the way in—right near the police horse stables. Get yourself a plate of shrimp and a few beers, and I'll see you at nine."

*

After a nap on the beach, he woke with his feet in the water and went to check into a motel. A spot called the Blue Yonder reminded him of the rundown hotel his family had always stayed at during summer trips to Myrtle Beach. He showered and smoked a few cigarettes on the balcony, watched the girls skate by a few stories below.

He still had time to kill before meeting with Felix, and he never did know how to deal with free time. Not a patient man, Keith.

He put on the closest thing he owned to club clothing, a white button-down and jeans and cowboy boots, and then he walked down to find Smoky's. The dive bar was on a houseboat docked up near the police facilities. A wobbly plank led to an outdoor bar. He enjoyed two baskets of grilled shrimp with heavy Old Bay seasoning and two twenty-ounce glasses of pilsner. He had the frame of a rooster, so he was buzzed as all get out.

The boat bar had a mix of patrons, mostly men. A few looked like salty dog captains. A few were in white suits and could have been investment bankers, though Keith suspected them of being in some less reputable line of work. A bald man with a big head and wearing a florid shirt sat at the end of the bar and appeared to be keeping an eye on Keith. At one point he raised his glass in salute.

"You got a problem, buddy?" Keith asked.

The man shook his head. "Just out for an afternoon libation," he said, and he took a sip of whatever was in his glass. Gin, maybe.

Keith flagged the waitress over and handed over a twenty to cover his tab.

It was still early when he shuffled his way up Ocean Drive to Felix Machado's club, but he'd needed to get out of the boat bar before paranoia closed in. The florid man and his gin, the white suits and their mustaches, the captain and his paunch: was there no one ordinary in this town he might trust? He felt itchy with anticipation.

Somewhere in the distance, someone played steel drums. The tourists had morphed from the scantily clad beach bums to the sharp dressed see-and-be-seen crowd. A fat man, sitting on a bench and smoking a cigarette, nodded to him as he came off the boat and headed up the avenue. Keith didn't look back but felt the fat man's eyes on him, sensed the man had gotten up to follow him. Could be a coincidence. Could be he turned back and the man was right where he'd been.

Keith stepped lively.

Willow 57 was a small club with a stage and disco ball in the back, flickering lights, synth pop, high ceilings. The neon blues and reds would be festive if anyone were out, but as it was, nothing was sadder than dance music and a near-empty club. The only patrons, a group of girls who had to be underage, grooved near the stage with shots and electric iced drinks. The bartender wiped down tables, a few other staffers stood in the corner near the stage. A heavyset man with a droopy mustache, wearing a leopard shirt and sporting a carpet of exposed chest hair, sat at one end of the bar but took no notice of Keith as he sat at the other. Keith felt the man's eyes on him but every glance he snuck, the man was staring off in the distance.

When the bartender came over, Keith ordered a beer. The man bobbed his head and cracked open a bottle.

"Mr. Keith!" a man said behind him.

Two men: the first was the fat man on the bench outside the shrimp shack. The thing about Miami, Keith was learning, there was always someone watching. He thought of the florid man in the boat, the tinted windows of the Japanese auto, and the men in suits on the beach.

The second man was a rail-thin Hispanic a few years older than Keith, with a lotto-winning grin and large white pants left over from the seventies. "Felix Machado," he said. "This is my associate."

Felix hadn't announced the hefty man's name, so Keith merely nodded to him.

"So how'd you wind up in Miami?"

"I got sick of my last job, and B.D.—Jim—told me there was a lot of work down here."

"He wasn't lying, amigo. This town has done quite well for itself over the last few years. He tell you anything about what we do here?"

"Just said there was plenty of work."

"You've seen the strip out there. Part of our economy is tourism, so there's always opportunities for someone wait tables or tend bar, same as any destination."

Felix ordered a rum punch. His associate crossed his arms and remained standing. The bar had mirrors on every wall, rimmed with red neon. The haze of cigarette smoke shimmered in the lights.

"Now, if you were hoping to make some serious income, we've got other opportunities. If you've got the right disposition."

Keith knew what the man was hinting at, and knew he had no qualms with certain businesses, no stomach for others. "What kind of opportunities?"

"Well, for instance, my employer has a logistics operation. Runs a supply chain around South Florida. Little of this, little of that. You'd be surprised how much goes on behind the scenes to keep a city in business. Point being, I thought with your experience in sales, you might be a good addition to our operation. We need someone who knows how to get something delivered on time, who can follow a schedule, that sort of thing."

"That's all I did at my last job."

"Exactly. I know from Jim that stocking convenience stores can wear a body down. The nice thing about our operation is we don't run our employees ragged. There's a variety of work, so as long as you get the work done, there's plenty of time to enjoy life down here in paradise."

Keith looked over at the girls near the stage. Felix smoked a cigarette, tapped his glass on the bar to signal another round.

The associate—still standing, still silent—narrowed his eyes and said, "I've seen that girl somewhere."

Felix glanced their way. "Which one? The girl in red? She's Bobby West's daughter."

"What's she doing here?"

"Drinking, it looks it," Felix said. "Bobby's one of our business partners. His daughter is, I don't know. Interesting."

The girl's ears must have been burning, because she looked up and smiled at the three men at the bar. She said something to her friends and then came their way. She sidled up to the bar in a slinky red top and a narrow band of white skirt that shined above her tawny legs. Keith sipped his beer.

"You the boss man?" she asked Felix.

"Me? Nah, our boss doesn't drink."

"That's no fun."

"Tell me about it."

Keith was swirling. He sensed danger in Felix, something unhinged in the man, but he clearly had charm. All he'd done was smile, but he'd taken charge somehow, cornered the girl, and she seemed to enjoy it. "And who's this one?" she said.

"This? Keith's here for a job interview."

"Oh, well don't let me interrupt."

"What are you drinking?" Felix asked her.

"Manhattans."

"Classy."

"I'm a classy lady." She had dark skin and long, lean limbs. When she crossed her legs, the way her short white skirt slid up her thighs made her seem pliable, like those legs could wrap around a man like an origami fold.

The bartender brought over a drink and then left as fast as he'd arrived. Felix pulled out a roll of cash, thumbed through a few hundreds and set a twenty on the bar. She watched and waited for what he had to say, the price of a free drink.

He said, "OK—what did you say your name was?"

"Holly."

"OK, Holly," Felix said. "I know we do business with your father, but we need to talk with Keith alone for a few more minutes. Wish him luck in his interview."

She flashed her teeth again. "Good luck, Keith."

When she was gone, the associate said, "That's not a coincidence, her being here."

"There are no coincidences, amigo. I'll have a talk with Bobby." Felix then turned back to Keith. "Our business is a little sensitive. Trade secrets and such. Her father manages several of our accounts, but since he's a vendor, if you will, I want to make sure he's being a good steward of our information. Anyway, where were we? Miami! A great city. Lot of *bonitas*, plenty of night life for a young man."

Keith's eyes had followed Holly back to the stage and he watched her as she settled in with her friends, fresh drink in her hand.

"That one, though." Felix chuckled. "She might be out of your league, cowboy."

Keith took a sip of his beer. He'd had a buzz since the shrimp shack, and knew if he weren't careful he would be plum drunk.

"So what do you think, Keith?"

"About what?"

"Your prospects in Miami."

"Maybe too soon to tell. Your company have a job opening?"

"I'll see what I can do, amigo. Give me a few days."

Felix Machado got up. The associate uncrossed his arms and stuck his hands in his pockets. Still hadn't uttered word one to Keith. Keith fastened his eyes on the girls by the stage. Holly was facing him and caught his eye.

"You hanging out here for a while?" Felix asked.

"I might."

Felix laughed. "*Bonita* like that, she'll wreck your life if you let her."

When they were gone Keith ordered another beer, nursed it by the bar, had nearly finished it when Holly came back up. "What's your play?" she asked him.

"Excuse me?"

"You finished your job interview. The boys left you here to mull things over." She sat on the stool beside him, eased her foot onto the rail between his feet, her leg tucked close to his. "Your mind's not on the job, is it?"

"Work's all the same."

"Exactly. So what are you still doing here?"

"How old are you?" he asked.

"Why do you want to know that?"

"Felix said your father was one of their associates."

"So are you worried about my age or my father?"

"Neither. Just curious."

She waved the bartender over. "I'd like another Manhattan. You want anything, Keith? On me."

His beer had a few ounces left in the glass. "I'm good," he said.

"Man knows his limits," she said to the bartender, who was already stirring her drink. "I always loved a Manhattan." She swallowed a cube of ice. "My father took me there on a business trip once. You ever been? It's not like the movies, your *Breakfast at Tiffany's*, where everyone dresses up and goes shopping. New York's a dirty place."

"I'd like to see it one day."

"Maybe you'll find a reason to visit one day. So did the goons hire you?"

"Jury's still out."

"Still, you're in Miami. Not a bad place to be in limbo, if you've got the money to enjoy it."

"That's what I keep hearing."

She swirled the cherry in her drink by the stem. "You going to make your million dollars here? Get rich and see the world? Throw money around like your friend Felix?"

"He's not my friend, yet."

"Uh-huh," she said. "You know, you look a little like a cowboy in that getup."

"Felix just called me *cowboy*."

"Did he. Maybe it's the boots. You a rodeo man or something?"

"What do you know about rodeos?" Keith asked. He knew next to nothing himself, had been to one with his grandfather and several of his cronies as a child. Bright lights, the clank of gates, the smell of shit.

"I know it's awful the way they treat those animals. In cages for our amusement."

"You got a problem with zoos?"

"Actually, I do."

"Well." He tipped his beer her way.

She pulled her leg back to her own stool, sipped her drink. "I won't hold it against you, if you're a rodeo man, but don't ever invite me out to one. I won't stand for it."

"Scout's honor."

"Good." She gave a quick nod as though something weighty had been decided. He couldn't figure what she wanted. Even with a few drinks in her, he could see she was intelligent, a quick wit and a fire in her eyes that told him to proceed with caution. She asked where he was staying.

"Why? You need a place to crash?"

"Too bold, Keith. You invite every girl over on the first date?"

"So this is a date now?"

"We're just getting to know each other. Same as you're getting to know the city."

"It seems nice."

"You have to be careful who you make friends with."

"Maybe I've found all the friends I need."

She cut her eyes his way and smiled. "Tell you what. I'm going back over to my friends right now. You want, you could give me your number. I can show you the real Miami."

She asked the bartender for a pen and scrap of paper.

"Everyone's lining up to give me a call," Keith said. "Why don't you give me your number?"

"A man who takes charge. I like that," she said. She wrote a number down, folded the paper in half, and handed it to him. "If I hear from you, I'll know you're looking for more than a one-night stand. Girl has to know you respect her. Treat her right."

She chuckled as she walked off. He watched her go, her limbs gliding her back to her friends.

One day in Miami, and Keith had gotten drunk, found a lead on a job, and met a girl.

B.D. may have been right.

The city seemed to have promise.

6

Keith lay low in the Blue Yonder for the better part of a week before Felix Machado finally got in touch on a Sunday to say he'd set up an interview with Mr. French.

"Actually, amigo, it's a job and an interview," Felix said.

"What's the job?"

"We need someone to tow a car back from Key West. You ever driven a tow truck?"

"I drove a dump truck once."

"You'll be fine then. We'll have the truck ready for you at the airport tomorrow. Long-term economy lot D. Plan to overnight in Key West. It's a fun bar town, you'll like it."

After Felix hung up, Keith dialed Holly's number.

"I wasn't sure you'd call," she said.

"Wasn't sure you'd remember me."

"Keith, if we're going to hang out and be friends, I'm going to need you to have a little more spine."

"I didn't know what we might talk about."

"You could ask me how I'm doing." She sounded more amused than anything else that she was having to lead him through the conversation. You'd think he'd never called a girl before, when in fact it was past history that made him hesitate. You get burned once, at the wrong time in life, it makes you cautious. He tried not to ask what she might see in him, how she might think he was more of a player with her father's associates than he was.

"How are you doing?" he asked in a robotic voice.

"Good God, Keith."

"I actually did have a reason for calling."

"Oh yeah?"

"You ever been to Key West?"

"Just once, when I was a kid. My mom said it was better before 'Margaritaville,' but I think my dad kinda liked it."

"Well, I've never been. I've got a job lined up and am going down there."

"My, my, you found that spine in a hurry, inviting me for an overnight. Aren't you worried I might be too young for you? That I might have school?"

"Do you?"

"I'm a senior. I can skip it."

It didn't occur to him that she might be lying about her age, or that he had all that much to worry about. It had sounded like she'd said yes. Without confirming if that was what she meant, he asked for her address and said he'd pick her up tomorrow after lunch.

The next afternoon she slid into his pickup in a skirt that certainly wouldn't pass the finger length test. She wore a cover-up over a low-cut tank top, but it was her legs that drew his eye. When her skirt slid up on the seat, he took a sip of coffee, kept his face neutral until she took his cheeks in her hands and planted a long kiss on him.

"Let's hit the road, Jack," she said.

"I've got to pick up my ride at the airport."

"Your ride?"

He said nothing, just drove them out the Dolphin Expressway and found the economy lot easily enough. He drove the perimeter and up and down a few rows until he saw, amid the lines of Chevrolets and Buicks and Fords and the odd Toyota, a tow truck backed into a space, Joe's Towing in cartoonish yellow font against the truck's red paint. If Keith knew anything at this point, it was that there was no Joe, and that whatever he'd be picking up in Key West, it wasn't the car Felix Machado was after.

"Are you kidding me?" Holly said. "That's your ride to Key West?"

"That's what the job is."

"Do you know what you've gotten yourself into?"

"Should I be worried?"

"It's your life, man."

"You want me to take you back?"

"Hell no, this thing just got interesting." She grinned and opened the passenger door. "What's up, boss?"

Felix's fat associate had climbed out of the tow truck and was coming over. Keith got out to shake his hand.

"What's she doing here?" the associate asked.

"I'm his new girlfriend," Holly said. "Didn't he tell you?"

"Felix didn't tell him to bring anyone along."

"Relax, I invited myself."

Holly danced around the side of the tow truck, hit the sides of it as she passed around in a loop. The associate said, "She's a firecracker. Maybe not the best plan to bring her."

"I think she'll be all right."

"Your call," the associate muttered, and handed over the keys and an address with driving instructions. "Park in the street. There's a room in your name at the Paradiso Inn. Mr. French will be in touch with you then."

7

The first rule of the Keys: Don't get in a hurry. To get to Key West you had to follow U.S. 1 through the rest of the island chain. A two-lane cut through the archipelago. Traffic bottlenecked and slowed every time a local in a jalopy turned into a bait shop and held up a stream of cars going back three miles. Reeds, marshes, flatland. The sun bled into the horizon and cast a pink streak across the waters, the bays and inlets and ponds, the foliage summer-green all year long. The seven-mile bridge splayed across the water like a straw.

"Hell, it's hot as a jail cell in here," she said. She began to unbutton her cover-up.

He glanced over at her. "How would you know a jail cell is hot?"

She flashed him a smile and finished with the buttons, jerked off her top. The tank was cut low, but she was alluring in other ways he couldn't pinpoint.

"Keep your eyes on the road, Keith," she said, and laughed. "Cool Keith."

As they rode on, his mind raced with thoughts of this girl beside him, of the adventure in South Florida, the rumble of the tow truck, whatever illicit work was ahead of him. A sexy girl, a life of style. It was a good move, getting out of Savannah.

They made it to Key West around sunset. He cruised down Truman, dodging bicyclists and jaywalkers, the stop-and-go shuffle of traffic lights, mopeds, college students and bikers all down for the party. She directed him to Simonton, then on up to Eaton, hang a right and you're there. He parked on a quiet strip across from a church tower. Outside, they could hear the party of Duval Street, but the Paradiso Inn was hidden behind a thicket of palm fronds, in a long lazy strip of mangroves and palm trees and stucco houses, shotgun style, porches, quiet sidewalks dark save for the faint glow of globe lighting. A few people sat on a second-story porch, feet propped on the rail. They sipped whiskey from glasses and followed Keith and Holly with their eyes, the Carolina rube and the Miami fashionista.

After checking in, they lit out for dinner and drinks on Duval. Tourists huffing like lost shoats. All the bars opened their doors and the party spilled into the street, beer in the gutters and ganja in the air. Old men with white beards and thin shaggy hair swayed on the sidewalks; middle-aged women in herds and too much lipstick waved their hands in the air and cheered for regaining their lost youth; a teenager sat at a café table and smoked, a nearby waiter pale and thin like an extra from *The Addams Family*; and a beggar leaned up against the pillar of a grand hotel, an old German shepherd at his feet. The scene a boozy blur of bright lights and colorful clothing and loud music—garage rock from one bar, slow ballads from another, steel drums from another. More wild than Myrtle Beach, for sure, but the same vibe Keith remembered from his childhood vacations. A girl on his arm this time, big brown eyes and no filter to her soul. They arrived at Mallory Square too late to toast the sunset, but enjoyed the swell of the crowd, the fire breather, the unicyclist, the tourist show. They ate at a Cuban restaurant, got smashed on fruit drinks, and stumbled back to the Paradiso Inn to find the tow truck missing.

"Of course," Holly slurred. "What did you think? Whatever you're picking up, it's not here in the tourist district. Plus, if you flunk your interview with Mr. French, you might not be going back to Miami."

She let that linger and went into the cottage.

He blinked a few times and stuck his hands in his pockets, shuffled after her. He wanted to ask her what else she knew, but instead he poured a glass of wine and sat on the couch beside her. She put her feet up on the coffee table. Dropped her chin and leaned into him and said, "So, Cool Keith, do you want to chat or what?"

He needed no other invitation and kissed her gently, then fierce. His mind reeled from the liquor at dinner so that the moment was a blur. She tasted smoky, slid lightly onto his hips and bore down, whispered, "Easy, cowboy," but kept him pinned to the couch.

He woke to a pounding on the door. It took a moment to disentangle himself from the girl, and was still buckling his pants when he opened the door, kept it half-ajar to hide Holly on the couch.

The proprietor said, "Phone call for you in the office."

"Who is it?"

"Didn't say," she said, already turning away. "You best come on. We don't like to keep the line tied up."

"Mr. Sorrells, thank you for coming," the man on the line said. Keith couldn't detect an accent, exactly, in the man's voice, though something about his inflection made him think of Eastern Europe, like maybe he had a bone stuck in his nasal passage. "Yes, Mr. Sorrells, Felix has had good things to say about you. Thank you for coming."

Keith thanked him for the opportunity.

"Tell you what," Mr. French said, "if you go out the front door of your lodging, across the street there's a shotgun house, pink, with a fabric store next door and white wicker furniture on the upstairs balcony. If you look out a window you can probably see me now."

Keith peered out the front window.

"Hello," Mr. French called into the phone.

A man waved from the porch across the street. A tropical bald man—shaved, not pattern baldness, though the shave could be a way to disguise the genes—wearing a pink sport coat over a blue and yellow Hawaiian shirt. He seemed familiar but Keith couldn't place him.

"Hello!"

"I see you."

"Yes. Well. You want to come over, we can start the interview right now."

Across the street, Mr. French met him at the front gate. Up close, the sport coat somehow seemed to increase his height and widen his shoulders so that, despite his beachcomber appearance, he had the air of authority, like a school principal monitoring crowds between classes, but his head was loose on his body. It swiveled like a startled bird trying to decide whether to take flight.

"Ah yes, Mr. Sorrells, hello," Mr. French said, as if they hadn't just spoken a minute ago. "Yes, come this way. We use the side door here." The air smelled of hot marijuana, as predominant in Key West as Confederate jasmine up in Savannah, and Keith inhaled deeply.

In the foyer, Keith noticed Mr. French's gaze settled on the middle of Keith's forehead rather than making eye contact, and as he spoke he rattled like a used car salesman.

"Yes, we use the side door here, and we explain it to our customers that it's a convenience. We could open the front door every time someone came in and out, but that would let this hot Key West air into the front lounge, and no one wants to wait in an intemperate environment. I do everything I can to make this environment pleasant for all our guests. We'll start at the top and work our way down."

Mr. French led him upstairs, where walls had been knocked down save a few support pillars. The house may have been old, but the floor was modern and sleek, several rooms partitioned off by glass and employees with headphones sat at desks with computer monitors before them and paperwork around them. Each room had a filing cabinet and a potted plant.

"This is our call center," said Mr. French. "We may have you do some collections work, if you're up for it. Don't worry—I don't have my people sitting in cubes all day. There's variety in my business, I'll say that. Do you have any sales experience? It's all about numbers, Keith. The law of averages. You'll learn it and you'll be amazed at the results. We offer a range of services, and we need someone who can handle more than one aspect of the business, sales to service to delivery, maybe even management."

"What is your business?"

"A&F Enterprises. Not the most creative—Alexander French— but our customers don't care what we're called. They're interested in our service, and everyone knows me by reputation. That's sound-proof glass there, which you won't find in any other call center in South Florida." Mr. French pointed at one of the rooms. "I want to give my salesmen top-of-the-line resources." He coughed. "Excuse me, but I just recovered from pneumonia—I'm not contagious but I have a leftover cough. I try to stay healthy. I work out five days a week. I get up at four a.m., but sometimes that's not enough. There's only so much you can do to control the body, but I have a few tricks. I've never had the stomach flu, for instance, not since I was a kid. You know what I do if I feel like I'm getting a stomach virus? Or if I'm around people I know are sick? I'll pop Pepto tab-lets—you just keep popping Pepto tablets and it coats your stomach and makes it hard for the virus to infect the rest of your body. I learned that trick from a secret service agent."

Mr. French delivered the tirade to Keith's forehead. Keith couldn't keep up, just smiled and nodded and wondered what kind of maniac he might be working for. Mr. French waved him back down the stairs and to the front room, decorated as though for a Victorian tea party—dark wood antiques and a musty, formal air, a piano in the corner.

"This is our customer parlor. So you know, we rarely bring cus-tomers in—most of our people go on sales calls, but if customers want to come in we want them to feel at home. That's marketing for you. We're not like a car dealership, where you have a salesman on one side of the table hammering a customer on the other. Here we try to have discussions, because what we offer sells itself. Our employees are just here to explain points of confusion and to facilitate the sale.

"Back here we've got the break room. The kitchen. And here's a café area because I want our visitors to feel right at home." At the back of the house, beyond the kitchen, was a well-lit room with café high-tops and barstools. The back door led to a veranda and a lush, shaded garden of brick walkways and green foliage and bright orange and pink flowers. "Our employees love this area. It's not just for our customers. We want a work space where you feel at home." Mr. French pointed to the wall. "I was frugal, though, with the paintings. I didn't want to invest in art so I took a few photos myself around Key West and had them blown up and framed."

"They look nice," Keith said.

"Now," Mr. French said, "this building is unique in that it's one of the few houses on Key West, or in Florida, for that matter, that has a basement. The Hemingway house has a basement because it was built on a hill—about a dozen feet above sea level. We're above sea level as well, though not as high up as Hemingway's house. The previous owners of this home spent a great deal of money installing and waterproofing a basement, and it's partly an illusion because the house is built a few feet up. You remember walking up to the porch before entering the front door? So the ground floor is actually four feet above ground, so the basement doesn't go as deep." Mr. French coughed again. "I promise I'm not contagious. Now, we use the basement for storage mainly, but we bring all new employees down here during the tour because I like for everyone to see the scope of our operation up front—just one time. Now, the rest of our interview process can be quite rigorous, so don't be alarmed."

Before Keith could register what Mr. French had just said, someone behind him placed a bag over his head and pinned his arms to his back.

Keith cursed, squirmed. His bony shoulders angled out, and he flailed like an unbroken horse. French's associate held him firm until he settled himself. When you lose your sight, the world takes on an abstract, dimensionless quality so that everything exists only in your mind, like the drama of program music. He tried again to struggle but it was like a giant hand had picked him up and squeezed him inside a fist.

"Now, now, it's just a precaution," Mr. French said, a less manic, more precise sentence than he'd spoken during the entire tour.

They dragged him down a flight of steps into a basement and threw him to the ground. A door closed, and he was left in the dark for some time. His arms were pinned tight to his back and his blood flow had all but quit. The basement was cool and smelled earthy, like an art classroom on pottery day. He called out until his voice was hoarse. He rolled over and stood up and felt around with his feet. His foot alighted on a wall, and he shuffled along the wall, tapping in front of him with the side of his foot until he bumped into a piece of furniture. He leaned against the wall and tapped at the obstruction, but the thing had a complex shape. Disoriented, he found himself surrounded by the furniture on all sides so that he could no longer find the wall. Careful to avoid getting banged up, he sat down gingerly and leaned against a support and rested, now lost in the bowels of Mr. French's business.

After a time—maybe twenty minutes, maybe an hour—someone returned.

A light clicked on and hummed, and Keith was grabbed by the collar and hoisted into a chair. The associate uncuffed his hands and removed the bag from his head.

A lone bulb, stained brown, burned from the ceiling, and below it stood a short, shifty, overweight man with big eyebrows and a receding hairline. He appeared boringly English. A rounded face, flat nose, big pores, sweat. He wore a white button down and black suspenders and a too-wide tie.

The basement was empty save for a water heater in the corner and a stack of window frames. Keith had grown disoriented in the corner where the window frames jutted up against the stairwell. Standing by the stairs behind the man, French held a cigarette between his thumb and middle finger. Puffing it as though it were a joint, he said, "I'm sorry for the odd nature of this interview, but we have to go through this process. Everyone does before they're hired."

"Everyone gets tied up and thrown in a basement."

"Afraid so. We like to know how people will handle being thrown into unfamiliar situations, which is a possibility for our business." Mr. French inhaled slowly as though trying to smell a literal rat. "Now, how do you know Felix Machado?"

"He's a friend of a friend."

"That so?"

Mr. French walked forward and leaned over Keith, who for his part still sat in the chair. He was free, but the associate's unblinking face suggested he'd be better off to sit and listen.

"I'm going to be honest with you," Mr. French said. "We've got a lot of elements to our business, and we value discretion over anything else. You won't be doing anything illegal or dangerous, but if you ever were picked up and harassed, by the police say, we need you to stay calm. Are you calm?"

"What is it you do again?"

"We're in the import/export business. Do you know how to fly a plane?"

"Never tried."

"Hmm. I can't have you just driving a tow truck back and forth to Miami. Fundraising is an important part of our operation. I need associates who will bring in business. But we can talk about that. Today we've got a car hooked up to the truck and need you to get that back to Miami."

"Whose car is it?"

Mr. French tsk-tsk'd him. "We partner with the folks who run Florida Air Transport, and own a stake in parking lots that serve the airline. You know how it goes. People show up late for a flight, they just park anywhere they see a space. Florida Air seems to have a problem with people abandoning cars, so we tow them up to Miami."

"Why Miami?"

"That's where abandoned cars go," Mr. French said, waving his hand. "Now. If you're going to work with us, we need you to appreciate our business for what it is. Felix can show you the ropes, see if it's something you're up for. In the meantime, don't ever bring a girlfriend on a job." French leaned in close, eyeball to eyeball.

"Pussy's for your own time. There's plenty of time for that, but on the clock's not one of them. Can you work with that?"

Keith nodded and asked, "Does the job involve any more trips to the basement?"

Mr. French leaned back and chuckled. "Not from us. Not unless you decide you're no longer a part of the team."

"In which case I'm cooked."

"Well, yes."

"But the money's good in the meantime?"

"Very good, but I should warn you: if the delivery doesn't make it to Miami, or if that girlfriend you brought with you creates some trouble, or if you ever decide you're not the right fit for our team, the basement is the least of your worries."

8

"Holly's gone," Isabel told him on the phone.

West sat on his quasi-girlfriend's bed, glass of bourbon in hand before nine in the morning, and tried to process what his ex-wife was telling him. "What do you mean she's gone?" he asked. "Gone where?"

"I wouldn't be calling if I knew that. Have you heard from her?"

"Not recently. Slow down and start from the beginning."

"The beginning is she's gone, Bobby. She told me she was spending Monday night with a friend and didn't come home yesterday. She never went over to her friend's house, so I don't know where she's been."

"Jesus! Why didn't you call me yesterday?"

"I did, Bobby. I filled your answering machine with messages all night. You didn't get them?"

"Must be broken," he muttered, already thinking ahead. Of course he hadn't been home yesterday to check his messages, no messages were ever worth receiving until your seventeen-year-old daughter disappears. Even if Holly returned in the time it took him to get to his house in Coconut Grove—his former house, for which he still paid the mortgage—Isabel would never let him forget this moment, the moment he failed in fatherhood. Another moment in a litany of failures, it seemed, when in truth they'd merely been an incompatible couple. She was giving him hell now, that exasperation all too familiar: "You never check in, you're always taking care of number one," she said.

He waited for her to finish, justified himself even as she called out his faults.

He'd never turned his back on Holly when she was a child, had always been the one to catch her just before she climbed up the bookshelf or dove head-first off the couch, yet now over the course of eight or so months he'd let his life slide, slide, slide. Isabel was still talking. The whiskey had gone down quickly, so all he had left in the glass were two cubes of ice. "I didn't catch that," he said.

"I said the police are on the way. Do you think you can get here to give a statement before they leave?"

"Where do you think she went?" he asked.

"Dammit, Bobby, if I knew that I'd already be out there searching for her. You know she's crazy. Always has been. That better be cereal you're chomping on."

He swallowed the ice and said, "I'll be there as soon as I can."

Next he called his secretary to let her know he wouldn't make the meeting, glad actually for an excuse not to see those other men, with their rambling committee attitudes, their inconsequential nit-picking. By the time he locked Diana's front door and got in his car, his morning's malaise had evaporated like dew, and he felt assured that his day would soon be back on track. Holly was seventeen. Teenagers did this, they went out with friends and gave their parents anxiety. Likely as not, she came home yesterday while Isabel was at work, and then lit out again for the evening. Maybe she had a boyfriend to stay with. Maybe she and her mother'd had a fight. He couldn't blame his daughter for that. Isabel was a manic, domineering, passive-aggressive parent unhappy in her bookkeeping job but unwilling to take responsibility for herself. Drove a man to drink, if for no other reason than to appear shabbier than the image of her family she wanted to present.

He peeled out of Diana's neighborhood, crawled through Miami Beach and onto the throng of high-end sports cars on the

MacArthur Causeway. Transplanted palms lined the highway, the tropical foliage a constant reminder that there was nothing natural about Miami, the city a strip of buildings in the barrier between the beach and the swamps. The downtown skyline gleamed and he once again felt grateful for the excuse to skip the quarterly planning session, where he knew nothing would be accomplished beyond half a day of counting seconds until he could get out and grab another drink. He bypassed downtown and followed the A1A down the Dixie Highway and mulled over the company's balance sheet. The company's finances were shakier than they appeared on paper, and the cash flow didn't seem all that good on the face of it.

In the lean years, something inevitably would fail. This time something had, the Artium Group's first-quarter balance sheet filled with skyrocketing debts, cash-flow shortages, and little prospects of recovery in what Reagan would soon term "morning again in America." Morning for some, perhaps. Holly certainly picked an inconvenient time to lash out. Such was the way of life. Smoke detector batteries always chirped their impending death at three in the morning. Children raised their voices right after you'd loaded your groceries onto the conveyor belt. It had taken West until middle age to realize he would never get used to the whack-a-mole nature of life. Right now the Artium Group's debt worried him. Life on the margin was fine in a boom economy, and none of the investors were concerned, the general attitude being that interest rates were down from the Carter years, so why not load up on new offices, corporate retreats in the islands, a suite of convenience stores in northern Florida, and executive bonuses to boot? The company owned a spread of low-margin businesses and owed a massive debt on their new downtown offices. West had advised they lease rather than purchase, but the board ignored him. If he'd had his way, West would have had the company in a one-story office park in the swamps, but no one here shared his midwestern frugality, nor his patriotism. The Artium Group was about money, not information, and the German CEO liked the idea of hosting his New Year's parties on their rooftop, where they could see the lights of Miami Beach and the blackness beyond, and perhaps think of Prussia or the failures of diplomacy and human nature that had wrecked his home country. Meanwhile, the attitude around West seemed to be: what good was going into business if you couldn't enjoy the profits of your labor? Or better yet, how could you find a way to live off the labor of others? Why should Hollywood have all the fun? Miami had its own glamour, its own ability to burn money. West knew the correction would come eventually, but what really concerned him was the second set of books he'd been keeping since January.

He left the Dixie Highway for Coral Way and zigzagged his way to his old house on 23rd Street. The neighborhood more or less unchanged in the year he'd been gone, another year of scum on the stucco walls, stray sticks and foliage on the terracotta roofs, a few more cracks in the sidewalk, the wrought iron gates still standing. The interiors of these houses were all nicer than the exteriors, Miami real estate low-slung in the flat landscape, defined only by shaggy palms and whether or not there was a fence around the yard. Even the nicer yards were freckled with clover. Banyan trees shaded his block and reminded him of the elms from his childhood. If they had to live in South Florida, he'd reasoned, may as well find those few comforts of home. He parked in front of his—no, Isabel's—house. A squad car was parked nearby on the street. He took a breath to prepare himself.

"He doesn't know a goddamn thing," Isabel said of Bobby West to the officer.

What Bobby West knew was this: their daughter was missing. Holly was in Isabel's care. Holly had not been seen since Monday, and now it was Wednesday. Isabel owed everyone—the two officers, West, and most of all herself—an explanation for how this had happened, but instead she'd decided to deflect everything onto West. Poor Isabel, the absent husband, the difficulties of single motherhood. All arguments he'd heard a thousand times over. Every time he picked up Holly for the weekend, she managed to be there to turn a cordial greeting—"Hello, how was your week, do you need anything"—into a litany of reasons the world was against her thanks to West's abandonment.

"What do you know?" she seemed to ask every time he saw her. "You have a career you like. You'll meet somebody else soon enough, if you haven't already—although she doesn't have a clue what's coming for her if she stays with you longer than a few months. But me? I put off my career to raise our daughter. I gave you the best years of my life, and now what do I have? I have to care for her and clean the house and work full time, and I have to do it all with a smile on my face. What do you know about a woman's life? What do you know about anything?"

How could he respond, except to say that Isabel's sour outlook caused him to withdraw from their marriage, to work longer hours, to pump iron at the gym rather than come home for dinner? In other words, he learned to dread their time alone together, where he felt he was expected to complete their lives with a magic that would never exist. *Irreconcilable differences* the technical term, a euphemism for silence, for one partner leaning out to get a taste of freedom. All their arguments over petty non-issues were symptomatic of West's lean away, symptomatic of their inability to understand the other, symptomatic of their giving up one degree at a time, brought to a boil so slowly that the poor creatures remained unaware of their impending doom until suddenly there it was, their marriage laid bare.

"Would you like me to take her more often?" he would ask.

"We decided it was best for her to stay in her home?"

"I'm not disputing that. I'm just asking if you could use a break."

"What? You want to take Holly from me too, after all you've already taken?"

"Dammit, Isabel."

"Don't 'dammit, Isabel' me. You want to take more responsibility, that's fine, but don't think you can just disrupt our lives any more than you already have."

"What do you want from me? You have our house, you have our daughter."

"You can't just blackmail me with your alimony payments. You're not paying for your freedom from responsibility."

"I'm just asking what you need."

"I need for you to leave."

"I need you to be reasonable. This isn't easy for either of us," he said.

"Oh, this isn't easy, he says. This isn't easy."

"And this temper tantrum isn't helping. We can be adults here. Adults have reasonable discussions, even when things don't go our way. I know things aren't going our way, but there's nothing to be done."

"Just get out of here, Bobby."

Those discussions always ended with her shutting down, with her putting her head in the sand, with her letting the water continue to boil around them. In a way it would be easier if one of them had clear grounds for divorce: an affair, in love with someone else, some manner of abuse. Something. But all they had were empty feelings toward the other. After these exchanges, he would leave with Holly, who doubtless overheard everything and had strong opinions of her own, opinions she never volunteered, for which he was grateful. Instead, she turned on the car's radio and fiddled with the dial to find a noisy British pop star. That seemed to console her. What would there have been to say, had Holly ever wanted to talk about the dissolution of her parents' marriage? West and Isabel married before they'd properly taken stock of themselves. He'd been a young and eager intelligence analyst, an ambitious Midwesterner with no friends in Florida and an outdated sense of how he should live his life—marriage, children, God, country—without taking into account just how long life was, and what longevity could do to a person. Such was the tragedy of this world: the young had all the talents but no perspective, and the old had all the vision without the ability.

Isabel, meanwhile, had been an accounts payable clerk who enjoyed the burgeoning mid-sixties club scene, the daughter of a Cuban exile, a self-made man here in Miami. It broke her father's heart to see her marry an American and settle in this country for the long haul, for no one at the time believed Fidel Castro would cling to power for as long as he would. The father-in-law had also been distressed by West's employer, whom old José had blamed for the death of a thousand freedom fighters at Playa Girón. America may have been a place for reinvention, but no one could reinvent the CIA. Always the same tricks, the same scandals, the same lowlifes. For her part, Isabel never quite understood America, its freedoms and its customs, the sheer size and bounty of what America had to offer. She always felt in want even when she had plenty. The world was an unsettled place, he knew, and people found solace in the familiar. Nothing was more familiar than the psychological traits that made us unique. Thus West's productivity became workaholism, in the latest parlance, and Isabel's want became need became a tendency toward victimhood.

Diana Burns knew what she wanted, and she took it. Isabel West née Hernandez knew what she lacked, and she cowered in fear. West wanted Diana, making him one more thing poor Isabel lacked, so it should be no surprise to find Isabel, that Wednesday morning, telling a police officer about what a good girl they'd raised, about where she could be, about her loser friends and what a terrible father West turned out to be.

"If I'd known this was how life was going to be, I would have listened to my father," she said to the officer, a buzz-cut young man who looked like he would be at home in a mud pit with a rifle. While his colleague circled the room like a caged animal, the interrogating officer nodded and obligingly transcribed her account:

"Yes, the last time I saw her was Monday morning before I left for work."

"Yes, she went to school that day. I already called the school to confirm."

"No, I didn't see her that evening. She called my office to say she was spending the night with her friend Lisa, but I talked to Lisa's mother yesterday. She wasn't there Monday night. They haven't seen her."

"Of course I'm not in the habit of just letting her go off whenever and wherever she feels like it, but you know how kids are. She's seventeen. You can't just keep her handcuffed to the bed, and it's not like I've had any help raising her for the last year."

She cut a glare at West that could melt a glacier.

"No, absolutely there's not been any odd changes in her behavior lately." She glanced down and West understood there was more to it. "Don't you think I'd notice there was something going on?" she said.

This time she turned to West as though expecting him to back her up, but she was on her own. He'd seen his daughter every other weekend for the past year, and she'd become a stranger to him. Sullen, distracted. Not anything like he'd expected from a teenage daughter, admittedly an old-fashioned idea of girls on the phone all hours, of unbearable boys trying to butter him up. Holly had given him none of that, instead passing their time together in front of the television, watching cartoons and puppet shows. This was the generation raised on television, and she seemed to find the same comforts in the simplicity of *Sesame Street* that he found at the gym. Mindlessness, the only cure for the anxiety of living.

"Bobby. Bobby!" Isabel would have made a fine commander. She could have stormed the beaches at Normandy, ordered men into the slaughterhouse, reduced Stalin or Khrushchev to a simpering child. She could have—

The officer spoke up. "I was just wondering if you'd noticed anything, Mr. West? Has she made new friends recently? Have you seen any strange vehicles driving around your neighborhood? Anything unusual you can think of?"

West licked his lips. An utterance came out.

"He doesn't know a goddamned thing," Isabel cut in.

The other officer, Fatso—West had forgotten both of their names—came in and said, "At this point, anything would help. If she's been gone thirty-six hours or more, she could be anywhere in the country. Does she have any money that you know of, or even a passport?"

Something flashed into West's mind: his neighborhood, a passport. He'd never considered Holly may have left Miami, and the image of her on an airplane off to some foreign land caused his heart to flutter. He felt hot in the back of his neck and couldn't say why. Surely his daughter was still in the city, surely she was in no real danger. He shook his head, turned to Isabel for confirmation.

She said, "If she's got any money, it can't be more than twenty dollars or so. Not like she's got a job."

"But a passport."

"I haven't taken her to get one."

"Would she need parental consent for that?" he asked.

Buzzcut said, "It's highly unlikely she would get a passport without either of you knowing it. She's probably still here in the city, but you never know. It helps to consider all the contingencies."

"Sure," West said. "I wish I had more to offer, but I haven't seen her in two weeks. I can't think where she might be."

Buzzcut looked right at him a moment too long, as though trying to determine how truthful a man Bobby West was. Men and their daughters, a fraught relationship. West knew the kind of questions this officer must be asking himself: What was the relationship between West and Holly like? Why were West and Isabel separated? How was each of them coping? She was clearly coping with anger, but what about West? Was he too calm? Those were the ones you had to watch, West knew. The ones who were composed, they were either exceptionally good men or serial killers.

West adored his daughter, had been caught completely off guard by her arrival, a man done for ever since. But adoration was one thing, a person's nature something else. Your true self came out under the pressure of parenthood, and West at his core could be careless and lazy. They weren't crimes, but in the rising heat of Isabel's kitchen, it almost occurred to him that he had failed in some elemental way.

Fatso's radio chirped, and he wandered to the kitchen before pressing the mic at his shoulder and saying, "Go ahead." Muffled conversation followed. A few moments later he came back and said to West, "We've had a report from one of your neighbors. There was some suspicious activity at your house last night."

The heat returned to West's neck. "You've talked to my neighbors?"

"We sent a patrol car out there to find you." He looked to Isabel. "She didn't know if you were going to be here. Were you at home?"

"No, I spent the night out," West mumbled.

"With?" Fatso asked.

"A friend." He refused to glance at Isabel.

"Well, one of your neighbors reported a strange car in the drive. A man and a woman came out of the house and took off. Didn't catch the license plate, but we've got it out on the wire. It may have been Holly and a boyfriend. Did she have a boyfriend?"

West's mind buzzed so he was unaware of himself saying, "No, no boyfriend."

Of course he had no idea if this was true, or if Holly had ever had a boyfriend. He supposed she must have, but she never talked about such things with him. She knew about the safe in his house, he knew that. He assumed she'd forgotten about it, but what if she hadn't? It came rushing to him that perhaps he knew nothing of his daughter's life, that perhaps she was much shrewder, much angrier, than he'd realized. Again, the thought almost bubbled up that there was some fundamental flaw in his approach to life, but in the same way habit settled into old dogs, middle-aged men were disinclined by nature to examine themselves too carefully.

Whatever turmoil lurked in his unconscious, West knew he needed to get home. First, he needed to keep these officers satisfied that he was who he said he was: an overworked ex-husband, concerned about his daughter, innocent of any malfeasance. With respect to Holly, all of this applied.

"Do you have a photograph of Holly?" Fatso asked. "Something we could take with us?"

Isabel got up and returned with a school portrait of a beautiful young woman with provocative eyes. Holly at sixteen, her parents newly separated, the world letting her down for the first time.

"She looks a lot like you," Buzzcut said, and Isabel blushed.

"Let's get this on the wire," Fatso said, "along with what we have. Thank you both. You've been very helpful. We'll need to take more in-depth statements later today, and we'd like to take a look around your house, Mr. West, when convenient."

"Of course," he said with no intention of letting an officer into his house.

"Right now, we'll get the word out. Call us if you hear anything. There's a good chance Holly's just gone out with friends and will come home on her own."

From the front window, West watched the officers go. Fatso spoke into the radio before getting into the car, and it seemed to take an obscenely long time for them to get settled and hit the road. He counted the seconds until they were out of sight.

Isabel was speaking behind him but he couldn't decipher a word she said. Instead, he tried to process what the officers had told them: Holly was gone, suspicious activity at his house last night, money, passports. He felt clammy, shaken with the blooming realization.

When he turned around, Isabel was quiet. She sat on the couch and seemed worn out. He knew she would welcome him joining her, that now was a time for parents to put aside their bickering and old wounds and take comfort in the familiar routines of us against the world.

Instead, he headed for the door and said, "I have to go."

"You have somewhere more important to be?"

Her weariness had flared to anger, but he lacked the energy to muster an argument. He needed to get home to confirm his suspicions, his fear.

9

They cruised out of the Keys, crossed bridges over the saddle bunches and channels, where the turquoise water was so shallow that trees grew right out of it, creating mini-islands. Along the side of U.S. 1 power lines sank under the weight of gulls. Tourists jockeyed for position on the cracked, gray, sea-salt-battered pavement, driving weighted-down station wagons and vans with squeaky hinges. He was in no hurry, the window down and his arm on the ledge grew red and burnt from the noonday sun. Top-heavy palms drooped over the roadside, and the yellow ends of their fronds danced in the wind. Men with coarse gray beards fished off one of the bridges. A young blonde with a gray tanktop and tight blue jeans stood on the side of the road, hitching a ride. A roadside crew sweated in orange vests as they mowed grass, picked up trash. They passed an RV park, and in a town called Summer Land an Ace Hardware sign read, *Everyone seems normal until you get to know them.* Keith drove on, and the mile markers ticked by. Cutthroat Drive, Snake Creek.

Strange to find himself once again employed, even if the work was nebulous. "Whatever's in that car, you don't want to know," she'd said as she climbed into the cab of the tow truck. "We going back to Miami?" Now the tow truck's hum had put her to sleep, and he kept the needle under forty-five and main-lined out of the

islands. He felt dislocated, same as he had in Savannah. He was a
grown man and could do anything he pleased, but with it came the
anxiety of life without a safety net. In Savannah time had passed in
a blur, each day bleeding into the next so that weeks would go by
without any development. He'd waited for life to unfold, for some
decisive point in the future, some rite of passage, some calling. Until
then, an aimless limbo of watered-down beer, games of pool, darts.
He'd called home on occasion, and his parents had been curious
about his life, but sounded far off, in another world. The trouble
was, no decisive moment had come, no urging from heaven. Just
one day after another. He'd blinked away the feeling as long as he
could, but eventually the dam burst and he'd shifted south. He was
determined now not to wind up in the same rut, the same dislocation. Maybe the girl beside him had answers.

They rolled into Miami with the scorch of late afternoon burning down on them, a foreshadow of a long summer to come. The
tow truck's engine grinded away, and the seat vibrated beneath him
and made his legs numb. Holly stirred, and he asked her to read off
Mr. French's directions.

Little Havana was a one-story section of town, low stucco
houses with terracotta roofs, chain-link fences, palmettos in the
yards. A cur dog stared lazily at them, and an old man shuffled
down the street with a newsboy hat on his head and a cigar poking
out of his lips. Could have been another country altogether, somewhere in South America for all Keith knew. South, south, south.
Lemon sunlight emanated from the driveways. Holly directed him
to a diner. The truck honked and jerked as he pulled into a space,
eased it out of gear. He left the truck at an angle and stretched his
limbs in front of the diner. Jose's Café, which struck him as funny.
Every business Mr. French touched seemed to be named after Joe,
whoever the hell that was.

"Wait out here for me," he told Holly, who replied, "Whatever."

Two men were already at the tow truck, disassembling the rig-
ging. The diner's door opened, and Felix Machado, clad in a black
T-shirt and khaki pants, said, "Come on in, amigo."

Keith followed him to a booth in the back of the diner. A waitress came over and Felix said, "Bring my friend a sangria. He's new in town." When she'd left, he templed his fingers on the table, said, "So what's new, my friend? How was your trip?"

"Smooth enough, aside from the interview."

Felix held his hands wide. "We've all been through it. Was the drive okay? You hit any traffic?"

"That truck's not all that comfy, but otherwise fine."

"Mr. French rotates his drivers for that reason. Some seem to like the open road, but they inevitably begin to complain of sore backs. Hence, we bring in new drivers."

The man was inscrutable. If you didn't know Felix, you might take him for a car wash operator or fast food manager—something sleazy and sad about his mustache—but he moved through the world with all the confidence of a New York playboy.

"You worked for him long?" Keith asked.

Felix batted the question away. "What do you want to do here, in Miami?"

"I don't know. Hang out, I guess."

"I've been in Florida four years and still don't understand the culture. Why didn't you go to college? Don't you want to work hard and buy a house in the suburbs?"

"Is that what you're doing?"

"Are you shitting me?" Felix said. "My father lost everything when Castro kicked my family out, but he came here and made a life for his family. No money for college but we had a nice little house in Hialeah, what you might call the suburbs, but I'll tell you something. My father worked my whole life to realize the American dream and rebuild what he'd lost, but he never was comfortable with it. Soon as I moved out and found work, he went down to the local pawn broker, bought a nine-millimeter, and blew his brains out."

Keith had nothing to say.

"He may as well have been dead all those years, just working away out of obligation. Castro killed him, far as I'm concerned. No,

I have ambitions, but they aren't to work hard and buy a nice little house in the suburbs."

Felix stuck his tongue out and stared for a moment. Then he hit the table.

"You brought the girl back with you, yes? What's your plan here? For tonight? To *hang out* a while?"

"I guess."

"Let's go out. Let me show you the razzle dazzle of Miami."

After the sun went down, the three of them headed over to Miami Beach. Felix had changed into club clothes, slicked his hair back, put on his game face. Keith wore the same baggy jeans and the battered shirt he'd worn up from Key West, but no one said anything about it. Holly: she hadn't taken long to convince. "I have to wear what I'm wearing," she said, but somehow she'd managed to spruce herself up in the bathroom at Jose's Café. She belonged in this city.

They rode in Felix's sedan, a beat-up beige Impala, which he had valet parked at an oceanfront club. Inside, lights strobed in time with the beats, a surreal wash of white pants and big hair and smoke. They got a private booth on the second floor, where a waitress brought them drinks without their placing an order. Then Felix lined up six stripes of cocaine on a mirror.

"No one cares," he said. "This is what it means to be in Miami. This is what it means to have money."

He snorted two lines and passed the mirror over. Holly took her hit and passed it to Keith, who wasn't prepared for how fast the coke hit him. Snorting it tickled his nostrils, and by the time he'd cleared his airway, his nose was leaking and his sinuses dried up and he felt a shot of energy.

"There you go!" Felix slugged his whiskey and club soda and slapped his arm across the side of the seat and bopped his head. "All right," he said, and slid out of the booth. They watched him jog down the stairs, and a moment later he was dancing with two women under the lights of the disco ball, flashing red and green dots under the pulse of the crowd. Sweat made Keith sticky and warm, and he felt himself flushed beneath the booth's lamp, the drumbeat of the club mix driving him onward into the great unknown. Holly pressed one of her legs between his, leaned forward.

"I can get us out of here," she whispered. She set a ring of keys on the table.

"You're not enjoying yourself?"

"Not here, the club. Out of Miami."

"What makes you think I want out of Miami? Maybe I like it here."

"You don't like it here. No one does. They just snort coke until they think they're having a good time."

He nodded toward the table. "Those are Felix's keys?"

"He left them here and didn't even realize it."

"Where do you want to go?"

She looked toward the dance floor. "How about New York? I've always wanted to go there."

"And you want me to take you there."

"I can get there on my own," she said. "I just don't want to go by myself. Besides, you don't want to get mixed up in this life. Mr. French's drivers, they all get swept up and burnt out."

"And then?"

She took a sip of her drink, through the straw. "Something will probably go down with these guys before you get burned out, but you don't want any part of it."

His mother had told him such a thing once. He'd been in junior high, and she must have had a sixth sense. Not three weeks later, he and several friends were busted spray-painting a fence, the flash of blue lights, the panic of running through a row of backyards, into the woods. Here he was at twenty years old and in the same spot, on the sidelines with a group of people who were about to do something venomous. His buddies were calm when the police walked up to them. They got away and laughed about it later. Only Keith, the son of a preacher, seemed to wrestle with the weight of it all, the fear of authority, the consequences, the walking through a door that would lock shut behind you.

Like some unholy rite of passage, the inversion of what he'd been searching for.

Holly said, "What if I told you I could get us ten thousand dollars?"

"I wouldn't believe it."

"You don't have to believe it, 'cause it's the truth." She leaned back and her head tilted forward as though her neck couldn't stand the weight of it. She was high indeed, high and sexy and her eyes shot heat right into him so that, by God, she could talk him into doing anything.

"Where are we going to get that kind of money?"

"My father keeps cash in a safe at his house."

"Whose cash?"

"Who knows? Mr. French's."

"Great." He slapped the table. "I'm on board."

She moved like she was about to get up. "Yeah?"

He sat back, took a sip of his drink. "Shit no."

"I'm serious."

"I am too," he said. "Didn't you just tell me these guys were bad news, and now you want to rip them off."

"Why not? They'll never find out."

"Do you know who Mr. French is?"

"Do you?" she asked.

"I met him this morning," Keith said, but said nothing about the trip to the basement, the gleam of amusement in Mr. French's eyes.

"How's he going to catch us?"

"I don't know. He's probably got a whole surveillance team lined up."

"It's a big country."

"Yeah, and you want to go to New York."

"Why not? You can get settled anywhere in America," she said. "Relax. Look at your friend down there. He's having a great time." Indeed, he was. Felix was already out of his mind, dancing with a large-breasted girl in a skirt and tights, his face buried in her chest, coming up for air before shaking himself back in. "Are you having a great time?"

He didn't have to answer her. She could tell he was dissatisfied in life, and the prospect of going back to work, even if it was illicit, was an endless grind. Humans were made for more than that, and with enough money, perhaps you really could start over. He said, "So we get the money and head north. What happens when the money runs out?"

"We'll find jobs. Or we'll come back to Miami. Who cares? Everyone wants something from you. Why not do a little something for yourself? It could be a good time."

Keith couldn't remember the last time he felt truly free. Holly was right, everyone wanted something from you in this world. Rent, a ride, a donation, a tithe. Say she was telling the truth, that her father somehow had a stash of easy money. Ten thousand wouldn't last them as long as she might think, but it would be a fun ride while it lasted. The question was how and when to get out of here.

He must have spoken out loud, because she said, "It's easy. Felix—he's going to be leaving with one of those girls in less than an hour. He'll forget all about us. If anyone asks, he won't know a thing, except we were here. We get in his car, drive over to my father's house, and take the money out of the safe. I have the combination. Then we head out of Florida. Simple as that."

She looked at him as if to say *don't be a pussy.* He sipped his whiskey and stared at the dance floor, where Felix still had his face in the woman's ample bosom, his hands shaking in the air like a tap dancer's. The music throbbed, lights pulsed. The whiskey seared his throat and his blood buzzed as a warm sense of unreality took hold of his mind, disconnected him from the here and now of his body. Whatever neurons created the sense of permanence, that created consciousness of the self as a visceral part of the world, they misfired in his brain so that all he could do was take another sip of his drink, chomp ice, and say, "All right."

The house was spare, with boxes piled in the living room, unopened, dishes in the sink. The television set had speakers beside it, the most put-together part of the room. A battered couch and an armchair faced the system, a tray table propped near one arm of the chair. Otherwise, everything looked uninhabited. Just a place for her father to store his stuff.

"Back here," she said.

He took her hand, felt like a teenager himself again, sneaking around the parents, wondering about the next step, what the other kids would think. A system he finally understood now that he was too old for it. He stopped and pulled her back to him, tried to kiss her.

"There's time for that later," she said. "Come on."

Down the hall, in the office, a folding chair was tucked under a desk, piles of paperwork spilled over and onto the floor. A shredder was plugged in, and in the back of the office, beneath a rug she kicked away, a safe was built into the floor.

"Wait a second," he said. "Were you serious?"

"What did you think I was talking about? Hey, go pack us some food for the road. Just take whatever looks good. And don't turn on any lights," she called after him.

West's kitchen was like something out of a department store, all show with no substance. He found a bag of chips and a gallon of spring water, a couple of apples. Everything else was dry goods—flour, uncooked pasta, peanut butter—nothing they would bring for the road.

Holly came in with a gray duffel bag. "Voilà!" she said. "You ready?"

Keith was still in his daze, half-drunk, the dreamy fog of misfiring neurons, but his face must have said enough.

"Don't worry about the food. We'll pick something up. Let's get out of here."

It took several moments before he said, "Wait, wait, wait."

"What?"

"You got the money?"

She slung the duffel bag over her shoulder and pulled a one-inch stack of bills out of her purse. "Easy peasy."

"We can't just take all that."

"Why not?"

He took her arm to stop her. "That's not a few bucks of walking around money. Your dad's going to miss it, and he's going to know who took it."

"He's a businessman. He's got plenty. You want to hit the road with me or not?" Then she said, "Relax. I didn't take all the money in his safe. He probably won't even miss it."

She adjusted the duffel bag on her shoulder, as if that settled everything.

He'd made five hundred a week selling cigarettes, and hadn't received his first paycheck from Mr. French. Ten grand would last them three or four months, but maybe she knew what she was doing. Her father's house, spare cupboards or not, was an expensive piece of real estate. Perhaps it was the gaudy surroundings, or the drunken high, or the sultry way she carried herself toward the front door, but Keith pushed out whatever suspicions he harbored and jogged to catch up with her.

He stopped her at the front door, slid the duffel bag off her shoulder. It landed with a thunk, but he was already kissing her and grinding his hips into hers with magnetic attraction. She snaked her legs around his and they shuffled back into the living room, toward the couch, where they fell over, and it was fast then, and when it was over he lay on top of her and took in the musky scent of her sweat and she pushed at him and said, "It's time to go."

She wiggled out from under him and readjusted her clothes. She kicked his foot and handed him a pill bottle.

"What's this for?"

"You're taking the first shift, so you need to wake up." She snatched the car keys from his pants pocket. "If you're not with me, then I'm on my own."

"Now wait a second." He tugged on his clothes while she stayed a few inches out of reach. He shuffled toward her as he buttoned his jeans.

"Pop one of those and meet me in the car," she said.

When she slung the heavy bag over her shoulder, he asked her what all she was bringing with her.

"It's my stuff," she said simply.

And then she was gone. He held the pill bottle in his hands, and stared blankly at its label. He heard the car start in the driveway. After just one more moment of hesitation, he went to the bathroom and washed down a Dexedrine tablet. It wouldn't take long to hit him, and he would feel pumped and steady all half the way up to the Florida panhandle, and by then it would be too late to change his mind.

When the sun rose they were on I-95 in north Florida. The light shined on the Florida swamplands, which would soon fade into the dusty red clay of the South. He tried not to think of Mr. French's basement, or the pound of flesh he felt he might owe someone for robbing ten thousand dollars and jettisoning north. Beside him in the Impala, Holly slept against the glass of the window, a halo of golden light around her head.

Thus they cruised north, into the blooming day, gradually out of the tropical paradise, its lush strips of sawgrass and condominiums and off to some new thing.

PART TWO

CENTRAL INTELLIGENCE AGENCY
WASHINGTON, D.C.

OFFICE OF THE DEPUTY DIRECTOR (INTELLIGENCE)

25 April 1984

MEMORANDUM FOR: Mark Brown
                     Special Operations, Latin America
                     Counterterrorism

SUBJECT: Events in Miami, Florida re: Robert West

The following is an excerpt from a transcript (edited for clarity) of a call between Robert West, senior officer, and Alexander French, Criminal Informant (CI), on Wednesday, 25 April, 1984, 3:59 p.m. Officer West placed the call from his office at the Artium Group headquarters, Miami.

WEST: We need to talk a few minutes.

FRENCH: Ah, Bobby, I was just thinking I needed to call you. How are things?

WEST: I've got a problem.

FRENCH: Nothing serious, I hope.

WEST: Nothing serious yet, but I've had a slight hiccup with this month's deposit. It seems my daughter has run off with someone, a boyfriend I guess, and she took the deposit with her.

FRENCH: I see. Um, this was from your home safe?

WEST: Yes.

FRENCH: And how much did she take?

WEST: About $3 million.

FRENCH: [whistle]

WEST: I know. Law enforcement is looking for her, and I've hired a private investigator. Assuming she's out of the city, he'll find her before the police do.

FRENCH: Bobby, that's a great deal of money.

WEST: I'll get it back, but I may have a problem getting everything to Felix on time.

FRENCH: I'm sure I don't need to remind you what's at stake if you miss the deposit with him. We need to keep everyone paid off, my friend. You'll have to find the money to float you. You met our friend Chekhov. Adriana's people are not like the banker men in your world.

WEST: Circumstances change. I'm sure she's familiar. But no excuses. She'll have her money. Felix will get yours. I'm just keeping you in the loop.

FRENCH: I appreciate the call. Do you need any help? A second investigator perhaps?

WEST: I'm fine.

FRENCH: And if your director catches wind?

WEST: I'll spin him a tale.

[END CALL]

10

The day had been about as dull as a tossed salad. Private investigator Ernie Falcon, age sixty-two and suffering no maladies except hair loss and blood pressure that bubbled a mite too high, was stringing up a set of old Christmas lights in his office when this woman came sashaying in like Rita Hayworth.

He balanced on his office chair, a spinning leather thing he suspected might twist out of control if he didn't keep one hand pressed firm against the wall to hold himself steady. She caught him in this precarious position because he no longer had a secretary to greet clients and buzz them in when he was ready for them.

"You hanging those up or taking them down?" the woman asked.

"Up," he said. "We had 'em up on our porch until last week when my wife tells me the neighbors are starting to talk."

He looped the lights over the last nail and let the string hang down to the floor.

"Joke's on her," he went on. "The neighbors have been talking since mid-January. I wondered if maybe she was going to let me keep the lights up all year and save me the hassle of hanging decorations come Thanksgiving."

The woman said nothing. She was a Latina—dark hair, dark eyes, but with skin pale enough that made him think Cuban descent—and she was all Miami in the way she carried herself. Short skirt, V-neck shirt, big wavy hair and enough gloss on her lips to blind a truck driver from a quarter-mile away.

Falcon was itching to know who she was and what kind of scheme she was about to rope him into. No wedding ring, so she wasn't here for him to photograph her husband with another woman. Dressed too provocatively to be a corporate mover and shaker. Possibly looking for a man who had run out on her, or wanted some help in an inheritance case. Nonetheless: these were lean times in the investigations business, so any sort of client was a welcome sight. Curiosity kept him alive as he sort of squatted to get off the chair without keeling over.

Safely on terra firma, he offered her a seat across from him and said, "What can I do for you, Miss—?"

"Hernandez. Formerly Mrs. West, but you can call me Isabel."

"All right, what can I do for you, Isabel?"

"I'd like you to find my daughter."

He nodded and resisted the urge to pull out a pen and notepad. "I can certainly try to do that," he said.

"If I wanted to pay someone to try, I'd throw a few dollars at a bum on the street. Your sign says you're a professional investigator."

He bit his upper lip, gnawed a few times before he said, "I'm a very good investigator, but the results depend on circumstances." He picked up his pen and tapped it on the desk. "How about you give me a little context and we'll go from there. How old is your daughter?"

She told him the girl was seventeen and had been gone for two days.

"And you've called the police?"

"The officers left my house half an hour ago."

"I take it they asked you about her friends, a boyfriend, that sort of thing."

"They filled out their forms and wished me a pleasant day."

"Don't be too hard on them. I spent thirty years as a Miami P.D. detective. You see enough crime, everything becomes a statistic."

"Yeah? What makes you different as a private eye?"

Clever woman, certainly more composed than your average parent might be if their kid had taken off. Either she knew where the daughter was, or had some inkling of what was afoot. He said, "It's my livelihood for one thing. Cops get paid either way, but my reputation rests on whether I can deliver results."

This seemed to satisfy her. People always liked the word "results," but that didn't mean they always liked the results he turned up. The world was an unpredictable place. Statistics suggested the girl ran off with her boyfriend, but Isabel's demeanor suggested there was more to the story. He liked her directness but would only trust her so far as he understood her motives.

"So your daughter—what's her name?"

"Holly."

"So Holly's been missing since, what, Monday?"

"Went out that afternoon and never came back."

"Do you know where she went? Who she was with?"

"She's got a couple of friends, Lisa and Nicole, she runs with. I don't know what all they do. Go to the mall, the movies. She told me she was staying with Lisa Monday night."

"Any boys in the picture?"

Isabel's mouth opened but she had nothing to say.

"We can come back to that," he said, and he made a mental note to ask the friends for their insights. "Does Holly have a car?"

Isabel shook her head. "She drives but takes the bus to get around. That, or her friends pick her up."

"Have you been in touch with her friends?"

"They say they haven't seen her. I called each of them yesterday, but neither knew where Holly went."

"You believe them?"

"I don't know. They're not bad kids. Anyway, the police have their names, and I'm sure they won't lie to the police."

"You never know. Authority isn't what it used to be, among the young."

He leaned back and thought, okay, here's this woman, divorced recently enough to be self-conscious about it, worried about her teenage daughter gone missing, involved enough in the daughter's life to know her two closest friends but not enough to know the boyfriend—and there was surely a boyfriend—and no mention of the ex-husband, the Mr. West. Several threads to pull here. The question was where to start. Falcon occasionally landed a missing person case, usually the type where the standard police involvement was undesired. Unpaid debts, a spouse run off. You knew the person was alive and well. They just didn't want to talk with his client. He found these people easily enough, through paper trails, sometimes even a simple search in one of the national registries. Florida was a state of transients. No one remained still for too long. He asked Isabel about Holly's father.

Isabel snorted. "The man's no help. He came over this morning, talked to the police, and promptly went back to work."

"What line of work's he in?"

"He's in finance. Real estate holdings."

"Really? How's his business doing these days?"

"The market's booming. He does commercial properties. Matter of fact, his company owns this building."

"The Artium Group."

"That's right."

Falcon had subleased the place when the money ran out for his Brickell office. Let the secretary and the ocean view go and downsized. When he approached the Artium Group about an office space in Riverside, not only had the agent been eager to talk with him, the company wanted to invest in Falcon's operation. Free rent in exchange for occasional information, a front for some government agency. CIA, most likely. Falcon had agreed, in part because he'd needed the money (he could draw Social Security and his pension from Miami P.D. this year, but he had another three years on a mortgage he wanted to pay off first) and in part because information was a central currency in Miami. Everyone had a hustle going—drugs or guns, politics or fundraising, sales or land development—and there was a time when everyone was assumed to be on CIA payroll. Money sifted from hand to hand, and every bum had an eye on you. Falcon had no qualms typing a monthly report on the neighborhood. He kept his clients confidential but had no particular loyalties to anything that went on around him. Most of his retail neighbors were moneylenders of some sort—payday loans, pawnbrokers, bail bondsmen—so this strip had its share of lowlifes. If Holly's father was the moneyman for a CIA operation, this case might be more than your garden-variety teen angst.

"How long have you been separated?" he asked. Isabel straightened up, so he continued, "I don't mean to pry. I'm just trying to get a picture of her home life. Might give me a bit of insight into her motivations."

"We separated last year, in the summer."

"Recently."

"Doesn't feel like it."

"How's she taking it?"

"I haven't noticed."

Falcon cocked his head.

"I mean, we had a few heart-to-heart chats about it. It was an emotional couple of weeks right after he left, but she and I kept the house. She sees him every other weekend and occasionally other times. Between school and her social life, it's not like she saw all that much of him before he left."

"Does he have another girlfriend?"

"I think he has someone he spends the night with sometimes."

She said it coldly, which made him think the woman might have played a role in the dissolution of their marriage. He switched his line of questioning.

"You have a boyfriend?"

"Why is that your concern?"

"Like I said, just trying to get a complete picture."

"No, no boyfriend. No one in the house that would drive her away, just me and a cat. Far as I know, nothing's changed in Holly's life since Bobby found a new place to live last August. Whether he's got a girlfriend, or a prostitute he visits regularly, I couldn't say, but I don't think Holly knows anything about that. I haven't even told her we signed the divorce papers."

"Really?"

"There hasn't been a good time to tell her."

"You think she may have stumbled onto them? Seen them around the house?"

"I keep everything at the office."

"And Bobby?"

She pinched her forehead, and said, "I really can't say."

Falcon knew he'd pushed her far enough for this first interview. There was more to the story involving the ex-husband, and maybe a boyfriend in the picture, but if he pressed her too hard before she signed a retainer agreement, she'd walk. Private investigation was a client services business. The trouble with this business was that too often, the client was at fault. They hired you to look into one issue, but the solution lay within them all along. Like being a psychotherapist, a private investigator at times had to nudge clients outside their comfort zone. Falcon made sure he had an agreement in place. Getting paid was job number one.

He opened his desk drawer and transitioned to the nuts and bolts of business. "OK, Isabel, I've got enough to get started in finding your daughter. I've got my standard agreement, where you'd have me on a retainer, either until I found Holly or you decide I should stop." This was the awkward part, talking money. This is where an office assistant would come in handy, to separate the service from the fee.

"What do you charge, Mr. Falcon?"

"Two-fifty a day plus expenses."

"Jesus."

"Big chunk of that covers my overhead." He nodded around the room, never mentioned he had a deal on the real estate. In truth, he had to charge a premium to cover the feast or famine nature of his business. "I'll need a one-week deposit and will give you an accounting statement every month, though of course I'll be checking in with you regularly."

When she was gone—after signing the agreement, reluctantly— he smoked half a cigarette and thought about what to do next. Days like these, he was tempted to pack it all in, take his fat retainer and play a round of golf. He thought about blowing everything off to take his wife out for lunch, but he suspected he might actually call it a day if he headed out of Riverside. They lived in Biscayne Park, in a little bungalow they built in the fifties during the post-war real estate boom. Fifteen minutes out of Miami once the interstate was complete, the bedroom community made a nice respite from the city's go-go hustle culture.

Holly Hernandez lacked the makings of a case that would change his worldview forever, though the way his life was heading these days, it wouldn't take much to unmoor Ernie Falcon in a way nothing—the changes to the city, thirty years on the police force, the estrangement of his children, not even the war—ever had.

He scooted out of the office to deposit her retainer and grab a quick bite for lunch. A slice of pie, perhaps, from his old taqueria.

Falcon had an appointment for a late luncheon that he wished he could back out of. Miami was a young city, and he was a man staring down the barrel of old age, and wished only to spend his time at work or at home. But he was infallibly polite and found it difficult to say no when someone wanted something from him.

On his way, he called his wife to check in on her. She was in good spirits, and good health, these days. Last year she'd been diagnosed with MS after a dispiriting period of symptoms ghosting in and out. The numbness, the tremors. The diagnosis had shaken him more than her, the first time he saw what real sickness was about. The doctor, the MRI, the specialist, the late nights of worry, the early morning appointments, the letters from the insurance company: one step after another but what had really gotten to him was how dull and ordinary it all was. The offices were all sterile, the medical staff all friendly, but he'd felt like he and Mary Catherine were part of a system operating in silos, like a Soviet bureaucracy. Fill out this form, wait your turn, don't ask too many questions. The mysterious disease with no known cure would be a part of their lives until the end. The halogen lights had given him migraines.

"I'm fine," she told him today on the phone. "I spent the morning in the garden. I bought some Thai basil for you."

"I thought you already had basil in the garden."

"I had Italian basil, but now we'll have both."

"I didn't even know there was a difference."

She laughed softly, more of a breath.

"I've got lunch with Frank Navarro today," he said.

"What do you want to meet with him for?"

"He called me up and invited me out."

"I know you've heard of the word *no*."

Falcon knew she wouldn't like it, but he had to tell her, felt he owed her that much. "Can't hurt to see what he wants."

"Isn't that how it started the last time?"

"The last time he was my friend, or I thought he was. This time I'm just curious." When she didn't say anything, he said, "I'll be home this evening."

"Don't get into anything with Frank today," she said.

"You know you don't have to tell me that."

"And don't kill him," she said as an afterthought.

His appointment with Navarro was for one o'clock at a taqueria near the river. The drive took him through his adopted city, where he'd spent all his adult life. He felt protective of the place even now as he'd outgrown the Miami of today and dug into the Miami of yesteryear. Incorporated in 1896 and soon a popular destination for out-of-state industrialists—Rockefeller, Carnegie, Vanderbilt, the titans of America's Golden Age—who all set up in Flagler's Royal Palm Hotel, Miami's beginnings set the tone for the city as an upscale destination. In the early years of the 20th century, tourism boomed, and with it came a rash of land speculation. In the history of urban development, water stars in the central role: rivers and seas for transportation, sewer lines for public health, rain for agriculture. You had L.A. in a drought, and here they were in Miami with altogether too much water. South Florida was a swamp, the everglades ever wet. As developers drained the water out, real estate went up, a casino of hotels and subdivisions whose random walk of prices seemed to go nowhere but up. But when the hot streak came to an end in the twenties, the bust came like a hurricane and washed away the speculators, allowing Miamians to breathe for a few decades before the next wave of growth crashed on their shores. Waves continued throughout the century: the post-war boom of veterans, the Cuban exiles, the mobsters sick of the mist and slush of the northern boroughs.

Because of the city's youth and these waves of growth, no one was truly from here. The oldest residents—whether the Jews in Coral Gables or the mobsters in Miami Beach—could only claim a generation or two of history in 1984. Ernie Falcon's family drifted around during America's agriculture years. His mother was from Missouri and his father's family hailed from the Florida panhandle. Ernie grew up outside Tampa, where his father worked in a packing plant, but he fell in love with the Miami sands during naval training in 1944. After the war he returned to the city, met and married Mary Catherine Simms, had two children and eventually settled in the up-and-coming enclave in Miami Shores, where they'd lived since 1957. Since then, the city had reincarnated once again with the Cuban influx, and for the majority of Falcon's professional life, Miami was an outpost of the Cold War. Not a formal battleground, exactly, but a simmering pot of propaganda fueled by anger among the exiles who'd lost everything to Castro's revolution. Newspapers and radio stations served as voices for a liberated Cuba, street marches and political rallies the bully pulpit.

As a former police detective, Falcon considered all of that through the lens of public safety. You put a diverse group of people in a tight space, all with different political agendas, and you watch as the federal government allows the pot to boil with frustration that action isn't fast enough. What did that do for your average Joe, who just wanted his beer and his evening sitcom? In truth there were no average Joes, not in Miami. Everyone was a potential menace. You never knew what lurked in a person's basement. Drugs, explosives, objects of sexual deviance. Falcon was not surprised the gang violence and drug cartels had taken over. Shoot-outs in shopping mall parking lots were new for suburban America, but here they were mere signs of the existing unrest, an insurgent tantrum, a power struggle. Falcon sympathized, not with murder but with the frustration. He knew first-hand the CIA had operations here, with a focus on Cuba. He also knew FBI agents kept tabs on those in the echelons of power to ensure Miami's corruption was no different from the corruption at the heart of every American city. The clear lines of arresting bad guys blurred, and the landmines became too much for detective Ernie Falcon. He cashed out after thirty years and set up shop as a private investigator. The work was neither steady nor glamorous (he received jeers from his former co-workers, when he saw them, about the sleazy nature of private investigations), but at least the aims were clear and the goalposts seldom moved.

The taqueria had a bright red door and a delicious chocolate cream pie. He'd told Mary Catherine about his meeting with Frank Navarro, but he kept the pie a secret. She worried about his blood pressure. Assumed fats and sweets and salt were equally bad for him. Maybe they were.

Falcon arrived early but Navarro was already in the booth. He wore a realtor's grin and cowboy boots and stood up to shake Falcon's hand. Falcon positioned himself to avoid the one-armed man-hug. He wasn't near killing Navarro, but he wasn't about to pretend they were friends.

"You're looking well, Ernie," Navarro said as they took a seat. "You haven't aged a day."

This was untrue. Since leaving the force seven years ago, Falcon had put on ten pounds, his hair had gone gray, and he'd taken on the disheveled cut of a man well into the back nine. Aging happened in fits and starts. He was a young man until suddenly he was middle aged. Then he was middle aged until suddenly he was old. "I feel good anyway," Falcon said. "How you doing?"

"Just fine, just fine."

Navarro picked up a menu and the proprietor came over to greet them. He said hello to Falcon, asked if he was having the usual.

"Sounds good," Falcon said.

"Cream pie today?"

"Course."

Navarro grinned. "That sounds like a winning order right there. Why don't you bring me one of those as well?"

"Very good," the proprietor—Ricky Something—said as he took the menus.

"So," Navarro said when they were alone. "You're wondering why I asked you out to lunch."

"Crossed my mind."

"How's your wife doing?"

"She's fine."

"Kids? What did you have, two of them? Must be grown now."

"They are. Both out on the West Coast."

Falcon thought it polite to ask about Navarro's family in return, but the truth was Navarro kept his affairs to himself. Came to Miami P.D.'s criminal investigations unit in 1972, and Falcon worked in the same division with him for five years. They were never in the same poker game, but were friendly enough. Still, at the end, when internal investigations started digging into Navarro's investment in a developer with a connection to a bank robbery in Illinois, Falcon knew almost nothing about Navarro's home life. The man was born and raised in Miami (one of the few) but was cagey about everything else, from his family to his ethnicity. With the name Navarro, he likely had a hint of Spanish in him—Mexican, Dominican, something—but he could easily have been a well-tanned white dude. In that respect, he fit the mold of Miami today, a multicultural melting pot where everyone was some shade of tawny. And he'd been equally vague about his home life. Wore a wedding ring but never talked about his wife, and denied ever having kids. Made it difficult to be polite at the water cooler, to say nothing of a holding cell.

Fortunately, Navarro liked to talk, always had a hustle going, and today he failed to notice—or didn't care—when Falcon kept silent. "Well, I tell you," he said, "I'd love to catch up all day but I do have some business to discuss, if you'll hear me out."

"I can't imagine we have all that much to discuss," Falcon said.

"I know my last venture sort of hung you out to dry."

"That's putting it mildly."

"I apologized for it then, and I apologize for it again today. I chose the wrong business partner, and I got burned as well."

"You both should have landed in prison."

"I never knew where his money came from, and never would have worked with him if I'd known about the federal investigation. You know that. I had my ass on the line as well, and got burned just as badly."

Ricky brought out two plates of tacos.

"Here we go," Navarro said. He unrolled his silverware and tucked the napkin into his shirt like a bib.

Falcon said a quick blessing while he unfolded his napkin. They ate in silence for a few moments. Falcon regretted accepting Navarro's invitation, and regretted suggesting this taqueria for a meet-up. Now that Navarro knew he was a regular, Falcon might never shake him. He'd gotten out of Miami P.D. on graceful enough terms with his thirty-year pension intact, and he'd assumed he would never hear from Frank Navarro again. Yet here he was, tilting his head into a steak taco like he and Falcon were old school chums catching up.

"What are we here for?" Falcon finally asked.

Navarro dabbed his lips with the napkin, leaned back. "Here's the thing. I've got another opportunity."

"You've got to be kidding me."

"Now hear me out. This isn't like last time."

"What, you gave up on land development and got in bed with the cocaine cowboys?"

"Ernie. Really."

Falcon set his napkin on the table, reached for his wallet.

"Hey, lunch is on me."

"Leave Ricky a good tip."

Falcon slid out of the booth.

Navarro leaned over and laid his forearms on either side of his plate. "Wait, wait, before you go."

"We've got nothing to discuss."

"Talk to the guys at the precinct. You still in touch with them?"

"A few of them."

"Talk to them. Mark. Ron. Charles. Bill."

"Bill Johnson?"

"They're all with me on this. I have a line on a security gig. Good prospects. Business is booming in America these days, not like last time. Now you can get rich through honest work."

"And you're looking for another investor."

"It takes a team effort. This is the 1980s. We can't have mavericks anymore."

Falcon went over to the counter and waived Ricky over. "My buddy said he's taking care of the bill. Better make my pie to go. If he stiffs you, on the tip or anything, let me know."

"I'll be fine," Ricky said, already moving toward the bakery case.

"This is the real deal," Navarro called from the table.

Falcon took his slice of pie, thanked Ricky, and said to Navarro, "You have a good day."

"Talk to the guys. That's all I ask."

Falcon opened his mouth, and then shut it.

Navarro leaned back and grinned, while Falcon hoped never to run into this man again for the rest of his life.

After lunch he traffic lighted his way back to the office. His mind had already cast Isabel Hernandez and her missing daughter aside for the offer from Frank Navarro. Lord knows what kind of scheme the man had cooked up. Tough to tell whether he was an inveterate optimist or a snake-oil salesman. Maybe a bit of both. Falcon wanted no part of it. He would have words with the guys at the precinct next time he dropped by. He might go down there tomorrow anyway on the off chance he could scare up something about the missing Holly Hernandez. Might smack Bill Johnson in the back of the head and ask the fool what he was thinking to get involved with Frank Navarro. Frank Navarro was the kind of man who—

Falcon's office door was unlocked and a man sat in the chair in the front room. Square-faced and freckled, the man was sort of frumpy, like a pet bird in too small of a cage. He got up when Falcon walked in.

"How'd you get in here?" Falcon asked.

"Door was unlocked."

"No, it wasn't."

"Well, I just walked in. Maybe the lock malfunctioned."

"Who are you?"

Falcon walked back to his office, set the slice of pie on the desk. The man followed and introduced himself as Bobby West. It took a moment for Falcon to peg him on two fronts.

He said, "What can I do for you, Mr. West?"

"I'd like you to find my daughter. Why don't we take a seat?"

"This is about Holly?" Falcon asked as he sat across from West.

"How'd you know her name?"

"Your wife was in here right before I went out for lunch."

"Ex-wife."

"Your ex-wife then."

"She wanted to hire you?"

"What she said."

"How'd she find you?"

"I didn't ask. I'm in the phone book."

"Yeah, but why you?"

"Why not? Not like there are all that many investigators in Miami, but I might ask you the same thing. How'd you find me?" Falcon already suspected, but wanted to see how forthright this Bobby West would be.

"I asked around."

"Yeah?" Falcon took out a pack of cigarettes. "You mind?"

West shook his head. "You did some work for one of my colleagues awhile back. She was in a divorce, and you got the smoking gun photo of her ex with his girlfriend in Key West."

"I do a fair amount of that. Doesn't explain why you came to me about a missing girl."

"I told you, I asked around."

"Doesn't have anything to do with your employment at the Artium Group?"

West cracked a half-smile but said nothing.

"Well, regardless, your wife—ex-wife—filled me in on the basics. I've taken her on as a client, so I'll let you work it out with her how you handle the payment."

"What's she already paid you?"

"Seventeen-fifty."

"Jesus! What am I paying alimony for?"

"Why don't you tell me a little about Holly," Falcon said.

West stewed a moment before he said, "What do you need to know?"

"I presume you don't know where she went. Any ideas where she might be? Who she might be with?"

West seemed to fidget but shook his head.

"She have a boyfriend?"

"No."

"Don't answer so quickly," Falcon said. "Take a minute to think. Any mention of a boy? Someone she may have mentioned off-hand recently?"

"She's never shown an interest."

"Any arguments with you or the missus?"

"None that I know of."

"When was the last time you saw her?"

"Week and a half ago? I see her on occasional weekends."

"And how'd she seem?"

"Like you'd expect. She watched TV, didn't say much."

West kept fidgeting his hands beneath the desk. It wasn't an obvious tell, but Falcon could hear the man's fingers rubbing together, even as he kept his eyes locked straight into Falcon's.

Since the wife—ex-wife—had already paid the retainer, Falcon had nothing to lose with West. He said, "I have to tell you, I don't believe you."

"What?"

"Cases like these, either the girl's run off with a boyfriend, or she's had a disagreement with the parents. There's got to be something back there you're not telling me about your relationship with her or your ex, and if you want me to find your daughter, I need to know what it is. Otherwise, you're going to be paying me to chase my own tail."

Falcon could see West sizing him up, trying to decide whether to establish trust. When business was slow, Falcon tended to accommodate squirrelly clients, the ones whose secrets, often as not, tied to the case. He had no training in psychology, knew vaguely a cigar was not always a cigar, except when it was. In the case of Bobby West, he suspected the man was beyond repair for an armchair professional. He couldn't say exactly what it was about the man that made him think he had a severe problem inside his brain. West had a brown dot in the white of his left eye, like a permanently burst blood vessel. Falcon noticed it because West rarely blinked, simply stared with those icy blue eyes, while beyond the eyes, inside his mind, neurons fired a volley of thoughts.

The man said, "I need to know I can trust you, Mr. Falcon."

"I tell you, you can, though I know that doesn't mean much."

"You mentioned the Artium Group, so I assume you know my company owns this strip and has you on its payroll."

Falcon said nothing.

"I also assume you know we're not gathering information for the fun of it, that we're part of an agency interested in the security of South Florida."

Falcon still said nothing.

"We run background checks on everyone on our payroll, so I know your story. Thirty years with the Miami P.D., decorated officer, not a scratch on your record until the end and that business with Frank Navarro. I also know that wasn't your fault, that you were suckered into a bum deal by a man you thought you knew."

"What's your point, Mr. West?"

"Point is, I know you do good work, and you're discreet. All I want is to get my daughter back, but there are certain contingencies around her disappearance that, if true and they come to light, would compromise more than just my own job security. You know Miami is on the front line of more than one proxy war? Cuba, drugs. Take your pick."

"You think Holly may have been kidnapped?"

"No, no, nothing like that, but the police officers in charge of finding her have started nosing around my neighborhood. Sounds like Holly may have stopped by my house last night, and I'm not sure what for."

Falcon knew the man was lying again. He'd slid into the rhythm of clicking his fingers together. He let him go on.

"I worry she may have stumbled into something, maybe got spooked and took off."

"What might have spooked her?"

"I keep a lot of paperwork at my house. Maybe she was going through some of it. Maybe she realized she was seeing something she shouldn't see."

"If that's the case, why didn't she just scurry home?"

"I don't know," West said. "That's what I need you to find out."

11

West had a seven o'clock meeting with Alexander French and a cashier's check for seventy-five thousand dollars. He'd tapped his retirement accounts and cleaned out his savings for what was nothing more than a drop of the money he owed Mr. French, but he hoped it was enough to buy time for Falcon to find Holly and recover the money. He'd spoken with Felix Machado on the phone for just long enough to convince the man West had a problem and needed to meet with Mr. French face to face.

While he waited for time to go by, he sat in his office and read through a stack of memos in his inbox. He stared at some of the company's recent financial statements, account balances, inflows and outflows and carried interest. He needed the cash returned to him fast. The money from Mr. French's operation was officially on the books for the Artium Group, $3 million and change currently hidden in a security bundle and masked with an accounting trick to keep the financial reports flat. It didn't matter for now that a major asset existed only on paper, laundered through a safe in West's floor, but you couldn't keep that kind of money hidden for long.

He rang up Isabel to see if she'd heard anything about Holly.

"Where have you been, Bobby? I called your office, but your secretary wouldn't put me through. Said you were out and could she take a message."

Isabel pronounced *secretary* as if Vicky were the woman West was sleeping with. He told her he'd been out most of the day.

"I assume you're bringing professionals into this search for our daughter," Isabel said.

"Every resource I can muster," he said.

"Because if you just went back to work, I swear to God, Bobby."

He gnawed his upper lip. Despite his ex-wife's change in timbre, he felt euphoric with the knowledge that he wasn't alone, that Isabel felt as out of control as he did. Granted, she knew nothing of the missing money, but the emotions were the same. This was a consequence of a long marriage, even one that breaks. You were never alone. "I've hired an investigator and am going to D.C. tomorrow," he said.

"You think that'll help?"

"It can't hurt. You haven't heard from her?"

"Do I sound like I've heard from her?"

He sighed. "I heard you went to visit Ernie Falcon. I presume you know he's one of Artium's tenants?"

"He better be a good investigator," she said.

"I went there to hire him myself. We don't both need to be paying him."

"Why not? Now he's got double the incentive to find her."

"Let me take care of it," he said.

"Like you take care of everything else?" She took a heavy sigh. "I'm going to blame you forever for this, Bobby, so you know. I'll say this now, why ever she left, and whatever happens when she comes back, I know it was her decision, but I have to blame you for it all."

He doodled on the back of a memo, a request from a county bureaucrat who needed some licensure information from the Artium Group. Everyone wanted something from you, everyone wanted their cut. Blue ink smeared, so he threw the pen down. He would take the blame, and blamed himself—for their marriage falling apart, for not seeing Holly enough, for the mysteries of fatherhood.

"We'll find her," he offered. There was nothing to be said. "Look, I got to go," he told her, and hung up.

The woman was impossible. He sat in his darkening office and bit an overlong fingernail. As their divorce moved at a frenetic pace toward completion, their phone calls had grown more and more tiresome, even when there was no crisis to avert. A few months ago, she would have been the one to hang up on him, no doubt feeling empowered and decisive, but now she seemed only to want to cling to him, as though he had more to say and surely if she gave him the time to say it, all would be well. What she didn't seem to realize was that by hanging up on him, she saved both of them from frustration or anxiety or outright boredom, for he was out of words and only wanted a graceful way of ending the conversation. Boredom and grace, the twin pillars of modern American life. These were complications no one prepared you for when you were young and searching for a role in life.

West had come a long way from Sandwich, Illinois, a post-war paradise he no longer believed existed: row houses on numbered streets, children walking to school, elm trees before the Dutch blight. His mother stayed home and put dinner on the table at six. He and his three siblings would clean up after. His father worked in a brake factory in town that produced parts for Ford. Though never a manager, he considered his role integral for the company. West took that lesson to heart because, with three other siblings, his family was large enough that any extra money their father brought home went to pay the bill collector. West's father always found the money, somewhere, but he also lacked any kind of a life outside the home. Didn't go to the race track, didn't drink, just went to work and came home, went to work and came home. Other boys' fathers would go out to the races and drink on Friday nights, and they'd lose crucial money and keep drinking so that when they came home they were so numb that if they woke their wives the argument wouldn't escalate. Two or three drinks, they started losing money. Four drinks and they'd lost serious money and felt guilty about it. Five or six or seven drinks and the guilt burned so much they might kill someone—their wives perhaps—who called them out on their losses. But after eight or ten drinks, their minds confused nouns and verbs, couldn't raise an argument even if they wanted to, which they never did because all the residual guilt had been buried in no-memory.

But these men, fathers of West's friends, wouldn't always have the money for the bill collector, and when the creditors came calling they were forced into Chicago back alleys to take out a loan from some skulking figure who would then come out to their suburban homes, or send a guy out, walk right into these men's suburban homes and give them a shakedown, a rap on their knuckles maybe, or just take pieces of their wives' jewelry to cover the loan. West's father never took out such a loan, but it cost him his life. His life was bringing money home for the family. And the family stayed together. West knew he had a rosy view of the world he came out of, but no one had given him a thing, he might say, yet here he was. He'd made it through the turbulent sixties without getting swept up in the anti-war protests, the women's movement, Civil Rights. He wasn't against any of that, but he had his own interests that didn't always align with the front-page headlines. True: the world had changed. Women worked now and schools were integrated. Post-Kennedy, post-Vietnam, the world a big global community. Isolated countries no longer existed, not even Cuba, dependent as they were on the Soviet Union. Japanese automobiles sold well in America. Terrorists could come from anywhere—Beirut, Tehran, Northern Africa, Miami. And today, especially in Miami, the drug wars had become so lawless that instead of a rap on the knuckles for a bad loan, you'd get shot up in a shopping mall parking lot by an automatic weapon in broad daylight.

Isabel would expect him to call her back. She'd hired the detective, same as he had, and if Falcon found the girl, Isabel would take the credit. If Falcon didn't find the girl, West would take the blame. Maybe he deserved it, and maybe he could one day atone. For now he had too many other concerns. It was his daughter out there, his money missing, his life at stake if both didn't come back in one piece. He had nothing to say to his ex-wife. Instead, he scratched out a few numbers on the back of the memo. Three million in bogus assets meant $3 million in cash could be his, though it would put the company at risk. If the market got spooked and investors came knocking, or if regulators caught a whiff, the CIA would shut the Artium Group down under cover of darkness and liquidate rather than face the scrutiny of the financial media. The government could cover the losses, but West and everyone else would be out of a job—and West would likely be brought up on charges of fraud. Still, if it came to it he could fly to New York to beg for Wall Street money. While Falcon did whatever he did to scour for Holly, West would start with Tiny Mark Brown in D.C. tomorrow.

He had one more obstacle tonight before he could go home and drink himself to sleep. He closed up the office, unbuttoned his throat and loosened his tie in the elevator, rolled up his sleeves in the lobby, and shuffled into the downtown streets. It had not been a good day on the market, what would prove a minor correction at best, but still the financiers drank in shirtsleeves like the defeated men of Edward Hopper's Americana. Days such as this you saw how precarious was the thread that held you afloat. A man in a chicken costume clucked on the roadside, advertising Wings 'n Things. *For Sale* signs checkered residential lots and commercial storefronts, a bubble in the making despite the grinding interest rates.

A veteran stood on the street corner with a sign:

```
Lost job
Need work
Anything helps
Praise God
```

The same man who had been on the corner every day since Reagan slashed funding for mental health services, but he took on new meaning today.

Life in the middle class was unstable. You could be next.

Thanks to Daylight Savings Time, the sky clung to its bleeding pastel hues, but you could feel it: time neared its end.

Like most American metropolises, Miami contained several cities in one. While the financiers built Brickell into a gleaming powerhouse of corporate success, an influx of the flamboyantly young were laying the groundwork to reshape Miami Beach, and while Cubans and Haitians and Colombians had set up quarters that may as well have been a different country, the city's black population huddled in tenement housing near the river. West drove into this district with a cashier's check.

Mr. French owned an abandoned condo complex, eight empty floors with his entire drug distribution operation on the ninth. West parked in the street out front, and a man came out and searched him on the sidewalk. The man then took his keys and said, "Your car won't last long here. I'll take it to our garage."

The man nodded toward the elevators inside the lobby, where another man stood with an AK-47.

Inside, the second man punched the button on the elevator and said, "You're on nine."

The ninth floor had boarded up windows. The entry office was nicely decorated like a bank, complete with an attractive young woman at the front desk, clad in blue business attire, big hair and pumps.

West introduced himself and said he had an appointment with Alexander French.

"Just a moment," she said, and she dialed a number on the phone. "You can go on back," she said when she hung up.

She buzzed him through a locked door, and he walked into a surreal set of offices. Beyond a series of glass partitions, women in panties and masks and nothing else sat on stools amid swirls of scales and beakers and wrapped bricks of heroin. In front of the partitions, men stood with machine guns and took no notice of Bobby West.

"Mr. West!" Mr. French shouted. "Come on back."

Mr. French's office, if that's what it was, had a computer and a ham radio and a series of circuit boards and soldering irons.

"Glad you could make it." He gestured at a chair with a stack of empty cardboard boxes. "Just clear all those out and take a seat."

"Quite an operation you have here." West set the boxes on the floor, gingerly.

"We keep it simple. Drugs come in, we process them, drugs go out. We're always tinkering with our processes, a tip I learned from the Japanese. You ever been to a Toyota manufacturing center?"

"Never been."

"Paragons of efficiency and quality. It's no wonder they've out-paced Americans. No unions or bureaucratic bullshit to stand in the way. Just them and the customer, a model I try to emulate. I'm careful who I hire, and who I do business with, and if something doesn't work out, I cut my losses in a hurry."

Mr. French steepled his hands and let West squirm a moment. Not all that long ago, West had been the one behind the table.

"Of course in all this, another thing I try to do is keep the money separate from the product, sort of a wall between art and commerce, if you will. You noticed all the security, even for the product. Nothing to worry about. The neighborhood is perfectly safe even if it is a slum. Street-level hustlers leave you alone. They know what we do here and how it benefits them, or at least what happens if we cut bait and close our operations."

"You're not worried about a big hit? A professional?"

"Where would they go? Everyone in this business knows I work with the biggest, baddest clientele around the world. You take a brick of heroin from in there, try to fence it in, say, Chicago or even Cleveland, someone's going to want to know where it came from. If it didn't come from the Sicilians, that means it came from Florida, and that means you need permission from the Sicilians to distribute. They're not going to grant it, but even if they did, they'd let me know who is doing what, and even take care of any problems. You understand what I'm saying?" Mr. French pointed at West. "Now, I'm hoping you've got good news for me about your money situation."

West reached into his jacket pocket and pulled out an envelope. "I've got a proposal to square everything up."

"A proposal."

"The money's gone. I don't know where it is, but I've got a private investigator chasing it down. I also have two backup options. First, I've got a meeting with my director tomorrow. I'm bringing

Felix as a Cuban informant, so we can discuss Cuba Omega and the possibility of funding. It'll take a few months to go through, but if it's approved, I'll have a slush fund I can tap to pay everyone off and fund some additional business, if you like."

"What's your second backup?"

"Second, the Artium Group is on the financial edge. We've got debt and a few bad properties on our books, but: I also have some financing options to keep us afloat. If push comes to shove, I can go to Wall Street and sell a repurchase agreement. The details don't matter. It's an accounting instrument that will give us a short-term influx of unsecured cash. I can borrow the remainder, maybe as early as a week, and because it's filed under a repo agreement, it'll be off the AG's books."

"So you want to borrow money from Wall Street to pay me, and then borrow money from the CIA to pay your company back."

"In a nutshell," West said.

"What do you have there?"

"Call it a good faith down payment, or an interest payment on the money until I get the full amount."

"If you've got the money coming, why bother with a down payment? Where'd you get that? Cash out your savings?"

"To be frank, there's a very good chance my daughter has run off with the money. I know a lot of people are eager to get paid, and I don't want anyone to worry—or take unnecessary action."

Mr. French leaned back and grinned. "You're thinking of our friend from Amsterdam."

"She didn't strike me as the kind of woman to have much patience with I'll-pay-you-Tuesday promises."

Mr. French studied him and seemed about to say something else. Could he know anything about the robbery? An inside job? Could Holly's disappearance be a coincidence? Then Mr. French shook his head and said, "You need to find that money in a hurry."

12

"Wake up, honey. Hey, wake up." A man shook her roughly enough to send bad dreams back to her subconscious, like roaches scattering under a light. Holly stirred, her head against glass, her body upright. It was the first blue blush dawn, and she was in the passenger seat of a twenty-year-old Impala with flecks of rust on the doors, a sun-cracked vinyl dash, and an automatic transmission. In the driver's seat was an unshaven man with pimples on the scruff of his neck. Keith from Miami, rangy dude she'd aligned her fortunes with. He smelled like leeks.

They were at a truck stop, a bright casino-lit parking lot littered with coffee cups and napkins. A brown Ford truck in a handicapped space, big rigs parked in rows across the way in a long black plane of pavement, dim-lit by the white light of a streetlamp. Way back in the shadows, a covered line of pumps for truckers. Then nothing, like the world ended beyond the lights of the Speed-Mart.

"What time is it?" she asked.

"Around six. You want anything from the store?"

"Where are we?"

"Not too far from the Georgia line." He shut the door and leaned in the window, said, "Come in if you need anything."

She sat in the car a minute and then got out and stretched her legs. The morning cool in a way Miami never was. She still wore her club clothes, a skirt and spaghetti strap shirt. Hadn't showered since God knew when and she felt the grime. They'd lit out of Miami around when—one? two?—and as the rush of the theft faded, she'd sunk into a deep sleep. Too tired to consider where they were going. Wherever it was, they had plenty of money to get there. She thought he'd said something about an apartment in Georgia, but that could have been nothing but a dream.

Inside the station the neon lights stung her eyes and she roamed the aisles in an aimless wander, stared at the beef jerky and candy bars and soft drinks and beer. T-shirts with American flags and rebel flags and deer and race cars imprinted on them. A door slammed in the back of the station, and she saw a sign for the showers. She asked the woman at the register—a tiny young thing with blonde hair and a delicate face—how much the showers were.

"Dollar-fifty." Her voice was high and lazy, in the real South now.

"Hey now, we ought to keep going," Keith said. He wanted to get over the state line before anyone knew they were gone.

"It'll only take a minute."

"I'll take ten on pump five," he told the clerk. "We'll be at my apartment in a few hours, and you can shower long as you like."

Something caught inside her, and she felt like digging in her heels. A line in the sand, perhaps. "I'm going to the restroom," she told him.

"Don't linger."

She walked off to the showers and left him at the register. When she'd disappeared, Keith turned to the clerk—a small-time hick who liked to talk big—and he asked her what he was supposed to do here.

"Sounds like your girlfriend's in charge."

He shook his head.

The clerk rolled her eyes and wondered for perhaps the eightieth time why all the wackos came in on her shift, made for a long night even with the day creeping in.

When Holly returned from the restroom, they walked out of the gas station and into bad news. A sheriff's cruiser had parked

Jon Sealy

between their Impala and the clerk's pickup, and a deputy shoul-
dered his way out of the cruiser, put on his hat to look mean, and
cut them off at the door. Behind them, the motion sensor for the
sliding doors picked up their shapes, and the doors opened and shut
testily.

"Where you folks heading?" he asked.

"Savannah," Keith said.

"You start early or been driving all night?" When they didn't
answer, the deputy looked at the car, the South Florida dealer logo,
and then back at the two kids. "You visiting someone?"

"I live there," Keith said.

The deputy turned to Holly. "You?"

"Girlfriend," she said.

The deputy was a youngish man but already had the paunch of
middle age puddling over his belt. He studied them a moment and
said, "Y'all got any ID on you? Registration for your car?"

Keith walked to the passenger side, opened the door, and began
rummaging around the glove box. The deputy shined a light on
Holly's license and then took the license and registration from Keith.

"It's a rental?" the deputy asked.

"We borrowed the car from my cousin," Holly said. "I thought
it was his."

"What's his name?" the deputy asked.

"Felix Machado."

The deputy sucked his teeth and eyed them for another moment
like he was thinking, even though it was clear what his next move
was. He said, "We've had some trouble with boys coming up from
South Florida. Drug mules heading for Atlanta or D.C. or wherever
it is they go. Do me a favor, will you? Take a seat in the back of my
car while I call this in."

Without looking at Keith, Holly did as she was told. What
did she care? Her father would come get her and forgive her for
stealing the money. Poor Keith would be collateral damage, not her
problem if things went south. She'd thought he was cute, if not
totally capable, when she latched onto him, but in times like these

114

you didn't need cute. You needed an alpha to take charge. In front of the deputy, Keith drooped like wet noodle.

They sat in the back of the squad car while the deputy called in the car's information. The car was registered with a private rental agency out of the Miami airport. The call from the Nassau County sheriff's station went through a switchboard to a bored agent working the late shift. Calls came in like this on occasion, law enforcement wanting to know who had rented what car and when.

The bored agent said nothing to the officer on the line as he rattled his keyboard through one screen after another, no doubt thinking, *Jeez, if they've got cause to arrest somebody, arrest them, why bother with the background checks.* He wished their computer system, which filed everything so clearly, could miraculously sync up with police departments so they didn't have to bother him. He had a magazine article about volcanic activity in the Pacific to get back to. "All right," the agent said, "the Impala was rented out to Felix Machado of Delray Beach on, wow, March 11."

The officer thanked him.

"Hold on," the agent said. He clicked the secondary drop-down. "Secondary driver is listed as Keith Sorrells. Doesn't list an address, which is strange because we ordinarily get all that information."

"Thank you," the officer said again.

The call came back to the deputy in rural Georgia: the kids were clean. The deputy knew something wasn't right here, but he knew he'd never see them again, and that if he raised a stink, tried to search their car, he'd be filling out paperwork to the end of his shift. Easier just to send them on their way and fill up with a cup of coffee.

"You're good to go," he said as he opened the door of the cruiser. "Next time, tell somebody it's a rental."

13

Adriana Chekhov had just returned from a meeting with a buyer in Istanbul, a Shia defector with possible ties to the Iranians. Chekhov had fiery hair and gypsy blood and steady eyes. A hawk, a bird of prey. Her contact was a rotund, fish-faced fellow who appeared agitated to discover his weapons salesman was a woman. No matter. She let him buy her coffee and a pastry and listened to him wax poetic about the nearby Anatolian hills. Istanbul was a poetic place, of course, but Chekhov had long ago lost any feeling she once had for the beauties of a city. Everywhere in the world had its glamour and elegance, as well as the shadows and dirt of human life, and the unyielding chill of the natural order. Istanbul was just another city, no different from any other.

She would never hear from this man again. Perhaps he was onto her from the start, knew she had no nuclear material to offer. Perhaps he would send someone after her, or perhaps he would be arrogant enough to believe he was in no danger, when in fact a team of Israeli special forces were in his hotel room now, sussing out his contacts and tracing the chain of communiqués from his time in Turkey. They would pick him up and, without fanfare, take him to a warehouse near the border with Iraq, interrogate him, and hand him over to Kurdish officials. Nevertheless, on her way back to the Hilton, Chekhov took extra precaution to shake any possible tail.

In the hotel lobby, the concierge flagged her down.

"Mrs. Martin, Mrs. Martin."

Turkey a free country but not a place where an unmarried woman would check into a hotel alone. Not in 1984.

"You received a call," the concierge said. "Mr. Adam Fields. In France."

He handed her a folded up piece of paper.

"In France?" she asked.

"He didn't specify, but this is a Parisian number."

She took the paper, glanced at the message. A name and a number.

"I appreciate it," she said.

"The caller spoke very good English."

"He's an ambassador," Chekhov said. "Just visiting France, I'm sure."

"Of course. Well, if there's anything else I can do."

She left the concierge in the lobby and went upstairs to pack.

Her job in Istanbul was over, the next no doubt on its way as soon as she placed the phone call. Mr. Adam Fields may have given her a Parisian number, but she knew exactly who and where he was. She also knew the call could only be bad news, for no one called her otherwise. She inverted the code and wrote down the South Florida telephone number. Her assignments came from all over—government agencies, private contractors, mercenaries—and it never ceased to surprise her how far this man's reach extended. Everyone seemed to know, and fear, the Miami businessman at the center of the Cold War: Alexander French.

Later, after she'd called Mr. French and gotten word of her next assignment—in America, this time—she packed her suitcase and checked out of the hotel.

"We had you for another three nights," the concierge said, unable to mask his disappointment. "I hope your stay was satisfactory."

"Everything was fine. My husband has an unexpected business engagement."

"Well, I wish him the best. Tell him I'm sorry I missed him."

"I'm sure we'll be back soon."

She left the hotel and abandoned her identity as Caroline Martin, caught a taxi for the airport. Mr. French's company had purchased a redeye to get her to Miami via Newark. Mr. French had been vague on the phone—a problem with "our friend Bobby" and a missing $3 million—but assured her a quick assignment followed by as much R&R as she wanted on his estate in the Marianas. Whatever had gone wrong, she knew it was nothing French couldn't handle on his own. No need to bring her in as the janitor unless there was more to the story. For now, she slid through airport security under the identity of a Canadian opera singer, bought a packet of winter-green chewing gum from the nearest kiosk, and found a dim corner of the airport to sit and await her flight.

The trip from Istanbul to Miami would take twenty-five hours with stopovers in London and Newark. Standing in the burnished husk of evening, Adriana Chekhov was wired on coffee and ready for the flight that would carry her across the bleak Atlantic and deposit her in Newark at dawn. Her eyes flickered over the crowd in Heathrow, the passengers shuffling and bumping into each other as they boarded the plane, forced their oversized suitcases into overhead storage, fastened their seatbelts. The skinny ones shrank in their skin to take up less space and hovered as far away from their companions as they could, while the obese gurgled and sweated and spilled over the armrests, into other seats, into the aisle, against the windows and tray tables.

The dense stink of old fabric and fuel and the negative ions in the air did strange things to everyone. Children cried out for safety while their tired-eyed parents shushed them and chuckled nervously. Flight attendants smiled as though the trip was one delightful show, or they were stoned beyond cognition. Meanwhile Chekhov considered the physics of the whole enterprise: a metal bird, sealed shut, fired up and launched itself five miles off the runway and aimed for another, dodged other planes and added to the spirograph pattern of air traffic control, all piloted by a man with 20/20 vision and directed by cold figures who were guided by radar towers. This was where the grand teleology of human progress reached an end. We are green blips in the night, panasonic starbursts of flesh and blood.

The door closed with a hiss and the passengers were locked in the tube. They sat with magazines and newspapers, closed their eyes and prepared to wake in a new place, their faith in operations beyond their comprehension. What if the plane never actually moved? Perhaps the rest of the world moved in a rumble around them. After all, they remained station-less, relativity of motion, two trains side by side on the tracks, impossible to tell which is moving. The slippery, unclear structures around us dependent on mathematical coordinates, vectors X, Y, and Z, differentiated from space-time onto a three-dimensional plane. Numbers, calculus, probability, the very odds that reality even existed.

When she dozed off somewhere over the ocean, she understood a system was in motion, the first domino had been tipped. Tomorrow she had to confront the mysterious Mr. French, whose people had misplaced $3 million. On the plane she had to trust all the pieces were in place and that the laws of motion would do their work, that chaotic interference would not disrupt the system. Her job was to play it cool. She could do cool. In Newark, she ate a banana and a bowl of oatmeal and read two newspapers. Nothing new. Nuclear testing in the Kazakh republic, another spat between the Palestinians and the Israelis, U.S. policy debates over Nicaragua. The noise of the world like the endless playback of a cassette, fragmented sounds of a corrupted world.

In Miami, she chewed a piece of wintergreen gum while the plane taxied to the gate. She counted seventeen men on the plane with her, thirteen women, and only one of them—the big African man with a barrel torso and a black knit cap on his head—seemed to understand they'd survived a miracle in landing this plane. The African leaned forward to pray, and Chekhov found that comforting, to be in the presence of someone willing to pray in public. The two women in front of her were named Delta and Cammie, southern girls here to enjoy spring break at the beach. Delta had long blond hair cut to mask plumpness in her cheeks, a signal of the long entropic slide into middle age. Cammie, however, was a bit gaunt, her face like a celery stalk, and she might one day come into her own, if she could ditch Delta. You had to go it alone in this world, and the sooner you learned, the better off you'd be—especially if you were a woman. The world was not kind to women.

The plane made a sucking sound when the hatch opened, like a vacuum seal being broken, and the planeload of people rose and reached for their luggage out of the overhead compartments. Bags fell and bopped into neighbors, and men checked their pagers. The African stared out the window, as did Chekhov. She wore no pager. As far as anyone in the world was concerned, she was not here. She did not even exist. A spook. A shadow. The person who carries your garbage away at five in the morning, the maid who remakes your bed while you're away, out seeing the sights, snapping photos.

She placed two phone calls from a booth near baggage claim. Then she changed in the bathroom into a tight tank top and a flower print skirt, flip-flops and sunglasses. Just another tourist. Perhaps a woman with a broken heart hoping to find herself over a few cocktails, to feel the sweat bead up on the glass and to taste a sweet liqueur and flirt recklessly with men on vacation and generally believe herself to be living the good life. She rented a car and drove into the city, paid cash for a motel room on the Dixie Highway. She left the door unlocked while she took a shower, fingered shampoo into her hair, stood under the water until her skin reddened and the mirror steamed. The towel was thin and coarse, so she dried quickly and began to dress. This was not the Hilton, but she never had expectations about where she stayed. Although born after the war, she'd grown up with a sense of dread and vague understanding of Hitler's atrocities. No one in her family had spoken of it, but she'd gradually come to understand why Israel existed, why she had no grandparents, what it meant to live comfortably, without fear.

When she came out of the bathroom, a duffel bag had been placed on the bed. She locked and chained the door, and returned to the bathroom to dry her hair before examining the bag. Inside the bag she found a Florida driver's license, three hundred dollars in various bills, a Glock 42, an M89-SR semiautomatic rifle, a Schmidt & Bender telescopic sight, several rounds of ammunition, a demolition block of C-4 and a charge assembly. She tucked the driver's license and cash into her wallet and slid the Glock into the back of her pants, hidden by a shawl. She zipped the bag and carried it out to stow it in her rental car's trunk. She scanned the parking lot and, seeing nothing of interest, got into the car and pulled onto the Dixie Highway.

14

In standard missing person cases, the first twenty-four hours are your window for gathering leads. Footprints, phone calls, eyewitnesses: if you don't catch these things early, you may never catch them. Memory blurs. Crime scenes destruct. Holly Hernandez, a.k.a. Holly West, had last been seen on Monday morning, was reported missing on Wednesday, and now it was Thursday. Falcon knew his former colleagues at the Miami P.D. were compiling information on the girl and her family, sending out releases to neighboring police departments, and would be expanding the search nationally soon if they hadn't already done so. Falcon knew these things were happening behind the scenes, standard procedure, yet he was surprised the girl's disappearance had not made the local news. He'd expected to see her innocent face blown up on last night's eleven o'clock news, or at least in the metro section of this morning's paper.

Nothing. News of how some fellow high on cocaine wrecked his Porsche in the everglades. Cops estimate he had it up to a hundred and twenty, a quarter-million dollars in the trunk. These days in Miami, that kind of cash was chump change. Enough for a fine night out on the town, maybe pay cash for a boat.

The first thing Falcon did after settling into the office today was call his buddy Juan Delgado at the newspaper.

"First I've heard of it," Delgado said.

"You sure about that? Seventeen-year-old white girl gone missing from her suburban home?"

"Sounds like front-page material to me," the reporter said. "It's possible we've pulled something off the wire, but no one said anything about it at our eight o'clock run down. You can be sure I'll ask around as soon as we get off the phone, though."

"Gracias, amigo."

"You got any more details you can throw my way?"

"Hey, I called you for information," Falcon said. "Figured you'd be in the know."

"Seventeen-year-old white girl, gone missing from her suburban home," Delgado echoed. "Who hired you to look into her case?"

"Call the Miami P.D."

"You're not freelancing for them now. I know they've had budget cuts, but still. It's got to be the parents."

"If there's any story for you, the cops are your sources."

"The girl got a boyfriend? On drugs?" the reporter pressed.

"Call me if you learn anything," Falcon said.

When he got off the line, he leaned back and put his feet on the desk.

First the mother comes to hire him—not the standard procedure for parents of missing children. Usually private investigators were a later resort, a last chance when the police turned up zilch and the case went cold. Then the father, Falcon's landlord, comes in to hire him for the same job. Fair enough. No one said a divorced couple had to start communicating just because the child went missing. You never knew what kind of bad blood existed between ex-lovers. But now the *Miami Herald*'s star reporter Juan Delgado says he's not heard a peep about young Holly Hernandez. Didn't take Sherlock Holmes to see this case was out of the ordinary.

Falcon's only question right now was who had been bullshitting him. His money was on dad first, then the mom, then the reporter, but Falcon had been in this business long enough to appreciate this space of not knowing. Most professions forced you to know something, or at least put up a good enough front to act decisively. It happened in police work too. The cops who rose up the ranks eventually became politicians, and politicians always knew something. The reason Falcon couldn't hack the promotional ladder was the same reason that made him an exceptional investigator. He reserved judgment and was comfortable with the sentence, "I don't know." Simple, but so many would-be leaders in this world refused to confront their limitations. Falcon was no relativist, but knew enough to know the truth could be a long time in emerging.

He placed another call, to the Miami P.D. this time, asked to reach his old pal Donnie Ray Callahan. The detective on the other line—whom Falcon had never met, sounded like his voice hadn't finished changing—said Donnie Ray was out of the office, on patrol.

"Can you get him on the radio for me?" Falcon asked.

"We don't do that anymore."

"Do what?"

"Radio for detectives when a CI calls in."

"Hell, I'm not a CI. I used to work there."

"Regardless, I can't raise him on the radio for you. I can leave a message."

"What's he got a radio for if you're not going to use it?"

"Those are for internal coordination only. New regulations."

"What if I were his wife, calling to say his kid's been in a car wreck."

"I'd take a message."

Falcon felt his blood pressure spiking and didn't know whether it was out of frustration with the kid on the line—kids today all swagger behind a fence of regulations, never had to make a decision without a safety net—or that he missed his old job and wished he were still in the loop. He tried another tack and introduced himself. "I need to catch up with Donnie Ray. What do you recommend?"

"I can take a message," the kid said again.

"All right, well take this down. The victim in one of your investigations has hired me to look into her case. I'm about to piss all over it and wreck whatever strategy you're taking, and I thought I'd call Donnie Ray as a courtesy."

"You know it's a crime to impede a criminal investigation?"

"Of course I know it's a crime," Falcon said, "but I spent thirty years in that department. You let Donnie Ray know I called, and if he wants to talk, he can call me."

"What case is it?" the kid asked.

"Missing girl out of Coconut Grove."

"Tell me your name again," the kid said.

A few minutes later, Callahan called from what sounded like a pay phone near an artillery range. Even though the detective was yelling his voice hoarse, Falcon could barely understand him.

"I said, I'm walking a construction site in Brickell, the new office tower by the water. Can't hear much of anything."

"I can be there in ten," Falcon said.

"Why don't you meet me at Spring Harbor Baptist? High noon? We can grab lunch."

At a quarter to noon, Falcon hung his closed sign, locked up the office, and drove into Little Havana to meet up with Callahan. He drove past a man on the street hawking newspapers and wondered if his pal at the *Herald* had managed to unearth anything this morning. Doubtful, unless he had a better contact with the M.P.D. than Falcon did. He intended to find out why the police hadn't issued any kind of press release. People went missing all the time, but Falcon was old-fashioned enough to believe a clean-cut teenager who disappeared from the suburbs was somehow different from the man who walks out on his family, the drug dealer who doesn't show up for Sunday dinner, the car thief who skips bail. He supposed this was city life: neighbors were strangers and crime was the norm. A missing girl was just another statistic, nothing for the newscasters to interrupt the soaps over.

The church where he was to meet Detective Donnie Ray Callahan was an old pink motel a few blocks off Calle Ocho, one of several in the area converted to an iglesia over the past thirty years. The neighborhood branded itself a haven for the Cuban population, but in truth the Cubans had taken over more of Miami than a few square blocks. They'd come in waves since the revolution but already had a population base from the thirties. Falcon grew up in a white and black Florida, but the Miami of his adulthood had always been an odd mix, where motels were churches, parades were protests, and fashion was a political statement. Cubans with frozen assets built a new capitalist life for themselves while many of the natives, thanks to the beneficence of government programs, couldn't find a leg to stand on.

At noon on the dot, Falcon pulled into the church's parking lot, pulled up alongside a shaded playground, and stopped next to Callahan's unmarked Crown Vic. He leaned out the window and said first thing, "Who's that prick taking messages in the office?"

Callahan sipped soda through a straw like he was puzzling out the Rosetta Stone. Then he smiled and said, "Who, Henry? He's harmless. A field mouse."

"Jesus," Falcon said, "you're gone a few years, no one knows your name and all the rules have changed."

Falcon and Callahan went back to academy days, both rural Florida boys in the big city. Neither had aged well, but Callahan in particular looked like he'd been soaking in brine these past ten years. They say a person's nose and ears never stop growing, and you could see the Jurassic face Callahan was aging into. He shook his head and explained, "We had a narcotics officer running a CI in one of the north end projects. One day, his CI calls up the station, says he needs to see the officer lickety split. Got a hot tip on some high-up crime boss. Desk sergeant radios the officer, the officer goes up to meet his informant." Callahan took a sip of soda, slurped the bottom of the cup, went on, "Alone, mind you, dumbest thing he could do, but I guess he thought he knew the guy. Anyway, we found him three days later strung up like Christ himself in a half-built condo complex. They'd cut off his left foot and burned cigarettes all over his chest and back."

"Good god."

"Another day and the man would've been graveyard dead. He's on leave pending a full investigation. Internal Affairs doesn't know whether the cop was dirty or what. Someone clearly wanted information out of him. That, or there's a new level of cruelty out there I don't even want to think about. Anyway, so we don't radio officers anymore when a civilian calls in. All calls are logged, all meetings are recorded, no one goes alone."

"Yet here you are," Falcon said.

Callahan grinned. "I got a pair of officers up the street watching us through binoculars."

Falcon saw nothing at first. Then he saw them, another unmarked sedan at the end of the block. "You think they could be any more conspicuous?" Falcon asked.

"You didn't see them," Callahan said. "Anyway, they won't bother us. May even take off once they see you're not about to kidnap me and string me up."

"How do you even stand it?"

"Oh hell, Ernie, couple of babysitters, tag teaming every operation, it's all part of the new operations structure, even before our narcotics crucifixion. Top brass thinks we need to be more nimble, which really means they're cutting our budget but want to make sure crime rates don't rise."

"Do they know what's happening on the streets?" Falcon asked.

"Not really. They think coke and heroin are the same as pot was in the sixties, nothing but recreation for long-haired young men with misguided politics."

Callahan took one last slurp of his soda, tossed it on his car's floorboard.

"They don't realize the dealers are organized, they got established trade routes coast to coast. I tell you, bud, we've got bad times coming our way. There's a new drug out there, a modified form of cocaine? Purer than anything you've ever seen, spreading like a virus. One hit and you're hooked, top brass don't even know it's out there."

"You've got to get out. How many years you have left?"

Callahan breathed out. "I could buy out and be gone by Christmas, but what would I do?"

"Private investigations get you out of the house."

"Don't mean to be disrespectful, but I like an office with a big team around me. Makes me feel less alone."

"Clearly, you're bringing the office with you." Falcon nodded his head toward the unmarked sedan. "You have to be comfortable being alone in this line of work, but old age is nothing if not lonesome, when folks start dying off. My biggest fear might be dying at my desk and not having anyone around to find me."

"What can I do for you, Ernie? Henry got on the radio talking about how you were about to jam up a case."

"I'm looking for a missing girl, Holly Hernandez? She should be in your unit by now."

Callahan worked criminal investigations for M.P.D.'s central station. If they were really trying to be nimbler, the unit was likely small enough these days that any scuttlebutt should have gotten around. But Callahan said he hadn't heard much. "It came in yesterday. How'd it land in your court so fast?"

"The wife came in before lunch, and then damn if the ex-husband didn't come in right after lunch to hire me for the same job."

Callahan whistled.

"Neither of them could tell me much. Girl gone missing, no boyfriend, friends hadn't seen anything. Dad was a bit cryptic about his work. He's with a holding company, rumor has it CIA might be connected. He seems to think maybe the daughter stumbled into something and got spooked. Wouldn't tell me what, and didn't give me anything to go on."

"Sounds about right," Callahan said. "The officers that caught the case spoke with Mom and Dad that morning."

"Together?"

"Yeah, at Mom's house. Dad showed up in the middle of the interview. Neither of them cooperative, but that may just be because they hate each other."

"Who's on it?" Falcon asked.

"Fat Steve and Maker's Mark."

Falcon thought for a moment. Everyone had a nickname at the precinct, and you didn't have to be gone long before you missed a name change or a shift in the power structure.

"Steve came out of sex crimes first chance he got," Callahan explained. "You may have run into him when he was an errand boy, but doubtful you ever worked with him. Mark has an uncle on city council."

"They know what they're doing?"

"They're good police, but we're all overworked."

"Haven't heard anything about the girl on the news yet."

"That one's not our fault," Callahan said. "Word's come down for us to keep this discreet."

"Which is why you're out here with me, against regulations." Falcon shook out a Pall Mall. "Who put out the order?"

Callahan shrugged. "Lieutenant said keep the media out of it, we kept the media out of it."

"You know they're going to get their teeth into it eventually."

"Who'd you talk to?"

Falcon breathed out a cloud of smoke. "Juan Delgado."

Callahan started laughing. "I imagine her photo's going to be on the front page tomorrow then. Jesus, you really did smear our investigation."

"Maybe, though I didn't mention her name."

"Good reporter like Delgado?" Callahan shook his head. "Front page tomorrow."

"Well, I didn't have anything to tell him. In fact, I was hoping he might have some intel for me."

"It was bound to get out some time," Callahan said, "though it might close some doors for you if Delgado lets slip you were his source."

"So you don't have anything on the girl yet?"

"Not that I've heard. They're knocking on doors, probably on the assumption she's off with a boyfriend. I know, I know, everyone says she doesn't have a fella, but."

"I didn't say anything," Falcon said.

"They're also checking on strangers, anyone who saw her. The usual."

Falcon flicked his cigarette butt on the parking lot. "You give me a call if they find anything?"

"I'll let you know," Callahan said, "assuming you do the same with me."

"I'll swing by the station soon. I want to do a little more digging on Dad. You still up for lunch?"

Callahan checked his watch, which he wore on the inside of his wrist. "Have to take a raincheck, unfortunately. You could ask my colleagues." He nodded his head back toward the surveillance crew.

"I'll pass unless you're buying. Any chance you could run a quick background on Bobby West?"

"I'm sure Steve and Mark have already run one. You got a card, I'll have them fax it your way this afternoon."

Falcon dug a crumpled business card out of his wallet and passed it over. "Oh hey, let me ask you, before you go. I ran into Frank Navarro the other day."

"Oh yeah?"

Callahan didn't sound surprised, which meant Navarro had approached him as well.

"Invited me to lunch out of the blue," Falcon said.

"I hear he's been doing that lately."

"Yeah? He called you up for lunch?"

"He knows better than to call me for anything."

"I thought he'd know better than to call me," Falcon said.

"Yeah, you'd think so. What'd he want?"

"Said he had an opportunity, and several of the guys at the station were into it. Sounds like he's investing in a piece of property. Offered me a ground-floor entry."

Callahan grinned. "Man never changes, never gives up."

"I guess not. He threw out Bill Johnson's name."

Callahan curled his lips and rubbed his chin a moment. "Bill's been out of it for a while now. Pushing paperwork, slowed way down. If he's agreed to anything with Frank Navarro, Frank's the one likely to get screwed."

"I figured as much. Just wondered if you'd heard anything."

"You going to take his offer?"

"I'll see you, Donnie Ray," Falcon said.

*

The lunch hour traffic was still jamming up the causeways, so rather than fight it back to the office, Falcon got off 12th Avenue and parked on a side street. He knew a local bar in the back of a Latin grocery where he could wait it out. His intention was one drink and then onto the office, but he ended up staying three rounds to mull over Holly Hernandez, Bobby West, and Frank Navarro. One would have been trouble enough for the week—for the year—but two made him wonder if he'd earned some bad karma. His children would say yes indeed. His wife might come back with a hung jury.

He sipped the beer slowly, and no one in the cantina seemed to mind his presence, even after he'd polished off a plate of plantains and marinated pork. The clerks were busy stocking shelves in the grocery, prepping for the after-work rush. The bartender doubled as the chef, complete with a folded white paper hat and a grin on his face. The beer was cheap here, seventy-five cents a can. Of course it was three dollars for a six-pack at the front of the store, but Falcon wasn't at the point of just buying beer to drink in his truck, or in the office. Civilization's fluorescent lights and smiling faces were a relief.

When he got back to the office, he saw Callahan had come through and faxed over a three-page file on Bobby West, a handwritten cover note that said West had high enough security clearance where most of his records were hidden from casual public view. Falcon couldn't say what the feds were doing, but M.P.D. was limited to property records, credit histories, run-ins with the law. Still, with the right kind of search equipment, you could build a dossier on anyone.

Trouble was, Bobby West's file was totally vanilla. Married in his mid-twenties, family deferment for Vietnam, one daughter, now estranged from his wife. He'd been in Miami for years, owned two houses here now, one for him and one for his ex-wife. The man paid all his taxes, stayed out of debt, had a million-dollar credit report and not even a speeding ticket to his name. Falcon flipped through the pages a second time and knew that any other cop would take

West for the model citizen who'd played the game straight and who had been justly rewarded in whatever public-private hybrid operation the Artium Group was. The company had been listed in the Dun & Bradstreet directory for years, Robert West listed as the chief financial officer, in charge of $100 million in receivables. West's accumulated wealth might irk some of the guys in the P.D., those who had gambled away regular chunks of their salaries on illegal poker games, but a lot of those guys had alimonies to pay themselves. They'd sympathize with the man, his wife getting that great big old house and him having to pay the mortgage and Lord knew what else.

But Falcon wasn't a man to let go of an idea once it had taken hold. So much of this job still relied on instincts and hunches, on feeling your way through the dark, and he felt Bobby West was up to no good. Falcon would stake his pension on it. Maybe the daughter was a red herring, or maybe she had stumbled into something nefarious. Either way, you could feel it just sitting near Bobby West. The man was one step away from a felony. Falcon tapped the sheets even on his desk and muttered, "Bobby, Bobby, Bobby. What are you up to?"

He leaned back to catch his breath. Needed to lose a few pounds. Needed to get in shape and eat healthier so he could cut back on his blood pressure medication. Cholesterol would be the death of him, his wife always said. The booze, too, was a problem. He was still lightheaded and sloppy from his cantina fare, and he dozed off for a few minutes.

The telephone woke him. He'd drifted into a dream, the details of which became fuzzy as he emerged to the waking world.

In the dream, he'd bought a farm, a genteel piece of property up in the horse country, to build a retirement home for him and his wife, a place for Mary Catherine to convalesce. He could smell the sawdust, the drywall, the pungent scent of earth turned up. Mary Catherine had come with him to look at the home, and frowned at the sight of it. "What is it?" Falcon asked her. She marched into the framed structure, held her hands on her hips as she took everything in. "Careful!" he called to her, worried even in the dream about her safety, always certain she would stumble into something. She put her hands on her hips and spun around and around, and then said, "That wall's in the wrong place"—pointed at a load-bearing structure—"and this whole sight is dirty." He joined her and said, "It's a construction site. It's supposed to be dusty." "Yes, but do they have to leave their cups out like that." It was true, a Styrofoam cup was on a board balanced between two sawhorses. "They'll clean it up," he said, but his wife had morphed into Frank Navarro. Navarro was short, like he was in life, and had a wide lower lip like a bill, which he curled whenever he went into project management mode. "Hey!" he called up to one of the workers, who was framing the second floor. He rattled off a string of Spanish in a tone Falcon knew to mean *Let's tighten this operation up.* He waved his hands around and whistled and shook his head toward Falcon. He opened his mouth as if to say something further.

The telephone rang again, and this time Falcon fought through the fuzz and picked up the receiver.

"You all right, buddy?" Juan Delgado asked on the other end.

"Yeah, just distracted here."

"I wake you up from a siesta?"

"What can I do for you, Juan?" Falcon asked, his dream vanished like an ebbing wave.

"I did a little research on your missing girl, and I have to tell you, your colleagues at the Miami P.D. are about as uncooperative as I've ever seen them."

"Yeah, an old friend there told me the word is to keep it quiet."

"We're running a blurb tomorrow, but we don't have much on record. Why I'm calling is, what do you know about the girl's father?"

Falcon grinned. "So you are an investigative journalist after all. I asked around about him with my old Miami P.D. colleagues."

"And?"

"He's a businessman with possible CIA connections, or he's a CIA man with a business front. That's par for the course in Miami."

"Yeah well, his business front is something you ought to look into to find his daughter. They've been hemorrhaging money for years now from some bad real estate investments. Got in when the interest rates were pushing eighteen, nineteen percent. It makes sense, if their financial officer is just a front man for keeping an eye on the Cubans."

"What does this have to do with the missing daughter?"

"Maybe nothing, maybe everything. These guys have a deep well of money from Washington, so it's no big deal that they're losing so much, but I can't get a line on any of their private equity."

"Speak English to me," Falcon said.

"OK, the CIA set up an operation down here, and they want to at least pretend they're being discreet, right? So they set up the Artium Group as a 'legitimate business,' pour a bunch of money into the company and buy up a string of properties. Now the company is a real estate developer. Maybe they hire a crop of legitimate employees and let them go to work, figuring, hey, if they screw up too badly, they'll just fire them and get another loan from Washington. The problem is, you can't do too well in this world without drawing attention. If I open a burger joint, no one cares. If I open fifteen franchises, McDonald's or somebody looks at me and says, wait a minute, this guy's eating into our margins. So they buy me out. That's the American dream: get big, sell out, get rich."

"You're thinking the Artium Group got too big."

"Have you seen their balance sheet? They're a giant. I'm sure the other Florida developers have their eye on the business, and have probably already made offers to buy a stake. The problem I'm running into is I can't figure out who's made what offers."

"Why does it matter unless the Artium Group accepted?"

"How do you know they haven't?" Delgado asked.

"Well, you told me they had an unlimited slush fund out of Washington. Why would they accept developer money?"

"Ah, there's the rub. Ask yourself, what does everyone here want? The people in Washington, the CIA, they want to know what's going on with Cuba. They want to take Castro out if they can find a way, and they want to make sure the exiles here in Miami don't cause too much trouble. We assume Bobby West wants something along the same lines—to do a good job as a company man."

"I'm with you."

"Well, everyone else down here just wants to get filthy rich. Sure, there are exiles who want to have the Bay of Pigs all over again, get on the first boat and invade Cuba, but most of them have turned capitalist. They support taking out Castro in name, but that's because Castro froze all their assets. It's spite versus greed, and greed eventually wins out. My money says that someone down here figured out what was what with the Artium Group, and went in and cut a deal with Bobby West. Someone saw a chance to get rich and pull one over on the CIA, convinced Bobby West to take private equity to further his cause."

"You're saying some developer invested in the Artium Group, promised a lead on Castro, but stands to make a bundle of money in the meantime."

"It could happen," Delgado said.

"What happens if West actually starts something? Organizes an invasion of Cuba?"

"Then spite wins."

"So you think this investor is a Cuban exile."

"That's where I'd put my money," Delgado said.

"But you don't know who."

"I don't know if there is an investor. I'm just making up a story to explain why no one's ever heard of the Artium Group, how this company can burn through so much money without drawing in the leeches, and—maybe—why the company's CFO is all of a sudden in hot water."

"So you think the girl has been kidnapped."

"I don't know, Ernie. I can't print a word of this. I'm just saying something doesn't add up here. Maybe it's totally random. Maybe she's just another face on a milk carton, picked up by a crazy man, or maybe she hitched her way out to Hollywood. But if you want to find her, my money is on Bobby West."

15

Bobby West met his contact Felix for breakfast at the Café Arugula in South Beach, a pleasant shop with six tables on a patio behind a wrought iron fence. A waiter in black with his shirt tucked in and a white pad of paper sticking out of an apron stood by one table and listened to some numbskull jabber about whatever floated his gastronomical boat. The pretense of the café made West uncomfortable, but he'd suffered through worse places. The good news was that Felix seemed at ease here, like he was on patio in Little Havana surrounded by his brethren, *la lucha*. Although Felix was Cuban, he had light, almost white skin and very dark curly hair. He had a flat face and a hook in his nose, like a beak, and a line that made his chin look like a butt.

There was no way for West to know what the man thought about his plan, but until West found his daughter and got the money back, he didn't see an alternative. Mr. French wouldn't be mollified for long, and the U.S. government seemed to be the best place to turn. After all, they were bankrolling the Artium Group in the first place. Artium may be generating enough profits from the business fronts to start Radio Martí broadcasting to Havana, but it wasn't enough for an operative to do what really needed to be done about Cuba.

"What you need to understand about Tiny Mark Brown is that he's got no field experience," West said. "And when I say no field experience, I mean zip. Never even served in the Coast Guard. Purely academic. Maybe he could tell you all about Clausewitz and Jomini and what Mao had to say about insurgency, but the simple fact remains, he's never been in the field, yet he's in charge of all CIA operatives around the globe."

Felix took this in without a word. Just sipped his coffee and waited for West to say what he had to say.

"What this means is that he doesn't always appreciate what we do, how long it can take to run an assignment, and how sometimes obstacles get in the way. He's like a sales manager offering weak leads to his team and then asking why they aren't closing enough. Now, I'm a good closer. It's what I do. But, fuck it, you can only do what you can with the resources you're given to work with, and it's like Washington wants us to fail.

"When we go up there, just let me handle the discussion. I want you there so he has a face to put to the name, but he's not a curious man. He won't ask you any questions, and he might not even remember the meeting after it happens. But we want it on record so that once we hit the first domino, there won't be any hitches to keep the others from falling."

"You trust him?" Felix asked.

"I don't have to trust him. Our plan is bigger than Tiny Mark, so once we get started, there won't be a thing he can do about it."

The waiter came over and offered more coffee. Felix turned him down. West asked for the check. They had an eleven o'clock flight to D.C. and a late-afternoon meeting with Tiny Mark.

"Why bring this man in at all, if we don't need him and he's not a solid ally?"

"That's a good question. With our organization, it's all about records. If it's not documented, it didn't happen. So we meet with Tiny Mark, that's one document. I file a white paper, that's another document. If you can get me some intel on your pals in Cuba Omega, that's another. These documents all remain classified, but they start to build a picture in the agency: Cuba is no longer contained. The exiles are getting restless, and we have an opportunity to leverage them."

Felix grinned. "That's a new one for me. Leverage."

"That might be the most important word in a capitalist society. When you have it, no one can mess with you. We leverage the exiles, we can get a line on toppling Castro. We topple Castro, the U.S. earns a return on its investment. Our job is to sell it so we get the investment in the first place."

Felix lit a cigarette and took in his surroundings with a curious look.

Bobby West believed he understood *la lucha*. The Cuban exiles, now fifty-six percent of the population of Miami and nearly all with a burning hatred of Fidel Castro. They came to America in waves following Batista's overthrow. They viewed Batista as America's stooge—which he was—and felt ignored by the CIA post-Bay of Pigs—which they were. It was America's responsibility to free Cuba, and America had let them down. What began as a temporary exile had lasted a generation now, long enough for them to rear children and regain their lost wealth and grow exceedingly nostalgic about life in their homeland. Such is human nature, always pining for the good old days, what used to be, which saved us from the terror of the present. The exiles were revolutionaries, or counter-revolutionaries, who knows what, but they wanted action and they'd wanted it now for nearly three decades. Through the Artium Group and his dealings with Mr. French, West had seized the opportunity to enact real change despite the CIA's bureaucratic best efforts.

But right now he needed money.

It was clear Holly was gone with the money—$3 million lifted from the safe in his house without a thought—so West had arranged for a meeting with the deputy director of operations, Tiny Mark Brown, whose office was in a nondescript building on F Street, a few blocks north of Pennsylvania Avenue, a base of operations outside of Langley. He and Felix, posing as a Cuban national, flew to

Northern Virginia, over the southern Piedmont, the tobacco fields, the factories along the I-95 corridor, and landed in a hot mess of manicured infrastructure. Green grass, clean cement, dark windows, smooth pavement: forget Wall Street and fuck Hollywood. Washington was where the money was in this country. Somebody spent some money to make America's capital look modern and clean-cut, but driving into the city from NoVa, you just felt like there were spies all around you.

A helicopter screamed across the sky. Wheels hummed on the asphalt. Buildings reflected the blue skies and the green grass like a small-town, swinging-dick sheriff's sunglasses. Who knew what eyes were upon you?

In the city a blinding sunlight reflected from the concrete. West and Felix dodged tourists and schoolchildren and walked into what could be the lobby for a car rental or travel agent. A well-dressed administrator stood from her desk, offered them coffee and pastries while she rang for Tiny Mark.

"Mr. Brown will see you now," she said a few minutes later. She pushed a button and the wall beside them came unhinged to reveal an empty corridor leading to a freight elevator.

As they walked away from the lobby, West said, "This was our original headquarters, back before we were even OSS. FDR wanted a foreign intelligence service to monitor global finances during the Depression. He hired a bunch of out-of-work bankers and newspapermen. The spy games didn't start until Germany invaded Poland."

The freight elevator clanged to a stop on the eighth floor. The doors opened across from a halogen-lit conference room where Tiny Mark greeted them without formal introductions.

"Bobby, good to see you. Take a seat."

Neither mentioned Felix, who followed them in and sat next to West.

Extremely tall and almost emaciated, Tiny Mark looked like a lamppost, dim-lit and dim-witted. He was a mover and shaker in bureau politics, knew everyone from General Westmoreland to George Bush, and he would likely one day be a candidate for the directorship. He wore amazing bifocals and had this phlegmatic voice that should have made him a bit player in life, but somehow, without any military or field operative experience, he'd crawled his way from a Rust Belt sewer to the highest echelons of operative service. CIA operations conjured up images of paratroopers in Southeast Asia, underground men in East Germany, binocular vision in Latin America, yet this man, who couldn't strategize his way out of a paper bag and would never survive a week in the jungle, nearly outranked the president in the D.C. cocktail class.

Tiny Mark opened a folder in front of him, studied the file a few moments.

West was impatient. He'd called this meeting and had a five-minute agenda, yet for the sake of politics, he let the deputy director believe himself in control. Finally, Tiny Mark said, "So you're in charge of Cuba."

"I suppose I am."

"I read your white paper on last year's hijacking. A compelling read."

"I'm working on another about our strategy in South Florida."

"Six rogue Cubans wanted to go home, and thought they'd do it in style." Tiny Mark flipped a page in the folder, which was not West's white paper. If history was any guide, that report was gathering dust on a shelf, would be de-classified and released to an indifferent media in thirty years. "Thought they could make a statement—part homecoming, part theater. And now that we've opened flights back up, I would think we're in a good place. No more cause for hijacking, correct?"

"Maybe. The exiles seem glad to have a way of going home, but that doesn't solve our long-term problem. These people have never assimilated, and they're growing agitated with our inaction."

"I read your conclusion." Tiny Mark flipped another page, read: "*It seems inevitable that another act of political theater will occur, perhaps on American soil.* Domestic terrorism, you mean, which is a matter for the FBI. I know it's all connected—just because things don't function in Washington doesn't mean we're all obtuse—but we've got our mandate from the president, so right now that means keeping a lid on Cuba."

Batista, Castro, the CIA, Communism: all players in the decades-long struggle to rid Cuba of the Communist dictator, to open up the nation so the exiles could return home to democracy. Because West had been with the CIA since Johnson's administration, he understood politics. He'd watched director after director step down, he'd seen brilliant ideas shelved, he'd dealt with agents on the lam, and he'd watched Cuba fade on the CIA radar. Well, now it was his turn in the wringer, and he was about to make something happen. He said, "I believe we can keep South Florida quiet for now, but the exiles aren't going away. We need a long-term plan."

Tiny Mark narrowed his eyes. "We're all under a lot of heat here. Miami's a thousand miles away, and right now the perception is that the exiles are assimilating. There are bigger problems in the world. Our eyes are focused on the Middle East."

"With all due respect, sir, you're underestimating Fidel, and the exiles."

"And who are the exiles?" Tiny Mark asked. "Are they organized? One homogeneous group? No. They're all freewheeling would-be revolutionaries, and we're not here to corral them. That's where Kennedy went wrong. He thought the world was a logical, organized place."

West said, "Organized or not, you can't ignore them. We don't give them something to focus on, they're bound to get restless, start acting irrationally. Fidel's the target, the bull's eye."

"He's a rat, and all he needs is just a little hole to slide through. So from my point of view, what I need from you is to keep a tight ship. No holes for Fidel."

"You're right," West agreed, "he is a rat, and still very much a problem. But so are the exiles. The newspapers don't cover them, but they outnumber the Anglos in Miami right now. They're angry. They think we've abandoned them. They think we're in cahoots with Fidel."

"Preposterous."

"Maybe, but we've got intelligence coming out of Miami that the prevailing attitude among the exiles is that we're content to do nothing."

Tiny Mark turned to Felix. "What do you think?"

"I think he speaks the truth," Felix said.

"Hey, no one is happy with the situation."

"I appreciate your position," Felix continued. "Not all of my friends in Miami do, but I know you've got a whole world to deal with."

"You both follow the news, don't you?" Tiny Mark's voice rose.

Felix droned on, "Cuba is just an island. It's contained."

"Iran is biting our asses right now."

"No more nuclear weapons down there."

"And no one's playing a gentleman's game."

"Just farmers and socialists," Felix said.

"You want courtly manners, go back to the nineteenth century."

"A bunch of angry peasants."

"This is bloody, bare-knuckle boxing in this town."

"But when the next revolution happens—"

That caught Tiny Mark's attention. "Say that again. What revolution?" He turned to West and said, "What is this guy talking about?"

West grinned and shook his head.

"I'm telling you Miami is not stable," Felix said. "I appreciate your position, but I'm not sure you appreciate the mood among the exiles. With all due respect, we're more organized than you believe, so it's only a matter of time before, well."

"And what exactly do you recommend I do here?"

"Ideally? Take a group of commandos in and get Castro out of power. Make it a black op if you need to, but let the exiles go home."

West was still grinning like a hayseed, but he wanted to step in before Felix said something to really piss off Tiny Mark. The man put up with agents, whatever their politics, because he knew information meant more than ideology. West gave him that. But, still, dude had as much testosterone as any other man. He said, "Since that's not an option right now, we've got a few alternatives."

Tiny Mark sat back, Felix already forgotten. "Such as?"

"First, as a stop-gap, I've had an opportunity to funnel money into Felix's organization."

"Not from us?"

"No, from a business deal with the Artium Group. Totally legit."

"That's what I want to hear," Tiny Mark said.

"You might not like the rest."

The deputy quit smiling.

"Despite the DEA's best efforts," West continued, "drugs are still pouring into Miami, and there's a real war between the Colombians and the Cubans. In exchange for aid and information, some of the exiles have agreed to do business with us. We'll help keep the Colombians at bay, invest in a fund so there's a paper trail, and there's plenty left to launder for whatever we want."

"What's in it for them?"

"Our implicit support of their political organization."

"Can't do it," Tiny Mark said quickly.

Felix cut in, "We're not asking you to take out Castro."

West waved his hand. "Felix and his colleagues just want to be reassured that we want him out of power, and that if they can start an uprising, they want to know we'll support them."

"Can you step into the hall for a minute?" Tiny Mark asked Felix. When the Cuban was gone, he said, "I'm all for the money, anywhere we can get it, but you're asking for me to approve a partnership with drug runners. Hell, you brought a dealer right into my office—what's wrong with you?"

"Felix isn't a dealer."

"But his friends are, he might as well be. What is he then? Where did you find him?"

"Does it matter?"

"Bobby, Reagan is more committed than ever to this war on drugs. He *believes* we can win it, that we can totally eradicate everything down to the thinnest ounce of marijuana from this country, and that means as a United States agency, we support our leadership."

"You know as well as I do that politicians come and go."

"The winds change, but right now we've got a prevailing wind blowing hard in one clear direction. If we went for what you're proposing, the president is not going to know about it. We can't have a line of U.S. currency going from drug runners to Cuban revolutionaries. We'll all be sentenced to treason for that kind of thing."

There it was. Everyone in Washington had careers to manage. It wasn't about serving the country up there, it was about serving yourself. The fact that drug shipments from Colombia had been funneling money into Miami for more than a decade concerned no one, nor would it concern them to learn the CIA was secretly profiting from drugs coming in from central Asia. But the knowledge that Bobby West was redirecting this money to exiles plotting to overthrow Fidel Castro might turn a few heads.

"Don't worry about a paper trail," West said. "I've already got us a system to keep it off our books."

"The guy in the hall."

"He knows the people and the language, and he's ready to help."

"How much does he know?"

"He thinks containment is a bluff, and that as soon as the exiles begin a coup, Washington will intervene."

"And when the revolution doesn't materialize?"

"He'll leak information to the exiles, which will at least keep them stable for the time being."

"And then?"

"My second recommendation for you," West said. "Felix is right, Miami isn't stable. If, God forbid, violence picks up and moves domestic, I recommend you put something on record, in our budget, so we can respond swiftly."

Tiny Mark leaned back, and the glare of light on his bifocals hid his eyes. This was the moment West had come for. All the rest, the bluster about revolution and finances and drugs—all a front to get Tiny Mark to commit to more financing, the idea being that if there was a fall—and a fall was already in place—West would have the resources to keep his world contained. He was betting Tiny Mark would bite. You could never go wrong by positioning your request as an insurance policy. As much as leadership hated to make bold decisions, they feared being the last man standing when the music quit. The way it worked in the CIA, operatives around the world could do anything they wanted. You could be gathering information or fucking prostitutes, as long as your corner of the world stayed silent. Everyone liked quiet. West made it seem he was here to protect Tiny Mark, so the man could rest easy in the knowledge that he would make it to retirement without some scandal wrecking his career. West needed to stand firm here. In order for Tiny Mark's dream of a peaceful retirement to remain intact, he needed the right winds to blow his way from Washington, which could only come through a $3 million investment in Cuba Omega. Fake training for a revolution. Arm the exiles for a guerrilla war that would never happen. Hang them out to dry if they tried to invade Cuba. Containment. Plausible deniability. Expense reports. All part of the centerless system of American government.

The deputy said, "All I can do is put something on file, a recommendation from a leading field operative. Specific appropriations won't come until July or August, so all I can do is put it in as a line-item and hope it doesn't get vetoed."

"That's all I ask."

"That's all you ask." Tiny Mark shook his head and licked his lips, like a reptile sensing the world around it. "Anything else?"

"No, sir." West rose to go, extended his hand.

Tiny Mark said, "You know, people don't seem to respect a handshake agreement anymore."

"Still all-American, in my book."

"Stay out of D.C. this summer."

16

They somehow made it to Savannah, Holly and Keith, arrived at his dusty apartment mid-morning, exhausted, and slept in his unwashed sheets until dusk. He woke to find her reading a John D. MacDonald paperback in the living room. Not much else passed for entertainment here. He'd made decent money in convenience store sales—not get-rich money, but enough to buy a color TV and keep his fridge stocked with beer and popsicles. Still, the apartment was a one-bedroom on the ground floor outside the city, the cable was out, and there was nothing but a baseball field in walking distance.

"Why do you have this apartment?"

"I never gave it up when I left for Florida."

"What about all your stuff?" she asked. "You just left it?"

He shrugged as he put on a pot of coffee. "Didn't really think about it," he said.

Such was the nature of his existence. He came from quiet, pragmatic parents who ushered him through the tasks of living from feeding himself as a toddler to making it through high school. The closest anyone in his home town came to self-analysis was on Sunday morning when the preacher said they were all sinners and needed to look into their hearts to find Jesus. A true southern Baptist, Keith found Jesus in the sixth grade but had lost Him by the time he got out of high school. In the Lord's place was an empty chamber in Keith's soul, a place he tried to fill with chicken fingers, bad TV, and now this makeshift existence with a girl far out of his league. They ordered take-out and slept some more, Holly leached of energy and Keith coming off a two-week high in Florida, more adventure than he'd ever had in his short life.

The next evening they ended up at J.E.B. Stuart's on River Street, where he knew he'd find the old crowd and could at least show off the girl to save face for lasting all of two weeks in South Florida.

"So this is your idea of a big time," Holly said but she sounded more amused than unkind. Where he saw a homey bar that served cheap beer and always had a lively conversation, she saw a crowd of roughnecks with untamed beards and missing teeth, a far cry from the house music and syrupy drinks she was used to in Miami. What had she expected, coming up into the heart of America? She wanted adventure, and this was adventure, or what would pass for adventure until she could find her way along to some other, more cosmopolitan setting. She knocked back three or four shots in a row while Keith's crowd cheered and banged the table and generally dragged their knuckles around the barroom, and after the liquor hit her blood she no longer minded the ugly and sad. She climbed onto a chair, brushed her skirt down her legs in a false show of modesty and said, "You boys are about the most fun I've ever had in a bar."

They hollered in reply. "How many bars you been to, girlie?" one man asked.

"Enough to know proper etiquette is for a gentleman to buy a lady a drink."

The man grinned and turned his ball cap around backward and raised a hand toward the waitress. "Damn, Keith," he said, "I believe I might have to go with you next time you take off for Florida. You staying here or heading back?"

Keith took a swig. "Maybe a little early to tell."

"You not have any luck finding work?"

"Oh, I found work all right."

"You caught up with Felix?" B.D. asked from behind them, laying a hand on Keith's shoulder.

"Yeah, I did," Keith said, and took another swig. "He hooked me up with some kind of tycoon."

"Mr. French! You meet him?"

"Just the once," Keith said. He wondered how much B.D. knew about his girlfriend's cousin's operation, if he'd ever met Felix Machado or been dragged into the basement. Something told Keith that B.D. knew what was what, and had wisely opted to stay out of that game.

"I never met him myself." B.D. took a seat on the other side of Keith, pulled him into a sidebar. "Job work out for you?"

"It's more of a contact position. He gave me the first assignment, but I don't think it's for me."

"Ain't easy getting rich in this life. Who's the girl?"

"Some stray I picked up."

"She's pretty. You sleep with her yet?"

Keith swirled beer around in his mouth.

"My man. I'm going to get a drink. You need something other than a Budweiser."

When B.D. was gone, Holly availed herself of the others and sidled next to Keith. "You're going to have to drive me home." Her eyes bobbed in their sockets like the bead in a level jostled out of plumb. She laid her head on Keith's shoulder and said, "I like this place."

"I wasn't sure it was your speed."

She giggled. "I've got all kind of speeds."

The waitress set a bourbon over ice in front of Keith, nodded toward the back wall. Keith looked over, and B.D. waved at him from the back hall where the restrooms were.

What did Keith know about B.D.? Ole Big Duck. He was the closest thing Keith'd had to a friend on the sales circuit. They partnered up regularly, spent long hours traversing North Georgia back roads and the South Carolina low-country, talked about music and cars and girls and movies. He was the kind of guy you'd trust to drive you home at the end of a long bender, but not enough to invite him to crash on your couch for more than one night. Something about B.D.'s wild hair and shifty eyes, his giraffe-like frame, gave you the impression he could corner you in an alley, turn you upside down and shake out all the loose change and secrets you kept in your pockets.

The alcohol was hitting Keith too, and he grew quiet like he always did. With Holly nearly passed out leaning against his shoulder, he watched the boys he used to sell with, some in jeans and cowboy boots and others in slacks and loosened necktie knots, they all drank merrily and pushed each other around, and then when "Piano Man" came on the radio they all leaned their heads toward the ceiling and grew weepy around each other. He'd worked with them for three years but hardly knew any of them, except when and where they graduated from high school and how many women they said they'd slept with. All lies no doubt, but young manhood was a murky enough state that you couldn't trust anyone with anything. Any semblance of order was a mirage. What Keith was unable to articulate, watching his former colleagues enjoy themselves, the girl beside him giving off a musky smell of sweat like cooked pasta, was precisely the sense that life was all empty chaos, and that the *this-ness* of things, existence itself, was nothing but one moment stacked in front of another. It terrified him.

He drained the bourbon and looked around for B.D., or anyone who could talk to him and help him forget the weight of his life right now: the runaway girl, the $10,000 she'd swiped from her father, the stolen car, the South Florida businessman who might bury Keith were he to return to Miami.

B.D. was on the payphone in the back corridor. He glanced up and saw Keith staring at him, and waved. When he returned to the bar, Keith had another beer in front of him. Holly had gone off to put change in the jukebox, sobered already like only young drinkers could do.

"I ever tell you about my old man?" B.D. asked. "Mean as a hornet when I was growing up, over in Aiken. He never beat me or my brothers, but he could play some Jedi mind games with you to send you cowering beneath your blanket. I used to think it was something personal, like we never measured up as kids."

"Sounds familiar," Keith said.

"Then when I got into high school, I decided my old man was just an asshole."

"That sounds familiar too."

B.D. smacked a pack of cigarettes against the bar and went on like Keith wasn't even there. "I had the whole thing figured out. I had him psychoanalyzed, how he couldn't help being an asshole because of the way he was raised. My granddad was an asshole too, and he put up with him same as my mother put up with my father. He was in the masons. Your old man up with them?"

"Nah, but my grandfather was."

"They put on a show at the lodge. Ku Klux Klan kind of stuff, dress up in garbs and all kinds of secret ceremonies. I had that figured into the equation with my father as well, what all you give up when you marry yourself to an organization like that. That's why they wear those rings, they're married to the masons. Anyway, I had this whole social-familial explanation for my father and why he was such a tyrant, and I couldn't wait to get out. You know what I did? I left home and never went back. Six years, I haven't set foot in my hometown nor said word one to my parents."

"Long time," Keith said, unsure of where B.D. was going with all this.

"Fucking A, it is. Oh, I've kept up with my brothers and a few friends. And some of them have passed word from my momma to me, but I just didn't have a thing to say to her, nor him either."

B.D. finally lit his cigarette and took a long drag. He watched Holly over by the jukebox do a little shimmy to Marvin Gaye.

"That's a hell of a song to be playing in a bar called J.E.B. Stuart's," B.D. said.

"She's from Miami. She doesn't know what it's like in the real South."

"That's what I'm talking about. Baggage. We're all assholes here. It's not my father, or my grandfather. It's all of us, and at the end of the day, he just was a lousy father. Nothing to do with me or my mother or the freemasons. We've all got talents and weaknesses, and my father's big weakness is fatherhood."

"Sucks for you."

"Ha!" B.D. slapped him on the shoulder. "Yes indeed. Anyway, I just called him to tell him that. First time in six years, I called my father and told him I forgave him for being an asshole, and that I understood I was an asshole too. I don't know. Something about seeing you and that girl and things not working out in Florida, made me want to call him up. Just felt the need to make peace with the man. You at peace with your parents?"

"More or less."

"You ought to follow suit. Give them a call, tell them you love them, make your peace with them."

B.D. gave him a strange look then, but Keith only had eyes for Holly and her little shimmy.

17

Chekhov knew Bobby West was in D.C. for the night, had heard from Alexander French in the afternoon. "He's trying to pull the wool over the eyes of his superiors," Mr. French had said on the phone. "Went up there to try to land CIA funding for our operation."

"That's good, if he succeeds."

"He won't succeed. I just heard from his boss, an operations deputy, who's planning to throw West to the wolves."

"So we carry on as planned."

"He'll be back in the morning," Mr. French said before he hung up.

She'd waited for dusk and now parked up the street from his home near Sunset in Coral Gables. West lived in a two-story white stucco bungalow with a thick palmetto in the front yard and a waist-high chain-link fence. She watched the house for a few minutes, took note of a beat-up old sedan, which idled at a four-way and then rolled left. Not a car you would expect to find here. West's temporary lodging wasn't as upscale as his familial hearth in Coconut Grove, where his wife and daughter—still missing—lived, but the temporary neighborhood nevertheless had its share of Buicks, Oldsmobiles, and a smattering of foreign imports, cars tucked in narrow drives like the jars and boxes no doubt organized neatly in upgraded kitchen cabinets. This was a neighborhood of housewives and appearances, and Chekhov saw nothing further of interest beyond the errant sedan.

She walked up to West's house, closed the gate behind her, and quickly jimmied the lock on the front door. Inside, she shined a flashlight around the foyer until she found the switch and flooded the downstairs with light. A few moving boxes were stacked in a corner, emptied. The dining room (16 x 10) and kitchen (with sink island and solid surface countertops with a backsplash) were off to the left, a few bowls stacked in the sink, boxes of cereal in a row over the fridge, unopened mail and a cup of pencils and pens and a chicken-scratched notepad on the counter. Through a double door-way (louvered door, tucked into the wall), she turned on a lamp in the den. Again, nothing of note: one couch, one coffee table (copy of *Seventeen* magazine at an angle), a TV and cable box on the only nice piece of furniture, a heavy dark-wood media stand with chips in the stain. Along the back wall, a half-filled bookcase with an encyclopedia set, a few reference books, a history of western civilization, a stack of paperbacks: Louis L'Amour, Nelson DeMille, Ken Follett. On the top shelf were a few framed photos of West and his daughter, his daughter's school portraits, and an elderly couple. No sign of West's ex-wife, nor the mistress that wrecked his marriage.

(Chekhov did not actually know whether a mistress wrecked the marriage, but she knew that whether there was another woman, something wedged itself between West and his wife. People make choices. Actions lead to reactions. Chekhov was not here to judge, only to record.)

Off the den was the room she had come for, West's office, a messy cluster of papers and filing cabinets. A desk was on the rug in the center of the room, and beneath the front of the rug a safe. She didn't know the combination and wasn't here for the safe any-way, but she was conscious of it as she pulled the rotary phone off the hook, unscrewed the voice cap, and implanted a bug. Then she flipped through several of the papers, mostly balance sheets and financial audit reports, executive summaries and memos. She already knew what a disaster the Artium Group's balance sheet was, and she understood the entirety of West's financial situation, his limited savings, his alimony payments, his over-extension with his ex-wife's house in Coconut Grove. He had a good interest rate through a special program for select government employees, which seemed to have given him the sense that he could take on more and more. In that respect, he was the ideal American baby boomer, a producer and a consumer, his world bounded by secure transactions within the letter of the law. And he was an idiot.

Although Chekhov was several years younger than West, she understood the limits of what she knew—what anyone knew—and operated comfortably in the space of not-knowing. A man like West operated by spreadsheets, risk analyses, his decision theory grounded in the belief that people behaved rationally and acted according to fixed principles. From his files, he appeared not to be a religious man—church on Sundays when he was married but nothing on his own—yet his view of the world was fundamentally American, which was philosophically religious in nature. No one said this about the American mind, but those Protestant consumerists were grounded in a centuries-old faith in education, hard work, doing right by the Lord, and reaping the benefits of salvation in this world and the next. Lunatics may take to the streets with signs of Jesus and the Second Coming, and politicians may rattle sabers about abortion and natural laws, but even secular Americans were hoodwinked by a story of redemption, the fall and eventual rise of the stock market, the annual raise, retirement savings, the good life always just around the corner. What men like Bobby West could not abide was the thought that their entire premise had been wrong, that people were not rational, but were merely animals with ancient instincts and mutated genes. Family members betrayed one other, the body betrayed the mind, and the world would betray America, just as America betrayed the world.

In the end, there was no god, no angels, no salvation, nothing but neurochemistry and physical forces and ciphers like Adriana Chekhov to correct your worldview when you teetered a little too close to the edge.

She made a pass through the upstairs to glance at the bedrooms. Not that she expected to find anything, but she wanted to make sure she understood the layout and commit to memory an image of Bobby West's home life. The daughter's bedroom was the saddest room in the house, a twin bed with a desk and a few posters on the gabled ceiling (Madonna, U2). The room lacked the knickknacks and private journals and cosmetic accoutrements to signify a teenage girl spent much time here. Without the posters, the space would resemble a convent, which Bobby West surely took to mean his daughter was wholesome and happy. Not much surprised Chekhov any more, but she did smirk in bemusement to think how ready American men were to misjudge their daughters, and to misjudge their relationships. Daughters tended to become stand-ins for the aging wives (beautiful, flirtatious, innocent, and completely open with their fathers) or they grew secretive and hid their inner lives behind a mask of complacency. Holly Hernandez had clearly been the latter, which meant there would be few clues to her whereabouts in this house.

Chekhov glanced through West's bedroom and the upstairs bathroom and, finding nothing, turned off the lights and headed back downstairs. When she reached the bottom of the stairway, the front door opened unexpectedly.

A blonde woman came through the door and said, "Hello?"

The woman paused when she saw Chekhov, and her expression shifted from expectant to skeptical.

"Um, hi," Chekhov said in her most unassuming American accent. Her hand went to brush the side of her hair, which she had pinned up in a bun. She cleared her throat and took the last step, angled away from the door so the woman could enter.

The woman remained in the doorway, blocked Chekhov's exit. She said, "Who are you?"

"I'm Adriana."

"Is Bobby here?"

Chekhov affected a blush, and brushed her hair again. "No, he isn't. He had a crisis at work and had to leave. Can I help you?"

"I'm sorry," the woman said. "Who are you again?"

"Adriana." Chekhov extended her hand. "I work with Bobby." The woman ignored her hand.

"Would you like to come in? I was just about to leave but could fix you a drink?"

"What are you doing here?"

"Well, I was just straightening a few things up," Chekhov said. "Are you the cleaning woman? Because we're having a few issues with the scum in the upstairs bathroom, in the shower."

The woman held up her hands and shut her eyes. She had a twitch, where her eyes rolled up and her lids closed as she composed her thoughts.

Chekhov waited. If the woman was West's lover, that would make her Diana Burns. French had faxed materials to Istanbul, and a page covered West's associates. This woman could do better. While Chekhov sympathized with her—it wasn't every day you found you didn't actually know someone you were close to—she also had to get down to business. Women were stronger than men. While Diana would weep for her lost love, if it was love, she would show only anger here. Chekhov wanted to be far away from that anger, the defensive anger of a cornered animal. You couldn't do anything to halt our most primal instincts.

"You're not the cleaning woman," Chekhov said.

"No, no I'm not."

"Sounds like we both have things to discuss with Bobby then."

"Do we?"

"I do, at least," Chekhov said. "It appears I've stepped into a situation I'm not exactly welcome in."

"Where are you from?" the woman asked.

"I can be on my way."

"Your accent, it's not local, or Latino. Eastern Europe?"

Chekhov smiled. "Next time you see Bobby, tell him Adriana wished him well."

She shoveled her way past the woman and opened the front door. The woman said, "Wait—" but Chekhov pulled the door shut behind her and took a breath on the porch.

No matter how many times she had been in such a situation, it never grew any easier. She'd learned to control her pulse and her breathing and to put on a stoic veneer, but inside she was all nerve. Electrical signals pulsed, kept her eyes focused, her mind sharp.

The evening had clouded over, and the breeze blew ragged through the palms. She skipped down the walk and back toward her car. As she rounded into the corner, she saw the beat-up sedan—a nut-brown Plymouth with an older, heavyset man beside the open passenger door—slotted in the street. She took note of the license plate's first three letters, BBC, and kept walking.

18

From his car, Falcon had watched the redheaded woman enter West's house. She walked with purpose, like maybe she was his mistress, but then she jimmied the lock. He'd known many skilled burglars in his days as a cop—and were he still a cop, he'd be forced to arrest her now for breaking and entering—but this woman was a true pro. She glided in like a housecat and immediately began to turn on the lights. No doubt she had a cover story if anyone confronted her.

Night had settled in over the city, the sky still aglow from light pollution. Bats flittered overhead, while at street level palmettos and mangroves took on a life of their own as shadows flickered against the backdrop of sodium street lamps. Falcon shifted and stretched his neck and back, and squinted at West's house. The man lived in a fine two-story bungalow, stucco and terracotta staples of Miami homesteads, yet the chain-link fence and overgrown grass suggested a fall. Here was a man carrying two mortgages, saddled with alimony and child support, leveraged to the hilt and unable to afford private lawn care. Some folks did fine taking care of their own yards—Falcon had never paid someone to mow his grass—but this was a city of excess. Whether you splurged for lawn care said something about your character. You are who you hire. All the lawns on this strip were on the verge of unkempt, the houses settled like a man in middle age grown soft around the middle. South Florida would do that to a piece of property.

He got out with his camera in tow and crept up to one of the downstairs windows. Over sixty, he was too old to be clambering around in the bushes, but he caught a break when she came into the living room and turned on the light. He held his camera up and snapped a few photos while she walked across the room. When she got closer, he ducked down beneath the windowsill and held his breath. Although it was dark out here, there was no guarantee she hadn't spotted him, somehow, or heard the shutter and the winding film. Falcon eased away from the window, startled to see her figure so close but with her back turned.

He scampered out of the shrubbery and limped back to his car. Whatever photo he took would have to do. He wasn't yet ready to break cover, not until he figured out who all the players were in Bobby West's life. The CIA, the Artium Group associates, his family. If Juan Delgado was right, the company was into something untoward, which could simply be hidden investments, repurchased loans to hide financial activity, cooked books with Wall Street, lobbyist support.

Or it could be the CIA was into something with the Cubans. Another Bay of Pigs? Surely this administration would never go for that, even with the bluster and proxy wars with the Evil Empire, which meant there was more on heaven and earth—or at least the U.S. government—than Falcon knew. That, or Bobby West had gone rogue. Stranger things had happened, but if that were the case, it didn't bode well for finding his daughter. She could be held for ransom, smuggled into an East European gulag, chained in some nefarious reptile's basement. The most likely answer was she'd simply run off, grown fed up with her bickering parents and lit out for the territories.

Falcon never got to tease out the rest of that thread in his thinking, because someone else had pulled into Bobby West's driveway. Another woman: blonde, professional, upscale. She gathered her hair and straightened her skirt before floating up to West's front door and pulled out a key.

The lights upstairs clicked off, and a moment later a funnel of light spilled out of the house as the front door folded away.

Falcon cursed to himself. He may no longer have a duty to stop a break-in, but he sensed the redhead meant business as she let the blonde in. Whoever the blonde was, Falcon wanted her to leave the house alive.

At his car, he swapped his camera for the revolver he kept in the glove box, checked the rounds. He hadn't fired his gun off the range since he couldn't remember when, had only drawn it a few times in his career. Back then, in his prime, the point of having a gun was knowing you wouldn't need to fire it. Knowing you had it, but leaving it in the holster.

Before he could get himself together to intervene, the redhead jettisoned out of the house. The blonde was behind her, shaken but uninjured. His plan was to let the redhead go and check on the blonde, but as she rounded out of the driveway, the redhead snuck a glance his way and quickened her pace.

Seeing as the blonde appeared to be fine and the redhead certainly wouldn't be returning—she knew she'd been marked, and anyway likely had whatever she came for—he made a snap decision to follow her rather than staying with the blonde.

The redhead got into a Chevy coupe, nothing to write home about, which Falcon knew was how she wanted it. He followed her off Sunset and onto the Dixie Highway, where he hoped traffic would mask him. The evening rush hour was long over, but there were still a few commuters and taxis hissing up the highway.

He left a good fifty yards between him and the coupe, tailed her past pawnshops and check cashing offices, fast food joints and gas stations. A carnival of bare necessities for the down and out. You didn't have to go too far off the main highway to lose the paycheck-to-paycheck crowd and enter the world of million-dollar homes. How oil and water co-existed in this city would remain a mystery.

A few miles south of Miami University, the woman pulled into a motel, the Motor Inn, which may as well have renamed itself Bates Motel.

Falcon cruised past and made a u-turn at the next light, aiming to get a spot on the opposite side of the highway to see which room was hers. License plate, room number, maybe a photo, and he'd be on his way to the suburbs.

Instead, she'd pulled her own u-turn and bumped her way over the curb and back onto the highway in the opposite direction. She jogged east at the next intersection, and Falcon hit the steering wheel. He hung a left and rode parallel to her a few streets down. He wended his way through a series of four-ways and up a pair of alleys, but by the time he'd edged closer to her street, she was long gone.

Ahead, he pulled into a shopping mall entrance. This was the site of the shooting a few years back, the first volley in the South Florida drug wars. Tonight the mall had returned to its place as an outpost for leafy suburbia. Its windows glowed as a beacon for hungry consumers. Falcon circled the lot twice and, seeing neither brake lights nor a Chevy coupe, he gave up and headed back to West's house. The blonde was gone, and she'd apparently taken the trouble to shut off the lights and lock up. You would never know anyone had been here, as though the owners had fled north for the summer.

Mary Catherine was still awake and on the couch when he got home, which surprised him. "You're home late," she said.

"I'm working a new case."

"The missing girl?"

"That's right." He wasn't sure she'd been paying attention when he told her about Holly Hernandez over breakfast. Her attention slid from point to point like a moth flitting at a window at night, never able to reach the signal it so longed for. It pained him to see her weaken, especially given they'd not reached old age, or what he considered old age (at least ten years beyond their current age).

"Have you eaten?" Her voice had the squeaky catch it got when she was near sleep. Never a night owl, Mary Catherine.

"I had a sandwich on stakeout."

"Not good for your blood pressure," she said. "You can't keep doing that."

"You're right. I'm getting too old for it."

"Honey, you were too old for it twenty years ago."

He kissed the top of her head from behind the couch. "You reading?"

"Trying to." She pointed with her foot at a thrift edition of Jane Austen, her favorite for the forty years he'd known her.

"Why don't you come on up to bed?" he asked her. He guided her upstairs and helped her get into bed. After tucking her under the covers he turned off the light and said, "I'm going to go have a beer. I'll be back."

She was already asleep.

A few minutes later he settled on the back patio with a beer and a pack of Pall Malls.

Their house backed up to a fence with a couple of old-growth live oaks between him and the neighbors, so he could almost imagine himself back in the rural Tampa outskirts of his childhood. He never regretted coming to Miami—it had been a fine life—but he did rue the way the world had changed around him. As a young man, he'd felt at the center of everything, his life imbued with meaning, every occurrence somehow a reflection of his world. He'd arrived on this rock and by God enjoyed his time in the limelight. More and more these days, he felt himself at odds with the world. The newscasters, the younger police officers, even his clients all seemed to march to a different tune, out of step with his old ways. He liked a pen and paper, and one-on-one human inquiry when the world had gone word processor and global supply chain. He thought about his rural upbringing: the darkness of night, the quiet country, the lazy days in the woods. He'd lived most of his life in the city now, and knew he could never go back, not just because the country wouldn't be there (though he knew Tampa to have sprawled into his old stomping grounds) but rather he wouldn't enjoy it. True quiet would drive him nuts. Mary Catherine would be the first to tell him that, and would laugh if tonight she saw him with a clear head.

Of the two, she'd always been the practical one. She'd served in the Marine Corps Women's Reserve and operated the telegraph out of Camp Lejeune. Eighteen years old and seeing the world for the first time, she found she rather liked it and was less inclined to put up with any man who merely wanted dinner on the table at six o'clock. Fine by Ernie Falcon. He'd fallen in love with her firecracker wit and her self-confident approach to the world on its own terms. Oh, they'd laughed their way through the late forties and finally settled into their suburban home thanks to the G.I. Bill. They'd raised two children who seemed to have inherited the most extreme aspects of their personalities—Mary Catherine's surety and Falcon's lackadaisical nature—which later translated into their children abandoning the parents for the West Coast. The boy was all right, an executive now for a health care system, but the girl had gotten swept up in whatever happened in the late sixties. In college she'd spoken of the patriarchy and accused Falcon of misogyny, which he found laughable, and told her so, to which she thanked him for proving her point.

Mary Catherine had talked to the girl, had tried to reason with her, but, according to his wife's report, the girl had suggested his wife file for divorce. Ever since Mary Catherine's diagnosis, the girl had refused even to speak with him, still infected with the virus she'd caught in college. Not that Falcon had been too deeply troubled. The boy was doing all right, and Falcon and Mary Catherine had a fine life, and he figured the girl would come around eventually, or she wouldn't, and he would die, and that would be that.

"You don't understand a goddamn thing, do you?" she'd said the last time he'd spoken with her. She'd only called to check in on her mother, she'd said. "Why can't you understand that? I don't care about your life."

"My life is your mother's life, and her life is mine," he'd said.

"You. Just. Don't. Get. It."

"Explain it to me then."

"What's the point? You'll never see yourself as you really are."

There was no arguing with her, but tonight, as he puffed one Pall Mall after another to its stub, he wondered if she'd had a point.

How little we know ourselves when we're young, and how little we know the world as we grow older, wisdom nothing but a cosmic joke whereby you understand only after crossing the Rubicon. He'd always attempted to engage his daughter on his own terms—after all, he was the center of his own world—but now that he was witnessing all these events coursing around him, he understood all his daughter had wanted from him was a little humility, and humility had been the one thing he'd been unable to grant her. He'd thought he was protecting her, when all he'd done was drive her away.

Perhaps the same had occurred with Bobby West and his daughter. Perhaps there was no CIA plot, no Soviet interception. Perhaps the two women were each mistresses unconnected to young Holly. Perhaps Holly had simply seen her father for what he was, an arrogant man, and let out a primal scream on her way out of town. Falcon closed his eyes at that thought, and drifted off to sleep on the uncomfortable chair on his patio, where he spent the rest of the night.

19

Jim Coffey, a.k.a. Big Duck, a.k.a. B.D. got off the phone with Felix and returned to the bar where Keith and Holly were strung out from the road and too much liquor. Should have known the kid wouldn't be able to hack it down in Miami, but there was no way to know he'd fuck up this badly. Who steals $3 million and goes right on home where you came from? And after going through the interview with Mr. French at that. B.D. had never met Mr. French, but he'd heard enough stories to know the man meant business. Anyone who had ever met him and lived to tell the tale had the same response: *I'll go to my grave trying to take care of Mr. French's business, because if I don't, I won't even have a grave.*

After feeding Keith some bullshit about the freemasons and suggesting the kid call his father, he walked them out of the bar, asked if Keith was all right to drive, and sent them on their way. He thought maybe he should take care of it right now, before they left the bar, but where would Keith go? Maybe he was sober enough to get laid one last time. B.D. could give him that, and it would be better to do it in his apartment, away from River Street.

Handle it, and five percent is yours, Felix had told him. *You botch it, we send Chekhov to get your five percent.*

And me? B.D. asked, though he already knew the answer.

You get gone, amigo.

*

The bright orange Econoline van pulled into the Pine Breeze apartment complex around two in the morning. One headlamp was dimmer than the other, and the van squeaked over the speed hump at the front entrance.

Officer Dewey Donaldson's hearing was shot, so he didn't hear the squeak from his parked patrol car, but he took note of the headlamp, and would put that in his report tomorrow morning when the apartment complex was a crime scene. For now he yawned and scratched his chin, took a sip of cold coffee from the Styrofoam cup, looked over at his partner asleep in the passenger seat beside him. The two officers were on their third night of the twelve-to-eight shift, and the third night was always the worst when you were trying to transition from day shift to night shift. Let the man sleep, he thought. Hell, he—Donaldson—was in no mood for police work. They'd been farmed out to crime watch zone, no doubt because some old lady had called about her neighbor's bass beats in the apartment above her or the trash collector leaving a few scraps in the parking lot. It all meant the world was going to hell, and it was up to the police to restore order. The broken window theory, they called it. You let one broken window remain unfixed, it was a sign the whole neighborhood was up for grabs. Soon enough you had drug runners on the corners and shoot-outs in the parking lot. So Officer Donaldson and his partner were slammed into the night (their stats were down on day shift, and the department's way of issuing a reprimand was to give you the shit shift).

When the Econoline parked, two men got out and walked into the outer hall at the end of one complex. A few moments later, a window opened in one of the apartments and a kid hopped out in his boxer shorts and scurried across the grass.

Officer Donaldson took another sip of his coffee.

Maybe there were drugs in the apartment, or maybe the kid was shacked up with the wife of one of the men from the van. Either way, Officer Donaldson wasn't about to chase after some teenager, especially when the kid stopped on the lawn, turned back to the apartment, and then crept back to the window. In his report, the officer would deny hearing a gunshot, and would cite his tour of duty in Vietnam.

The light came on, but Donaldson couldn't see anything. The kid crawled back into the window and shut the blinds. Officer Donaldson's partner coughed a few times, and Donaldson thought about waking him up for what must be a show. When nothing happened for a long time, he started to doze off himself.

The officer was half asleep when the apartment light clicked off at dawn and the kid—Keith Sorrells—and Holly Hernandez got into a beige Impala and fled the apartment complex in a panic, two dead bodies in Keith's old unit, a date with a prison cell the best thing either could hope for.

PART THREE

CENTRAL INTELLIGENCE AGENCY
WASHINGTON, D.C.

OFFICE OF THE DEPUTY DIRECTOR (INTELLIGENCE)

30 April 1984

MEMORANDUM FOR: Mark Brown
                    Special Operations, Latin America
                    Counterterrorism

SUBJECT: Events in Miami, Florida re: Robert West

The following is a transcript of a call placed from Alexander French's office in Miami to a Wall Street investment firm. The investment associate is believed to be Jay Stimson, the son of a college fraternity brother of Robert West. The woman who placed the call is unknown. She identifies herself as a representative from the Securities & Exchange Commission.

WOMAN: What can you tell me about your meeting with Robert West?

STIMSON: I'm sorry?

WOMAN: You had a meeting two hours ago with Robert West, of the Artium Group. He showed up on a flight registry today, and we've checked in with the compliance officers at all the big firms. He met with you, and we'd like to know why.

STIMSON: I'm not sure that's your business.

WOMAN: Actually, it is our business, if he's committing fraud, and it is our business if you are in any way complicit in his misdoings. Hang on, before you say it, I know you are not involved in anything untoward with Mr. West. I know there is no business relationship between the Artium Group and Farrier Securities. Nonetheless, Mr. West was in your office, no doubt requesting some manner of loan, and I need to file a report on his activities. Now. Please fill me in.

[LONG PAUSE]

STIMSON: You really did trace him here quickly.

WOMAN: It's our job.

STIMSON: I didn't even realize my compliance officer was tracking my meetings.

[LONG PAUSE]

STIMSON: What can I tell you? He's a friend of my father's and came asking for a loan.

WOMAN: Personal or business?

STIMSON: You know, I don't really know. He said it was business, but I got the feeling he was having personal financial trouble.

WOMAN: Do you have another appointment with him?

STIMSON: There's nothing I could help him with. I told him that, and he left.

WOMAN: Do you know where he is staying? We'd like to ask him a few follow-up questions.

STIMSON: What did you say your name was again?

[END CALL]

20

Felix Machado was no fan of dawn, preferred instead the quiet of the dark when the rest of his adopted nation slept. For Felix, and the rest of Cuba Omega, and all of *la lucha*, this was not their country, which meant more than a Social Security number and a passport. What the Anglos failed to understand was that *la lucha* was a spiritual cause as much as a political movement. Like the Jews expelled from Jerusalem, the Cuban exiles lived in diaspora while a Caesar occupied their homeland. Fidel Castro: the great Satan. The Anglos all lived in a state of permanent dislocation. This was the definition of America, a tree separated from its roots. The Anglos were homeless but didn't realize they lacked a home, for their home was as abstract as the Garden of Eden. But *la lucha* had a home and craved reunification. Reunification was the mission of Cuba Omega, announced last year after the hijacking of Flight 3232.

During what should have been a routine flight from Key West to Miami, in the brief moment aloft at cruising altitude before the descent, six men—*exilios*, Cubans—rose from their seats and pulled out switchblades somehow undetected by airport security. They announced their intentions: The plane is theirs, the pilot is to redirect. Passengers screamed in mass hysteria, but no one dared to stop the hijackers. They had knives, they had the power. Everything would be all right with cooperation. They redirected the plane to

Havana. Somewhere on the ground, an air traffic controller—eating powdered doughnuts from a bag at his desk, hot coffee sloshing around in his belly—noticed the green blip change course, some strange torsion from the geometric curve charted out for the day. He wiped the sugar from his hands, got on the radio, and said, "Flight 3232, do you read? Come in Flight 3232, is everything all right? Over." One of the Cubans got on the radio and said there had been a change in plans. It all sounded like a B action movie. One could picture Charlton Heston in the back of the plane, his ears perking up. A change in plan, they have the power. But no, they didn't, our hero would growl. This was America, where anyone can grit his teeth and by God get something done.

What could anyone do? Retake the plane? There were six hijackers with knives, and Americans are not the heroes portrayed in the movies. Someone would get stabbed, and for what? Who was in imminent peril here? The hijackers had announced a destination—Cuba was off-limits, beyond the edge, but at least it was nearby. The passengers sat by and waited as the plane charted a new course, which only took thirty minutes. The Cubans spoke to air traffic control in Havana. A landing strip was arranged. The Cubans landed the plane softly—expertly, they must have taken flying lessons—and the passengers breathed a collective sigh of relief. For now, whatever happened, they wouldn't die in a plane crash. Then a strange thing happened. You expect negotiations. What? A bus, maybe, to come out and take the hostages before the terrorists take off again. Or some kind of negotiator at least, a fat man with a white shirt and a sport coat and a badge that hung from a chain around his neck, here to talk trade, this hostage for that reward. What was one human life worth?

Instead the Cubans requested a ladder, and they opened the door and exited the plane. They were home. They had the power, and they used it to be the first ones out, to breathe the Caribbean air on the tarmac. To feel the heat of the sun, their home sun. Men with guns came out and surrounded them, and the terrorists raised their arms and bent down to their knees, clasped their hands to their heads, and the men placed the barrels of their guns to the terrorists' heads, yelled at them, *"Acuestase! Acuestase!"* And the men lay down. They had the power, and what did they want? To come home, even if only to be thrown in jail. They had the power, and they were home now. They knew what they wanted and they took charge.

That was the promise of America, and she lived up to her promise.

The truth, Felix knew, was more complex. The men had come to America in the Mariel boatlift and found no opportunities here as unskilled laborers with limited English. They wanted to go home. They wanted to make a statement. They wanted the end of Castro. They'd accomplished two of the three, and Felix knew the hijackers, his uncle among them, either were in a Havana prison cell or had been decapitated on a dirt road. Felix had been a part of the boatlift, a teenager then, with full faith in a better future that had not emerged. His uncle was gone, and his mother was ill. But his English was good, which may have been how he earned a place in Alexander French's organization, a translator with connections in all pockets of Miami.

He'd met Bobby West late last year when the CIA agent had shown up at a rally for disaffected Cuban exiles to speak their minds.

```
            CUBA LIBRE
   Don't let the Communists win!
       Speak your mind at
     "La Voce por Cuba Libre"
      Tuesday, December 21
```

This sign, hung on telephone poles throughout the Calle Ocho district, attracted more than a dozen locals, mostly the homeless in need of free coffee and shelter for the evening. Felix came and sat in the back while a few angry men launched complaints against Castro, the same tired arguments people had been circulating for nearly thirty years.

Bobby West had stood in the back of the room, a small auditorium in a defunct elementary school now converted to a civic center of sorts, arms crossed, eyes steady. Felix his mark: intelligent eyes, sitting quietly, taking it in, not drawing attention to himself. The kind of man who could absorb information and report on it, who could show up at a gathering of any size and leave un-remembered. After the event, standing on the curb in front of the old school, West invited Felix out for a cup of coffee in a different, discreet part of town.

"So, who are you anyway, man?" Felix affronted, unused to being singled out. He had his own secrets to keep. A player recognizes a player. A hustler, a hustler. A mole, a mole.

"Relax, I want the same thing you do," West said, "and I have a plan to make it happen."

"What makes you think you know what I want?"

"You're here, aren't you?"

"And what does that tell you?"

West stared for a long time, sipped cold coffee from a Styrofoam cup. "Am I wrong?"

Felix was silent.

"Hey, if I'm wrong, I'm wrong." He tossed the cup into the gutter. "You heard about the last hijacking? You know anyone on board?"

Felix narrowed his eyes.

"A little information and we might be able to make both sides happy. Open up flights for your people, ease some of the political strain on my people."

Flights to Cuba had been reopened for *los exilios*, a week here, a week there to see old relatives and smell the Promised Land. Felix had not been back since 1980, and he had no plans to return until Castro was gone. But now here was this hulking, sinewy, American businessman offering him the chance to make history. After agreeing to feed West some information about Cuba Omega, a group of underground rebels quietly organizing, he brought the CIA agent to the attention of Mr. French. Mr. French, of course, saw other opportunities. Felix distrusted both men, distrusted the CIA, distrusted America, but his life was determined by forces put in play long before he was born—by guerrillas in the Cuban jungle, by a bear named Joseph Stalin, by a long history of aristocracy propagated by human nature itself, Eve taking a bite of the apple.

The serpent was in the grass then, and the serpent was in the grass now.

The evening after his return from D.C. with Bobby West, the shadows grew long in Little Havana but the evening remained warm. Men on the sidewalks continued their games of dominoes, puffed cigars. The restaurants on Calle Ocho opened their doors and windows and mambo beats spilled into the streets. You could almost imagine yourself in Havana proper here, in your homeland. The promise of America was that anyone could rise up and make something of themselves. Thus far Felix's life had been one of luck, or lack of luck. He was a cork bobbing in the ocean, but now, it seemed, he'd caught his wave. The question before him was: Now that Bobby West had lost the $3 million, would Mr. French cut ties with him or try to pry something more out of the CIA? Was it possible the CIA might divert money or guns to Cuba Omega?

Where should Felix place his bet, with the government criminals or the organized criminals?

21

An afternoon rain shower filled the gutters and slowed traffic every-where in the city to a crawl. In front of the police station young cops with dark and starched uniforms huddled under the awning and stubbed out one cigarette after another, talking about whatever it was young cops had to discuss—girls, probably, Falcon thought. A puddle had formed by the door from the warped sidewalk, right where you'd want to step as you walked into the building. Falcon did a little sidestep but somehow landed his foot right in the puddle, and after a delay, water seeped warm into his sock. One of the officers tossed away another cigarette and nodded to Falcon.

"Fellas," he said. His wet shoe squeaked with every other step into the building.

He was late for a meeting with Callahan, waylaid by cheap Chinese takeout, fortification for a long afternoon of digging into Bobby West's affairs in the police database. His old pal Callahan had arranged him access to the station library and also said he had news about the woman Falcon photographed a few nights ago. The girl working the desk—Stephanie O'Shea, who had sharp eyes, pouted lips, and the sober reserve of Lauren Bacall at her finest in the forties—let him into a conference room and asked if he needed anything, coffee or such. "Donnie Ray will be in shortly," the girl said in a chipper, innocent voice. She would have made a great small-town cheerleader, and had likely stumbled into the wrong line of work. Give her a few years, Falcon thought, and she'll be as surly as the rest of them.

"I'm all right, honey," he said.

"Well, if you need anything."

He thanked her and when she was gone, thumbed through his folder on West. The latest item a news clipping from this morning's paper. Juan Delgado had finally picked up the story and ran a blurb about it on the front page of the metro section: "Girl, 17, reported missing in Coconut Grove." The paper included scant details, left out the girl's name and the name of her family as she was underage. The report was so vague they may as well have left it out altogether. Falcon thought about calling Delgado to see what the deal was, were they getting pressure to ignore the story or what, but it was Saturday. Only the hungry reporters would be answering the phones this afternoon. Falcon lacked access to the investigating detective's files on Holly Hernandez, but he knew the incident report would be as thin as Delgado's reporting. The girl would be a presumed runaway. Seventeen, divorced parents, rumors she was at a club with a boy the night she went missing, reports she frequented the club in South Beach. Falcon knew the detectives wouldn't write her off, but unless the media made a stir, they had other cases to chase.

Rain thwacked against the windows. The HVAC system hummed. A steady downpour, too long for ordinary, too soon for everyone to clear out of the station and hunker down. Falcon pulled out his background report on Bobby West and wondered yet again who this man was. Civilians thought police had access to untold amounts of data about them, from bugged homes to interviews with ex-girlfriends. Too much fantasy in their lives. James Bond, George Orwell. No, the Fourth Amendment put the onus on law enforcement. You still had a fundamental right to privacy, and no one practiced spy games in America, at least not at the local level. Falcon couldn't speak to Bobby West and the CIA, so he had to rely on property records, credit histories, and run-ins with the law to build his dossier. Trouble was, on paper, the man was as legitimate as they came, middle American to a T.

Callahan entered with two men, gangly disheveled types, pants hitched too high, shirts tucked in off-center. They carried themselves like philosophy professors or scientists rather than cops. Callahan introduced the first as Agent Blair, who had a wild poof of hair and a mustache that hid a crooked grin, and the other as Agent Gibson, who wore round spectacles with some kind of film on them that reflected the light and masked his eyes.

"You boys with the Miami P.D.?" Falcon asked.

"They're with a private agency," Callahan said.

"You're contractors?"

"Federal contractors," Callahan said. "We brought them in to research your mystery woman."

The agents had yet to speak, which unnerved Falcon. They all had connections to the law in this room. He was used to FBI agents being a bit too buttoned up for their own good, but even they reserved the suspicious silence for the bad guys. These guys, he didn't even know who paid their salaries.

"Good news, bad news, Ernie," Callahan said as the three of them took a seat around the conference table. "These guys have traced the photo of your mystery woman."

"That was fast."

"We're efficient," Agent Blair said. Falcon noticed the man kept his crooked grin at bay, perhaps embarrassed by a gap between his front teeth.

"So who is she?"

Agent Blair pulled out a blow-up of the photo Falcon took in front of West's house. "Adriana Chekhov. Slovakian Jew with several close family ties to Israel. Her father was a chemist who escaped the Iron Curtain with his family in tow, and she was raised in Quebec, but then she fell off the grid for a number of years. We don't have a record of her ever graduating from high school, or opening a bank account, or ever really showing up in the system as an adult. In fact, for the majority of record-keeping organizations on earth, she does not exist after age fifteen."

"Well, how did you boys stumble on her?"

"She did contract work for the Israeli military about ten years ago. She listed her father in one of their forms, which likely sped up her process to get into their system. A number of his siblings emigrated to Israel after the war, so it helped to have blood ties to the country."

"What did she do for them?"

"We're not at liberty to say," Agent Gibson cut in.

Agent Blair continued, "Once she got into their system, she went deep undercover, but through a series of assumed names we were able to trace some of her movements over the past decade. It wasn't easy. She's almost a statistical variant, an errant blip on the radar."

"Just enough to know she's there," Agent Gibson said.

"And?" Falcon was tired of the woe-is-me hard work of investigation. He investigated for a living, and this conference room's stark lighting was making him anxious. This was not a room he frequented when he'd actually been a detective. Detectives belonged in the street, working cases, knocking on doors, taking action. All he wanted now was to know who the hell the woman was and why she was in Miami, in Bobby West's house.

"You had a close call, my friend," Callahan said. "Not many people run across this woman and get away to tell the tale."

"Lucky me."

"Very lucky," Agent Blair said. "As near as we could piece together, she's a mercenary with some of the vilest contacts around the world. Seems she's done everything from facilitating arms deals in the Soviet Empire to scooping up lost nuclear material for the Chinese to running the drugs out of Afghanistan."

"What's she doing in Miami?"

"Our guess is the drug trade."

"Colombians?"

"It's possible, but more likely she's importing heroin out of Afghanistan," Agent Blair said. "Most intelligence agencies see heroin as funneling east into Asia, but we found one source who said there's a direct line into the United States."

"Where do you find these guys?" Falcon asked Callahan. To the agents, he said, "So you think this Adriana is running that line."

"Appears so."

"Is the CIA involved with that?"

The agents looked at each other.

Callahan asked, "What do you mean?"

"I mean, I photographed this woman in Bobby West's house. He's CIA, so I wondered if she had any connection to him."

"The CIA is not involved in the Miami drug trade," Agent Gibson said.

"Did you look into it?"

"They're not involved."

"Well, Jesus, what are you telling me? Did you look into Bobby West and the Artium Group?"

Agent Blair said, "We believe her contact in South Florida is a man named Alexander French."

"Why do I know that name?"

Agent Blair pulled out another photograph of a late-middle aged man with a shaved head and loosening skin around his face. He could have been a member of the VFW in a small town somewhere, but he also had an earring and a floral shirt that gave him the rakish cut of a pirate. "Alexander French. He's been a known quantity down here for several years. A bit of a gadfly in certain circles, he's also a serial entrepreneur in the criminal trade. Running direct mail scams with the elderly down in the Keys, working with shady developers to cut land deals, and now, we think, financing the drug trade between Afghanistan and Miami."

"So he's in partnership with the woman," Falcon said.

"That's our guess," Agent Gibson said. He'd been the silent one among them, but now he said, "He's got very deep connections with politicos, lobbyists, business owners, foreign dignitaries, you name it. It's tough to say how seriously they take him, but he's financed enough clout that it doesn't really matter. What this means for us is that we can keep an eye on his operations, which we've been doing for some time, but he's built a largely bureaucratic machine around him. His employees aren't your average numbskull criminals looking for a scam. He's hired people who want nothing more than steady work, and he pays them to fill out form A or form B, like the IRS or the Soviets."

"Or the Nazis," Agent Blair cut in.

"You know how bureaucracies work," Agent Gibson continued, waving his arm around the room. "They're giant machines. Once you put them in motion, everything is pre-determined. Form A, form B. Alexander French's criminal empire is like trying to penetrate the IRS. It's a labyrinthine system with wheels of its own."

"So you've got no shot at pinning something on him," Falcon said.

"Correct. You know how if you have a problem with the IRS, you're rude to one of their workers or what have you, they can put you in a special file. They fill out form C, and suddenly you get audited. Your assets get seized. I'm serious. Ask any business owner in America. The IRS is the most terrifying organization in the country. Better under Reagan, but there's no greater threat to American freedom than a bureaucracy."

"Gibson," Agent Blair cut him off.

"My point is, Alexander French's operation works the same way. You go after him, you might find your pension has dried up. You find yourself with form C associated with your name, you've got no recourse, with the government or anyone else."

"Hence private contractors," Falcon said.

"That's a big part of it. Our organization operates off the grid, same as French's, which gives us a bit of leeway. My advice to you, however, is steer clear of French or Chekhov. Find a different case to work."

"OK, fellas, I hear what you're saying, but all I've been hired to do is find Bobby West's daughter. She took off five or six days ago, and now Bobby won't return my phone calls. He's in deep with some bad folks, it sounds like. He disappears for a day, and this Adriana Chekhov breaks into his house. I don't need the details, I just want to find the daughter. His ex-wife is my primary client here."

"I'm afraid we can't help you with the daughter," Agent Gibson said.

"Well, what are you here for today?"

"We came here to explain the gravity of your situation."

"You're telling me to back off."

The agents said nothing.

"And the girl? What am I supposed to do about her?"

"Refund your client and tell them she's gone. She'll probably turn up on her own, run out of money or get sick of the boyfriend. Or maybe she won't. She's, what, seventeen, eighteen? Children grow up and leave their parents all the time. Sometimes it's genetic, sometimes it's bad parenting, but it's not your job to solve problems beyond your control."

Falcon thought of his own children on the West Coast. The boy called home as an obligation but the girl wanted nothing to do with him. He'd grown resigned to the estrangement but it bothered him the way the girl could be so callous toward her mother. Mary Catherine had been nothing if not a paragon of decency, made sandwiches and carted the kids to every inane practice and event. Falcon believed in freedom as much as the next American, but he also believed in duty. You had obligations in this life, even if people failed to recognize it.

While the agents packed up the files and photographs, Falcon leaned back to catch his breath. He needed to lose weight. Needed to get in shape and eat healthier so he could cut back on his blood pressure medication. While his stomach rumbled in digestion, he looked out the floor-to-ceiling window, at the rain and the gray day, the mist that seemed to hover in the air like snow on a TV screen. A weak signal muted between the air and the antenna and the device.

Callahan, who had remained silent through most of the meeting, stood and opened the door for the agents, said, "You can see yourselves out, right?"

When the agents had gone, Callahan closed the door and sat across from Falcon.

"Well that went well," Falcon said.

Callahan shook his head. "You got to be careful what you say around here these days."

"You too, Donnie Ray?"

"Eyes are everywhere, my friend. You may want to tell your buddy at the newspaper as well."

"Eyes are one thing, but it sounds like these boys are colluding with criminals and letting drugs pour into the streets. You still do any police work around here?"

"I'll see you, Ernie."

Falcon stood and left his old colleague in the conference room, alone with the halogen lights and whirring HVAC system, the patter of rain against the windows.

Outside beneath the police station's front awning, he bumped into Frank Navarro, who stopped and gave a mock grin, as though he hadn't been expecting to run into Ernie Falcon here. Falcon suspected of course the man knew he was here, had found out somehow, and intended to ambush him. That didn't stop Navarro from extending his hand and saying, "Ernie! Good to see you! Twice in one week, must have a good luck streak going on."

"Hey, Frank."

"What brings you down to the station?"

"Oh the usual. Doing a little research for a case."

"Good, good."

"What about you?"

"Me? Oh, I keep close ties with all my friends on the force. Building up that business opportunity."

"Surely not every cop is interested in whatever real estate scheme you've got cooking."

"Real estate? Where'd you get that idea? No, I'm in the security business these days, Ernie, and I can always use a good cop. Speaking of, why don't you let me take you to lunch again next week? I'll put together a few details and maybe we can arrange a formal offer."

"I'm not in a place to make any investments these days, Frank."

"That's good, because we've got all the VCs we need. It's your time and expertise I had in mind."

"I've got a full caseload these days."

"Maybe I can help you on that front."

Falcon shook his head.

"Think it over. These are dangerous days for our country, and the government doesn't have the resources to manage everything. Private security is the future, mark my words."

"Enjoy your weekend," Falcon said.

"I'll give you a call next week," Navarro said to his back.

Falcon scurried through the rain to his old Plymouth Valiant. His hand slipped on the handle but he finally was able to fold himself inside and turn on the engine to get the heat going. The day was warm but the rain had chilled him. He wondered what to do next about West, Chekhov, Mr. French, and Holly Hernandez.

Years past, he might have driven off somewhere, perhaps to see Isabel, perhaps to talk things over with Juan Delgado. Something, some action. Actions were for younger men. Now he saw the wisdom in sitting still and allowing a mystery's secrets to come to him. He'd developed this patience too late in life for it to help him much, but at least it might give him a hint of insight into Bobby West and his missing daughter.

When he pulled out of the parking lot and rumbled down the street, he saw Frank Navarro outside a van, his hand on the roof. Inside the van, on a bench seat, Agents Blair and Gibson bobbed their heads. When Falcon passed, Navarro gave a little wave before returning back to the contract agents.

22

They took I-95 to I-26 out of Savannah, neither of them speaking about what they'd left behind as they sped through the swamps and kept an eye out for police. Keith was wired on No-Doze, coffee, and adrenaline. His breath stank like a cap gun and made him self-conscious. He breathed through his nose, avoided exhaling in her direction—though for what? He was terrified of what she might be capable of, but for her part she seemed equally traumatized.

They barreled into South Carolina and right into the first hills of the piedmont without letting off the gas or articulating where they were headed. Keith only knew so many places in this world, and he damn sure wasn't going back to Florida. Couldn't stay in Savannah either, which meant his old hometown was the only place he knew to go. Could tell his parents he needed another loan. Mull things over.

Holly slept, woke, fiddled with the radio stations—nothing but country music and big oldies in this part of the world—and stared out the window before sleeping some more.

Thou shalt not steal. Thou shalt not covet. Thou shalt not kill.

Phrases popped into Keith's mind, instructions from his devout upbringing. He'd not been to church in years, but now that he was back in his home state, trail of wreckage behind him, he understood how he'd shifted his life in some permanent way. He saw himself from two perspectives: then-Keith the cigarette salesman, bumbling through young adulthood with a vague promise in his future if only he could find the right key or go through the right door, and now-Keith the outlaw: a stolen car, ten grand and a girl in tow, bodies in his old apartment.

He'd walked through a door all right, but now the door had locked behind him. Although he wasn't certain whether he'd made a fatal mistake, he understood the permanence of last night's decision: wrap the bodies in the shower curtain, one at a time, and drag them into the apartment's hallway, prop them up behind the vending machines. They'd cleaned out the apartment as best they could, but Keith knew someone would eventually come knocking. A man with a badge and the law behind him, or a man with a gun who operated by a different code.

When Keith was a child, his father had preached about sin and the limited seats in heaven and the depravity of life, those old Calvinist tropes that made ordinary folks flee from the church in the late twentieth century. He'd flipped through his parents' Bible, read the verse about plucking out one's eye, and understood himself a sinner. How could you be responsible for your very thoughts? How could something beyond your control lead to your damnation? It made him sick then, a boy of ten, and it made him sick now to know not only was he a sinner in his mind and heart, but also in his action. Even if God were a fiction, and sin nothing but a story to keep men in check, there would be no hedging for the stolen money, no optimistic platitude—*Trust in Jesus*—to save him from the likes of Mr. French.

They pulled over at a rest stop north of Columbia, near a Wal-Mart distribution center and not much else. The area was nearly vacant, just a few families with roof racks on their vans, hamburger box-shaped cargo, dogs walking in the grass, sniffing the clover, raising legs to the bushes. Keith took a piss and sighed in relief. In a nearby stall, a man grunted and appeared to be boxing the toilet paper dispenser. Pop-pop. Pop. Pop-pop. Holly was asleep in the back seat, and Keith cracked the windows and leaned the front seat back, dozed for a long time.

He dreamt of bloody shower curtains, of lemon soap and the sound of a vacuum cleaner. He was not a smart man but knew even in his dream that his reckoning would come. You could only run for so long before the wave of your past came crashing down on you. People more innocent might be able to stay afloat until Judgment Day, but Keith knew he and Holly would see judgment in this life, the here and now.

When he woke, half the day had passed and the sun had begun its fall from the sky. He yawned, covered his mouth, felt as though he were emerging from thick sludge. He found Holly squatting on the sidewalk in front of a child. Thick blond hair, maybe four years old, cherubic. She reached out her hand. "It's okay, it's okay," Holly said as if to a dog. Her voice had a bit of a lilt that made Keith wonder if she'd taken something.

When Keith got out of the car, the child backed away. Holly swatted Keith back and said again, "It's okay, little guy. What's your name?"

Keith glanced around for the parents but saw no one around. He found a pair of sunglasses in the Impala's glove compartment. He put them on, leaned against the car, and watched as Holly made friends with the child, hoping she wouldn't get it into her head to bring the kid with them. Where did that thought come from? Something about the way her mothering instincts seemed to kick in, that combined with her brazen approach to the world and her lack of self-understanding. She seemed capable of anything.

He'd returned to the apartment after hearing the gunshots. Even though he'd been in boxer shorts and had neither keys nor cash, he knew his best move was to get out of there. Instead, he'd found her shaking at the foot of the bed, a pistol on the floor, two men bleeding out in the living room. "Good goddamn," he'd said, "what happened?" She'd remained catatonic while he checked the dead men for pulses, recognized B.D., thought about Mr. French's basement. He'd gotten dressed and asked her again and again,

"What happened?" Finally, he said, "We need to get out of here." Only then had she looked up and nodded.

Before Keith's rumination gave way to out-and-out fear, a woman ran up and said to the kid, "Spud, where have you been?"

She took the kid's hand and looked up at Holly apologetically. The woman was frumpy and thick and had the greasy crumpled hair of a belle long past her prime.

Holly stood. "What kind of name is Spud?"

"It's just what we call him. His name's Jeff."

"You ought to call him Jeff, then." Her voice was too loud. Keith pushed off the car and headed toward her. "And you shouldn't be letting your kid roam off like that. What if we were kidnappers? We could have snatched him and hit the road. You'd never see him again."

The woman backed away, holding Jeff's hand, and she squinted at Keith and Holly as though she could see into their hearts and knew their past and future in a godlike stroke of insight. Holly sickly and deranged. Keith, in the sunglasses and still wired from caffeine and the road, doubtless looked the same.

"We were just on our way out," Keith said.

In the rear-view, he watched the woman watching them. She still held onto her son, who for his part was already lost in his imagination. Keith watched her head over to the row of payphones by the brick building, and that was all he saw before pulling onto the interstate.

He sped north and pulled over at the first exit, turned left onto a state highway and made another immediate left to get back on I-26 heading south, thinking that if highway patrol did decide to investigate, they'd head north, the only way to go out of the rest area. He kept it at sixty-five for three exits and pulled over at a McDonald's.

Holly hadn't asked questions, but she seemed pleased to be off the road again. She bounded out of the car and started singing.

"What are you doing?" he yelled.

He chased after her.

"I want a milkshake."

"I can buy you a milkshake, but keep your voice down," he said. He put his arm around her and pulled her toward the entrance. "We got to lay low and be smart."

He heard sirens in the distance and hurried up.

"Take it easy," she said. "You're hurting me."

He opened the door for her and said, "What flavor milkshake you want?"

She pulled away from him and went to the bathroom. He took a guess and ordered her a chocolate shake, and a large fries and a Coke and chicken nuggets for himself. She stayed in the bathroom an awfully long time. He watched the door nervously. He had the keys, so she wasn't going anywhere and anyway, if she did, he told himself he could go on without her. Still, he was relieved when she came out and sat quietly at the table in front of him, stole a fry, sipped her milkshake, sat quietly.

They were on the road again an hour later. They topped off the gas tank and bought a map. To evade the law, if the law were on their trail, he outlined a route that seesawed through the Carolina upcountry. He was tired of driving but didn't dare give up the wheel to her. When they passed a sign for Presbyterian College, the old Protestant guilt burned in his chest again. Folks around here would not take kindly to a young man who quit a good job out of greed or lust for a different life, and who immediately got swept up in the Miami excess and violence. Too late for second thoughts, but damn if they weren't in a tight spot with no plan.

They continued through South Carolina meadowland until they reached the corporate sprawl of Greenville-Spartanburg. They left the interstate for country back roads. Billboards advertised God and admonished *Stop Drop and Roll Doesn't Work in Hell.* Crumbled barns and country gas stations. Local yokel speed traps. Keith cruised at five miles over the limit with his jaw clenched. When a tractor-trailer passed them, Holly said, "You drive worse than my grandmother, and she's got Alzheimer's."

"You want to explain to Barney Fife what we're doing on the road, in this stolen car, with ten grand in your purse?"

She fiddled with the radio.

*

They ate dinner at a strip mall Mexican restaurant called Los Hermanos. The waitresses wore colorful puffy shirts pulled down to expose bony shoulders. Keith ordered enchiladas and stared out the window at the empty parking lot with an empty mind, long shadows and a bruise of light. All afternoon the silence between him and Holly had been thick and swampy.

When the waitress had left with their order, he walked back to the restrooms and placed a call on the payphone. His intention was to spend a few nights lying low in Six Mile, a community of five hundred north of Clemson near Highway 11, but he wanted to avoid his parents. You never did grow up in this life, but things grew difficult to explain. Such as: what was the nature of their relationship? What had he been doing with his life? Why was he here?

No, he had no intention of accounting for his life this evening, so he called up his old buddy Kennedy.

"I got us a place to stay tonight," he told Holly.

She yawned and stretched.

"It's a friend from high school. He's got a wife and baby but said we were welcome to the guest room."

"How old is this guy?" she asked.

"He's my age."

"Good God, people make some choices, don't they?"

"Could be worse things than having a wife and kid at twenty," he said.

They snacked on chips in silence while night continued to fall over the dingy southern wasteland. They were too far out of Greenville or Atlanta to be part of the world, but not far enough into the mountains to be attached to the old ways of life. Keith had grown up in the between spaces, and he pushed his thoughts away from the variations of what he and his high school classmates were doing with their lives. Many were in college, while others had picked up odd jobs over in Seneca or Anderson. Milliken still had a plant in the area, and of course there was the nuclear station. They were widening the interstate in Greenville, but Six Mile was far enough off from any epicenter of business that maybe Kennedy had it right: get married, have a kid, get your life over with, because it's not getting better. High school all over again: the boredom, the Friday night ball game, the occasional meal out at Ryan's steakhouse buffet, the cakewalk at the fall festival. Keith had grown up amid this historical detritus. Such as it was. The sweep of time, details, interpretation—all that belonged in the classroom, and classrooms were irrelevant to the marrow of his life. Out here, we were all inconsequential specks, no more important to the annals of history than a mote of dust, the flecks of salt he swept from the table when their food arrived.

"Y'all got ever-thing you need?" the waitress asked.

"Believe so," Keith said.

"Holler if you need something."

A police cruiser sped past with lights flashing, and Keith quit chewing and waited for the neon flare of blue to fade. The pulse of the lights mirrored his quivering heart. He resumed chewing and a few minutes later spat out a piece of ceramic broken off his plate. He remembered from school a demonstration once about Mexican serving ware, how it was radioactive and would make a Geiger counter clack like a radio dialed slightly out of tune. He wondered what it meant to eat off such a plate, if his food would glow in the dark of his stomach, if he'd weakened his teeth by biting into the ceramic. He set down his fork, unable to finish the enchiladas. They'd cooled and congealed to a salty sludge. Plus the lingering fear from seeing the local police in such a fury had wrecked his appetite.

He pushed the plate aside and asked, "What happened back there?"

"I told you, I shot them."

"Where the hell did you get the gun? And learn to shoot it?"

"My father."

"What?"

"My father. It was his gun, in the safe with the cash."

"Jesus, what else did you take from him?"

She shrugged. "We needed protection."

"Protection! Protection from who?"

"Clearly, your buddy from the bar," she said. "And besides, where were you, Mr. Out-the-Window?"

"I told you to come with me."

"But I stayed," she said.

"We could have gotten out."

"With the money?"

"Who cares about the money?" he asked. "Ten grand's a lot, but it's not murdering money. Why the hell were they coming after us?"

She opened her mouth and then snapped it shut.

"What are you not telling me? How'd you know how to fire a gun?" he asked again.

"My father used to bring me to the firing range."

"What kind of man brings his daughter to a firing range?"

"The type who wishes he were a different kind of man," she said. "He spent his life as an analyst and always wanted to be in operations. It's why he got in that scheme."

"What scheme? What are you even talking about?"

"My father. He's CIA."

"Har har," Keith said in mock laughter. Then, "You're serious?"

"He's a legitimate businessman, but the CIA bankrolls him."

Keith's heart was a stone in water, straight to the bottom of his belly. "You're telling me we stole CIA money. Jesus, not only will they come after it, they'll know how to find us."

"Get real. They couldn't find a drop of water in the ocean. Besides, it's not CIA money."

"Whose money is it?"

"Same guys you were working for."

Keith tried to make the connection, how some CIA-backed businessman was in cahoots with Mr. French and the South Florida—what? Mafia? Drug runners? Whoever Keith had been in business with, and whoever this girl's father was, neither meant a long and free future for Keith and Holly.

"He was smuggling it or whatever you call it," she went on.

"Laundering."

"Yeah, he was laundering the money for the guys you worked for."

Keith cursed, thought of Mr. French's basement. Still, that was heavy muscle to be sending over ten grand and a stolen car. There must be something else. "Anything else you're not telling me?" he asked her. "You expecting any Soviet agents to poison our enchiladas, anything like that?"

"Just don't tell anyone where we're staying tonight," she said.

When they left they saw a passel of cop cars down the street, lights flashing, circling a nearby motel like cowboys around a wagon, or the Bolivian Army gearing up to execute Butch Cassidy. He couldn't tell what was going on, but it appeared dire. He hoped he and Holly were safe where they were. A helicopter hummed overhead, the news media or police or a stray bird connected to the nearby military facilities. The thumping blades sounded into the night like white noise, the after-hours static on broadcast television. Keith checked the trunk of the car and saw the duffel bag was still there, the butt of the gun jutting out of the side pocket.

"You coming?" Holly sauntered to the passenger side and drummed her fingers on the roof. "I want to get away from those cops."

He told her that was a good idea and closed the trunk.

23

In a bar near the office, West ordered an expensive scotch and drank like a bastard. With an empty bank account, the promise of CIA money mere illusion, and no word from Ernie Falcon, he needed to fill the hours. You'd think he would have learned some patience by this point in his life, but when things went wrong, time crawled like rush hour traffic. His heart drummed as though someone stood on his chest.

When he ordered a second scotch, a woman with red hair sat beside him and tapped a pack of Gauloises on the bar top. She ordered a White Russian and had a familiar thickness to her accent, an inflection not quite right. Then she was gone, merged with the crowd before it registered with him that he'd met her before. His heart clenched.

He sipped his scotch and looked around for her with growing unease. His mind wouldn't stay focused long enough for him to pinpoint his troubles, so he got up and went to the restroom. The lights against the white tile walls, the checkered white and green tile floor, were startlingly bright. You'd expect a dim and dank bathroom to match the bar outside, but with these fluorescent bulbs it was like a thousand watts beaming straight at him—should have given him a suntan. The future so bright, he's got to wear shades. There was a fly floating in the urinal, and he aimed the stream at the fly and the fly fluttered its wings, bobbed up and landed on the walls of the urinal and flew up again when West flushed.

When he returned to the bar, the woman still was nowhere in sight, but he did see Vicky, his leggy secretary, who wore a provocative violet dress cut low on her chest and high on her thighs. She matched West in a stupor, leaned her buggy eyes forward and raised her cocktail like she was about to give him a piece of wisdom, and said, "I could use a refill."

"Let's see if we can do something about that. Step into my office."

"I don't know if I should do that."

"I meant the bar over here," he said.

"Oh. Right."

When she sat on a stool, and crossed her legs, he tried hard not to leer. He really did, knowing he had no business ordering another drink, nor getting close to anyone he worked with, especially someone much younger and who reported directly to him. She could be his daughter, poor Holly, off with his money. Young women, these vixens, they set traps for men, he was sure of it. Yet rather than heed his better instincts and go home, check on his ex-wife, he watched Vicky knock back the drink in her hand, ordered another scotch for himself, and turned to her.

"I'll take another gin and tonic," she said to the bartender.

"How can you drink gin?" he asked.

"One sip at a time."

He shook his head. "It's 'cause you're still young. Are you even thirty yet? That's when it starts going downhill."

"Uh huh." Her eyes drifted away, and he kicked himself for bringing up her age, which implicitly brought up his age, which was not something he wanted to consider. When the drinks arrived, however, she turned back to him and said, "How can you drink scotch?"

"One sip at a time," he said, and he took a drink.

"Is that something that happens when you turn forty? You start drinking scotch?"

"Touché."

"What you doing out here?" she asked.

"Trying not to lose my sanity."

"Some of us, from the office, we come here every Friday for happy hour."

"Where are they at now?"

She stirred her drink. "I think I've been stood up."

"That's no fun."

She re-crossed her legs, and again he tried not to watch. Although he kept his eyes focused firmly above her shoulders, his attention focused on everything below. Smooth skin, toned muscle. He imagined her exposed skin was cool, and there was nothing he liked more than to rub up against cool skin, to inhale the fresh and sweet scent of a woman's shampoo or body wash, to hold her to him.

They exchanged a few more empty words, which he paid no attention to, thinking only of her impossibly long thighs.

"There you are," said a woman behind them.

Vicky's face sobered and she smiled and stood up to greet her friend.

"You know Bobby, right?"

West had never seen the woman before, but they both looked at each other with the secret fear that they had met, or should have met, so they awkwardly said hello without answering Vicky's question.

The woman sat on the other side of Vicky, and the two began chattering. Others soon joined them.

West ordered another scotch, was unable to stay here in the bar now that Vicky was occupied. A market correction was on the nightly news on the TV behind the bar, the somber-faced anchors gesticulating with their hands in motions that presumably meant doomsday was around the corner. The Artium Group had a relatively safe portfolio, stocks of consumer staples, a money market, and, lately, municipal bonds that funded projects of nebulous origin and investors with no financial provenance. Nevertheless, it was West's job, as the ostensible financial officer, to maintain the company's fiduciary stability. The missing cash from his home safe made him nervous, because if their investors panicked, that cash on paper was the only thing between West and the wolves, and the cash belonged to the wolves.

"What do you think, Bobby?" Vicky asked.

He shook his head to wake up. More from the office had joined the party, three young men in suits. West knew them, but not well. Brokers. Salesmen, essentially. He said, "About what?"

"About Hoffman."

"Is he a Nazi?" one of the men, Peter, asked. Thick black hair parted neatly, a mustache to make him appear older than twenty-five, the lean frame of a Frenchman and the self-assurance of an asshole.

"Bobby doesn't know that," Vicky said.

"Of course he does. He knows all the executives."

Another man, Sam, said, "He's not going to give us the scoop."

West took a sip of his freshened drink and said, "I can assure you Hoffman's not a Nazi."

"He's from Germany, isn't he?" Peter persisted. "When did he come to America?"

"I don't know when he came here, but—"

"There you go. Where do you think Artium got all its money?"

"No," Vicky said. She turned to West.

"Yeah," Peter said. "Probably a guard like in *Sophie's Choice*. Stole money off the Jews and came to America to start a business."

"Oh my god," the other woman—West still couldn't think of her name—said. "That was such a horrible story."

"People did that, you know."

"Did it in Vietnam, too," Sam said.

"Can you imagine being put in that position?" the girl said.

"There wasn't any money over there to steal," Peter said.

"Never stopped us from stealing food and setting fire to some villages."

"What do you know about it? We were all in elementary school."

"What do you say, Bobby?" Sam said. "You in the service?"

"I never was," he said.

"Good man."

West didn't feel it. His one regret in life was that he had never seen war. When he'd joined the CIA payroll, he'd had visions of himself as James Bond, running Black Ops while his fellow young men set fire to Vietnam. As he aged he began to realize the consequences of never serving in battle, for men of his generation were divided into those who knew war and those who played war. No matter how many push-ups West did, no matter how many weights he lifted to tighten up, he still lacked the true cut of a military man. He was not a part of that fraternity, and never could be, no matter what he did in the name of patriotism.

The girl looked like she was about to cry thinking about Meryl Streep, a train station in Germany, one child lives and one child dies, your choice.

"You think we'll ever know what went on over there?" Peter asked.

"We don't want to know."

"He's not a Nazi," West said.

They all stared at him in silence.

"Hoffman." Hoffman was the Artium Group's CEO, a German immigrant who went from owning a line of Volkswagen dealerships in the sixties to starting a holding company in the late seventies. In truth he'd been a double agent during the fall of the Iron Curtain. Hoffman was a true James Bond, now a filthy rich capitalist with a private boat and a direct line to the Secretary of Defense.

Peter pulled out a pack of cigarettes, smacked the bottom of the pack, repeatedly, before sliding one out. "Yeah?" he said, easing the cigarette into the corner of his mouth. "What makes you say that?"

"For one thing, he's in his fifties. He would've been a teenager during the war. But his parents came to the U.S. before the war."

"You'd know best, boss."

"Peter," Vicky said.

He moved the cigarette to the other corner of his mouth, cupped his hand over, and lit up. West'd had just enough scotch to take the little prick's bait. One more scotch, and he would've been too far-gone to care. One less, and he simply would've looked the kid up in the directory tomorrow and had him fired. As it was, he said, "You make a habit of disrespecting your supervisors?"

"Nah, man, but Hoffman's not my supervisor."

"He's all of our supervisor."

"What about you?" Peter blew smoke away from West. "What do you think of him?"

"I think you don't know a thing about him."

"Enlighten me, then. How'd we do in the market today?" Peter's eyes glowed with interest, and West suddenly understood the boy had more knocking around his brain than he let on.

"We took a hit."

"You think it'll come back?"

"It always does."

"Not back in Hoffman's day."

"That was a different time."

Vicky said, "I don't get how the market can just drop like that."

"Traders," Peter and West said together.

"Bunch of assholes," Peter added.

Vicky seemed confused, but West wasn't about to explain the inner workings of Wall Street to her. When he was younger, he'd considered abandoning a career in intelligence for a career in moneymaking, but he lacked the stomach for Wall Street. Late nights of studying numbers, running over uncertainties, sucking down coffee or cocaine or Coca-Cola until their skin was pale and slick and their hands shook from the adrenaline rush. This was what they lived for, the danger of it all, the thrill of it. Gambling, a high stakes game of poker, of probability. Finding the pattern running through random numbers in aggregate. To cope, one man would play three rigorous games of squash tomorrow, another might break a stranger's nose in a bar, another might have violent sex with his wife, or a whore, and another still might do serious meditation with the barrel of a gun in his mouth. It was all in the cards.

He swirled the last melting cube of ice in the bottom of his scotch. His head felt full, and the noise seemed to close off around him, as though he were in some pre-dawn hour, beyond time. How fragile the body became, healthy life an illusion. Illness came for us all, and on hapless occasions we saw a glimpse into what the grim future held. Around him, the others were in conversation, Vicky laughing hysterically at something one of the boys said, her concern over the stock market vanquished by the siren call of good times. Hearing his own echoing heartbeat within his mind, he set the glass on the bar, took a last glance at the growing crowd, Vicky among them, and shuffled out.

This was not the first time in recent memory he'd found himself chasing the never-ending bottom of scotch-based cocktails. If he'd learned one thing in life, it was this: sometimes moral objections had to be placed in the background for the greater good. West was rich because of his work at the Artium Group, and he'd allowed the money to steer him away from his youthful idealism, the thought of going after Castro and saving Cuba, of life in the shadows behind the Iron Curtain, slaying the bear in the woods. Pro patria mori. Instead he'd shuffled money around for twenty years, skimmed his percentage, and old Castro was still terrorizing his people. Just ask young Felix. The boy had fire and ambition, and believed in the mission to sell Tiny Mark on Cuba Omega, whereas Bobby West had no fire, merely fumes, dying coals, and wanted only to sell Tiny Mark on saving him—West—from Mr. French's wolves. Perhaps this was a moral failing on West's part, but he'd seen men held in higher esteem stoop to lower means. He'd voted for Nixon both in 1968 and 1972, and he'd paid no attention to the Watergate scandal, for it seemed obvious that the world of politics worked one way and everything else worked another way, and if you were in politics you had to suffer certain failings that would be moral failings in the other world but that in the world of politics were merely failings. The question was, which world did West exist in? The world of politics or the world of everything else? And could one really make such a distinction and remain a whole person?

Same question applied to the world of love and marriage. He'd married Holly's mother, who worked as a secretary in the business office at the time, a spicy young thing back then. The two of them shared a bond, and West was rooted until Holly came into the picture. As more and more Cubans immigrated to Miami, Isabel grew closer to her roots. The split had come recently, but the fault line had been there for years, waiting for the hammer to tap the right spot. Things had not worked out, and neither West nor Isabel made any apologies, and that was how it was and there wasn't anything interesting to say about it. If West were more introspective he might ask why, but instead he'd had sex with Diana, the woman-who-was-not-his-wife, who would never be his wife, and accepted his cash payments from Felix Machado and Mr. French, padded his bank account and tried to right-size the Artium Group. It had not taken a robbery for his days to end with noxious amber liquid numbing him to the ails of his REIT funds.

In the street, no more Sam and Peter and Vicky and the nameless girl: the cocky, innocent young. How many of those businessmen—those financiers with fumbled stock plays—had crossed a line others would object to? How many of them considered their business necessary within the world in which they did it, and therefore was no great sin? His boss Hoffman was no Nazi, West was certain, just another immigrant working his way to the top of American society with a few hidden secrets. Everyone had them: the carnal desires, the prejudices, the ill-gotten gains, the family shame, the psychological damage from their childhood. West imagined the people in the street, drunks and bums, businessmen and call girls, young and old, confronting a genuine reckoning about the way they were living. He imagined most of them would talk their way down from a moral failing to a mere failing, which was bad enough. To fail. Even the ones, like West, flush with prospects and whose cocks still worked and who still had hair on their heads (even though he felt soft around the middle, bulky, aged), they too must have the unflagging suspicion that their lives somehow had not turned out right.

With a lonesome heart he got in his car and drove out to Miami Beach, where he hoped Diana would comfort him. He weaved like a teenager over the MacArthur Causeway and cascaded up to Diana's neighborhood. She lived in a side street townhouse that was at least half a century old. Advantage: classic charm, a brick exterior, elegant interior wainscoting. Disadvantage: drafty rooms, radiator heat, massive insurance costs because the house wasn't bolted to the foundation and thus would be blown away should a major storm come through. Diana's allure lay in her nonchalance about such things. She wanted to live in a home with character. If this relationship was to go anywhere, though, West would move her out to his new home in Coral Gables, which, he felt certain, would survive anything mother nature had to throw at them.

All the lights were off. He didn't know what time it was, and beneath the scotch, a voice suggested he might be better off leaving her be. He pissed on a hedgerow and banged on her door. He hummed the standoff theme from *The Good, the Bad and the Ugly*, sucked in his gut and thought of himself as a lone cowboy, kindred spirit to Clint Eastwood. He knocked out the beat on her door, and then he stepped off the stoop. A few minutes later, the light came on and she opened the door.

"Whoa," he said. She wore a ratty white bathrobe and had smeared dark makeup under her eyes. Oily hair helmeted her head like a storm trooper. "Well hey there."

"What do you want?" she asked.

"Just in the neighborhood. Thought I'd stop by."

"You couldn't stop by in the day, like a normal boyfriend?"

"I had things to do."

"Things to drink."

He walked up the steps and took hold of the railing. She didn't move aside to let him enter. "Well, I might've had a sip or two, to take off the edge. But so what? It's Friday night."

"Where have you been?"

"Oh, out at the office."

"I mean this week."

"I had a business meeting up in D.C. yesterday, why?"

"I stopped by your place."

"Oh did you?"

"I had it in my mind I'd take you out for a nice dinner, maybe take in a movie, see where the night led."

"Oh yeah?" He leaned in. "The weekend's just getting started."

"You know what happened?"

"When?"

"When I stopped by."

"No, what?"

"I bumped into your friend Adriana."

West took a step off the porch.

"Maybe you should just go," she said.

"Wait," he started, but he had nothing to say.

She waited nonetheless.

He said, "What do you mean, you bumped into her?"

"She was in your house."

"My house?"

"She let me in, and then said to tell you she said hello."

He pinched his nose and leaned his head back.

"Goodnight, Bobby."

"Wait," he said again, but this time she closed the door on him. "It's not what you're thinking," he yelled after her, but no longer cared what Diana was thinking. The woman in the bar, the redhead, he knew now it was Adriana Chekhov, no doubt here to settle a debt. It made no sense. He'd made a down payment to Mr. French, got the wheels in motion to get funding for Felix's group from the CIA. Everyone should be happy.

His mind truly was in a fog when he started his car this time and backed into the street, driving cautiously because he knew he was drunk and believed extra vigilance would save him. Which it did, as always, but in the sobering hours of post-midnight and pre-dawn, he knew *always* only went so far. Meantime, in-between times, these hours where anything could happen: a shoot-out, a shoot-up, or Jesus Christ himself could come down from the heavens.

He knew one thing, Jesus Christ had not come back to earth to save Bobby West. Instead, the lord had sent his messenger, Adriana Chekhov.

His mind flashed to back alleys in Chicago, hard times where friends of his father's would beg for money from a snake. Those snakes were bad, but the men West owed money to now were worse. He would gladly take a rap on the knuckles in a back alley over a bullet to the brain. Did the snakes exist today? Surely. The world was rampant with them. But could West find a snake who could loan him enough to cover his loss, and what would be the price? Crazy thinking any way you looked at it. You didn't have to be a drug runner to know when you have $3 million in a safe in your home, and the money turns up missing, you're in something deeper than just paying back the people whose money it was to begin with. You had to figure out who stole it (in this case, Holly), and why (greed, adolescent angst, daddy issues), and where it was now (God only knew). It wasn't until you knew where your money went that you could consider what you would do about getting it back.

He might have to kill someone to keep from being killed, and he'd never thought he would be in the position of having to make that choice. He'd missed his shot at the war years, the testing of manhood. He was a middle-aged bureaucrat and accountant. The thing to do was stay rational. This was Mr. French's plan to begin with, so surely Mr. French had a contingency plan. If not, West worked for the CIA. Surely the CIA wouldn't leave him to the wolves. Surely Tiny Mark's money would come through before Adriana Chekhov decided to announce her presence to Bobby West's face. And surely his daughter would come home to him alive and well. If he could only make it through the next few weeks, surely things would be all right.

24

When Bobby West stumbled out of the bar, Chekhov finished her drink and placed two calls from the payphone at the back of the bar. The first was to Alexander French, who answered from somewhere with a loud whining in the background, like a band saw or vacuum cleaner. She pictured him with a finger in one ear, the phone pressed tightly to his other ear. He spoke too loudly. "No sign of the money then?"

"Not in his house. Not in his office. Not on his person," she said.

"Sounds like it was a legitimate robbery. We've had some trouble with one of our employees, which might be related."

The sound behind Mr. French spiked, and Chekhov had to ask him to repeat himself.

"We shouldn't discuss this on the phone. Can you meet me in South Beach in an hour? The usual spot."

After hanging up, she placed a second call to her backup contact in this whole mess. The movies portrayed spies as glamorous daredevils who jumped out of planes and walked into dangerous situations and lit a cigarette when they should have been calculating the odds of their survival. There really were men like James Bond, Chekhov supposed, but they either died young or never came close to the core of what was real, the bottommost layer. The secret of her line of work was that daredevils were not to be trusted. Yahoo cowboys made for good television, but the quiet, humble, meek men in the corner, the ones you wouldn't suspect of doing anything more than fetching coffee or filing papers or perhaps teaching British literature, those were the ones with secret inner lives, the ones who calculated the odds and took on ill-advised ventures no one else—the others who spent their days in the limelight, taking risks and showing off—noticed. The ones you trusted were the ones you never heard about, the ones who lived conservative lives and kept their mouths shut. Chekhov had a file full of those contacts, and spent her life making phone calls to them.

The reality of the world was that glamour and rebellion only carried you so far, whereas bureaucratic systems reigned supreme. Chekhov was no spy, but rather a supplier for the system. She worked with CIA, MI6, Mossad and others, but they were all the same. They paid for information, or for black market goods, and they all knew what their colleagues in other organizations were doing, all part of the global network, each hungry for their piece of the action. *Give me a lever and a place to stand, and I will move the world.* People—governments—wanted information, and the system put up barriers that created opportunities for people like her. The world was saturated with information. Advertisements, TV, newspapers. Billboards, street signs, flyers and bumper stickers and license plates. People in restaurants and bars and airports and college classrooms and in stores. The mall, the filling station, the post office. People everywhere, in pairs or groups or even alone, all wanting to say what was on their minds. You couldn't get away from the information out there, and Chekhov's skill lay in acquiring it, filtering it, interpreting it. Information was easy but ultimately a chore. She could have accepted a fat paycheck from one of those organizations or some other government, but then she would be removed from the wellspring. As part of the system, she would have the same roadblocks, the same meetings, the same cautious approach as the people she contracted for now.

The man on the other line picked up, took her number and called her back from a secure line. "I'm meeting with French in an hour," she told him. "Sounds like the money might be with a rogue employee."

"Anything about Bobby's daughter?"

"Not a thing," Chekhov said.

"The girl's been missing since Wednesday, and Bobby's pulled all kinds of agency strings trying to unearth another pot of money to cover the loss."

"He's not embezzled it?"

"No, he's not the type," the man said. "When you find something, let me know. Or if you need more in your burn account. Just do what you need to do to get this train back on the rails."

She thanked him and hung up.

Mr. French was already at the bistro in South Beach when she arrived.

He sat at a table and stared at the pedestrian traffic along Ocean Drive. Pale tourists sweated in the South Florida heat, vicious even in the evening hours in April, but they were no doubt glad to be shed from their coats and scarves and hats and gloves. Probably calling home at night to brag, their friends up in a Lansing or a Springfield or a Harrisburg. Some union-friendly, heavily trafficked, industrial city-town they couldn't leave behind even while on vacation. We like to be known, to be part of our network. You can remove yourself for vacation, but you'll find yourself in a bar feeling lonesome, and the only way to cheer yourself up, you think, is to share your good fortune with others—to brag—when the cold bare-bones truth is that you've been infected with the village virus and don't actually enjoy leaving for vacation. You anticipate the vacation, and you have fond memories afterward, but its actual occurrence is a letdown.

A man held a yellow python and plopped it on a tourist who stopped to stare for too long, and offered to take the tourist's picture—"Ten dollars, ten dollars." The inevitable hustle. Chekhov had seen it all. She'd seen it in New Orleans, in Barcelona, in

London. Mexico, Kingston, San Francisco. The same everywhere, so you became inured to it.

Chekhov put out her cigarette and clasped her hands and leaned forward and rested her forearms against the table and waited.

"We hired a new guy a few weeks ago," Mr. French finally said, "and now he's disappeared with one of our cars. Seems he might have had more than a passing acquaintance with Bobby West's daughter, and maybe the two of them have the money."

"Any idea where they are?"

"Actually, yes. The boy, Keith, was a referral from a guy up in Savannah. We got in touch with our guy, but now he's dropped off the radar."

Chekhov pulled a pen and notebook out of her purse and said, "Give me their names."

Mr. French pulled a folder out of his briefcase. "Names, addresses, family members, the whole nine."

She put her notebook away and flipped through the folder for a few moments. Then she said, "You need this fellow back to Miami?"

"All I want is the money, minus your commission."

She guzzled half her beer in a single draw. "At West's house the other evening, there was a man hanging around on a stakeout."

"He's hired some redneck private investigator to chase down a few leads, but don't worry about him. He finds anything, we'll be on him fast enough. Go up to Savannah, see if you can find out what's happened with our man Keith or the girl. I wouldn't think this kid would be too hard to track down. Doesn't have a clue what he's stumbled into, so my guess is you or this private eye will find him soon enough. We good?"

In response, she took another large swig of the beer, and worked her throat to make the foam go down quicker. She quit when she realized Mr. French was staring at her, as though he understood she was a mere animal after all, attacking the bottle like a hungry dog.

25

Six Mile started as an old trading post in the late eighteenth century, named for a nearby mountain with an old Indian legend attached to it. A love story between a local Choctaw maiden and an English trader in a settlement ninety miles away. To warn the English of an imminent attack, she rode on horseback and named landmarks along the way: Six Mile Mountain, Twelve Mile Creek, all the way to what is now the town of Ninety-Six. The two lovers then holed up in Stumphouse Mountain, which today is known for the dead-end tunnel of a failed railroad passage through the Appalachians. The nearby town of Six Mile has kept itself small, a couple of families who owned everything from the hardware store and filling stations to the tracts of woods and farmland in the country. It had been a nice enough place to grow up, nestled in the shadows of the Blue Ridge, but it was also the type of town that told you exactly where you'd be in twenty years if you chose to stay.

Keith rocketed along Highway 133 north of town, the road a seesaw of hills and curves, and turned onto the county road, crossed a bridge over a wide branch of Crowe Creek. Although it was full dark and he was driving fast, he took note of the black shadows on the wind-chopped water below. Power lines stapled the road. A pair of shoes hung by their laces from one of the lines. A few minutes later he pulled up at the house on Cedar Street, a single-story on the corner near Keowee Park, way out in the middle of nowhere, big cedar tree in the front yard and a chain-link fence out back. Kennedy's old Pontiac sat in what served as the driveway, a patch of land stripped of grass in the side yard next to the porch. By the front door, a urine-yellow lamp lit up a dusty green couch and three or four planks of wood strewn about.

"This is where you hail from," Holly said as she got out of the car.

"It's the town," he said, and those were the only words they would exchange about Keith's origins. He rubbed his hand over his facial scruff, popped the trunk and pulled out the duffel bag, which was startlingly heavy.

"I've got it," she said, and reached for it.

"I don't mind."

"It's got some of my stuff in it." And she pulled it out of his hand, returned it to the trunk. "It's fine just to leave it in the car."

He wondered what else she brought along for this joyride. Cash, coke, guns. She'd said nothing of committing murder, no concern over sin or the law or the sheer inhumanity of taking a life.

"We going in?" she asked.

He couldn't tell if she was being flirtatious, or what she wanted from him. The novelty of this venture had worn off quick for the both of them, and he felt like a pinball already set into motion. Her father's safe the spring, B.D. and Savannah a flipper, the rest stop a bumper that bounced them from the South Carolina midlands up here to Six Mile, where he feared yet another lever waited for them inside the dilapidated house.

"Maybe don't tell Kennedy about the money," he said.

"No, I thought I'd tell him the whole story, see if he wants to invest in some real estate with us," Holly said, already marching up to the porch.

Someone scuffled inside the house, and then Kennedy greeted them by saying, "Keeeiiiithhh," and extending his hand for a slap-shake.

Kennedy stood a few inches taller than Keith, muscular, heavy-set, downright fat in the face. He had big glassy eyes and a red nose and cheeks. Without waiting for introductions, he led Keith and Holly into the house—the walls thin as cardboard—and swayed over to the easy chair. Holly followed him into the dim living room. Light streamed in from the kitchen on one side and from a floor TV on the other side. Two quarts of vodka, a liter of whiskey, and two emptied pizza boxes were on the coffee table, as well as the butts of stubbed out Swisher Sweets cigars and a twenty-ounce of Mountain Dew.

The house was no worse than Keith's old apartment, but he felt embarrassed here with Holly. He'd seen her father's house, albeit briefly, and knew she came from larger circumstances. It wouldn't take her long to tire of this hick on the run with her, and although he was distraught with her mood swings, he didn't want her to leave him alone. He put his hand on the small of her back and guided her to the couch.

Kennedy sank into the chair and propped his feet amid the mess on the coffee table. He pointed at Holly and asked, "Girlfriend?"

"We're friends," Holly said. Then she nodded at the vodka on the table and said, "All right?"

"By all means." Kennedy picked up one of the vodka bottles himself and took a swig. Then he said, "Friends are all right. Keith tell you we went to school together?"

"He mentioned it," she said. "Nice of you to set out drinks for us." She handed Keith the whiskey bottle and kept the second vodka for herself.

"We like to accommodate. My wife will be home shortly. She got hung up at work. Kid's asleep or I'd introduce you. You mind?" He picked up a sack of pot and a cigar and began peeling off the cigar's wrapper. "You hear what happened to Max T.?"

"Haven't heard from him since graduation."

"He's around." Kennedy bobbed his head and lined the cigar wrapper with flecks of the pot. "Anyway, he was over here the other week, sideswiped a line of trees on his way home. Tore up the side of his truck, knocked off the mirror, lost both hubcaps and bent—bent—his front axle. He had to wait around for a tow truck and shit at three in the morning."

"He drunk?"

"Fell asleep. Said he woke up and was like, 'Hmm, I've landed in some trees.' Hasn't changed since we were kids."

Keith said to Holly, "Max T. was one of our best friends. The three of us spent I don't know how much time hanging around out at the lake."

"Oh yeah?" Holly said. She tucked her feet under her on the couch and eyed Kennedy's joint.

"Boomer's Landing still out there?" Keith asked.

"Nah, they shut it down to Chinatown." Kennedy sparked his lighter and then passed the joint around. "So what are you doing now?"

Keith took the joint. As he breathed out he said, "I had a job down in Florida. Recent job, where I met her." He passed the joint over to Holly.

"You seen your parents yet?"

"Hadn't planned on it."

"You just passing through? Where you heading?"

Keith and Holly looked at each other.

"I don't know," Keith said. "Just taking a trip."

"Nothing wrong with that." Kennedy took another long drag of the joint, and then chased it with a slug of vodka. "I wish I could just take a trip, but I can't do that. I got a wife and kid, so I don't do anything but work. We hang out here most every night." He took another sip of the vodka. "My advice? Don't ever get married. Y'all look cozy and all, but marriage is something else you can't even understand."

"We're not getting married," Holly said.

Kennedy whistled. "That's direct."

"We're just having a good time," Keith said.

Kennedy shook his head. "Well as long as y'all are both enjoying yourselves. You know what you ought to do, you ought to drive on up to Manhattan. You ever been there?"

"Never been out of the south," Keith said.

"I have," Holly said.

"Oh yeah?"

"With my dad on one of his business trips."

"Manhattan?" Kennedy asked. "I went up there once, with my family. Came home with a Gucci t-shirt and a new appreciation for the rednecks below the Mason-Dixon line. You're a smart man, for never going north."

"Didn't you just recommend it?"

"Hell, I don't know what I'm saying," Kennedy said, and laughed. "Actually, yeah, I do recommend it once in your life. Ask your girl. It's worth visiting once, right?"

"Oh yeah," Holly said, and Keith felt the odd man out in the equation. He wasn't opposed to traveling anywhere the girl wanted to go, but New York never crossed his mind. He figured they'd end up going west, maybe into Tennessee. He'd always wanted to visit Nashville, had a cousin or two in Knoxville.

A baby began to cry from beyond the kitchen. Kennedy got up, unlit cigarette tucked into his mouth, and went back to check on it. While he was gone, Keith put his arm around Holly, and she slid into him, a surprisingly quiet comfort given all they'd been through this week on the road. His foot tapped the coffee table and he wondered if they'd be sleeping on the couch, or a spare bed, or what. The house was a rental, which Keith thought maybe belonged to Kennedy's parents. The dude hung out like a good old boy but came from money, or at least what passed for money in South Carolina's dark corner, which didn't take much.

When Kennedy returned they watched TV in silence for a while. The house was spring-warm. Crickets and other night callers sounded in the immediate darkness, but in the distance, the quick shatter of glass made Keith nervous about the money in their trunk. He doubted anyone, no matter how rough the neighborhood, would do anything with a ten-year-old Impala, especially bust into the trunk, but he still felt a reckoning on the near horizon.

After Holly drifted off, Keith and Kennedy passed another joint back and forth. No more glass broke, nothing but the chirring of insects, so Keith relaxed for a time. Then someone pounded on the door. Keith stirred but Kennedy kept his eyes on the TV. When the pounding strengthened, Keith muttered and got up, unlocked the deadbolt, and opened the door.

A young blonde with a dangerously low-cut shirt and a thick cake of makeup on her face stormed in. "What are you doing?" Kennedy yelled at her, not in an angry voice but rather perplexed by this hurricane now in his living room. The woman wore a fir-green shirt and white pants, the uniform of a waitress down at the Bluebird Café. She carried a white plastic bag with a Styrofoam box in it.

"I locked myself out!"

As she pranced into the kitchen, Keith wondered what frumpy families who patronized the Bluebird thought of her cleavage. The men likely gave her bigger tips, but the women—who knew? The church-going wives maybe wrote her off as a fallen woman, but once you got past the rampant gossip and judgment, southern towns could be remarkably accommodating to the daughters of their own.

"Goddammit, can't you use a key instead of making all that noise?" Kennedy asked.

"No, goddammit, because I left my keys here," she yelled from the kitchen.

Kennedy turned to Keith. "You see that door? You see what she did the other day? She locked her keys in, so she broke the goddamn doorknob to get back in. Now all we got is our deadbolt, and she can't even deal with that."

"Shut your face," she said, stumbling back into the room, carrying the bag and box. She flopped onto Kennedy's lap and pulled out a chicken fried steak sandwich. "Who're our guests?"

"You remember Keith, from school."

"Hell yes, I remember Keith," she said, though Keith had yet to place her. "I'm Leesha," she said. "I was a year younger than you."

Keith studied her, but she seemed not to care whether he knew her or not, nor what Holly's name was, nor why they were there or how long they were staying. Kennedy lit his cigarette, and Keith asked him what he was smoking.

"I always go with menthols," Kennedy said. "Keeps my lungs clean."

The baby cried again from the other room. Leesha continued snacking on her sandwich, and Kennedy let his cigarette burn and kept his eyes on the TV. The baby was still crying a few moments later, so Kennedy said to Keith and Holly, in the same tone you might tell someone you preferred red wine to white, "We're not bad parents. The kid's always crying, and he needs to learn to be independent."

With her mouth full, Leesha said, "You're just too lazy to check on him yourself."

"I was just in there. He cried, and then as soon as I walked in the room, he shut up. He needs to learn. You're so concerned, go check on him your own self." To Keith, he said, "He's always crying, and the second one of us goes back there, he stops. He needs to just go to sleep already. It's late."

It grew later still while the four of them sat there, none with a thing to say. Leesha finished her sandwich and announced she was going to bed and asked if Keith and Holly were staying the night.

"We got a spare bedroom anyway," she said. "You're welcome to it."

"Appreciate it," Keith said. "We've been on the road all day."

Kennedy showed them to the kitchen, the bath, their bedroom. "I'm going to sit up a while," he said.

Holly went on back, but Keith stayed up with his old friend. They smoked another joint and took to sipping liquor. When the TV went to static, Kennedy turned on the radio to a pop station that played the latest from the Eurythmics, Madonna, Duran Duran, weak tunes that depressed Keith with their gloss. Synthesizers were surely a sign of the Last Days. It was a race between artificial intelligence and a nuclear winter, each just around the corner. You could hear it in the flat rhythms of computer-generated sound, the glory days had passed.

"Savannah didn't work out for you?" Kennedy asked.

"Wasn't for me."

"Least it got you out of the county."

"For a while, it did."

"You staying?"

"We'll probably head on tomorrow."

"Then it got you out. Everyone comes home for a visit. Long as you don't marry the first girl you knock up."

"How did you end up married with a kid?"

"I told you, I married the first girl I knocked up. Easiest way to keep her father from coming after me with his twenty gauge."

Keith swished whiskey around in his mouth. He'd drunk half the bottle without intending to. Must have been the stress of life on the lam coupled with a return to his hometown. He'd gone off as far as he could at eighteen, because that was what you were supposed to do, leave home. It never occurred to him simply to stay put, to find work at Duke Power or Milliken. He'd never been a self-reflective planner, but had floated along like driftwood and finally beached in South Florida.

"You ever think about your immortal soul?" Kennedy asked.

Keith swallowed. "Not if I can help it."

"Remember when we went to that cola wars festival, at Springs Mill Church?"

Keith wished he'd forgotten, a Baptist youth program's bait and switch. Come for games and soda on a Friday night, then listen to a sermon about how you were damned but could still repent. Why this mid-twenties youth leader thought he had the keys to Keith's immortal soul, he'd never know, but he'd not felt right since. "Why do you ask?"

"Just remembered it, is all," Kennedy said.

It seemed there was more on his mind, but Keith wouldn't pry. Too many landmines. They'd spent many an evening talking church or politics, and came down on the same line in many respects, but Keith felt like a fraud. Easy to dismiss Reagan and containment, Jesus and salvation, but difficult to shake a lingering suspicion in his bones that he was in fact a sinner on the road to Hell. His parents were thoroughly Baptist, gentle (if slightly judgmental) souls who tiptoed around the politics of religion, abortion and homosexuality. The father a minister, so they'd brought Keith to church all his life, but it occurred to him now they'd never actually asked him what he thought about his immortal soul. Had instead simply given him a bible at five years old and spoke often of accepting Jesus into his heart. Father and son, his mother the holy ghost in their familial trinity. Keith's father kept his own bible in a drawer in his nightstand, and his mother read nothing but paperback mysteries, books she churned through thanks to a weekly trip to the public library. They were kind, simple folks, conservative, good neighbors, and so thoroughly introverted they provided no models of social life for Keith. Instead, he'd gleaned what he could from Kennedy in high school, or Big Duck in Savannah. He felt he had no wisdom about the meaning of life but at least some sense that his true life was just over the horizon.

Neither friend spoke again for a long while. They polished off the bottles, and Keith stumbled into bed with Holly and slept a dreamless sleep, a four-hour blackout that ended abruptly at four in the morning. He lay shaking and feverish, clammy with the mild throes of a looming hangover. The girl snored softly beside him, a furnace of angled bones. Before dawn he rose and went out and smoked a cigarette on the back porch, which overlooked a copse of trees. His hangover had settled in but wouldn't debilitate him all day, though a shower and a shave and a plate of bacon would help. Out of nowhere, he thought of Jesus. Carolina was the land of crosses and churchyards, billboards and cemeteries, all the stark reminders of death and the need for salvation. This was no country for young men, men full of earthly desire and human error. To be back in Six Mile, to come home to his parents, seemed like defeat, when anyway there was no going home, not with a sack of cash in the trunk and a female time bomb in tow.

A helicopter whirred somewhere in the distance. He wondered if the bodies had been discovered yet, if a manhunt were underway, how long it would take investigators to trace the damage his way.

Curiosity overtook him, so he lit another cigarette, hopped off the porch, and walked around to the Impala. He popped the trunk, opened her duffel bag. He'd been expecting clothes and makeup and maybe a bag of cocaine, but he found bricks and bricks of hundred-dollar bills. He took a step back and looked around. There had to be more than a million dollars in there, maybe several million.

He sat thinking about it for several moments.

When you took this kind of money, he knew, people came after you. No wonder B.D. came after him. He wasn't sure if her father worked for Mr. French or some other South Florida kingpin, gangster, or drug mule, but this was not an insignificant ten grand. This was murdering money. The question was: who would they send next? And could they find him in Six Mile?

He picked up the gun, a heavy, greasy automatic, which was the extent of what he knew about guns. The weight of the pistol surprised him. He aimed it at a tree in the distance, pictured the way the bark would splinter if he fired a bullet into it. He didn't know how to fire the gun, wouldn't know how to defend himself if anyone came after them, so it made him feel safer to tuck the gun in the spare tire well, out of sight.

An engine backfired in the distance.

He jerked up, looked around. Tomorrow would be a breaking point with Holly, the girl unhinged and a danger to everyone. He crept back into the house, rummaged through the kitchen and found an empty paper grocery bag. He returned to the car and filled the bag with the cash from Holly's duffel bag, pulled out one stack of bills and stuffed them in his front pocket as a contingency.

He slammed the trunk shut and looked around again. No one was about.

He folded down the top of the grocery bag and circled the house. He found the entry to the crawl space and stuffed the bag in a corner under the house. In the morning, after Holly had taken the keys and driven off while the others slept—a fitting move for an outlaw—he would feel for the stack of cash in his pocket, debate whether to retrieve the grocery bag, and ultimately opt for a ride from Kennedy to his parents' house. The prodigal son home with his tail between his legs. For now, though, he returned to bed and curled against the girl and focused on his breathing, tried to relax and eventually slept through what remained of the merciful dawn.

He was down deep, below dreaming, when the girl stirred and slid out of bed. She listened to his snoring as she slipped on a cotton dress and sandals. Then she noiselessly grabbed the car keys from the dresser and crept out the back of the house. Seeing where Keith had come from, meeting his friends and sleeping in rural South Carolina, had worn off the magic of their adventure. She had no plan, only knew she was not meant to stay here. She was busy congratulating herself for waking early and successfully sneaking out of the house, so she didn't notice Kennedy on a rocker on the front porch, cigarette in hand, bemused expression on his face. He watched the girl drive off, took another drag of his Camel Light, and leaned his head back to wait for night's end.

26

The girls were of no help. Lisa and Nicole, Holly's closest friends in school. Falcon contacted their parents, who agreed to allow him to interview the girls together with the families present (they'd already been interviewed by the police, also to no effect). Falcon met them at Nicole's house, and the girl's mother offered him coffee and said how terrible it was that Holly had gone missing. The girls sat on the couch and said little. Did they know where Holly had gone? No. Had they seen her the night she left? No. Did she have a boyfriend? No. Any idea where she might go? None. After half an hour, Falcon thanked them for their time, thanked the parents, and fled the neighborhood. He'd never felt comfortable around teenagers, could never gauge just how much they understood about the world. When he'd been seventeen, he'd felt wise and invincible, but by the time his own children came of age, they seemed dangerously unprepared for the world's perils. Now he believed anyone younger than thirty to be playacting in the world. He needed to get out of his own head and was immensely relieved when, upon driving to West's house on Saturday afternoon, the man answered the door in his bathrobe, eyes bloody and face haggard. "Tell me you're here with good news," he said as he opened the door for Falcon.

"Nothing yet. No one I've spoken to knows anything about your daughter." He followed West into the den and set his briefcase on the coffee table. The man fixed himself a screwdriver.

"No thank you," Falcon said to the offering. He lit a Pall Mall. "I talked with Holly's friends today. It sounds like she hadn't taken the divorce very well."

"What kid does?" West asked. "I grew up in a 1950s sitcom, so no one ever got divorced in my neighborhood. People these days, my generation, we're all failures as parents."

Falcon said nothing about his own children. Divorce wasn't the only thing to drive a wedge between a father and his daughter. He said, "Maybe you could walk me through the past few months, see if you remember anything unusual."

"Such as?"

"Well, had the girl stayed out past curfew more than usual. Or maybe she came home smelling like alcohol, or cigarettes. Cars driving by. Anything that might indicate she was keeping any secrets from you." Again, Falcon tried to remain focused on West and Holly but couldn't help thinking of his own family, the secrets all of them kept. He'd kept his own secrets, he supposed, his own inner life, and children picked up on those emotional walls.

West slugged his drink and fixed another. "I told you the other day, nothing unusual. Isabel would know better than me, but she just seemed normal and happy."

Falcon stood up and walked to the mantel and studied the photographs on display. An old picture of West with Holly on his shoulders, the girl about ten at the time, the best age for a daughter. He shook his head. "I just can't help but think there's something more going on here, something you're keeping from me."

"Like what?"

"Like where were you the other night? Thursday? I came over here and waited for an hour for you to show up."

"I had a business trip."

Falcon returned to the sofa, sat and rested his arms on his knees. "See," he said, "that's strange to me, your taking a business trip."

"I couldn't get out of it."

"Not even when your daughter's gone missing?"

"Not even if—" West kept his eyes away from Falcon. "We've got things going on at the Artium Group that can't wait. No one is paying any attention to what's going on. Market forces are pushing us into quick action."

Falcon pulled a photograph out of his briefcase. He handed it over to West, who looked at it without saying a word. "You know this woman?" Falcon asked.

West shook his head.

"You can see, she's in your house here."

West continued to stare at the photograph with a blank expression. He took a sip of his screwdriver and dribbled liquid down his face, which he quickly wiped on his sleeve before handing back the photo.

"Another woman came by as she was leaving, though I didn't get her name or photograph."

"Good-looking blonde?"

"You know her then?"

"I was sort of seeing her."

"Was?"

"I'm not sure she'll be taking my calls anymore."

"And this woman?"

"What do you want me to say, Ernie? Are you looking for my daughter, or are you investigating me?"

"I'm looking for your daughter, but you haven't given me much to go on."

"Goddammit, I don't know her anymore." West mopped his head with his hand and looked toward the mantel. "I don't know how far back it goes. Maybe Isabel and I were doomed from the beginning, but somewhere along the way, I got busy with work and she got caught up in her fashion lifestyle, and we just had nothing to tell each other at the end of the day. I lost some money, got into debt, and hid it from her. She kicked me out for lying as much as the transgression."

"I'm not here to judge your marriage," Falcon said.

"Well, my marriage is the root of everything. I've only seen Holly two weekends a month lately, but she turned into a different person years ago, at fourteen. You have kids? Then you know. Hell, we all used to be kids, and we all had to grow up eventually. But when your daughter grows up without you, there's not a whole lot you can tell the private investigator about her whereabouts. Maybe she did have a boyfriend. Maybe she drank and smoked or shot heroin every weekend. Hell, the entire world is getting high."

"Maybe not the entire world."

"But all of Miami is," West said. "Some days it seems this city's got enough drugs running through it to keep us all catatonic to the new millennium."

"Your daughter, Bobby."

"All I can tell you is she robbed me and fled into the night."

"Robbed you?"

West leaned his head back and cursed. "Yeah, I keep a safe in my office. I think she broke in and took some cash before she disappeared."

"You tell the police? Isabel?"

"I didn't know the money was gone until after we filed the missing person report."

"Was there any sign of forced entry?"

"No, but she had a key."

Falcon wondered at the stupidity of this man. With enough money, the girl could be anywhere in the world, when Falcon had assumed she was holed up with a boyfriend across town. Maybe she still was, but the money changed the calculus.

"How much did she take?" he asked.

"I'm not sure."

"Can you give me a ballpark? A hundred bucks? A thousand?"

"Several thousand. I had a stack of cash in there and she took it all."

"But you don't know how much," Falcon said.

West shrugged, unable to carry the lie any further. Lord knows how much money she'd actually run off with, but Falcon supposed it didn't matter. If it was five thousand or five million, it was enough for the girl to do some damage. "I take it this money wasn't yours? The woman in the photograph, she's come looking for the money?"

West said nothing.

"You in trouble, Bobby?"

"I'm all right," he muttered.

"Can I see the safe?"

West quietly led him to the back office, where the safe was uncovered in the floor. He knelt down and spun the dial through its combination and pulled open the door. Empty inside. Large enough to hold a million-plus.

Falcon looked around the office, saw what appeared to be ordinary paperwork—bills, invoices, credit card advertisements, spreadsheets—and ordinary office supplies—pens, paperclips, a stapler, a hole-punch, envelopes. Nothing to indicate West was up to anything beyond your average household bureaucracy.

Falcon would say nothing about meeting with the Feds, nor what he'd learned about Adriana Chekhov. Whatever West was into, Falcon was sure the man knew his daughter was in danger. He suspected the only way he would find the girl would be to figure out what else West was hiding, see where the girl might have gone and with whom, and then try to get her out of harm's way before whatever shoe was hovering overhead dropped and squashed Bobby West. Falcon didn't care about West, but the girl, and Isabel, deserved better.

The first thing Falcon did when he left was place a call to a guy he knew at the airport, a security specialist and former Miami police officer. "I need you to look up a flight record," Falcon said.

"You got anything more to go on than a name?"

"Just that he flew out sometime Thursday and returned on Friday. I don't know if it was commercial or private, or where he was going, but I need you to find out, and I need you to find out if he was traveling alone or with someone."

"Jesus, Ernie."

"Hey, Roger, I've got two clients paying me for the same case-work, so charge what you need to get it done, and fax it over to my office. This afternoon if you can."

"Let me get back to you," he said.

Rather than go to his office, Falcon went down to the central library to read through the news reports of the drug trade, to see if he could get a handle on what was happening in the city around him. Donnie Ray Callahan at the police station or Juan Delgado at the *Miami Herald* might have certain insights, but for now Falcon needed to think. South Florida had long been home to smugglers, who ran rum during Prohibition, marijuana and heroin through the sixties and seventies, and cocaine in the eighties. None of that was a secret, and in fact reports of shootouts in suburban shopping centers had made national prime time news. But something West had said—*the entire world is getting high*—made him think there might just be a connection between his missing daughter, this Adriana Chekhov, and the South Florida drug trade. If West had his hands in anything dirty, chances are drugs would connect. Maybe that wouldn't get him any closer to finding Holly, but it would at least give him a sense of the murky world in which Bobby West might be operating.

He found a whole lot of nothing. In Miami—and in South Florida more generally—the Medellín cartels ran the drug trade, primarily marijuana and cocaine from South America and imported by a network of boats and airplanes into the Keys. There were rumors swirling about the mix of races and ethnicities and nationalities, and who had what drug and what territory. Some reports suggested Cubans had an edge in the heroin market, which ironically boosted Colombian profits due, in one journalist's word, to "synergies." Falcon may as well have been reading *Barron's* or *Forbes*. Innovation, supply and demand, saturated markets, big business. The general consensus was that small-market entrepreneurs in the system were eventually swallowed up by larger players. The business of America, after all, was big business.

The heroin market had taken an interesting turn in the eight-ies. During the Vietnam War, drugs came in via the Pacific. Again, nothing but hearsay and possibilities, but the CIA kept popping up in reports. What was known, in April 1984, was that massive quantities of heroin were synthesized in Afghanistan tribal regions, a major source of employment for displaced villagers and hungry masses still trying to regroup following the exodus of the Soviets and the CIA. A few covert operatives remained to oversee the establishment of light infrastructure, nothing more than dirt roads and a few shanties for chemical processing. It was suspected that a steady supply of heroin was cut and packaged and then shipped into Miami via a secret network of arms dealers and other international operatives. Then it was cut and packaged once again for street distribution.

It was stunning to see how much history had been written on the national pages of the *Miami Herald* and other newspapers. It was all there in plain English, just waiting for someone to connect the dots.

Back at the office, Falcon's fax machine had spit out a copy of a flight manifest from Thursday morning, a direct flight out of MIA to Dulles, two tickets paid for out of Bobby West's expense account for the Artium Group.

A handwritten note on the first page of the fax read, *Call me.*

Falcon dialed his security contact Roger, who said, "You're stirring up some trouble, aren't you, Ernie?"

"Always. What's up now?"

"You get the flight records?"

"What am I looking at?" Falcon asked.

"Your man Bobby West took a flight up to D.C. with a fella named Felix Machado."

"OK."

"It's a slow day down here, so I did a little digging."

"Did you now? Look at you."

Roger ignored him. "Your man Bobby West flies out regularly enough. Sometimes pays for his own tickets. Sometimes they come out of an expense report for the Artium Group here in Miami, and some times they come out of an expense report out of a D.C. agency."

"So?"

"So the D.C. agency? Code for CIA."

"CIA's been buying him tickets?"

"Gets even better," Roger said. "The Artium Group is a CIA front, set up to monitor the Cubans in Miami."

"Ah. Callahan said something about CIA connections. How'd you get all that so quickly?"

"Sources, my man."

"Maybe you need to come work for me," Falcon said.

"Nah, pension's too good with airlines. I show up, run the occasional background check, and read Mickey Spillane all day. Anyway, if you're chasing down a CIA spook, good luck."

"It's his daughter, actually. West and his ex-wife are paying the tab."

"Then you'll want to look into this Felix Machado."

"Oh yeah?"

"There's not a whole lot out about him. Immigration records say he came in with the Mariel boatlift. Lives in a housing project, with no job and no family on record. Lot of those folks, they get a little vocal about Cuba Libre. If your man's CIA and he's hanging out with a Cuban exile, you can bet this fella knows some rough characters over in Calle Ocho. It also seems—" and here Roger paused for dramatic effect.

"What?"

"There's also some indication he's working for Alexander French."

Falcon whistled. "You think there's something going on between French and the Cuban exiles?"

"I doubt they're connected. You ask me, your man Felix just couldn't find a better paying gig. Still, it's interesting enough that I would think it's worth looking into."

"I don't have any other leads," Falcon said. "You got an address?"

27

West returned to the vacant condo complex where Mr. French kept office hours. This time the man in the lobby didn't buzz him up, but instead instructed him to sit on the sofa and wait. A few minutes later, Felix Machado came down and said, "Tell me you're here with more than a low-ball cashier's check, amigo?"

"You've got to call her off."

"Who?"

"Chekhov. She's in town."

Felix squinted at him. "I don't know anything about that."

"Well, go talk to Mr. French. Is he here? Let him know I'll get the money, either from the thieves who took it or an investment from my director in Washington."

"I'm sure you mean well, but come back when you have some results."

"I can't get results if I'm dead, if that woman comes after me."

"I'm sure she's not coming after you."

"I just saw her last night, in a bar near the Brickell building."

Felix started edging toward the door. "Well, I didn't call her, and I'm sure Alexander didn't call her. You've met her, though, so you know she's unpredictable. But keep in mind, she's also in business. She's not going to go against her own self-interest."

West followed him into the street.

"We've got a cargo plane coming in tonight," Felix said, and he looked at his watch. "Lands around two. You're welcome to go with me, if you want to chat more. Otherwise."

"You'll talk to Mr. French? About Chekhov?"

Felix sighed. "You're very high strung, amigo. I know you're under pressure, with the money, but worrying about what Adriana Chekhov is or isn't doing won't help you get the money back. Mr. French might be chasing his own angle, but what you need to be thinking about is how to find your daughter and talk her into bringing the money home, or how to get your Mr. Brown to speed up his advance for the Cubans. Why don't you come with me? You might learn something about the exiles that can help you with your bosses in Washington."

"I understand them well enough."

"You understand America's interpretation of them. You understand an idea of a people, but you don't understand what drives them. If you're so invested in them that you'll bankrupt yourself and your company, you should see everything they're about."

"And watching a shipment of heroin come in will do that?"

"History turns on a dime," Felix said. "Come with me, and forget about Adriana Chekhov for the time being."

They drove through Miami's back streets, along the river district and then up the highway to the airport. West believed he might be shot out on the airfield but he believed he might be shot in a day or so anyway, if the money didn't turn up. They stopped at a dilapidated Howard Johnson that was so close to the runways that the building appeared to shake during takeoffs. The lights of a jumbo jet soared overhead, and they felt the tremors under their feet. West followed him up the leaky concrete steps to a room on the second floor. Felix carried a duffel bag up and banged on a door.

"Might be better if you didn't say anything while we're in here," he said. "No disrespect, but these guys aren't going to know who you are, and they won't give you the time to explain."

"Hey, this is your gig."

Before Felix could answer, a shirtless man with a cigarette dangling from his mouth answered the door. Neither of the men asked Felix about West, either because they trusted him or because he was in charge or because they wanted something from him and lacked the stones to question his decisions. Either way, West was happy to wait by the door of the motel room while Felix went into the bathroom with one of the men. The other man lay on the far bed with his hands crossed behind his head. He kept his eyes closed, but West knew from the rate of his breathing that he was awake, and West also suspected the man had a gun beneath the pillow within easy reach. A young woman lay on the floor between the beds, her leg resting on one of the mattresses, a needle stuck in her foot. Her shorts rode up and West could see her panties. Her leg was thin and long like a gazelle's, and her eyes had that dreamy look that meant somewhere back in her mind, thoughts fizzled like sparklers, or like candles guttering in the wind, on the way to darkness.

The woman grinned at him, and West thought that even in her stupor there was something sleazily attractive about her, the way she held herself, the way she was framed, her lean and flexible body. He tried not to leer, instead focused on the quiet parking lot out the window. Traffic shuttled by on the nearest highway, and the lights from airplanes circled the sky like disoriented shooting stars. When he'd seen all he needed to see out there, he rested against the wall, crossed his arms, and kept his gaze neutral, in case she snapped to attention and wanted small talk. The man on the bed had not moved.

West licked his dry lips. He felt tired but not sleepy, like he'd been up all night and had a Dexedrine tablet at four in the morning to prolong the crash. He said to the man, "You speak English?"

The man opened his eyes, pursed his lips, said nothing.

"*Hablas Ingles?*"

"*Un poco, pero no quiero hablar la lengua del Diablo.*"

"Well, goddamn it, *no hablo Español.*"

The man shut his eyes again. His body never moved, never flinched, just lay there like a palace guard, stone-still security. West tried to listen to what Felix and the other man were saying in the bathroom. They spoke in Spanish at just louder than a whisper, but he caught enough to know it was petty, street-soldier shit. After they'd arranged whatever it was they needed to arrange, Felix returned with a blank face. "You ready?" he asked West. He left the duffel bag they'd come in with and took another with him on their way out.

In the stairwell, Felix grinned, held up the bag, and said, "Another delivery underway. How'd you enjoy your first drug run?"

"Reminds me of delivering pizzas as a teenager."

"You ever skim anything in a job like that?"

"That goes against my values."

"No man is that honest," Felix said.

"You'd be surprised. I like to know I'm doing the right thing."

"Only because you think someone is watching. Maybe you were smart enough to know what would happen if you ever got caught."

"You think there's a difference between honesty and fear?"

"Only one of them is real."

"I'm not sure either of them is," West said.

"That's because you've never been afraid. Or never known when you were afraid."

"I learned all I needed to know about fear in basic training."

"You in Vietnam?" Felix asked.

West shook his head. "Went straight to domestic intelligence."

"You don't know fear then," Felix said as they reached the car.

Felix drove them across the way to the airport, and at a security check he flashed a badge and was waved through to a runway, where they taxied to a hangar away from the commercial area. It was 3 a.m., late enough for air travel to be on hold, the redeyes gone, alarms going off across town for the earliest travelers who would arrive in a few hours. Nevertheless, the airport glowed like a beacon in a lunar landscape, some alien industrial complex.

They parked in front of the hangar a short distance from a Corvair 440 badly in need of repair. Felix got out with the second duffel bag. They met the plane's pilot, a young man who appeared vaguely Arabic, or at least some kind of un-American, though he wore a flight suit with an American flag stitched on the sleeve. Without introducing West, Felix shook the pilot's hand and passed off the duffel bag. The pilot took the bag and loaded it beneath the plane's wing and climbed into the cockpit. The window in the cockpit was down and the pilot sat with his elbow out the window, a toothpick between his lips. He started the plane and began to taxi, and the window stayed down until just before takeoff. Like a toy duck in a bathtub, the plane bobbed and weaved down the runway before sputtering into the night sky. The wheeze of the engine, the groan against gravity, faded to a dull hum.

Felix turned to West and said, "You like how things work in Miami? A phone call in the middle of the night can change the course of history."

West shoved his hands in his pockets. Wind blew across the tarmac. His ears rang. He had nothing to say because he couldn't tell whether Felix was threatening him, or what message the Cuban was trying to deliver.

"Just so you remember, this is bigger than drugs," Felix said. "You may get your loan from your Washington bosses, and it will most certainly help you float with Mr. French. But there are more people in this system than you and Mr. French and Ms. Chekhov. Yours isn't the only life at stake. We're all in it. You, me, my friends in Cuba Omega, those junkies at the hotel. We're all one network. Everything connects. One piece fails—money goes missing, a skim disappears—the whole system fails. Remember that."

"I'm aware of my situation, and of what happens when the money runs dry."

"Let me put it to you this way," Felix said. "There are two kinds of people in the world, those who want to go along and those who want to build something. The go-alongs, they work, they watch TV, they shoot up. The builders are also the destroyers. These are the people who are aware of the big picture and who pull the strings. They write the shows and they import the drugs. They design the system, and we're all a part of it. You won't do heroin? Fuck you. Heroin is nothing. This, amigo"—he waved his hand at the empty runway—"this is what runs the world."

28

On Sunday, Chekhov flew to Savannah and rented a car to visit Keith Sorrells's apartment complex. She wondered if the boy was truly dumb enough to steal $3 million and return with it to his old homestead, but then she was used to dealing with a higher class of criminal, men who covered their tracks and led her on a puzzling trek across three continents, say Montreal to Hamburg to Bangkok. She wasn't sure if he embodied American innocence or the foolishness of the young, but either way she was ready to collect her fee and get out of this backwater nation.

Alas, there would be no easy resolution. That much was clear from the police tape around the apartment complex, the two police cruisers stationed at either end of the parking lot. She circled around and headed a few blocks away, pulled into a drug store parking lot. There she went in and picked up a copy of the daily newspaper, flipped through to the metro section.

"You gone buy that?" asked a perm-frosted clerk from behind the register.

"Just wondering what happened at my apartment this week," Chekhov said, carrying the newspaper to the front counter. "I was away on business, and now there's caution tape everywhere."

"They's a double murder last night. You didn't hear about it?"

"Just got back."

The clerk whistled. She rang up the newspaper and put it in a bag, set the bag on the counter and said, "Whew, it was vicious. Two local boys shot execution-style and left propped up by the vending machines. I live there myself and didn't hear a thing. Woke up Friday with blue lights all over my back parking lot."

"Lot of drama, huh."

"Yeah buddy. That'll be fifty cents."

"Thanks, but I don't need it," Chekhov said.

"Well, why didn't you say so?" the clerk called after her.

Chekhov waved, and the automatic doors binged as she went out.

Back at the apartment complex, she took a chance and picked the lock to Keith's unit. The door swung open into a dark room smelling of bleach and drywall. She clicked on the light in the front hall, shut the door behind her. The apartment was clean. No bloodstains, nothing to indicate anyone had been here recently except the mail on kitchen counter, direct mailers sorted and stamped for this week. The bed was made neatly. She pulled back the covers and found a few long dark hairs on the pillows, the stink of sex on the sheets.

She sat on the couch in the living room for several minutes. Mr. French's notes indicated the boy was from the upcountry, about five hours away. Seemed a fair bet the boy knew better than to go back to Miami, and if he'd caught the two goons here, he'd need to go somewhere.

She locked the apartment and sat in the rental with the windows down for a while, waited for an old Impala to show up. When none did, she pulled out a road atlas and found Six Mile up in the corner of the state. Long drive for no return, but she'd been in this business long enough to get a feel for the men she was chasing, the way a good fisherman knows where to drop anchor. She continued to wait.

At dusk she was on the road out of Savannah, and after midnight she checked into a motel in Clemson, a few miles from where the boy grew up. She took a hot shower in a bathroom that stank of mold, the tub lined with cold ceramic tile. A luxury compared with some of the places she'd stayed but she thought it might be nice to retire soon and spend the rest of her days in civilization, which the Carolina upcountry was not. Before climbing into bed, she peeked out the window, studied the ghost-lit landing and the parking lot, but saw nothing of interest.

The boy and the girl and the money were close. She could feel them. Could almost write the story. Tomorrow, she would drive into Six Mile, visit the boy's parents, find out which friends were still in town, and find the money in a day or so. Mid-week, she would be out of the country, back to brokering plane flights from Amsterdam to Miami, out of the weeds of this sour operation.

29

Falcon kept his own church on Sunday. In the fall he enjoyed a few beers while he watched the Dolphins, and the rest of the year he puttered. Occasionally he would thumb through the bible or put some thought into his soul, but it had been many years since he believed in much of anything. Raised a Methodist in Central Florida, he kept up appearances early in his marriage to Mary Catherine. She wanted to set a good example for the children, so like good Protestants they went to church and had Sunday dinner as a family. You never simply quit believing, but as you aged the world took on its own life regardless of your thoughts about God. Jesus said the Sabbath belonged to man, and he had no truck with the law. Denounced the priests and Pharisees and money lenders with equal vigor.

As one whose job was to uphold the law, Falcon had never fully come to terms with the biblical teachings, had instead kept his faith private, comfortable in the knowledge that at the end of his life, either he would get his reward or his light would be extinguished. There was everything to gain and nothing to lose from private prayer. The children must have been teenagers when they finally raised enough stink about waking up for service, and he and Mary Catherine left them home. Dinner that day had been silent, with everyone in the family adjusting to the new program. Was this a one-off or a permanent freedom for the children? It meant nothing to him, he'd realized that afternoon. Mary Catherine would be disappointed to give up the church—and indeed she'd continued for years afterward, alone—but Falcon and the children had disappointed her enough that she only had enough fight left for her own soul. This had been the mid-sixties, those heady days that changed the world.

Now, twenty years later, neither husband nor wife went to service regularly, though he did accompany her on the major holidays. She'd been too ill for Easter last weekend, and he'd gone for the both of them, sung the songs, feigned the good news but felt nothing of the joyful occasion. Joy was not an emotion he experienced much these days. While his peers seemed to enjoy life as grandfathers, or had found second—younger—wives, or took up golf or joined the freemasons, Falcon continued to investigate humanity's mysteries, which were plentiful. Most of his cases were forgettable distractions. Photos here, court records there, the occasional call to a bounty hunter. Holly Hernandez was different. Her disappearance had shaken him to his core, perhaps because of so many unknowns around the Artium Group, but more than that, it was dwelling in the muck of a parent's worst nightmare. Even bad parents, he was convinced, those hapless souls who took a lackadaisical approach to raising children, even they cared what became of their progeny. For a girl to go missing and for no one but an aged private detective to care, that was tough to stomach.

Falcon had lost his own children, not through disappearance but through a fissure that developed in their adolescence. He'd expected the fissure, saw it as a natural part of growing up, and believed his children would eventually come to respect him, the same as he'd come to respect his own parents, and Mary Catherine her parents. Instead, the fissure widened so rapidly that he and Mary Catherine eventually came to realize the rift was permanent. His daughter had become a psychology major in college, and had come home one Christmas talking about *holistic family strategy,* and becoming *self-actualized,* and how he'd never respected her *autonomy.*

"You never gave us creative freedom as children," she'd indicted him at all of nineteen years old. "We'd be enjoying harmless play, and you were always, 'Cut it out, or I'll beat your ass.' You thought you were ingraining character in us, but instead you were driving us away. Do you never wonder why we don't come home?"

Today the girl lived on the west coast with her creative freedom and would only speak to Mary Catherine, never Falcon, and instead delivered to his wife caustic invective against him. He suspected it was cover for her own failures, because her life sounded like a wreck. In her early thirties, she'd suffered a failed marriage, was in myriad types of counseling, and seemed to be self-prescribing psychotropic treatments for anxiety. What she never learned, it seemed, was that freedom and anxiety went hand in hand. No one promised life would be easy, least of all Falcon who'd tried to set up walls around the kids to teach them boundaries but also to protect them from the abyss of total freedom. While the girl made her feelings clear, the boy was more circumspect about his discontent with Falcon. He at least feigned security, worked long hours and bought big cars and a big house and ate in plenty. He rarely visited home, but he was invariably cordial and gave no indication that Falcon had been a failure as a father or as a man, which seemed to be the common complaint for men of his generation.

Had he somehow failed? What could he have done differently? The older he got, the less he understood about the world. What would possess a teenage girl to take off without a word? How did the CIA and the South Florida financial realm and the drug-dealing underworld all connect? Did they connect?

In the afternoon he found his wife sitting at the table on their backyard patio, and he went out to join her.

Mary Catherine gazed at the drooping palms, which appeared to be weeping into the backyard. "The girl turn up yet?" she asked.

He shook his head. "How you feeling?"

"I'm here," she said.

"Anything I can do? Bring you?"

She gave a heavy sigh and pressed her lips together. It had been like this for the past year, since her diagnosis. The doctors had all been optimistic that her disease's progression would be slow, and she could still enjoy her daily life for some time, but her daily life was filled with fatigue that made them both wonder about what was worth living.

"It's like being pregnant all over again," she said. "I just want to stay in bed all day."

As when she'd been pregnant, Falcon had tried to indulge her, but he lacked the energy he'd had as a younger man, and shut himself away with his work. He'd told her about Holly Hernandez, of course, but he thought it was just another case to her until she asked, "You think the girl will be okay?"

"I don't know," he said. He told her what he knew.

"Must be tough being a young woman today," she said. "The world's a different place from the one we grew up in, and the one we raised our children in."

"You heard from either of the kids lately?" he asked.

She shook her head. They'd not overtly discussed the children in a long time. If he answered when they called, he would shuffle the phone over to Mary Catherine, who would give him a cursory report. Some things were best passed over in silence.

To change the subject, he filled her in on the case, his suspicions of Bobby West's secret dealings with the Florida underground.

"What are you going to do?" she asked him.

"I don't know. See if I can catch up with the Cuban fella. See where he takes me."

"All these lines of investigation," she said.

"I know it's taking me nowhere, but it's what I do. What I've always done."

She returned her gaze to her plants. Her green thumb had given them a bounty of backyard foliage: flowers, herbs, ferns. All was in bloom now, the hibiscus and hydrangeas, the lilies and roses. The smell was overpowering. Although Miami lacked the dramatic seasons, he'd come to appreciate the symbolic nature of spring. He loved the tropical colors and felt blessed to live in such a paradise.

He felt a loosening in himself, like maybe their long marriage could endure an honest appraisal.

"Do you think," he said, but nothing followed.

"What?" She turned to him.

"I don't know. I lost my train of thought."

"You're getting old, Ernie," she said with warmth rather than malice. "We both are, I suppose."

They sat in silence then, as the sun went down on the last ordinary day they would ever experience.

30

The past five days had been among the toughest Bobby West had ever experienced: his daughter missing on Wednesday, cashing out his savings to put a down-payment on the missing $3 million, and his negotiations in D.C. on Thursday. With the knowledge that Chekhov was onto him and that everyone who ever touched the money—West, Holly, Felix—was in danger, he bought a plane ticket to New York and landed there early Monday morning to commune with the loan sharks. He needed an immediate infusion of cash, and venture capitalists ran the dollar's church. While many VCs had come from Christ-haunted backwaters, they had all traded in their God for an intimate knowledge of interest rates, earnings reports, and the ability to sell the devil to a preacher. Now it was West's turn to sell, a scheme to a schemer, with the promise that everyone would get rich.

When the plane flew in, it circled out over the choppy, unforgiving Atlantic. Turbulence stirred the overhead compartments even though the morning was nearly cloudless. Scuds in the horizon, the sky hydrangea-blue. He thought about the plane going down, any number of mechanical errors or a bird in one of the engines, and that would be it. A wing would hit the water first and send the plane into cartwheels, and mousetrap its passengers into the ocean.

Although they could see the shore, it would be too far to swim, and a race against the clock before hypothermia set in. He remembered when the plane in D.C. crashed after takeoff. Only five survived the frozen Potomac, with rescue efforts hampered by the ice, and it still frightened him to think how quickly the initial survivors died within earshot of onlookers. If the plane went down today, West prayed for death on impact, a mercy and a way out of his current troubles.

A few minutes later the plane landed without hiccup and taxied to the jetway.

He took the train into the city and got off downtown at the fabled Wall Street, towering heart of corporate finance. As a younger man, he'd considered coming here to work as a trader, to make his fortune and rise through the echelons of power. This was no world for men with a family, the long hours and high stakes, the searing possibility of failure. One wrong short, one bad purchase, you might find you owed more than the fortune you'd accumulated. In other words, you might find yourself in the same situation where Bobby West now found himself: in the clutches of drug runners and political operatives who only understood the bottom line.

Money was the real drug in the United States of America. The year had opened with predictions of an era of permanent growth. All the leading indexes were on the rise, a businessman was in the White House, and the crises of the 1970s were long forgotten. There was money to be made, and even General Motors had hopes of remaining profitable. On Wall Street, investment bankers had figured out how to bundle and sell mortgage bonds, which opened up a new line of ways for investment bankers to grow fat off the labor of middle America. *Gimme gimme* was the modus operandi. Economists were preening about growth forever while Chevrolet would soon proclaim itself the heartbeat of America. Strong, healthy, sleek. Beneath this veneer, however, you could see a bubble slowly forming in real estate, a crash was on the horizon.

No one foresaw the trouble already brewing on Wall Street, the booming bond market, collateralized debt, a casino of financing that eventually would turn Miami's real estate vacancy rate from

3.6 percent to 22.9 percent. Who would fill the vacant space? The junkies? The exiles? Deep-pocketed optimists said everything was fine, vote Reagan for another term and keep your eye on the Soviets. No one would believe the language of defaults, fire sales, and write-downs would soon enter the national lexicon, but Bobby West understood. He saw the imbalances in his company's budget and knew it was only a matter of time before he faced a steep reckoning. He knew the country was on the edge, and wanted only to finance his way out of trouble before history repeated itself and the house of cards collapsed.

The trouble, as he saw it, was the rediscovery of leverage in the 1980s. Leverage, a financial miracle, was investor-speak for debt, which in the mid-1980s had rapidly accrued in a series of mergers, acquisitions, takeovers and buy-outs—all fine while the economy boomed. But when the crash came, investors would find themselves in a panic. Investment bankers on Wall Street, holding companies like the Artium Group, men like Bobby West: they all weighed the scales against the bubble, but the rule of bubbles was that the higher you climbed, the farther you fell.

He believed he had a parachute to soften his fall, a friend's son who worked for Farrier Securities, a little-known investment bank that specialized in middle market corporations such as the Artium Group. *Little known* meant discrete, which is what West needed in a lender today. West believed the boy might be an easy mark for a business loan. The kid was twenty-three, had thick dark hair and nothing but baby down on his cheeks, a cocksure grin on his face. West felt weathered in the boy's presence, and also somewhat ridiculous. Was he really about to prostrate himself before someone young enough to be his son?

The boy, Jay Stimson, carried himself like he might have played football in high school. Now here he was, on his way to a managing director position and a seven-figure salary. Fifteen years, twenty tops, and he would be among a few hundred men running the country. He waved West into his office and clasped his hands in front of him and said, "It's a pleasure to meet you, Mr. West. My dad told me you were a real card back in the day."

West grinned. "You never forget your college friends. You're probably still too close to those years, but they weigh on you as time goes by."

"I'm sure. I can already tell, they'll be important years for me."

The kid had an edge to his voice. West let the age difference drop, and asked after his father.

"Oh he's fine. You know he never left the Midwest. Doesn't trust anyone from elsewhere."

"That's how we Midwesterners are. We like our college football. We believe in American values. We mistrust cities and the government."

"You know my father," Stimson said. "Well, what can I do for you today, Mr. West?"

"I'm here to see about a loan."

"Certainly. You mentioned the Artium Group to my secretary, but I've not heard of them. The D&B directory only had the bare minimum."

"Sure," West said. "We're a holding company, based in Miami. We've been around since 1959, and we specialize in commercial properties." West opened his briefcase and pulled out an executive summary of the firm's finances and operations, a detailed prospectus he'd drawn up the night before, and a balance sheet. While the kid flipped through the materials, West continued, "What I'm looking for is a short-term note. I was thinking a repurchase agreement on some of our assets."

"Mm hmm." The kid studied the balance sheet.

"You'll see in there we have a number of tangible assets. We've got good long-term profitability and a rock-solid strategy moving forward. But as I'm sure you know from most of your clients, businesses hit these knuckles between periods of heavy growth."

The kid finally set the paperwork aside. "Of course everyone hits a few road bumps, which is why I'm here, and I'm sure we can work something out. Couple of red flags here, though, I wonder if you could clear up. Most businesses, when they hit those 'knuckles,' as you call them, it's really due to one of three things." The kid counted on his thumb and fingers. "Number one, they try to grow

246

too fast and get wrung out. Number two, something happens in the market, outside your control, and requires a short-term bridge. And number three, they change strategy. Now, in each of these cases," the kid went on, leaning back, "I can go over a business plan, or a balance sheet, and see what went wrong and how you're planning to right the ship. I'm thumbing through your materials, but I don't see any of those things at work. The market's steady, and if anything interest rates are in decline. Doesn't look like you're changing strategy, or really doing anything unusual, which leads me to wonder what's gone wrong. Not that we can't fix it. I'm here to help you out, but I need to know the situation."

West bobbed his head. "Sure, Jay," he said. "We are about to change strategy. It's not in the paperwork there, but we've got a line on a local enterprise down there, and we're in acquisition talks. I can't go into the details"—he held up his hands and the kid nodded, say-nothing and secrecy the levers of corporate finance—"but it's a good venture. I need some working capital to strengthen my hand."

"All right, well, we are going to have to go through some of the details. I don't have to see a business plan, but we do have to file a number of forms for regulatory purposes." The kid shuffled the papers on his desk, opened a file drawer. "Can you start by telling me the nature of this venture you're looking at?"

"See, I can't go there. If I say more, it might wreck our deal."

The kid closed the file drawer.

West knew he had nothing, no logical reason to ask for the loan, no responsible reason for the kid to give it to him. He was no different than a beggar in the street, a junkie in need of a fix. The kid was polite about it, never let on that he understood West was serving him a snow job.

"I'm sorry, Mr. West," he said, "but I just don't see how this is going to work."

"What if I made this a loan in my name?" West asked. "I've got an LLC, for occasional consulting work, but I could put a plan together."

The kid's face brightened. "How fast do you think you could put something together?"

"If we could get the paperwork started today, I could fax you something from my office tomorrow."

The kid cleared his throat. "And how much were you looking for?"

"Three million."

"Jesus, man," the kid said.

Sentimentality and the old boy's networks would mean nothing to Stimson, given the circumstances behind West's request, so he said, "I know, I know."

"We loan that kind of money often enough, but not to private LLCs."

"Could it hurt to put the paperwork through? You haven't even seen my business plan." Groveling now, West hated himself.

"I don't know that anyone here would come up with that kind of loan for you. Maybe one of the bigger firms, but I'm not even sure where in the market you'd best be served. Maybe some kind of private equity, away from Wall Street?"

The kid maybe meant simply away from the SEC and the trading floor, but West heard the inference. Not even a Chicago back alley knuckle-breaker could come up with that kind of dough. Even the mob had standards.

"I'm sorry, Mr. West, but I don't see how I can help you."

"Of course, you're right." West stood, and he found himself shaking. Years and years in boardrooms, different meetings with heated moments, tense negotiations with millions of dollars, countless jobs, entire companies at stake, and he'd managed it all in stride. Now, a brief meeting with a kid half his age, and he was shaking and on the verge of strangling someone.

31

On Monday, Falcon sat in his car and watched the Cuban refugee sitting on a bench in South Beach. Felix Machado, allegedly a
member of an outlaw group of would-be revolutionaries and a thug
in the employ of Alexander French. There were so many strings
to West's operation—the partnership with South Florida gangsters,
some form of bad business with the international assassin, the
Cuban financial arrangements, the CIA payroll—any one of which
could have something to do with the missing girl. Or nothing at all.
The girl still could have decided on her own to pack up and hit the
road with some boyfriend. There was no telling. All Falcon knew
was that the more he looked into Bobby West's affairs, the more
room for error he found, a man on the edge on so many fronts.

Falcon breathed heavily and rolled a fist over his chest. Still
promising himself he might eat a few more vegetables one day, worrying the valves in his heart might be irreparably clogged. Too much
sludge in his diet. Not enough blood-pumping exercise. The story
of men in his generation.

The Cuban had been here half an hour, with his backpack, and
now checked his watch every thirty seconds. He'd apparently taken
no notice of the heavyset ex-cop on stakeout. No reason to, this
whole city filled with spies and counter-spies. What was one more
fat man in an ugly sedan?

Around twelve-thirty, another man joined Felix and the two of them began walking down the quay. The other man wore a muscle shirt and walked with the lopsided gait of a bodybuilder.

Falcon got out and trailed them to a recently revitalized strip, where neon lights and Afro-Cuban beats and the sleek young on roller skates created a vibe unlike anywhere else in America.

They went into the Café Arugula, a pleasant shop with six tables on a patio behind a wrought iron fence. The maître d' led them to an outdoor table.

Falcon found a bench to sit on and pulled out a Pall Mall. One more bad habit taking a toll on his heart. He puffed away on his cigarette while tourists promenaded up and down the street. A pair of skates popped on the cracks in the sidewalk, the beat of a metronome as a bodybuilder glided by. A dog took a dump on a patch of dirt from which grew a palmetto tree, and the owner walked off with the dog, leaving the steaming pile of dog shit where it fell.

The bodybuilder friend got up first, and a few moments later lurched out of the café's front door and headed south. Then Felix nodded at someone across the street and got up as well, leaving his backpack in place at the table, and a moment later was sprinting down the sidewalk.

Falcon got off the bench and huffed toward the cafe, already knowing he wouldn't catch up, already knowing he was being lured into a mousetrap. He quit running, but before he could recombobulate himself, the café exploded in a white cloud of smoke and knocked him to the ground.

32

West had booked a room in the Plaza Hotel. He thought he might set up more than one meeting while he was in New York, and he needed to put on the appearances of success. The meeting at Farrier had shaken his confidence, and after leaving Stimson's office, he'd walked all afternoon from Wall Street up to 58th Street, with a stop for an espresso in midtown. His options were limited now. He could wait for the money from Tiny Mark. He could pull an accounting trick to stave off the gangsters for the short term. Holly could turn up with the money.

As he neared the Plaza on Fifth Avenue, he tuned out the lunchtime buzz of clanking trucks and hungry pedestrians and entered the hotel lobby. A porter looked him over, sweaty and ragged from the urban hike, and the desk clerk smiled nervously. He passed without a wave and, as he rode in silence up the musty elevator, he remembered traveling here with his family, years ago, doing the tourist version of New York. Holly had been excited to stay in the hotel where Eloise used to skate up and down the halls. He remembered reading those books to her, embellishing spots, hamming it up for his only child. The memory gave him a twinge. Of course she had to grow up, and into a Miami very different from the sheltered walls he'd provided. They both had lost something, even if she had not run away.

Once settled, he dialed Tiny Mark Brown, left a message with the director's secretary.

A few minutes later, just long enough to make a statement, Tiny Mark returned his call. "Bobby, I haven't even thought about Miami since you left here."

"I know you've got a full plate, but things are heating up down there. I don't want to miss our opportunity with Cuba Omega."

"Down there?" Tiny Mark echoed. "Where the hell are you now?"

"New York. Accounting issue with several of Artium's investors. Nothing to worry about."

"You ever get tired of running a double life? You've got enough experience running programs that you could come up to D.C. Maybe redirect some things in Langley."

"You know Castro's what drew me into the agency."

"Rooting against Castro is like rooting for your Cubs. You'll be dead before anything changes."

"Twenty years ago, I would have challenged you," West said. "Now, I don't know, but we've got an opportunity to move the needle. If that's all I do in my career, I'm fine with that."

If West still had a career this time next week, he would be fine with anything. He'd always thought he understood the forces they—the agency, the American operatives—were up against, but Adriana Chekhov and Alexander French had convinced him the world made no sense. No story, no plot, could explain West's circumstances. It was one bad action, one piece of bad luck, a role of the dice.

"OK, call me in a few days," Tiny Mark said, relenting. There was a click on the line, followed by muffled cursing.

"Hey, Bobby," he said a moment later. "You better get back to Miami."

"Why? What is it?"

"Turn on the news."

PART FOUR

CENTRAL INTELLIGENCE AGENCY
WASHINGTON, D.C.

OFFICE OF THE DEPUTY DIRECTOR (INTELLIGENCE)

7 May 1984

MEMORANDUM FOR: Mark Brown
                   Special Operations, Latin America
                   Counterterrorism

SUBJECT: Events in Miami, Florida re: Robert West

The following news article was published in the Sunday edition of a South Florida newspaper, and may be referred to in the upcoming Congressional inquiry.

Search for Bombing Clues Continues

By Juan Delgado
The Miami Herald

MIAMI—Police in Miami are still sifting the ashes of Café Arugula in South Beach for clues about the attack. What police are calling a pressure-cooker bomb went off in the trendy café mid-day Monday, killing seven and injuring more than 20.

Police are refusing to comment on the nature of the attack or any suspected perpetrators. A spokesperson for the Miami Police Department said officers are pursuing several credible leads based on a preliminary investigation.

"We know this act was intentional. We believe it was carried out by two or more individuals, who may or may not have been acting for any group," said Capt. Patrick Donnelly. "We're asking anyone with information to submit tips to our helpline."

Although Donnelly would not comment further, AP sources inside the police department are referring to the bombing as an act of domestic terrorism. Cubans, Arabs and white supremacist cells are all on the short list of people being investigated.

Additionally, sources say, the bombing resulted from two homemade pressure cooker devices believed to have been carried into the restaurant by two suspects.

While police continue their investigation, the café owner, staff and area residents are trying to rebuild their
lives.

"It's not something you ever expect," said Ellen Parker,
who co-owns Café Arugula with Karen Moore. "We've been in
business more than 10 years, and we have a lot of loyal customers whose support right now has been amazing. People have
come up to us and offered all kinds of help."

Parker would not speculate about the future of Café Arugula. The building is a shell, with debris strewn across the
sidewalk. Neighboring businesses, including a tax firm and a
convenience store, suffered minor damage but remain open.
For now, the café remains a crime scene.

Anyone with information about the bombing is asked to
call the police tip line at 1-800-HELP-FLA.

# # #

33

The city went on lockdown at approximately 4:45 p.m. Monday, April 30, four hours after the café bombing, when multiple suspects were believed to be at large in the city. Local and national media outlets had reported the day's harrowing activities—the bombing, the confusion, the wounded, the dead, the missing, the search, the police, town leadership, Florida government, federal law enforcement (or the initial lack thereof), and a host of related and unrelated issues that all culminated with one big unanswered question: Who had blown up Café Arugula?

Falcon had assisted cops and EMT personnel with triage at the scene of the bombing, and then he'd ridden into the police station to give a statement. "It was a pair of Cubans," he told Detective Callahan. "They were on the payroll for Bobby West."

"Mm hmm, mm hmm." Callahan wrote it all down. Then he pulled out a photograph of a white boy, seated in a chair in some kind of basement, crane tattoo on his bicep, look of terror and defiance on his face. "This your man?"

Falcon shook his head.

Callahan wrote another note and pulled out Falcon's picture of Chekhov, from the night at West's house. "What about her? You remember her?"

257

"She wasn't there either. I would have recognized her. I'm telling you, you're looking for a Cuban refugee, a guy named Felix Machado."

"Mm hmm, mm hmm," Callahan said.

The chief press officer, Capt. Patrick Donnelly, was fielding calls from reporters across the country and attempting to appease his superiors by providing the appropriate spin. "Caught completely off-guard" might be the analytic truth, but "appalled and saddened by this gruesome attack" was a more politic statement. "No suspects" became "several lines of inquiry." And the like. He had not slept Monday night and dreaded the statement to the press Tuesday afternoon to announce the police were declaring a form of martial law, had set up a dragnet around the city, and would be closing in on residents block by block. A private security firm, Navarro Security Company (NSC), would be leading the search, pulling in national resources from other federal contractors and ex-military combatants. Tactical squads stood by. A team of lawyers from Tallahassee had submitted legal briefs with consequences about due diligence, search and seizure, emergency response, freedom of information, and military privileges. The FBI had been briefed, and agents were at the ready, as were the National Guard, the Coast Guard, and a host of private government contractors, mostly ex-military, who had waited their entire lives for such an exercise. No, Capt. Donnelly was having a bad day indeed as the police commanders held secret meetings to determine whether Cubans, Colombians, or other drug-runners were involved, a dragnet mapped out from the swamps to the ocean, logistics and coordination not seen since the Works Progress Administration.

Meanwhile, Miami shut down for business. Offices closed, public transportation quit running, residents hunkered in their homes to wait as though a hurricane were on its way to rain destruction on the magic city. By four o'clock Tuesday, all citizens were off the streets with their televisions tuned to the local news while broadcasting around the nation was interrupted with special news bulletins that showed images of men in attack gear, militarized helmets, assault rifles. They roamed Miami's streets with flashlights and radios. Helicopters swirled overhead. Churning rotors hummed an omnipresent white noise, a constant reminder to stay alert. In City Hall, the mayor sat in his office and muttered, "Christ, Christ," like it was a saving mantra. His army of speechwriters and press officers typed one release after another, refined their messaging, brainstormed on chalkboards, paused frequently to chug sodas and coffee, smoke, and watch the news. Newsrooms lived for this: the ringing phones, the clatter and ding of typewriters, the buzz of impatient editors, the heated discussions about the fourth amendment, warrantless searches, privacy, and security. Terrorism, police theatrics, brutality, racialized violence. Police flashed up photos of a white boy, yet all races were tense with reports of harassment coming from all quarters. Cubans, Castro, Kissinger. The litany of twentieth century American foreign policy.

During all this, Falcon loitered in his office like a gelding put out to pasture. He seldom regretted his lost career with the Miami P.D., but an occasion such as this was a reminder of the service aspect of the job. Miami was his city, and whatever turbulence existed among local tribes, he felt compelled to assist. Plus, he enjoyed what he knew his colleagues were currently feeling, the rush of triage and project management. From the outside, the search would appear to be organized chaos, detectives (and security contractors, apparently) partnered off and sent with patrolmen to city hotspots: South Beach, the remnants of Café Arugula, an abandoned apartment nearby.

Across the river in Little Havana, another squad cruised the streets, went into barrios, harassed shopkeepers, kept twenty-four-hour surveillance on churches, snipers on rooftops. Cops pulled in the known street thugs, hustlers, drug dealers, junkies, petty thieves, and mean-looking dudes, anyone with any kind of a record. While choppers buzzed overhead and the compliant residents remained indoors across the city, detectives interrogated the criminal class for information. No one knew anything about Felix Machado, or whether he (or they) acted alone or for an organization, but in Miami you could never discount anything. In the absence of information, investigators nonetheless turned Little Havana upside down. That left the scene of the crime itself, where Falcon finally ventured on Tuesday afternoon, while the remainder of the city was on lockdown. His labored breathing cascaded through the empty shell of Café Arugula. Falcon had no business here as a private investigator, yet he believed he knew who the man was, and feared this entire situation was a fallout for Bobby West and the Artium Group.

Yellow caution tape blocked off the building. The remnants of the patio and the sidewalk had been dusted for fingerprints, hair, anything that may have been left behind. The salvaged fingerprints did not show up in any M.P.D. databases, but the forensics team had handed them off to NSC operatives, who had access to deep intelligence databases, but as a private security company, NSC had no duty to the public, much less to a journalist's FOIA request, and thus had refused to provide any information, not even to confirm the prints were clean. Meanwhile, federal agents (the FBI, ATF, and Marshals) hovered on the sidelines like jackals around a wounded beast, biding their time before going in for the kill.

In charge now was Frank Navarro.

Falcon met Navarro and two of his agents—Blair and Gibson—in the shell of the café's kitchen.

Navarro clapped his hands together and called, "Ernie! Welcome to the war zone." He was decked out in black cargo pants, a black tactical vest, and had a headset and microphone. "Search and destroy, just like taking back Hué City."

"I was too old for that war."

"Nothing gets your blood racing like when you're under assault. You must know that, or you wouldn't be out here."

"I didn't want to miss out on the action."

"I take it you know who we're searching for."

"Thanks to your agents over there," Falcon said, indicating Blair and Gibson. "You know, I really thought they were just the Feds."

"The Feds are bullshit," Navarro said. He was wide-eyed and blinking too frequently for comfort. He went on, "Even now, they got an army of lawyers analyzing the rules about marshal law. Meanwhile, my guys are combing every neighborhood in the city. What are you worried about, Ernie?"

Falcon shook his head. "All this when you know who did it? Why aren't you looking at Alexander French? Or dig into one of the Cuban networks?" .

"That's not what we were charged with," Navarro said. "P.D. brought us in to find the pair the top brass believes responsible, starting with your mystery Cuban but extending to a whole host of terror groups. Word is a gang of skinheads made it look like a Cuban revolution. Trying to start a race war, something like that."

"I was there, Frank. I saw who did it."

"Credibility, my man. You were working a case and think you saw something. The top brass believe they know better than eyewitnesses when it comes to terrorist investigation. They're floating a name—known criminal by the name of Keith Sorrells. You heard of him?"

"You don't believe that."

"That some dumb American kid blew up the café? Of course not. But I believe the intel came from somewhere, and if we can find this Sorrells kid, we can maybe figure out who's feeding us the B.S."

"You're talking about Alexander French."

"Doubtful. There's too much at stake for him to go around rocking the boat down here. But someone needs to dredge up whatever there is to know in this situation."

"I'm sure you're the man for the job."

"It's because I understand this city. This is the kind of place that pushes you into a corner. Here's what no one understands about violence. Everyone's looking for a cause, for a rational motivation, when we're dealing with insanity."

"It's not insanity," Falcon said. "An event like this starts with a person who wants something."

"In this case?"

"Bobby West, on the CIA payroll, has been working with Alexander French via this Cuban exile."

"Why?"

"I don't know what he's into, but there's money at the bottom of it," Falcon said.

"I'm not the one you need to convince," Navarro said. "I can submit a report, but people well above our paygrade have said we're looking for one Keith Sorrells."

"What happens now?" Falcon asked.

"We keep the city on lockdown till we flush out whoever we need to flush out."

"You think the city's going to stand for that?"

"What choice do they have? A maniac's on the loose." Navarro grinned the grin of a maniac himself.

Falcon gave him a wave and headed back the way he came.

Navarro called, "Find your Bobby West. Whatever business he's got going with French and the Cubans, it's about to go under. Least you could do is warn him. Whatever he was trying to do, he failed spectacularly."

Falcon continued on his way.

Bobby West, Holly Hernandez, Adriana Chekhov, Alexander French, a Cuban nationalist, and a mysterious kid named Keith Sorrells—all wrapped up in the bombing of a South Beach café. All these loose connections in a town Miami's size could mean anything. Everything was related. Nothing was related. Frank Navarro's security team and the constant buzz of helicopters and the otherwise silent city offered neither comfort nor insight.

In the coming days, the drone of choppers never left the skies, and the streets remained abandoned. Traffic lights changed, and neither cars nor pedestrians entered the intersections. Where could someone hide with tactical units kicking down doors, scouring abandoned buildings, entering citizens' homes? Miami offered no lasting refuge, no absolute truth, merely a long wait to be found.

34

Keith hadn't realized how time could slow until he returned home to his parents, the thing he'd most wanted to avoid. After seeing the girl had left with the car and receiving confirmation from Kennedy that, yes, Holly had snuck out in the early morning hours, Keith retrieved the money from beneath Kennedy's house and accepted a ride home. "You can just drop me off," Keith told his friend, who let the car idle a moment in the driveway before leaving Keith with the wolves.

His mother answered the door. Lean-boned with colored hair that appeared almost purple in the dim foyer, his mother was the type to dote and remain entrenched in everyone's business, especially her son's. Her immediate perplexity ("I'm just here for a few days," he told her) shifted to an interrogation ("A friend drove me up from Savannah," he explained, "I wasn't going anywhere in that job so I'm coming back to the upstate") shifted to a cautious joy ("Of course," he agreed, "it's great to be home").

His father, when he arrived home from the office, praised God and asked if his mother had set the boy up in his old room. "She's got me set up fine," Keith said, to which his father nodded and disappeared into his home office. Never a man for words when he was off the pulpit, Keith's father was inscrutable. Happy to see his son? Suspicious of Keith's motives? All knowing of the boy's recent depravity? He never tipped his hand.

Sunday was a day of re-acquaintance: church in the morning, a feast of a dinner, news of Kennedy and the other friends Keith went through school with. Most had either settled into the same line of work as their fathers or had flown the coop to Clemson or USC. Monday, his father went calling on his flock, and Keith watched TV all day. His parents wouldn't splurge for cable, so his options were limited to baseball, *The Price Is Right*, and reruns of *Dallas*. It was like summers in high school all over again. Meanwhile, the grocery sack of money, now in the bottom of his closet, felt more dangerous by the day. He'd seen no mysterious cars, no mustachioed men, no low-flying helicopters, but the small town where he'd grown up had its own eyes, its own mysterious knowledge. People waved from their yards and porches.

Tuesday afternoon he took a long walk around the surrounding farm country, beat-up and weathered barns on the verge of collapse, peach trees, chest-high tomato stakes, mist on distant mountains, hills really, deep green and flattened as though by a celestial hammer. Late in the day he found himself at the country church where his father preached, the man's pickup the only car in the lot. Keith wandered through the graveyard and rested beneath a water oak. No one he was close with had been buried here, but it was quiet and had always felt hallowed, though the bell of a nearby gas station clanged every so often to interrupt any sort of reverie. Streetlights and modern conveniences made it difficult to imagine the lives of those who lay buried, dates going back to the 1800s, Confederate days. His father's office light was on. It had been some time since Keith had set foot in a service, not since he was old enough to drive, but he had vivid memories of the musty and yellowed sanctuary and the comically rotund deacons who served as soldiers in his father's crusading army. How simple were the commands of the church, and how complex his life had become. He went in and sat on one of the pews to see if he could find some small comfort, some mercy, some remembrance of the belief his father felt, that he'd felt as a child.

The sanctuary was empty, and he sat in one of the velvet-covered pews halfway up. Three battered hymnals and a bible were in slots on the seat in front of him, but he had no use for either. He sat there for a long while and stared at the pulpit, the baptismal fount in the background, the cross looming overhead. He told himself a story that he was fallen and in need of Christ. He recognized the scenes on the stained glass—the wise men, Abraham and Isaac, Jesus and Mary, Paul and his conversion—and the glass was bright and beautiful but failed to lift his spirit to something greater than himself. This was no place for a genuine religious experience, you and God and the Holy Spirit conversing in a dank sanctuary. He could hear the rumble of a redneck's truck pass by and knew he was still too close to civilization, or what passed for civilization, to experience anything mystical. And he'd fled too far to rekindle any true communion with his home church.

He stood to leave, but then his father came out of his office and said hello.

"I didn't mean to disturb you," Keith said. "I was on my way home."

"Please, it's no disturbance," his father said. "You're always welcome here. I just didn't hear anyone pull up."

"I walked," Keith said.

"Come in and have a seat—excuse the mess." He cleared the paperwork and a Wendy's bag off the desk. "Too many meals at the desk these days."

The office had a tall window with white mini-blinds. It could have been any dull office, not the space for a preacher to do his work. The bookshelf had a few bibles and several hokey titles about faith and Jesus and Abraham and finding the peace within you.

"The office about like you remember it?" his father asked.

"I don't know that I've been in here since junior high."

"Your mom says I need to clean it up, do some decorating. Make it look more holy, I guess, but I just haven't had the time. How about you, Keith? Did you have an office where you were working?"

"I was mostly out on the road," he said.

His father nodded. "Nothing wrong with that. You remember what the bible says about work? Always give yourselves fully to the work of the Lord, because you know that your labor in the Lord is not in vain. Doesn't matter what the work is, though you want to find something that nourishes you. Sounds like your sales job wasn't it."

"I reckon I'm in transit," Keith said.

"The good book's full of men who spent time in transit," his father said. "Moses, Abraham. They were all in search of the Promised Land. I like to think we have a little bit of that here in Six Mile, if you think you want to come home."

He'd always spoken in terms of what Jesus or the Bible said, like Keith was just another parishioner. The man was an only child like Keith, and perhaps had never had the proper training in how to be a father. If that were the case, should he even have had a child? Where did his responsibilities lie? Did they not teach these things in the seminary?

"I don't know that I'll be staying long," Keith said.

His father scratched his chin. "Anything I can do for you today?"

"I don't know. Like I said, I'm just passing through."

"I could pray with you, if you've got something on your mind."

"I don't guess you've started doing confessions."

"That's a Catholic ritual," his father said. "The priests serve as intermediaries between you and God, but we believe everyone has access to God, if you're willing to approach Him humbly and listen to what He has to say."

"He hasn't said much to me lately."

"Have you asked for help?"

"I don't really know how," Keith said.

"Remember, you're saved for life. You accepted Christ into your heart once, so all you have to do is remember Him there." His father crossed his arms and thought for a minute. "You read the Gospels lately?"

"Sure, couple times," Keith said.

"But have you ever read them all the way through?"

"I guess not."

"It's interesting," his father said. "We all know the stories, but the tellers have different personalities. The picture of Jesus the bible gives us isn't a one-size-fits-all portrait. When I was a boy I used to believe there was one Jesus, and He was the Christ you heard about in Sunday School. But you read the Gospels, and you find out Jesus is just a man. My favorite has always been the book of Luke. Of all the narrators, Luke seems the most honest to me, maybe because he addresses you directly and lets you know he's telling you a story. What's really interesting about that book is we get an extended treatment of Jesus on the road to Jerusalem. That's where we get many of the most famous stories, including the Good Samaritan and the Prodigal Son. I guess I don't have to be telling you all this."

"I've only been gone a couple years. Not like I forgot everything you ever taught me."

"Sometimes I wonder," his father said. "I know we must have gone wrong somewhere, and I've asked the Lord for guidance, but sometimes all you can do is remain humble and wait for an answer to come in good time."

Keith listened to his father ramble and wondered if the man had a point. He'd long ago decided he couldn't tell his father he didn't care what the man had to say. He had bigger problems than Jesus could solve, and whether or not the Lord answered his father's prayers was beyond his concern.

But his father went on, "They never told me this in Sunday School, but Jesus was something of a rule-breaker. He was a real rebel, only he had a cause. He and his followers would go into the grain fields on the Sabbath and enjoy a snack, and the Pharisees would say, 'Wait a minute! You can't be out here on the Sabbath.' But Jesus just told them the Sabbath belongs to man and he would do what he wanted. When I read that story in college, it shocked me. Here was this scruffy, wandering preacher telling the man to stick it you know where. The Pharisees back then had all these rules. We know the Ten Commandments, but good golly they had a bunch of laws. You can still find them in Leviticus. Everything from no meat on Friday to no cheeseburgers. I'm serious!"

Keith cracked a grin but had nothing to say.

"And here comes Jesus to say all those rules don't matter. His only commandments are to trust the Lord and love your neighbor. That's so much easier to manage, don't you think? Anyway," his father said, "my point is you might feel like something's troubling you, like maybe you're in some kind of a jam, or maybe you're just lost in the world. But it's not that hard to find your way again."

He remembered this talk from his childhood, and he remembered the corollary to the forgiveness of sins, which was that sin was real and hell was its punishment. He thought of starting over, washed in the water and born again. He had little faith in redemption but knew he would find no peace here in his old home. He felt nasty and worn, and the almost demonic compulsion to find a bar without drawing too much notice, and enjoy enough drinks to get him through yet another evening. He stood to go and said, "I believe I'll head on."

"Being a searcher is the mark of a *holy* person, Keith. You know what holy means, don't you? It means *set apart*. There are those rare birds who know, and know they know, and the equally rare birds who don't know, and know they don't know. Most of us don't know what we don't know, if you follow me."

"Not really."

"Point is, Jesus was the former. He knew and spoke with authority. All most of us can hope to be is the latter, knowledgeable of our own ignorance." His father scratched his chin again while Keith stood in the doorway. Then he asked, "I know you walked here, but say you get in your car. You know there's the possibility that you'll get in a wreck on your next trip. It's quiet out there, but any of us could get creamed by an eighteen-wheeler in too big a hurry. When you get in your car, either you'll wreck or you won't, but you can't know for sure before it happens. That doesn't stop you, though. Most of us don't sit there and think, as we turn the key in the ignition, that today is the day some maniac runs a stoplight and slams into the side of us. You can't live your life like that. Most of us take our spiritual lives just as lightly. We don't live consciously. We grow stagnant, and our souls suffer entropy. It's all chaos, Keith, you understand? What I'm saying is, I can't save you, but I can point you to He who can. Only you can save yourself, by forgiving and asking forgiveness."

Keith was leaning out the doorway, unable to speak.

His father slapped the table, stood up, and said, "I guess that's enough of a sermon for one day. You want me to give you a ride home?"

Outside, his father started the old pickup and wrangled it into reverse. Neither man spoke on the short drive home, where they found a long gray sedan was in the driveway. His father said nothing as he parked next to the sedan, and Keith followed him into the house. At the dining room table, a redheaded woman sat with his mother, sipping a cup of tea. When the men came in, she smiled, and Keith's mother got up and said, "Keith, your friend Adriana is here to see you."

35

After his unsuccessful attempt to wrangle money in New York, West returned to the office in Miami. He parked on the fourth floor of the parking garage and thought about his next move on the walk across the echoing pavement. He owed Mr. French another deposit and would need the entire $3 million soon. He had no update to give, no way of getting in touch with his daughter. Falcon had been doing research all week but as far as West knew, he'd uncovered nothing of consequence, and he suspected the private investigator was no longer on his side, had perhaps stumbled onto something unsavory about Bobby West. Weren't we all soft, spoiled fruit, with bruises beneath our skin? Hadn't we all sampled the tree of knowledge and made our compromises? Whatever his subjective philosophy, he lacked the money from the CIA or Wall Street that could save his objective self, and his legal options for pulling cash out of the Artium Group were dwindling. Matter of fact, he'd already slid over the edge and was now on the verge of losing his last life-saving grip.

He got in the elevator and turned around. As the elevator doors closed, he thought he saw Adriana Chekhov sitting in a van, eyeing him silently. Then the doors cut her visage off, and as he rode to the ground floor, he debated whether to go back to double check, but decided he wasn't ready to confront her if she were there. No one had been tailing him since he'd returned to Miami. The highway into Brickell had been empty, the parking garage a dead zone. Chekhov couldn't have been behind him, and the odds of her staking out the office had to be slim to none.

His office building was remarkably quiet, and people—what few were here—seemed to speak in hushed tones, hunkered low in their cubicle corridors. He imagined everyone was nervous about the bomber on the loose. The HR director may have sent a memo out to send employees home, which was fine by West. Vicky was not in, so he let himself into his office and locked the door behind him, set his briefcase on his desk, and fixed a drink. He stared out the window at the empty city below him. The blue lights of a squad car flashed on a nearby street corner, but otherwise he saw no police activity.

He called Tiny Mark in D.C.

"Good God, Bobby, are you back in Miami yet?"

"Got in late last night," West said. "I take it you're following the news here?"

"Following? We've got agents up and down the east coast armed to the hilt and on alert in case this incites a war with Cuba, or the Soviets. You heard from your contact in Cuba Omega?"

"No, why?" West asked, though he saw where his boss was going.

"Have you not been paying attention? Who do you think set off that bomb?"

"I thought it was someone local," West said. The news had reported a young white male, and the sketch artist's depiction was nothing like Felix.

"The locals are chasing after some kid, but our intelligence says it was a Cuban nationalist trying to force our hand with Castro."

West cursed and sat down. Of course it had been Felix. Café Arugula was part of the Artium Group's business holdings, so this was a message—what Felix had hinted at the night he took West out to the airfield. West understood now that there was no escape.

"I presume you know what this means, if it was the contact you've been funding," Tiny Mark said.

"I don't see how it could have been him, or what he thought they would get out of it," West lied.

"Did you promise him money was on the way?"

"He was there. He knew I'd pitched you the idea."

"I must have given something away," Tiny Mark said.

"The money was never coming, was it?"

"You didn't need to know that."

"Felix didn't need to know that," West corrected him. "I'm trying to manage my agents, but I can't do it if I don't have all the information I need."

"It's all moot now," Tiny Mark said. "Now we're on damage control, for the agency and for all of us. Speaking of, I presume you're up to speed on everything with the Artium Group?"

"How do you mean?"

"Your financials."

"Everything's fine," West said.

"Good, because we got a call from the SEC. They were about to prepare an audit, and had called the administrator on record. Thank God our team here was able to talk them down for national security, but we have to shut it all down by the end of the month."

"Wait, what are you talking about?"

"I'm talking about whatever's going on with our Wall Street investors," Tiny Mark said. "Someone got suspicious and took a closer look at our account statements. I trust you that it's all together, because if it's not, you might find yourself in front of a grand jury."

"I'm still confused." West pinched the bridge of his nose.

"Bobby, the Artium Group's finances are toast. No one there can untangle the mess you've got in your accounting logs, and I don't want to know why you were in New York over the weekend or who you were pitching. But the easiest fix is we're shutting it down and having a fire sale of its assets. Meantime, I need you to chase down your Cuban friend and make sure he's contained. Keep him out of the hands of local authorities. We're going to have to get him on a plane out of the country. Maybe back to Cuba."

"Can you slow down a moment?"

"Dammit, Bobby, have you not been listening?"

"I have, but have you already initiated anything with the Artium Group?"

Tiny Mark was silent for a moment. Then he said, "Where have you been? The HR team should have sent everyone home. You'll need a core staff to wind down the payroll, and I'm leaving it to you to get yourself out of the accounting mess. I don't even want to know what's on those books. Just clear them, do you understand?"

Without waiting for an answer, Tiny Mark hung up on him.

A minute later, Tiny Mark called back. "Look," he said, "I'm going to give you a number. I know there's a lot of political horse-trading down there, so maybe this will help."

West took down the information from Tiny Mark. Then he put his head on his desk and lay there for several minutes and thought of nothing. It was a blessed peace he hated to end, but eventually he sat up and flipped through the paperwork in his files, gnawed on his lower lip. The majority of the Artium Group's assets would be easy to unload. They'd originally bought businesses useful to the CIA—boat shops, gun shops—but had their hands in enough profitable businesses now that West could separate everything and pay off most of his investors. Trouble was, the one tangle he couldn't unwind were the series of repurchase agreements he'd initiated the other day, the finance he'd buried off the balance sheet. He would have to buy them back, which would take away the company's excess liquidity. That meant he would have no options for paying back Alexander French, which meant, worst-case scenario, he would be a dead man.

He drove in from the office to Coconut Grove and turned into Mangrove Estates, his old house where Isabel and Holly still lived, a house Isabel could not afford and for which West would continue to be stuck with the mortgage payments until death did them part, it seemed. After pulling into the driveway, he got out and inspected the yard. His yard. Isabel had a landscaping crew come in, so the lawn was in decent shape. The fence could use a new coat of sealant, but overall he felt his property value had been well maintained.

The house even may have appreciated a bit over the past few years. Couldn't rule out a source of income.

He let himself in and called out, "Hello! Isabel, hello!"

She thundered into the foyer with blood-streaked eyes and her hair in a bun. "You can't just let yourself in. Who do you think you are?"

"I wanted to check on you, see if you'd heard anything. And how you were doing after the bombing."

She took a breath and asked, "And where've you been?"

"I had to go to New York, for business," West said.

"That's just great."

"You talked to Ernie Falcon this weekend?" he asked.

"Haven't heard from him." She looked at him with what you might almost mistake for concern. "Are you all right, Bobby?"

"Just worried," he said. "About all of us."

Isabel cocked her head toward the door. "You know your way out."

West and his women: Isabel, Holly, Diana, Vicky. They would drive a man to drink even if he weren't three million in the hole to a South Florida gangster and an Israeli assassin.

36

The boy's parents stayed out of the way, in the back office, muttering quietly between themselves. A cross hung on the wall in the dining room, the house cramped and smelling faintly of plaster and dust. The boy's mother had been accommodating when Chekhov showed up at the door, said she was an acquaintance of Keith's, and was here on a business venture.

"Do come in," the woman said. "I'm Mrs. Sorrells, Keith's mother."

"I don't want to be an imposition, if Keith isn't home," Chekhov said.

"He should be back shortly. He's gone for a walk. Always liked his exercise. Can I fix you anything? Cup of tea?"

"That would be lovely."

The house had dark wood paneling in the living room and meaningless figurines and crystals in a glass case near the foyer. The boy's mother was not all that much older than Chekhov, and by the way she dyed her hair it was clear she very much wanted to play a role in the world, though her options were limited, in this corner of the planet, to community bake sales and fall festivals.

They only had to wait a few minutes before Keith and his father arrived in the pickup truck. The boy's face fell immediately as he realized what must have caught up with him.

Jon Sealy

Chekhov smiled and said, "Hello, Keith."

If he was surprised to see her, he hid it well, gave nothing away.

Silence continued until the boy's mother said, "We'll give you two some space," and she motioned for the boy's father to follow her out of the room.

"Have a seat," Chekhov said when they were gone. "You know who I am?"

Keith shook his head but he sat anyway.

"Or what I'm here for?"

He nodded.

"You know," she went on, "I travel a good bit for my work and therefore have heard many of the different ways in which people deal with their own mortality. Philosophers declared God dead a hundred years ago but much of the world has not gotten the message."

"I'm not worried about God," Keith said.

"Nor should you be. I'm not here by divine edict." She tapped the table a few times. "I can tell you that while French philosophers today debate the meaning of objects in our world, and whether those objects even exist, you and I know this table sits between us. A table is a table, and its essence is beside the point. The true point is you have a great deal of money that does not belong to you. We could debate ownership and free society, but I would just as soon you set the money on the table for me and I move on."

The boy said nothing, and it was unclear whether he even understood what she was saying. Perhaps her accent had grown thicker as she'd waxed philosophical. In truth she was bored with the entire affair. Helicopter rotors thumped in the distance, and she knew she needed to get moving.

"Perhaps you have the money in your bedroom?" She slid the chair back. "I've come all this way. I don't mind taking a few extra steps."

He still said nothing, so she pulled a knife out of a sheath on her leg.

"This can be quick and painless, but it won't be silent." She lowered her voice. "If I have to slit your throat, I'll have to slit your

276

parents' throats as well, which I will do. A knife is a knife, and does its work efficiently. Is this your bedroom? The money here?"

She started for the bedroom off the dining room, heard something bump in the back office, and wondered if she needed to kill them all regardless.

"In the closet," the boy said quietly. "On the floor."

She re-sheathed the knife and found a paper grocery bag filled with stacks of hundred-dollar bills. No time to count it but she'd seen enough stacks of money to know it had to be close to the right amount. When she returned to the dining room the boy had not moved, but sat mutely like an animal shocked so many times by a cruel scientist that all the lights had faded from its eyes. The helicopter rotors had faded so perhaps the boy had a respite. A head start from whatever agency had tracked him here. Mr. French had sent her on the trail to recover the money, his deposit for the next drug shipment. No money, no delivery. No delivery, that was the end of the operation. Made no difference to Chekhov—she had other obligations and opportunities—but Mr. French had incentive to come after the boy himself. Plus, with the bombing in Miami, other forces had entered the fray.

She left him in a state of shock at his dining room table, got into her rental car, and eased out of the drive. On the highway she passed a row of black Broncos careening into Six Mile. She passed hay fields and electrical infrastructure and several country churches and pulled over into a gas station named Maw's. A cross-eyed fellow sat behind the register and grinned at her stupidly before asking if he could help her. "Telephone?"

"All we got's the payphone out front."

"You got some quarters?"

She handed over a dollar and accepted the quarters in exchange. Then she went outside and held the phone to her ear, waited for a helicopter to pass overhead, humming north toward the boy. Then she dialed Tiny Mark Brown in Washington, D.C., to tell him she'd recovered his money and ask what he wanted her to do with Bobby West.

37

While the city remained under the watchful eye of NSC surveillance, Falcon tried to find Chekhov. The Cuban bomber was a dead end, but if he could find the redheaded woman before she found West or the daughter, perhaps he could get a line on where the girl was and bring her in before anyone else got to her. It was clear now she'd run off with the boy, for whatever reason, and had put West in a jam with the missing money. Falcon had no illusions that he could help West, or any interest in helping a man who had gotten himself into such a predicament, but he still believed a teenage girl could be redeemed. Maybe not a young woman, like his own daughter, but surely a teenage girl was not beyond the Rubicon of a decent life.

He pulled into the Blue Yonder, the motel where he'd trailed Chekhov that first night he'd seen her at Bobby West's house. If she were still in Miami, this was the only place he knew to look. He had no plan as he strolled over to the front office, his detective's license in his wallet, a gun in his glove box. If he found Chekhov here, he knew he would be unable to bring her in, and knew she would have no answers for him. He just wanted to see her face and hear her voice. She was at the heart of it all, and he believed only she would be able to offer him a sense of closure.

The office was staffed with a lanky young man with greasy and curly hair, flipping through a copy of *Easy Rider*, his feet on the

278

desk. He kept his feet up even when Falcon came in and leaned over him.

"You need a room?" the dude asked.

"Actually, I'm looking for one of your guests." Falcon pulled his license out of his wallet. It wasn't a badge, but it looked quasi-professional, and at least signaled he was on genuine business. "A woman," he continued. "Single. Red hair. Checked in about two weeks ago?"

The dude pulled his feet to the ground and squinted. When Falcon pulled out two twenties and slid them over the counter and said it was important, the dude said, "Yeah, she's checked in a week at a clip. Hasn't let our maid service clean the room. I was actually waiting for her to come back, because we've got board of health regulations that say we have to at least inspect the room, but I haven't seen her in a day or so."

"She's probably not coming back."

The dude shook his head.

"Why don't you let me take a look, and I'll let you know how the room is when I'm done," Falcon said.

The dude looked over his shoulder to the parking lot, and then he got up and took a key from the shelf, tossed it over. "Don't linger," he said. Then he sat back and picked up his magazine.

Falcon looked around the barren parking lot before heading to room 9.

The room was dark and cold as a morgue, and the light and warmth from the open door did little to alleviate the immediate sense of gloom he felt upon entering. He switched on a lamp and checked the thermostat, which was set at fifty-eight. The AC whined from beneath the window, ruffled the drapes.

The room was otherwise in order. The bed was made and the towels were hung on the hooks in the bathroom. There was a black bag in the bottom of the closet, and inside were a number of handguns and rifles. He backed away and continued to look around at nothing. He sat on the foot of the bed and wondered what he was doing here. He'd been hired to find Holly, and no thanks to his investigation, the girl was still out there. West had gotten himself in over his head, but that was not Falcon's concern. In his days as a police officer and now as a private investigator, he'd trafficked in the worst of human intentions. He still believed that despite the fringes, most people were basically decent, but even the best of the lot could be their own worst enemies. Luck, good and bad, was contagious, and Bobby West had caught a deadly strain.

Just as Falcon stood to go, two agents in drab suits entered the room and shut the door behind them.

"Who are you?" the first asked. The other stationed himself at the window and peeked outside.

"I was just leaving," Falcon said.

The first agent put up his hand to stop him. "You have any ID?"

"What about you?" Falcon asked.

The man pulled out a badge for NSC security.

"It's okay, fellas. I used to work with Frank Navarro." Falcon pulled his investigator's license out yet again. "Looks like we've missed Ms. Chekhov."

"How do you know about her?" the first agent asked without looking at Falcon's license.

"Couple of your colleagues told me all about her the other week. You're trying to catch her, you're likely too late," he said again.

The other agent came over and frisked Falcon and, finding nothing, said, "We have reason to believe she'll be back."

"Well, if you find her, give me a call, will you? I'd love to talk with her about Bobby West."

"What do you know about Bobby West?" the first agent said.

"Not a thing," Falcon said.

38

The congressman had an evening engagement, black tie dancing and schmoozing to do, so he was not excited to meet with Bobby West, even though Mark Brown had called in several favors to set up the meeting. Brown was of the old Yale school of espionage: he innocently believed it was his civic duty to make the world safe for democracy, and felt politics was merely a means to accomplish moral ends. He should have known better. Wall Street was a more powerful entity than the government these days, so decorum compelled a man to chase money rather than ideals, which is exactly what the congressman was good at. The government was pouring a never-ending stream of money into intelligence these days, and the congressman was beginning to pick up on quiet grumbling about deficits and the cost of the Cold War. It was not expedient for him to be meeting a representative of the CIA.

Bobby West showed up at the congressman's office in Tallahassee two days after the bombing of Café Arugula. By now it was clear nothing would come of the Cuban connection. No one was looking for Felix for the bombing, and all the money West had funneled to Mr. French had been for naught. Everyone understood Holly had run off with the money, perhaps with a boyfriend, so the question was who found her first—Mr. French, Chekhov, the Navarro Security Company men—and what each party would do if they found her. If the boyfriend had any sense they were after him, he ought to be thinking about Canada.

The congressman was a young-looking man with black hair and horn-rimmed glasses. He had something of a reptilian head, something about the way his hair slicked back and the shape of his face, it just said "swoop," like he was driving down the turnpike at eighty miles an hour with the top down. His lip had a curl so that you couldn't be sure of the difference between a smile and a sneer. He led West back to his office, which was surprisingly small and cramped, no bigger than Bobby's own office at Langley, an office he hadn't seen in three years. The congressman's was overrun with files and receipts and folded-up pieces of paper sticking out of hastily torn envelopes. The room was hot, and the Capitol building was old and dingy, with ugly brown tiles on the floor that needed a buffing. West felt like he was walking into a Department of Social Services office, some lowly building bearing scars of overwork, like a battered briefcase left out in the rain. Surely this was not the office of a U.S. Congressman.

But it was.

"So?" the congressman said, offering him a seat.

"We know it was a Cuban exile."

"You do, huh?" The congressman sat across from him and put his foot against the corner of the desk. He leaned back and clasped his hands together. Cocky young thing. Before West could go on, the senator took control of the meeting, said, "I tell you, I got a call today from Alexander French."

West listened.

"He told me he had some information about this bombing. He told me he didn't believe it was the Cubans, but that someone from the federal government might try to lay the blame on them."

"Me."

The congressman smiled. "Looks like it. Now ordinarily I wouldn't take the word of a gangster to save my life, but he had specific details that led me to believe he was telling me the truth."

"Do these details have anything to do with a campaign contribution?"

The congressman flashed teeth and said, "Now that's out of line."

"Look, with due respect, you're telling me you got a call from Alexander French, a known gangster, as you call him, and you're telling me one phone call and you're willing to trust his word over a representative of the federal government that you serve? Of the Central Intelligence Agency?"

"Not by itself, no. But I passed this tip along, and as we speak the Justice Department is making a bust in South Carolina. They believe they found the terrorist, a disgruntled ex-employee of Mr. French's."

"You're kidding me."

"He's been on the road for a few days, was holed up with his parents in South Carolina. They're going to bring him in, see what he has to say, but it looks like this café bombing case will be closed by the end of the week. Now if you'll excuse me."

The congressman rose, and West sat in his chair and stared at him. After a moment he got up and left the room.

Downstairs, he placed a call to Mr. French, who answered on the third ring.

"This is Bobby West."

"Bobby, hello. I've been trying to reach you."

"I bet you have. What are you playing here?"

"Pardon?"

"I'm in Tallahassee, and I've just been told that they caught someone for the café bombing, and the feds are rounding him up now."

"My, that was fast."

"Alexander. What happened? I thought I had time here."

"Well, I spoke with Adriana, and she wasn't any keener than I was to have lost the money. She offered an approach, and it sounds like she found her man. Your robbery provided a very good scapegoat to keep Felix out of the news."

"But what's the angle?"

"The angle is you fucked me, Bobby. You let this kid make off like a bandit with my money, and instead of taking responsibility for it, you hemmed and hawed and tried to cut deals with the CIA, Wall Street, and now Congressman Rich. Who do you think you were working for here? I've got a legitimate, transparent business to conduct down here, and I can't have any half-wit messing around with a good thing."

So that was the end of it. Those months of money laundering, of hoping the finances might help him draw more out of his director, or that Felix might offer something about the Cuban nationalists—everything was irrevocably wrecked. He'd been a fool, he understood. He'd taken a gamble but dropped the ball. He felt faint, like he was going into shock from blood loss. The room grew hot and he leaned against a wall. "What now?" he asked.

"Adriana has led your government to our friend Keith Sorrells, and Keith Sorrells is already on the nightly news across the nation. A lone terrorist, with motivations unrelated to drugs or to Cuba. I presume Adriana will recover the money, and once she ensures the news about Café Arugula dies down, I imagine she'll pack her bags. Business as usual, I suppose."

"And me?"

"I don't particularly care what happens to either of you, Bobby. If Adriana is able to collect her fee and is satisfied with her three million, she might not find it in her best interest to fly back down here just to string you up for the inconvenience. But I can't say what she'll do. She's unpredictable like that, but I can tell you she's meticulous, thorough, and never forgets, which is why we hired her in the first place, if you remember. If she were predictable, she wouldn't be a good assassin. She'd work for some government, as you do, and she'd be bound by some kind of ideology, as you are. She wouldn't be of any use to me, or to you."

When Mr. French hung up, West stood in the phone booth and looked up at the Capitol building, where the congressman held his office. Why had he dedicated his career to the CIA and the Artium Group? Where had he gone wrong? It turns out the intelligence agency was just another career path, filled with incompetent colleagues, opportunities for advancement into irrelevance, the grand nothingness of America. This is your life. The global chess game will continue. No one wants mutual destruction. Everything is power plays and bluffs. Only the terrorists are willing to put their lives on the line.

He put in a call to Washington and left a message with Tiny Mark's secretary. She told him Tiny Mark had left a message to call an encrypted number, which he did. A woman told him plans were being made. Investigations were underway. The FBI was on it.

"The FBI?"

"They're claiming jurisdiction. Domestic event, domestic bomber."

"They've got the wrong man," he said. "It was a Cuban exile, not any kid up in South Carolina."

"You're expected back in Washington on Friday morning," she said.

"Friday morning—what's happening then?"

"You'll be debriefed before an interview with the FBI. They may need you for a Congressional hearing."

"Congressional—"

"Nine a.m. Langley." She hung up and left him wondering if he could even raise enough cash to head to Brazil.

39

The black Bronco had peeled into his parents' driveway the day after Chekhov collected her money, and from nowhere a helicopter swooped over the property as though delivering Army Rangers into a war zone. A line of long sedans materialized on the street, and even in the ensuing melee, Keith imagined his mother's socialite tendencies: *what will the neighbors think?* Two men banged on the front door. Both wore suits and scowled like bankers, could have been if not for the firearms they held in their hands. They each took an arm and dragged him to the Bronco. The men shoved his head inside a bag that smelled of nylon sweats. A string zipped tight around his throat, and he was wrestled into the Bronco. Someone cuffed his hands to the door handle. He called out, but no one answered. The bag was dark and warm, but spit had gotten onto the fabric and chafed at his lips. He could sense several figures in the Bronco with him, and he heard a rustling outside, more men, more cars, the whirr of helicopter blades. The vehicle spun out and his head slammed against the window. He cursed, yelled, but the only answer he received was the rev of the engine.

He leaned his head back and tried to relax. His heart drummed. He gasped for air.

Hours later, a light shined in his face and three men stood before him. They wore sunglasses and stood with their arms crossed.

They could be on the cover of a magazine. *G-Men Quarterly. The Federal Review.*

"What is your name?" asked one.

Keith was tied to a chair and his face was bloody and numb and one of his canine teeth was loose in its socket. He wiggled it with his tongue.

The man kicked his shin and repeated, "What is your name?"

"I've already told you," he said. Blood in the back of his throat, a wet pain pressed into his ribcage. He thought of muddy bales of hay, heavy from rainwater. Imagine that inside you.

"Tell us again."

He told them.

"Why did you leave Miami last week?"

"I went on a trip with my friend."

"Your friend or your girlfriend?"

"A friend. A girl. I don't know."

The lamp above him hummed and the bulb seemed to be teetering on the edge of burnout.

"What is her name?"

"Holly."

"Holly what?"

"Holly, I don't know. Holly."

"What does the name Bobby mean to you?"

Keith spat.

"Bobby West."

"Who the hell is that?" he said. He tilted his head back and tried to focus on the man who was speaking, but he couldn't force his eyes to focus, and he couldn't tell which one of the three it was.

"Bobby West is your girlfriend's father. You stole from this man. How much did you steal?"

"I didn't—I don't know."

The front man looked to his side, nodded.

A burst of electricity shot into Keith's testicles, and he screamed and smelled cooking oil, tar, insecticide. Burnt flesh. The machine cut off and that was the source of the hum. Not the light bulb.

"How much did you steal?"

"I didn't count it. We never counted it."

"And where is the money now?"

"I told you already, it was stolen from me."

"We'll be the judge of what we should and should not be asking."

"If you can't listen to reason, you've got to be the biggest fuckup I ever sat still for. Who you work for? It's not the police."

"That does not matter."

"You CIA?"

"Why do you ask that?" said the first.

"Holly said her father was connected to the CIA."

The men looked at each other.

One leaned in and took off his sunglasses. He had blue eyes and smooth alabaster skin. It startled Keith. The man smiled and said, "We're trying to make this as painless as possible, Keith. We've got unanswered questions, and we believe you have the answers for us. Please let's not focus on irrelevant details. Who works for whom, who did what and when. Let us focus just on the facts. The facts are you stole a great deal of money, which the U.S. government would like back. But facts are funny things. For instance, the two dead men in your Savannah apartment. Do you feel remorse about that? Another fact: the money has disappeared. We believe you had it until recently, and perhaps you still have it, hidden away, though that is not a fact."

"I don't know what I can tell you."

"Do you know who Adriana Chekhov is?"

Keith remained silent.

"I see." The man nodded and another electric current shot into his balls. "I know this is painful, but we cannot succeed here if all you can tell us is you don't know where the money is." Another shock. "So. Let's start again. Where is the money?"

Keith bit his tongue with the last shock, and blood leaked from his mouth. He leaned forward and drooled blood so as not to swallow it. He tongued his loose tooth and his mind faded, back to his home in Six Mile, Saturday afternoons when he and his friends would wander aimlessly up and down the main street, sitting on benches and tripping up pedestrians. The fence they painted on a lark. Kennedy and his wife and child. The thick stench of the Savannah paper mill, the grueling days of convenience store sales, the languid Florida air. All a dream to him now.

The man slapped him and grabbed him by his hair and pulled him up so that the chair he was tied to clanked and came off the ground, dangled from his limp body.

"You will talk to us," the man said. "That you will do."

A number of military training operations took place in the Tidewater region of eastern Virginia. Interstate 95 bisected the state north-south, cutting through Richmond, and everything east was a series of watersheds that flowed into a delta-like environment—old plantations, accents with a British strain, the *rivah*—all the way to the eastern edge of the country. The coast, Virginia Beach, the Chesapeake to the north and the Outer Banks to the south. Here in a jungle of brambles and other such foliage, CIA grunts bushwhacked and worked toward a kind of recognition within the agency, meaning they could go work in a room in Langley or they could be dumped into some hellhole—Beirut, Tajikistan, northern Africa—and be forgotten. Some wanted the hellhole and others wanted an office in the Pentagon. All went through Virginia.

Certain other organizations made use of the commonwealth's thick woods and friendly attitude toward federal contractors. Richmond provided a nice backdrop for tailing exercises, urban surveillance, interrogations. The city still had a small-town feel, a strange brew of old money and poor blacks. Looming over them all, though natives wouldn't always recognize it, were the shadows cast during the Civil War. Downtown fell east in a slip to Shockoe Bottom, an amalgamation of railroad tracks, old iron works, Civil War memorials, abandoned factories, and kitschy restaurants. In one of these old brick buildings along Cary Street was a law office, three stories of inaccessible business, for no one practiced law here and no one came here for counsel. This was only a few blocks from the state capitol, the governor's mansion, the federal courts, yet here was one of the most secret, most illegal, most non-governmental, most unofficially official outposts of the U.S. government.

Here agents from the Navarro Security Company held Keith Sorrells bound to a chair in a room with electric lights and an unblinking camera's eye gazing at him from the corner.

They'd flown him in via helicopter, in what could be days or perhaps merely hours, but now he was dirty and unshaven and stinking like a swamp pit, a bruised eye socket and a bloody eyeball and a missing tooth and a bastard of a smile if he could smile, blood all up in his gums like he'd been chomping glass. Every few hours a new official would come to him and offer some form of pardon, some form of release before proceeding to send an electric current into his bruised, battered, broken and bloody body so that Keith no more trusted these offers of redemption than he trusted there was a God in the sky above to protect him. Was this the natural progression? Here he came to the end of a long line that began with—what? Began with taking a sacrament when he was not converted? Taking money from the vulnerable elderly? Or was it a natural progression from birth, born bad, a sinner, and destined for punishment?

They fed him gruel and uncuffed him at night and left him in a cell to cower. He was not hungry so much as thirsty, for all the water tasted like dirt, like it had been tainted with coal dust. He drank it anyway, but could feel his body infected with the toxins in the water. All he wanted was clean water. By now he would have sold his soul for a drink of clean water, though he couldn't seem to find a devil to bargain with. Everyone had left him. Sinner though he was, the church did not teach of Hell on earth. One could always be saved.

A man came in wearing jeans and a Roxy Music T-shirt. A black-haired fellow with pale skin—he had to be British, a cold clammy Brit—and this man pulled up a chair and sat next to him. He held up a key and leaned over and uncuffed Keith and said, "How are you?" A perfectly American accent, maybe a trace of Midwest cragginess about it, like maybe he was from southern Ohio.

"Oh, you know."

"I see that. Anything I can get you?"

"Glass of clean water?"

"How about a bottle?"

"Perfect."

Another man came in with a bottle of water, which Keith had trouble opening but which he eventually cracked open and funneled down his throat.

"You haven't asked who I am yet," the man said.

"I know who you are."

"Yeah?"

"You're all the same," he said. They came down with different personalities—aggressive, kind, fatherly, brotherly, neighborly, mean-spirited, indifferent, smart, dumb, sinner, saint. They all came down and asked questions he couldn't answer. All turned angry and threatened Keith and eventually left. This man was brotherly.

"All the same, huh."

"You'll be nice, and when I can't tell you about a terrorist plot, you'll get angry and storm out, and I won't see you again."

"Keith, don't get angry," the man said. "I'm here to help you, and you're right, I do have questions for you, some of which you will be able to answer. But here's where you're wrong. If you can't or won't answer them, I'm not going to turn angry, because at the end of our session, your fate will be decided. I'm your last stop before you face a federal jury."

"And what am I supposed to have done?"

"Local authorities in Miami believe you may have blown up a café. They won't have the evidence against you. Your alibi on the road will protect you. But the way to make sure you never have to face capital charges is to work with me and my organization. We can assure Miami authorities you've never had any part in terrorist activities."

"I'm not a terrorist."

"Let's start from the beginning. You're from South Carolina."

"Yes."

"And you spent time in Savannah, selling to convenience stores."

Keith sat there.

"Traveling sales is hard work. I can understand why you might want to find something else. How'd you end up in Miami?"

"I had a lead on a job."

"Ah, and this lead, who is this?"

"A man named Felix Machado."

The man nodded in recognition. "We know Mr. Machado. Do you know what line of work he's in?"

"I don't know."

"Never brought you into the inner circle, did he?"

"I guess not," Keith said.

"That's too bad. That could have been useful information. What did you do for Mr. Machado?"

"His boss needed a tow truck driver."

"Who was his boss?"

"French was his last name. I only met him once."

"Alexander French, perhaps?"

"Could be. I never knew."

"Didn't you find it odd that he hired you, a stranger, to drive a tow truck? Because I sure would. I'd expect a background check at least." The man, who still had not said his name, drummed his fingers against his knee, which he'd pulled up so that his foot rested on the seat of his chair. It gave him an oddly flexibly, birdlike appearance. "Next?"

"As I've told your people, I caught up with this girl, and she'd stolen a lot of money from her father. I rode with her to South Carolina, where she took off on me. I haven't seen the money since."

"Ah, this is where your story gets a bit thin," the man said. "See, we were watching you for several days in Six Mile. Want to know why we moved when we did?"

Keith shut his eyes. "You saw the woman."

"Exacta-mundo."

"Then you know she has the money."

"Well, we've searched you and your apartment and your parents' house, but we haven't found the money. Nor any trace of the woman you now say took it. Did she give you her name?"

Keith shook his head.

The man leaned forward. "You have a wild story, Keith. A kid shows up in town, gets a job with the likes of Alexander French. He disappears with $3 million, and now you can't account for the money or the girl or your actions. This is a story for the movies, not real life."

"So is this warehouse you've got me tied up in."

The man smiled a politician's smile, as though he were caught on camera going back on a campaign promise and was trying to charm his way out of the trap. "Keith, are you a religious man?"

"Not really."

"I was raised a southern Baptist, which means I believe in accepting Christ in your heart and the possibilities of redemption. Unlike many of my friends, I wasn't baptized until I was twelve years old. I had to decide for myself to accept the will of the Lord, and I remember vividly being dunked in the pool of water. It was warm, which I'd not been expecting, and when the preacher dipped me, water went up my nose and I came up gasping for air. The experience didn't fundamentally change me, though I'm glad I went through with it. Have you been baptized?"

"Same here, Southern Baptist," Keith said.

The man nodded and pressed his tongue in his cheek. "What I'll tell you is this: You can talk to me now, and it might be a bit unpleasant, like getting water up your nose in submersion, but it might not fundamentally change anything."

Keith finished the bottle of water, screwed the lid on, set the bottle on the table.

"I can't say I was saved that day when I was twelve, but I can say there was a lot of possibility in that moment. I believe I *could* have been saved, if I fully believed in the transformative power of those waters. What I'd say is this: You have a similar possibility here. You can tell us your story—not about Alexander French and drug smuggling, but about the café and your act of terrorism. You will still have to face a trial—let's be honest here—but if you give us information in good faith, and you are willing to take that leap, you're in the best possible situation. It's like Pascal's wager. You can believe or not believe. If you don't believe, and the thing turns out to be true, well, you've missed your opportunity. Or you can believe, and if the thing turns out to be false, no harm done. But if you believe and the thing becomes true, then you're saved. Here too you can believe or not believe, but only belief is the true choice."

Keith made no reply.

"Do you wish to say anything? Anything at all to help save yourself?"

"I've said all I have to say."

"So this is your story? You know nothing?"

"That's all I know to tell you."

"All right." The man stood up and cracked his hands. "You'll be brought down to Miami tomorrow. They'll appoint you an attorney, and we'll see if Bobby West—the man you stole money from—and his daughter can back up your story. Maybe Mr. Machado or Mr. French will come forward. I wouldn't advise saying anything without counsel, although I'm not sure what can save you at this point."

True to his word, the man did not get angry and storm out. He turned and strolled out and left Keith uncuffed in the room. It grew dark. The metal walls around him faded, and wind against the building groaned and something shook. Scuffling upstairs. Pipes in the ceiling leaked. The camera's eye never blinked. The red light indicated it was always on, always watching.

The next day a man came in and put a black bag over Keith's head and carted him out to a van. They drove for nearly an hour, and when the van stopped and the door opened, he was led out onto squishy ground and marched across soft wild land and into a farmhouse, where the bag was removed from his head.

One of the men with him brought down the butt of a rifle onto his skull and he fell to the ground.

When he woke, light filtered in as though through fractured glass. The shadows were long for late afternoon. He lay in an empty kitchen with tacky farm wallpaper peeling off walls and a rusted washer and dryer set shoved against one wall. The appliances were the puke green of the 1950s. A wasp's nest hung from a corner. The air was warm and stale.

He sat up and felt the bruise on his head from the rifle. A welt had formed on his temple, and blood had dried in his hair. He felt woozy, and it took a long while for him to realize he was free.

Nothing bound him, nothing barred him from walking out the door.

He looked out the kitchen window and saw woods beyond a yellowed field. The back door was unlocked, and he went out and looked about and tried to decide which way to go. Farmland and woods all around, as far as he could tell. Was it this easy? Did they figure out he was no terrorist, and so decided to dump him somewhere? They could have bought him a plane ticket back to Florida; that would have been nice.

Just as he was getting used to his newfound freedom, a SWAT team came around the corner, men with helmets on their heads and visors covering their faces. Guns raised.

"Freeze! Freeze! Put your hands up, drop to your knees, turn around."

So this was how it was. He'd been released to the local police, and the agency spooks had fallen back to the shadows.

40

What led Holly Hernandez in the spring of 1984, after running north with a boy she hardly knew and then skirting away from the boy under cover of dawnlight, to the sudden realization she'd made a terrible mistake and that life would be no easy venture? The idea for the theft had been simple enough: her father had a safe full of cash just sitting there, and the man could use a lesson in what mattered. The last time she'd seen him he'd come into her room— her old room, in her mother's house, what used to be her parents' house, before the separation—all apologies for not picking her up from school on his Friday, his semimonthly time to be a father. She'd been dozing in her bed with the TV on, *Fraggle Rock* the only thing tolerable on at this hour, the new color 20-inch her mother had purchased to assuage the guilt of raising a daughter in a broken home, and he'd come in all calm and said of the TV, "That's new."

"Mm."

"I guess your mother bought that?"

"How'd you guess?"

Her eyes remained stuck to the screen when he came in and sat at the foot of her bed. He put his hand on her ankle, wanted her to sit up, let him give her a once-over, a fatherly hello, hold her close for shame at blowing her off. She knew this, and she wanted to show her father affection, to be playful with him the way they were when she was younger and everything was simpler, but the man needed to learn, he needed to learn she was a person, a whole person, not a doll to be pulled out of the closet when it suited him. She scrolled through a few commercials before landing back on the puppets. Pink and purple humanoid, colorful creatures romping around inside a cave-like setting, a city built up amid sepia-tinted rock formations. The puppets had orange hair and cheerful dispositions, no kind of analog for life.

"I thought we might grab lunch," he'd said.

"When this is over."

"You're sucked into the story?"

Holly changed the channel and gave him a look. On the screen, a woman stood on screen with a jug of detergent. *Isn't it hard when colors fade and whites darken? Try the all-new Palette so your colors stay colored and your whites stay white.* Up popped an image of a striped T-shirt paired with a blinding white sock.

"Come on," he said, and she dragged herself off the bed. She wore whitewashed jeans with holes in the knees and ragged cuffs and a beige T-shirt with a long-haired singer on the front, dressed in some kind of space outfit. "That's what you're wearing," he said.

Since it wasn't a question, she remained silent.

He shook his head. "I just have to say, it looks kind of cheesy."

That was her father, always thought he could tease his way out of a jam.

So she and Keith had the money and made it all the way to Savannah before she began to get an inkling of what a bad idea it was, to take all the money and the car and lie to Keith about how much she had in her duffel bag and not even mention the gun. She'd feigned drunkenness at the bar J.E.B. Stuart's and saw how furtive Keith's friend was, could tell something was wrong like a foul odor in the air. No sleep that night, and no surprise when the two men jimmied the lock to the apartment. The only surprise was how quickly Keith decided to scoot out the window with a half-hearted, "Come on," before leaving her to take the gun and open fire on the two shadows in the living room. At least he came back for her, not that he had any sense of what she was feeling, Keith just another self-centered man she needed to get rid of.

Which she did: got him all the way to his hometown and then slid off and hit the road, unsure of where she was or where she was going, drove on one highway after another until she found herself in a motel outside Knoxville. She realized her last mistake, out of all her mistakes this spring, was not verifying the money was still in the trunk when she slunk out on Keith Saturday morning. She popped the trunk to pay for another night in the hotel, and saw the duffel bag was crumpled over, empty save one stack of bills.

She paid for several nights at the motel and thought about what she should do. She spent a few days feeling sorry for herself and watching the soaps and ordering pizza. When the motel owner knocked on her door to tell her she needed to pay again or check out, she found her way to I-40 and headed west, unsure of where to go next. When the low-fuel light came on in the Impala, she pulled over at a truck stop near Nashville. She had enough cash to fill up the tank but not enough to get back to Miami, so she spent a night in the back seat at the truck stop, trying to ignore the honks and squeaks of the eighteen-wheelers.

At dawn, she got out to stretch. The air was cool and the sky had lowered so that there seemed to be no transition between the ground fog and the overhead clouds, one gray mist that prickled her skin and sent a chill up her spine. A man in a pickup leered at her as he filled up with gas. He wore sunglasses and a jean jacket, and had a thick mustache like a race car driver. A big man, of the type who might stuff her into the cab of his truck and hit the highway without breaking a sweat. She went into the gas station and asked the clerk for a key to the bathroom, which was attached to a hub cap and hung on the wall behind the clerk.

"You filling up?" the clerk asked.

Holly produced her last twenty, and the woman gave her the key. Holly went out to the bathroom and locked herself in and sat on the toilet to think for a while, and then the weight of everything caught up to her and she began to cry, a hiccupping wail that left her shivering in the stall. After a long time she caught her breath enough to stand up and go to the sink to splash water on her face, where she saw she had a burst capillary and a splotchy face, which made her well up again.

This was her life. This was where she was.

In defeat, she left the bathroom and returned the key to the clerk. The man in the pickup had driven off, so it was just her Impala in the lot. She rummaged through her purse for a quarter and then went over to the payphone to call her father.

41

Back from Tallahassee, Bobby West's mind floated scattershot: still no word from his daughter, no word from Tiny Mark, or Felix, or Chekhov, but everything in his existence was in arrears. He'd manipulated the books at the Artium Group and shuffled the company's debt around on the false belief that he could pay off French and keep the Cubans happy until CIA resources came through. But the CIA resources were not coming through, and venture capitalists would soon pick apart the Artium Group like birds of prey scavenging the bones of roadkill. In this respect, West was the vehicle and the roadkill, the agent and the result. It would only be a matter of time before the bean counters arrived at his malfeasance and called him to account for the fraud. Where had the money gone? He couldn't answer that question. Down the rabbit hole. The asset had been in his safe, had traveled to South Carolina, and had vanished like a puff of smoke, dispersed in the wind.

He'd already emptied his savings to pay Mr. French a down payment, so while he could still buy a plane ticket on credit, still had his passport to flee the country, he had nowhere to go and nothing to live on when he arrived there. Still, he knew he needed to get out of Miami, because this town was filled with gangsters, terrorists, refugees, hustlers, vultures, leg-breakers, drug runners, drug dealers, assassins, spies, miscreants, and vagrants. Here he was a focalizing point of enmity, a target. Therefore, he slept little the night he returned from Tallahassee and rose before dawn to pack a few bags. He lay in bed awake for a long time, ignored the early-morning chirp of birds, the blush of dawn, and the bump of the newspaper landing against his doorstep.

At six, Adriana Chekhov picked his backdoor lock and was sitting on the couch with a cup of espresso when he came down stairs. When he turned on a light and saw her, her hair pulled back tight on her face so that her skin was unlined and worry-free, he froze. He looked left toward the front door, but she raised a pistol and ushered him in.

"I would have brought you a cup of coffee," she said, "but I wasn't sure what you drank."

"I'd actually prefer a glass of whiskey, if you don't mind."

He made his way to the kitchen, fumbled with the glass and the ice and the whiskey's screwtop.

He wondered if she would have followed him had he left at five this morning, or let him sail off to Byzantium. Better yet, he should have abandoned his possessions and left straight from Tallahassee. But you were never prepared for what was coming for you. If it were not Chekhov in his living room this morning, it would be a car wreck, or cancer, or a random drive-by shooting.

Fate had a way of getting her man when the time came.

He sat on the chair opposite Chekhov, the bottle of whiskey in tow. He drained the glass and refilled it and set the bottle on the coffee table. She sipped her espresso and set the empty cup next to the bottle.

"I take it you know what I'm here for," she said.

"I don't have the money for you."

"I know."

"You can kill me, but it won't get you any closer to it. I can't get in touch with the guy who has it."

She picked up a duffel bag that had been resting at her feet beneath the coffee table. She set the bag on the table and said, "I've got the money. I had to go up to South Carolina to get it, but the kid was easy enough to find."

His chest hurt as though a slow-growing tumor had finally pressed into his lungs and heart. His neck grew hot and he found it hard to breathe.

"Your daughter wasn't with him," she went on. "I don't know where she went, but she's got nothing to worry about from me."

"You've got the money," he said.

"I do," she said. "The boy's with some of your colleagues. Apparently, people believe he's responsible for the café bombing, but we both know that was your department." She looked around the room as though genuinely perplexed by Bobby West's existence and her role in the world, like a drunk sobering at the end of the night when the lights come on and most of the guests have left. Then she lifted the gun and said, "I want you to know I don't take any pleasure in this."

"Why would you tell me that?"

"I just feel it would be good for you to know."

"Then why do it? You got your money. These people, whoever you're ultimately working for, they're not the type to quit. They're coming for you too."

"It's my profession," she said.

West crossed his arms.

She went on, "You know, I have been thinking of retirement. This whole business is quite dull. Hours and hours of sitting around, waiting. And I really hate flying, the smell of it."

West scoffed. "A woman shouldn't go into a profession she's bored with."

"Neither should a man, wouldn't you agree? In any case, you're right. You need passion in this life, and passion doesn't play well with what I do. Do you think I missed out on something in life? A family, a husband? The joy of femininity?"

"I doubt you'd be happy with something like that."

She chuckled. "That never would have been my strong suit. What about you, Mr. West?"

"What about me?"

"Do you enjoy what you do? Do you find passion in it?"

He thought for a moment. "I did, once."

"When you thought you could take down Castro, and the entirety of Communism while you were at it?"

"Something like that."

"Meanwhile you've spent your life at the Artium Group, negotiating with people like me and Alexander French, shuffling money around, preparing the stage for the messiah who will come in and create a new world order. Let me ask you, have you ever been to the Soviet Union?"

West shook his head.

"You can't live in these abstractions. The world is in balance now, as much as it ever has been or ever will be. Without the Communists, who would it be? Perhaps the jackals on Wall Street? Communism will kill itself in time," she said, "and then what would you do?"

"I'd retire knowing I did something good."

"Good is a relative term."

"Not to me, it isn't," he said.

"Then you're living with purpose. I salute you."

West looked toward the door, but he made no motion to leave.

"Well," she finally said. "You know Alexander was quite upset with you. He said it was dishonorable for you to be playing sides the way you were."

"It's my profession," he said.

"I told him, that first day in Amsterdam, I told him if he allowed you to funnel proceeds to the Cubans, the entire situation would blow up in his face. He thought he had you contained, or believed you had the Cubans contained. Never trust a greedy man who believes he has a line on a good investment. You'll never convince him otherwise, so all you can do in such a situation is protect your own interests."

"I've done my duty," he said. "I have to protect my own interests."

"I understand, and I wouldn't blame you if your actions hadn't been for nothing," she said.

"They weren't for nothing."

"They were for nothing," she said again. "You would do yourself a favor to admit this. It's no failure to admit defeat. You're looking well for yourself. This could have finished much worse for everyone. But the world turns. It's business as usual for everyone—CIA, the Cubans, Alexander."

"The Communists."

"For now."

"And how is Alexander?" West asked.

"He's gone west, I believe, to find his fortune in the Asian market."

"So he's out, huh?"

She smiled. "Never underestimate ambition."

Then she raised the pistol and shot West in the heart. He never heard the blast.

42

Then it was over. Chekhov thought about firing a second shot into the back of Bobby West's head to be sure, but she knew he was long gone. Perhaps his soul would find peace in the afterlife. Or perhaps death was the end: the light guttered, entropy took over, neurons grinded to a halt. She put the gun in her pocket and picked up the duffel bag from the coffee table, slung it over her shoulder.

In the kitchen the telephone rang. It rang, and rang, and rang. She finally grew tired of it and picked up the receiver.

"Hello?" said a woman. "Daddy? Are you there?"

Chekhov returned the receiver to its cradle and held her hand on the phone a moment.

Then she picked it back up and listened for the dial tone before calling Tiny Mark Brown's secure line in D.C. "It's done," she told him. "Do we need to talk about Alexander?"

"We've got our man in custody, so there won't be any Cuban uprising."

"Did he send anyone after me? Navarro Security Company agents?"

"Not that I've heard. Why?"

"Something Bobby West said."

"I wouldn't concern yourself. Those boys have a big bark, but we've got them on a leash."

"And Alexander?"

"Nothing to worry about there," Brown said, though she didn't believe him. Bureaucrats were all the same—they saw one piece of the story but failed to ask questions to get the full vantage.

When she'd hung up, she thought about what West said: *They're coming for you too.* Perhaps. She was in business with enough competing factions someone was bound to get her number. Such was the nature of Miami, it seemed, everyone was a free agent. Everyone worked more than one side. With her commission, she had enough to cash out. She'd dispensed enough of her would-be justice and believed she'd done enough. West was right about one thing. They would be coming for her: agents, mercenaries, businessmen, the Furies. They were all the same, all within a wheel, churning up turbulence.

She turned out the lamp in the living room. Then she vanished out the door she'd come in not thirty minutes ago, dawn light still struggling over the horizon.

43

When news reports came out that Keith Sorrells was in custody as a suspect in the bombing as well as a double homicide in Georgia, Falcon got up from the breakfast table, put on his cap and shoes, told Mary Catherine he had to get on with his day.

"What'd you read in the paper?" she asked, flipping through the metro section.

"That boy they brought in for the bombing, he was on the road with Bobby West's daughter."

"I thought you'd closed that case."

"I thought I had too, but it's not over, apparently."

"You did what you got paid for," she said.

"Well," he said. The girl had called home and reached her mother, and was now safe in Coconut Grove. Isabel paid the rest of her tab, which Falcon felt uncomfortable accepting given how everything had turned out. He'd not, after all, actually done what she'd hired him for, but instead had uncovered a mess he couldn't clean up. He leaned over to kiss his wife on the cheek. "You know that's never stopped me before."

"I know. I just worry about you. When does it ever end?"

He had no answer for her, and came up with nothing on the drive down the A1A to the police station. He hoped he could catch up with Donnie Ray Callahan, and that his old pal on the force could give him necessary insight into the Keith Sorrells situation.

An unseasonable cool front had settled over South Florida. A gray drizzle misted his windshield just enough to be obnoxious. People who came down here to retire must be disappointed to find the place had its own brand of lousy weather, and that paradise was a myth. Of course, those retirees must be equally disappointed to discover you could never escape human nature, and the same lousy problems from Michigan or Connecticut or Nebraska would be waiting for them with open arms in Miami. That pervasive disappointment might explain why this state was so inscrutable, and Falcon wondered if southern Californians experienced a similar dissatisfaction, a similar schizophrenic worldview.

The police station was surprisingly empty, but he found Callahan with his trademark Big Gulp on his desk and an unlit cigarette tucked over his ear.

"Jesus, Ernie," Callahan said once Falcon inquired about Keith Sorrells. "Navarro's security forces are going to put us out of business before it's all over. They picked this kid up in South Carolina and had it in their heads that he was our bomber. We asked the feds, 'What about the woman?' and they said, 'What woman? This guy's your man.' We asked them, 'What did Frank Navarro's guys tell you?' and they said, 'Who's Frank Navarro? We're in charge.' We've already caught a federal agent in our records department, and he couldn't explain what he was doing in there. I think he was trying to rewrite the story of our investigation, as though you could just wave a wand and say we'd been looking for a white boy all along, eyewitness reports be damned."

"So what are you going to do about the kid?"

"What can we do? We don't have a lick of evidence linking him to the café, or any kind of subversive group. As near as we can tell, he's been on the road for the past two weeks, and positively couldn't have set that bomb off. But tell that to whatever agency picked him up. Those guys will drive a man to retirement." Callahan slugged his soft drink and put the cigarette in his mouth but didn't light it. Through the corner of his mouth, he said, "We're going to hold him another day or two, just to satisfy our lawyers, but I've made it my mission to build an air-tight case against Keith Sorrells ever setting foot in South Beach, and will type up a fifty-page report myself to give to those federal assholes. Then I'm going to retire, because I can't do this anymore." Callahan lit his cigarette and blew smoke in the air. "What's your interest in the case?"

"Nothing," Falcon said. "I was working that missing persons case, and it turns out the girl was on the road with Keith when the café blew up."

"Good. So you can give me ammunition for my report."

"I can do that. Hey, I'd like to talk with Keith myself, if you can get me in to see him. Just want to tie up a few loose ends."

"Be my guest. He's up at the pretrial detention facility. Feds pressured the DA into charging him, so we're holding him like he did it until we can get the evidence otherwise."

"But you've got the evidence?" Falcon asked.

"Oh yes. We'll let him go in a day or two, and then I just hope he doesn't bring a lawsuit big enough to wreck my pension. Of course, Georgia law enforcement wants him in connection with a double homicide, but that's not my problem."

The Miami pretrial detention facility was across the river from the police station. The facility kept evening visitation hours, but thanks to a phone call from Callahan, an exception was made for Falcon as an independent investigative resource. Still, the staff kept him waiting for half an hour before ushering him into an interrogation room with Keith Sorrells. The boy was scrawnier than Falcon anticipated, and looked impossibly young and meek across the table. He had a Japanese symbol tattooed on his arm, and had a patchwork of faint stubble coming in on his cheeks and chin. Falcon introduced himself as a private investigator.

"I was hired to find Holly Hernandez the other week," he said.

"I take it you've found her?" the boy said in a country drawl.

"She ran out of money in North Carolina and called home."

The boy nodded.

"I talked with a colleague at Miami P.D. He says you'll be out of here in a few days. You need anything for right now?"

"I'd like a lawyer," Keith said.

"They should have appointed you someone."

"He came in here talking about plea bargain. I want a real lawyer, someone who understands I wasn't anywhere near that café."

"It wasn't the local police. It was another law enforcement group, they got a little overzealous. You should walk away with a clean slate, though I wouldn't blame you if you wanted to take some kind of legal action."

"What I get for taking an interest in the wrong man's daughter. Girl was a lunatic and about dragged me down with her. Her father tell you about the money?"

"Her father shot himself the other day."

The kid looked at the table between them. "You want to go around arresting people, you might start with the people he was working for. Especially that redheaded woman."

"And who is that?"

"She didn't tell me her name, but she came and picked up the money right before those bastards picked me up and carted me all over tarnation."

Falcon chewed on his lower lip a moment. He said, "I wouldn't worry about any of that now."

"Easy for you to say."

"You'll be out of here soon enough," he said.

"And then I'm off to Georgia to deal with that other thing." Keith put his hand to his forehead and leaned over the table like he might be ill. "I know I got involved in something bad here, but they haven't even let me get a lawyer. Who were those guys? The agents that dragged me into that warehouse?"

Falcon held up his hands. "Hey, son, I don't know what you've been through to get here."

"I suppose you wouldn't. No one seems to know anything."

"I used to work with Miami P.D. I have a few friends still in the department, and they tell me it's only a matter of days and then you're free. There are newspaper accounts of your arrest, so I wouldn't be surprised if a civil liberties attorney contacts you before it's all said and done."

"Yeah, but that won't change anything."

"I suppose not," Falcon said.

"You know, my father's a preacher. Right before I was picked up, he tried to talk with me about Jesus. Man to man, like he'd never done before. When I was a kid, it was all faith and damnation. You a believer?"

"Depends on what day you ask me, I suppose."

Keith nodded as if Falcon had passed some critical test. "He tried to tell me Jesus was this scruffy rule-breaker, always going in and creating a ruckus. I could get behind a man like that, but that's not how the world works, is it? We've got our rules, and you've got to know them and follow them, or they lock you up and throw away the key."

"No one's thrown away the key on you, son."

"Yeah, well, no one's calling me a savior either."

Falcon wanted to offer some piece of wisdom for the boy. Keith was not an innocent—none of them were—but he'd gone through an ordeal over the past week, one Falcon couldn't explain. He remembered his daughter telling him he just didn't *get* it all those years ago. Now he felt the old fool, couldn't even counsel a scrawny teenage boy in need of absolution. "You'll be all right," he finally said, and he stood up to go. "You want me to contact anyone for you? Your parents?"

"They can't help me," Keith said. "Can they?"

"I suppose not," Falcon said.

West's funeral was on a Saturday. The recent cool front had abated and summer seemed to have blasted its way onto Miami. Hydrangeas were in bloom all over the city, and the scent of hibiscus and jasmine hung on the breeze. Men and women alike wore white to the funeral, which gave the day a flair of joy, as though everyone were here for

an Easter baptism rather than the funeral for a suicide. This was
the unofficial word about Bobby West's death, a self-inflicted bullet
wound, perhaps a belated fallout for his recent divorce or perhaps a
response to the Artium Group's bankruptcy. Regardless of the cause,
the church had a respectable crowd of colleagues and friends.

Falcon sat in the back and took note of the crowd. No one
appeared overtly suspicious, a few suits who perhaps belonged to
some government agency but no Alexander French, no Adriana
Chekhov, no Cuban or Colombian drug lords. Isabel and Holly sat
in the front row with a number of other nameless relatives. Holly's
face was puffy and sad, but Isabel kept her resolve, kept her arm
around her daughter but let no emotions show. In a brief service,
the preacher spoke of God's love and forgiveness and Bobby West
in the kingdom of heaven—all the dead were in the kingdom of
heaven at a funeral. Sundays were for talk of sin and salvation and
the fires of hell, but funerals were for about comfort for the living,
not a call to repent.

Afterward, Falcon followed the receiving line to Isabel and
Holly. Isabel thanked him for coming, and he apologized for Mary
Catherine's absence. "She can't get out in this heat," he said. "It's just
too much for her."

"I wouldn't expect her to come out," Isabel said. "Good of you
to come."

He pulled her aside, out of ear's reach of Holly, and asked how
the girl was doing.

"She's been quiet since she got back. Won't say where she went
or what she was doing, or if her father knew where she was all this
time."

"I can assure you he didn't," Falcon said.

"He was a liar through and through."

"Maybe so, but from what I understand, she and boyfriend
took some money from Bobby and hit the road. They split up
somewhere along the way, and she ran out of money."

"That can't be the whole story," Isabel said.

Falcon looked away. What good would it do to try to explain
the whole story? Could even he explain it? Falcon's daughter,

paranoid as she was about the power structures in the world, would say Mr. French and Chekhov and maybe someone in the U.S. government had formed a kind of cabal that unraveled with the theft of the money. From Falcon's vantage, no one appeared that sophisticated. Everyone was a freelancer, out to make a buck, and Keith and Bobby had simply gotten caught in someone's way, deer in headlights. But then, that was Falcon's vision of the world: paranoiacs were emotionally damaged and looking for order where there was none.

He shook Isabel's hand again. Before he could get away, Holly came over and said, "Mr. Falcon? The gun wasn't in his house."

"I'm sorry?"

"The gun. They say it was a suicide, but I took his gun with me. Keith had it in the bag with the money, so my father couldn't have shot himself."

Isabel tried to pull her daughter to her.

"I mean it. He wouldn't have killed himself. It had to have been murder. Will you look into it?"

Falcon wished he could assure her, offer comfort or even the promise that he would seek justice, but there was nothing to say. He knew the girl was right, and he knew who had done it, but Adriana Chekhov had slipped out of Miami undetected. Perhaps Frank Navarro's security forces would find her, and arrest her. Or perhaps they would find her and hire her for their own purposes. But for now, Chekhov, Mr. French, Navarro, the CIA: they were all out of Falcon's reach.